SoniaLand

The Eminent Professor

The diary of a minor academic from a very minor university

TG Snowball

Lamoned G Snowball

16 December 2015

BECKSIDE BOOKS

First Published in Great Britain in 2015
by BECKSIDE BOOKS

Copyright © TG Snowball 2015

A CIP catalogue record for this title is
available from the British Library.

ISBN 978 0 9933886 1 3

Printed & Bound in Great Britain by
Clays Ltd, St Ives plc

BECKSIDE BOOKS
Publishers

www.BecksideBooks.co.uk

Dedication

For my wife, Jean
No more stories; at least, not these...

Acknowledgements

My sincere thanks go to David Thomas, the well-known watercolour artist from the East Riding of Yorkshire, for providing the cover illustrations.

The key events that happened during the last few days of the Beijing massacre were confirmed through collaboration with Feng Congde, who is probably the most reliable source of information from the student leaders on Tiananmen Square at that time. The other reliable source of information is Robin Munro, a Human Rights observer, who remained on the Square until the end. However, any historical error or omission is entirely the fault of the author.

'The greatest enemy of truth is very often not the lie – deliberate, contrived, and dishonest, but the myth, persistent, persuasive...'

John F Kennedy
Yale: November 6, 1962

Prologue

Sunday, June 4, 1989

I walked into the lounge and saw my family staring at the television watching the evening news.

I was horrified!

I saw armed troops, tanks crushing barricades, and buses and trucks on fire. In the background, I heard gunfire. The commentary talked about a brutal attack on Tiananmen Square, massacres, and the unofficial death toll being over 1000, with many more injured. There was a blurred picture of an armoured vehicle knocking down the Goddess of Democracy, a replica of the Statute of Liberty built by students on Tiananmen Square only last week.

The commentary said tanks and armoured personnel carriers had driven onto the Square indiscriminately crushing temporary shelters with many students still asleep inside. Another account said that as students left the Square, troops had fired on them, felling the first row of 100, and then the second.

I switched between channels and one commentator from the BBC reported that while watching from the Beijing Hotel, he saw troops shooting at students at the Monument in the centre of the Square.

Nothing made sense.

I was there just a couple of days ago.

Chapter 1

Tuesday, April 18, 1989

'**Dr Charles** Vincent?'

'Yes, and you must be Petter.'

'Was that you trying to get through the diplomatic channel at passport control?'

'It was.'

'You weren't successful then?'

'No.'

I decided I might try out my new, blue United Nations Certificate. While nobody explained what exactly the certificate was for, inside it stated, without going into specifics, that I had certain privileges and immunities, but the officials at passport control weren't interested.

'Let's go and find our luggage,' said Petter.

Our welcoming party from the university consisted of Professor Song, the dean of the faculty responsible for my teaching programme, and Mr Chou Ke-qiang, the director of the Office of Foreign Affairs. They were both smiling, unnaturally so, and we all shook hands. While Petter was discussing arrangements for his visit with Professor Song, I considered it polite to talk with the director.

'Err, Comrade Chou, what does the Office of Foreign Affairs actually do?' I asked.

'They call me Mr Chou.'

Why did I call him, Comrade?

'You are an eminent professor from a famous, foreign university, an honoured guest of Jaliang Number 3 University, so my office looks after you,' continued Mr Chou in reasonable English. 'We provide you with a car to go places. We arrange cultural visits for you in the evenings. We look after all foreign delegates.'

I looked at Mr Chou suspiciously to see if he was having some fun at my expense, but he appeared sincere. The problem was, I was not a professor, let alone an eminent one, and Pontefract Polytechnic was most definitely not a famous university. It's just a decent poly.

'I look forward to the cultural visits,' I replied warily.

'I have arranged a classroom monitor for you,' Mr Chou informed me. 'He will look after all your classroom needs such as photocopying handouts. You should submit student handouts for photocopying at least three days in advance. Things take time here.'

'A classroom monitor, excellent, Comr...err...Mr Chou.'

I never got that kind of assistance back at the poly.

'Yes, people are our greatest resource. We have a population of over a billion, and all have occupations and jobs,' explained Mr Chou. 'I can arrange for you to have two classroom monitors if you want.'

*I*t was April 1989, and China had already started its Open Door Policy.

I was involved in a well meant, save the world, United Nations projects. The UN International Business Organisation (UNIBO) based in Kuala Lumpur sponsored the project, funded through the Swedish government. The project manager for the programme was Petter Lyngstad, a tall and distinguished looking Swede.

It was pure luck that the original academic broke his leg in a car accident and I, at short notice, took his place. While it was unfortunate for the academic with the broken leg, it nevertheless allowed me to become a consultant for the United Nations. I was now an academic globetrotter involved in lucrative work outside the safe, affable, and boring confines of Pontefract Polytechnic.

They selected a group of talented young graduates from Jaliang Number 3 University to undertake a postgraduate programme in business management. They designed the curriculum to reflect the very best of western management theories, and a market economy, instead of the dour, commercial conventions of a centrally controlled command economy, as practised in China at that time.

At the planning stage, UNIBO excluded senior and older Chinese candidates because in all probability, they would be unsympathetic towards western business concepts and theories. They decided that young graduates would be more receptive to new ideas. They argued

2

that most of the young graduates were destined for senior roles within Chinese universities and industry. They would then be in a position to influence academic curricula and business management and, as a result, be able to introduce some of the concepts and theories they had learnt. Through that process, the academic multiplier effect should have some impact as China opened its doors to trade with the outside world.

I had a short stopover of a few hours in Kuala Lumpur, partly due to flights schedules, but mainly so that staff from the UNIBO office could brief me about the project. They had arranged for me to meet Petter at Kuala Lumpur airport before flying to Jaliang together, but we had obviously missed each other.

While I did not know all the details of what Petter was up to in China, it included organising the overseas work placements for my students. After the taught part of the programme, not forgetting the cutting-edge concepts of cross-management communication I was to teach, they were to attend work placements in large western companies around the world to experience all those new theories in practice.

As we drove to the university, Petter explained that a town like Jaliang was essentially a collection of compounds or communes, although that structure had fragmented in recent years. For example, the university compound contained all staff and student accommodation, a primary school, kitchens, buses, a fleet of cars, and so on. The State provided everything, but salaries were low. With the Open Door Policy, they allowed a little bit of free enterprise. The university wanted its share of free enterprise and had recently built the foreign-visitor guesthouse. The new guesthouse, attached to a much older building at one end, stood within its own small compound in the middle of the university.

Unfortunately, as it was late evening when we arrived, I couldn't see much of Jaliang itself.

'You are the first honoured foreign guests to stay at the new guesthouse,' Mr Chou told us. 'You can have your meals there. You are lucky.'

Although it was dark, I thought I saw Petter's eyebrows rise ever so slightly. 'This might be interesting,' he murmured quietly.

Chapter 2

Wednesday, April 19, 1989

I met Petter on my way to breakfast.

The breakfast room was comfortable enough and had the décor you would expect to see in a traditional Italian hotel, except robust, heavy, thick plastic replaced the marble. I looked out of the window but merely saw the guesthouse compound wall. The gardens within the compound looked unkempt. We chose a table and sat down.

We didn't exactly choose a table because there was only one set for breakfast, with two place settings. We were the only guests. A little, old, Chinese lady, who was to be our breakfast hostess for the next few weeks, came cautiously to the table. We exchanged a few bows and smiles.

'Engli brekfass?' asked the little, old, Chinese lady.

'English breakfast,' I repeated, nodding my approval, 'excellent.'

Part of being a seasoned traveller was to know that whenever you had the possibility of a hot bath or shower, you took it, and similarly, when offered food, you ate it. You just never knew when the next opportunity might arise. Food was on offer and I was ready to tuck into a good English breakfast.

Petter, I imagined, would have preferred raw herrings, or whatever Swedes ate for breakfast, but even he knew that would be stretching his luck. Since Petter spoke no Chinese, he tried to engage our hostess in conversation but soon realised she spoke no English. Anyway, she walked backwards into the kitchen muttering this and that. We then heard the comforting sounds of pots and pans banging in the kitchen. I thought the banging in the kitchen was excessive, but what did I know. After a few minutes, the little, old, Chinese lady appeared and presented us both with our English breakfast.

Apple pie and fried eggs!

The guesthouse had obviously done some research into English food, and I forgave any misunderstanding it might have made. Besides, I appreciated the effort made on my behalf and happily accepted my generous portion of what I took to be home-baked apple pie, with two fried eggs precariously balanced on top. I also knew, from my limited knowledge, that Chinese breakfast consisted of a glutinous mix of rice pudding without the rice; and I didn't fancy that!

Probably because he was missing his raw herrings, or whatever, Petter was having nothing to do with his English breakfast. Unlike me, he was an experienced, seasoned traveller and had a theory that if you were not firm from the beginning then you would never get what you wanted.

Petter must have looked, to the little, old, Chinese lady, the very worst smelly, big-nosed barbarian imaginable. That, I once read, was how the older Chinese generation sometimes viewed western foreigners.

'Omelette,' demanded Petter politely.

You might contemplate why a seasoned traveller, like Petter, would make a stance of principle over omelette and not, for instance, some Swedish delicacy.

Two reasons...

Firstly, when confronted with an uncertain cuisine, eggs were recognisable on the plate. Secondly, when language was a barrier to communication, chicken noises seemed to be universal. Petter, therefore, went into his chicken impression routine, with elbows flapping, making deep, resonant, Scandinavian chicken cluck sounds, then a mime of mixing eggs in a bowl, and whipping them into an omelette. Petter seemed pleased with his effort, gave the little, old, Chinese lady a big smile, and repeated, 'omelette.'

That seemed to work and our hostess smiled with recognition. 'Ah, omele,' she said slowly, and returned tentatively to the kitchen.

Mind, I would have liked to see Petter attempt a raw herring impression.

As I mopped up my egg yolk with the crust of my apple pie, the little, old, Chinese lady returned and presented Petter with his omelette.

Pancake!

Close, I thought.

Petter's resolve to be firm from the beginning faltered. He thanked the little, old, Chinese lady and, if a little disappointed or just plain hungry, ate his pancake without further ado. Since Chinese pancakes were quite nice, Petter must have been pleased with his chicken impression endeavours.

'I suppose you've heard about the demonstrations in Beijing?' Petter asked vaguely, deftly eating his pancake with chopsticks. 'There are students involved, I believe.'

'What demonstrations?' I asked.

'Oh, some chap died a few days ago. He was the former Chinese Communist Party leader forced to resign because he was sympathetic towards the 1986 student demonstrations. The Chinese government cannot quite make up its mind if he is a hero or villain. Students at Beijing University stuck posters on walls and hung banners from windows criticising the government and showing sorrow for his death. They went to Tiananmen Square to place wreaths.' Petter had heard that on his worldwide, short-wave radio that he always carried when travelling.

'Tiananmen Square?' I queried.

'It's big and a good place for protests,' replied Petter. 'Don't worry. Beijing is a long way from here. These things do not normally last very long in China.'

Whenever anyone told me not to worry, then I worried. Otherwise, why would they tell me?

I had not travelled halfway around the world to be involved in protests. They were not part of my contract, but I didn't dwell on that. My teaching programme, which started the next day, was a more pressing matter.

Chapter 3

Thursday, April 20, 1989

Zhuang, my classroom monitor, introduced himself. Although he looked about sixteen, Zhuang was, or so he adamantly informed me, in his early thirties. He was also a head shorter than I was.

While Zhuang walked with me to my classroom, I took little notice of my surroundings. I was too worried about my teaching programme. My preparation yesterday had not gone as well as I had hoped. I was finding the campus noisy. Loudspeakers kept coming on at irregular intervals during the day making it difficult to concentrate. They were blaring away while we walked to the classroom.

Zhuang took me to a three-storey, grey-concrete, flat-roofed building without architectural merit. It certainly didn't look Chinese. The window frames were metal, and suffered from corrosion, with those small glass panes, which, from how they looked, must have been difficult to clean. Bikes, those robust sit-up-and-beg types, old but well cared for, were parked in long racks immediately in front of the entrance.

My induction to the building was brief.

'Toilets,' said Zhuang, pointing to an open door in the corridor.

I looked inside and saw what looked like a cattle trough sunk into the floor running the width of the room, about a foot deep, and made from concrete. I stared for a few seconds trying to work out how it worked. On either side of the trough was a space – perhaps to place your feet. I could only conclude it was a communal affair where you all lined up, feet apart, with the trough passing below. You would need to keep a careful eye on anyone in front of you. Then you flush the trough with water, although I couldn't see how. In truth, I was baffled. I made a mental note to make full use of the guesthouse facilities. The toilets didn't have a strong smell, so perhaps were not in use.

The building itself had a smell, not strong, but it was there.

'Classroom,' Zhuang informed me.

My classroom, which was on the middle floor, was much like any other classroom. It comfortably fitted my thirty or so students. The students had old-fashion, wooden desks, laid out in disorderly rows. In the front of the classroom was a large traditional desk, with drawers down each side, for the tutor. The desk was on a raised platform so the tutor had a commanding view over the students. Behind the desk looked a good place to hide. The bare walls badly needed decorating.

They had provided me with an overhead projector with a white wall behind to act as a screen. Petter had briefed me well, and I came prepared with non-permanent pens and a box of transparencies. If I were to run short of transparencies, then my classroom monitor would wash and dry previously used ones for me.

Petter had managed to provide the university library with a range of textbooks to support the programme, but none for cross-management communication. It was, after all, a new academic subject in business management. That did cause me some concern. Apart from a couple of vaguely related textbooks I had brought with me, I had a selection of dubious articles from journals the poly library had managed to obtain through inter-library loans. Leaving aside my plan to keep one-step ahead of the students, I was worried about having enough material to keep me going for the six or so weeks I was to remain in China.

I gave Zhuang a pile of notes and handouts for photocopying.

My first session with the students was an introduction, finding out names and things. Since I was an eminent professor from a famous, foreign university, Petter warned me the students would take everything I said literally and without question. At the time, I didn't appreciate the significance of that sound advice.

Until I could provide the students with reading and background material, I had copied some of the summaries from my notes onto transparencies and hoped for the best. I assumed they were about cross-management communication; regrettably, I had never taught it before.

My students arrived punctually and sat down quietly. They were predominantly male, although I did see a few females among them. The male students mostly wore white shirts with dark trousers and black shoes. They were not in uniform; it was just the preferred mode of dress. All had well-groomed, bristly black hair, which would be mistaken for wigs back in Pontefract. The females mostly wore white blouses with modest skirts or trousers. I consider myself to be of average height, but I was distinctively tall in the company of the students.

The loudspeakers suddenly stopped, which was fortuitous. I did the names bit and briefly introduced myself, but I became bogged down with the eminence of Pontefract Polytechnic.

'Compared to Harvard, Pontefract has a better racecourse,' I offered flippantly. 'In England, polytechnic means university, more or less…'

The way to progress, I decided, was to tell a joke. Back at the poly, I had a repertoire of jokes for my lectures but, unfortunately, none for that particular audience. I then remembered a joke I had read in one of the Kuala Lumpur airport magazines; with hindsight, I wished I hadn't.

'There was a Chinese man looking for a job in London,' I started, 'his name was Zhuang.'

Zhuang was at the back of the room, and several heads looked in his direction. I had not yet learnt many Chinese names and his was the first that came to mind.

'I eh, don't mean Zhuang, the classroom monitor, literally, but just a Chinese man.' I pointed to two or three students in front of me to emphasis my point.

I decided to persevere.

'Zhuang, eh no, I mean, the Chinese man went to a building site and found the foreman to ask if there was work available.'

I had to clarify to the students that the foreman was the boss, but I won't go into that. To make things easy, I will continue the joke without the interruptions, because there were many…

The foreman was impressed with the diligence of the Chinese man and he decided to help him if he could.

'Can you lay bricks?' the foreman asked.

'No,' replied the Chinese man.

'Can you lay roof tiles?'

'No.'

'Can you make cement?'

'No.'

The foreman was trying hard to find something the Chinese man could do, and he had to think what else he could offer. A continual problem on most building sites was supplies and deliveries. Things never arrived on time or when required, and that caused continual delays.

'Supplies,' asked the foreman, 'can you do supplies?'

'Oh yes,' replied the Chinese man. 'I'm good at that.'

The Chinese man was duly employed, and the foreman went about his duties as usual. It was a busy building site and the foreman didn't think about the Chinese man until about a week later. He wanted to know how he had settled in and see how things were going. He wandered around the building site looking for the Chinese man but couldn't find him anywhere.

'Anyone seen the Chinese man?' shouted the foreman.

The foreman wandered around a bit more, looking here and there. Suddenly and without warning, from behind a stack of bricks jumped the Chinese man waving his arms wildly and pulling faces.

'*Surplies, surplies!*' shouted the Chinese man.

'Ha, ha...ha,' was all I could finish with.

If acting, there must be a moment when you know the performance has gone horribly wrong.

It was one of those moments.

All I could see in front of me was a room of blank faces. Things then took an unexpected turn. The students became quite animated and started to talk all at once, initially in Chinese among themselves, and then to me.

'How much did the Chinese man earn?' asked Hou, a student near the front.

'Did the Chinese man need a permit to work on the building site?' asked Yang, who sat next to Hou.

'Is it possible to work on any building site or only one chosen by the government?' asked Wei.

'Did the man bribe the foreman for the job?'

'Will we get our work placements that easy?' and similar questions...

I was baffled.

I tried to explain it was just a joke I had found in a Malaysian airport magazine – okay, a lame one at that. Would they listen? The students knew from Professor Song that Petter had come to China to discuss their overseas work placements, but did not seem to understand it had nothing to do with me. They somehow had the wrong idea.

I moved the session towards cross-management communication by placing my first transparency on the overhead projector.

'Oh, very interesting,' they said. 'Give the transparencies to the classroom monitor to photocopy. We'll read them later.'

Apparently, the students could get photocopying done almost immediately. UNIBO, who sponsored the project, had provided a dedicated photocopier with an unlimited amount of paper. Mr Chou had not informed me of that, and I was puzzled about the, '…submitting photocopying at least three days in advance,' fuss he spoke about a couple of days ago.

'Is it that easy to get a job in the West?' persisted Hou.

'No, it's just a joke, ha, ha!' I replied. I tried to explain the concept of an icebreaker to the class but to no avail. They looked out of the window and could see the weather was warm!

At the end of the session, the students were highly stimulated and full of enthusiasm.

'If you work longer hours in the West, you get paid more. That's right, isn't it?' was the last comment I heard from Hou as he and the others left the room.

That went well, I thought.

Chapter 4

Friday, April 21, 1989

The students had read and remembered everything on my transparencies. They had even managed to get the classroom monitor to photocopy my notes, and they knew them word-for-word.

I asked a question. They gave me the answer.

'Excellent,' I replied.

'Correct,' I encouraged.

'That's a good point,' I pointed out.

'Is it true that if you work hard in the West, then you might get promoted?' commented someone from the back.

The students wanted to know how much I was earning. I was reluctant to answer because I was getting my senior lecturer salary, an excellent consultancy fee from the United Nations, and extremely generous living expenses while working in China.

Rather than answer directly, I attempted a different course of action.

I provided a résumé of my life-style back in my small village on the outskirts of Pontefract. I explained that I had to provide and pay for my own housing and food; my university provided nothing. I gave them my monthly bills – mortgage, local tax, water rates, telephone, electricity, oil, and things like that.

I told them I needed two cars because there was no local transport and gave them the related costs of car insurance, road tax, cost of petrol, maintenance, etcetera.

I gave them the costs of the clothes I was wearing, which were some smart, new, lightweight, traveller-clothes, bought from the Rohan shop in York. I certainly looked the part.

I explained that I always went skiing at Christmas with my family, and that I had just bought a small apartment in the south of France and plan to spend Easter and summer there every year.

I indicated what my family living costs were, and what insurances I had. I told them that the government took away a certain percentage of my salary in tax, and I had to pay into a pension fund for my old age. I told them everything I could remember. I then asked them how much they considered I needed to earn to cover that.

'Is that normal for intellectuals in England?' they asked.

'For an educated professional involved in the realms of higher education, yes, this is about normal,' I replied. Admittedly, I over-elaborated a bit...

The students spent the next fifteen minutes or so discussing my financial situation and came up with their solution, which was far higher than my senior lecturer salary. I asked them to provide me with a letter of support for a pay increase from my head of school back at the poly.

'So it is possible to negotiate your salary in the West?' Hou queried.

Hou was obviously more confident than the rest. I had noticed he always had a group of students around him and wherever he went, the others followed.

It was Friday afternoon, and the students wanted to get away early.

'We have important things to do,' they said.

Not much different to the poly, it seemed.

They took my transparencies for copying and went away happily.

I could not understand what I had done to deserve such positive response from the students. By contrast, students at the poly never read handouts or prepared for lecturers. They never took learning seriously.

Because the students in Jaliang were extremely bright, I decided I had better be careful and planned a new teaching strategy, which involved keeping back the last few pages of any handout. Since I had the only source of learning materials, I would always know something they didn't.

Chapter 5

Saturday, April 22, 1989

It was the weekend and my first opportunity to visit some of the attractions around Jaliang.

'You are lucky,' Mr Chou informed us at breakfast. 'I have arranged a university car for you, and you will enjoy some of the magnificent achievements of the People's Republic. You will tour the port and then visit some of the factories in the industrial zone. This evening you are guests of honour at a banquet with Professor Song and some of his senior faculty members.'

'That's very good of Mr Chou to go to all this bother for us,' I remarked to Petter.

Petter, on the other hand, looked most displeased. He had travelled to Jaliang on numerous occasions, and didn't appreciate arrangements made by staff from the Office of Foreign Affairs. In any case, Petter lived in northern Sweden, in a village above the Arctic Circle. Apart from his regular visits to Stockholm on business, he had just spent most of the past winter months in darkness. He had had enough of snow, ice, and the cold. He wanted sun and warmth.

'With respect, Mr Chou,' Petter said, with greatest disrespect, 'you could have consulted us before you made these arrangements. I want to go sunbathing. This is Dr Vincent's first visit to China, and I am sure he wants to see other things.'

'But all the arrangements have been made,' protested Mr Chou.

What perplexed Mr Chou mostly was the concept of Petter wanting to go sunbathing instead of seeing the magnificent achievements of the People's Republic. In addition, the arrangements were arranged, and in China, you don't change arrangements!

'Look,' persisted Petter, 'I have seen enough achievements to last me a lifetime. I have visited many Chinese factories already.'

'But you haven't visited the port.'

It was true, Petter had not been to the port of Jaliang, and the main port area was quite close to the town centre.

After careful negotiations between Petter and Mr Chou, we agreed we would visit the port complex that morning. I had commented, foolishly according to Petter, that I wouldn't mind seeing the port as it might provide me with excellent background material for my lectures. I didn't think my standard British-based case studies would be relevant in Jaliang. I wanted to develop some local cases.

I also had another interest. I started my adult life as a qualified deck officer in the merchant navy before becoming an academic. I had spent my time on tankers and never had much opportunity to visit ordinary commercial ports. They invariably built tanker berths in lonely godforsaken places, well away from anything interesting.

'After visiting the port,' Mr Chou said hesitantly, 'the car will take you to the Friendship Store, which is not far away. You will then be free to shop and wander around. Later, the car will drive you to the hotel where the banquet is to be held.'

Petter could not find particular fault with these arrangements, although he was still unhappy about not being able to sunbathe.

'I will organise things so you can go sunbathing tomorrow,' promised Mr Chou, looking relieved.

'Why do I always feel I've been hoodwinked?' commented Petter.

The car that took us to the port office was comfortable but it was difficult to view anything through the windows. They had covered the windows with a grey plastic film to give the appearance of tinted windows, but unfortunately, the tint was too dark. The effect looked good from a distance, but close up, you could see the plastic film had been difficult to attach and suffered from inconveniently positioned air bubbles, which I wanted to prick with a pin.

The parts of Jaliang we saw were not very pretty. The trees that lined the roads were the only redeeming feature, giving a leafy appearance and softening the harsh dreary buildings hidden behind. Although I didn't have any expectations, it was not how I envisaged China to be.

The port office of Jaliang was a large building near the town centre. From a distance, the building looked like a multi-storey car park, but as we got closer, I saw windows in the gaps between the floors.

Our first act of enjoying the magnificent achievements of the People's Republic, as promised by Mr Chou, was to sit through a slide show presentation given by the propaganda department. They gave us the trade statistics of the port with lists of import and export cargoes, and presented us with publicity material with nice photographs of ships and cranes, and the like. I was impressed, but I could see Petter did not share my enthusiasm. Outside, there was a clear blue sky, and it was warm and sunny. Petter, no doubt, was probably sulking about the sunbathing he was missing.

Because I normally related propaganda with bias or misinformation, I was suspicious of information given to me by the propaganda department. Petter pointed out that such a department was common in China. They generally provided the usual informative and PR functions we were familiar with in the West.

Two members of staff from the propaganda department and Mr Cheng, the assistant-deputy port director, took us onto the roof of the port office, which provided excellent views of the port. I saw a wide estuary open to the sea. Beyond, there was a long breakwater protecting the estuary entrance from adverse weather. I couldn't see how far the river meandered inland because buildings and hills blocked the view. They told us that some berths were located near Number 3 University but not used for working cargo.

There were several large rectangular docks open to the estuary, lined with cranes at irregular intervals. The crane arms were sticking into the air at awkward angles giving the port an untidy look. I wanted to go and line up the cranes so they looked symmetrical. The buildings and sheds around the docks were grey with flat roofs, except one, which was a peculiar hexagon-shaped building, on stilts, with a green roof, quite modern looking compared to the rest of the port. Looking closely, on one of the sides of the building, underneath large yellow Chinese symbols, the sign Jaliang Passenger Terminal was clearly visible. Where might passengers travel? The water in the docks was murky and flat.

Mr Cheng, who was hospitable and friendly, could speak very good English. By contrast, the two chaps from the propaganda department were much younger and without charm; one could speak English, but not the other. Propaganda-man 1, who couldn't speak English, was constantly giving orders to the other. Besides continually jumping about, opening and closing doors, offering tea or Pepsi, and things like that, propaganda-man 2 was translating, to propaganda-man 1, everything said by Mr Cheng, Petter, and me.

'Unfortunately, we have a port congestion problem,' explained Mr Cheng, 'but—'

'But the ministry is providing funds from central government to build twelve new berths,' propaganda-man 1 informed us through his colleague. 'To get such funds allocated by central government is undeniably a great achievement by the port municipal central committee. Isn't that correct, Mr Cheng?'

'That is correct,' confirmed Mr Cheng.

'Does the port work a seven day week?' enquired Petter.

'Yes,' replied propaganda-man 2.

'So today is a normal port working day,' Petter again enquired.

'Yes.'

'I see,' commented Petter knowingly. I could tell from the tone of his voice that Petter was getting at something. Petter continued to gaze over the port complex. 'There must be about twenty-five or so berths we can see from here, don't you agree, Charles?'

'Yes,' I agreed.

'How many ships can you see in the port, Charles?'

'Three,' I replied. In a congested port, I would expect to see it teeming with ships and activity. This place was almost empty.

'Things are never what they seem,' Mr Cheng said quietly.

'That container berth over there,' Petter pointed out, 'the one with the yard piled high. How long do the containers stay there?'

'Fifty days is not untypical, perhaps longer,' replied Mr Cheng.

'Four days is normal in Sweden,' commented Petter. 'And the yards, sheds, and warehouses all look full to me.'

'Yes, they are all full.'

'Do you know much about ports, Charles? You were once an officer in the merchant navy, if I remember correctly.'

'I was on tankers,' I answered. 'We never visited proper ports but were always berthed in the middle of nowhere. Tankers are dangerous.'

Nevertheless, I could see Petter was right. Every space in the port area was crammed with containers, boxes, sacks, machinery, cars, and so forth.

While Petter was discussing technical aspects about the port with Mr Cheng, I talked politely to the two propaganda-men.

'Nice cars,' I said, pointing out some imported BMWs.

'Yes, those are for important government officials,' replied propaganda-man 2.

'And for escorting foreign guests,' said propaganda-man 1 pointedly. That was unfair because the large comfortable limousine we had was not a BMW.

Petter decided we would walk to the Friendship Store from the port office. It wasn't far.

Friendship Stores were one of the few official places where foreigners could legitimately spend their Foreign Exchange Certificates (FECs). Oddly, from the clientele we saw, we were probably the only foreigners in the place. The car park outside was packed with nice-looking foreign cars, including BMWs. It was a place popular with high-ranking Chinese officials.

On arrival in China, when I exchanged my currency, they gave me FECs, which was a special currency for foreigners to use in certain places like hotels for foreigners and certain shops. It limited where a foreigner could go or stay in China, although there were ways around that. On arrival at the airport, I had to declare all foreign currency in my possession, which they would check against my exchange receipts when I departed. It was the Chinese government's measure for controlling hard currency. Most Chinese people had never seen or handled FECs. In any case, if they were to have FECs, they could not officially use them, unless they were high-ranking officials.

Petter explained that it was difficult for foreigners like us to obtain Renminbi, the normal Chinese currency. As you might expect, there was an unofficial market for such dealings.

The Friendship Store was another unremarkable building. Inside, it looked much like any other department store, less cramped perhaps, slightly grimy, but without the crowds. In any case, people didn't visit the Friendship Store to admire its architecture and decor.

The store was packed full of the better things produced or manufactured in China, such as lacquered furniture, clothes and fine silks, jade and jewellery, porcelain, modern and old art, registered antiques, and a lot more. I couldn't resist the goose-down ski jacket, jade bowl, hand painted antique fans, or the freshwater pearls. I had the feeling there was a two-tier price system in operation, one for foreigners, and another for the high-ranking officials and their families. I was not complaining. Things were still cheap.

I made a mental note of what I might buy on my next visit, which included a lion, about twelve inches high, carved in heavy grey granite. Historically, they symbolically placed these in pairs outside the main entrances of palaces, temples, and the homes of state officials. Petter said you saw them around Jaliang outside offices and restaurants. Unfortunately, they came in pairs and I only wanted one, the male holding a ball under its paw, a bit like a proud footballer.

A sales counter had several shop assistants and half were asleep with their foreheads on the counter. The other half were in a huddle, drinking tea, and not doing much, not even having a good gossip. It was with great reluctance that someone would come and serve you.

After rummaging around the various departments, we went to the Friendship Store coffee shop to enjoy a cold Tsingtao beer, China's favourite beer.

'You seemed to have a long conversation with the two gentlemen from the port propaganda department,' Petter commented. 'Did they tell you anything interesting?'

'They told me about some of China's great achievements,' I replied.

'I thought you wanted case study material for your classes.'

'I'm working on it,' I said vaguely. I knew that wasn't strictly true, so I decided I had better change the subject. 'What about Mr Cheng?'

'He was very helpful,' Petter replied. 'He told me about the problems of the port. The port does suffer from congestion, but you could see there are plenty of berths. Poor road and rail links causes the congestion. They cannot cope with the volume of traffic, and imported cargo has to stay in storage within the port. That is why the warehouses, sheds, container yards, and parking areas are all full. Until they transport the cargo from the port by road or rail, other ships cannot enter to discharge their cargo. There is physically no space in the port to discharge or store further cargoes. Mr Cheng reckoned there must be at least twenty ships at anchor waiting to berth.'

'At least they are building twelve new berths to resolve the congestion,' I said.

'The problem is caused by the poor road and rail infrastructure between Jaliang and the rest of China,' Petter explained. 'The port looks fine. Unfortunately, the ministry responsible for the ports is different to that for road and rail. The port has the congestion and immediate problem, so the ministry responsible got the investment grant. All it can do is build more berths. It certainly cannot improve the road and rail infrastructure because that is the responsibility of a different ministry. One ministry isn't likely to hand over a large investment grant to another, is it?'

'No, I suppose not.'

'But you know all about that with your shipping background.'

We both sipped our beer and watched the senior officials and their families scurrying around the Friendship Store, buying all sorts, and then loading their bags into the ample boots of their large foreign cars.

'Those ships at anchor must cause another problem,' I commented. 'When a ship arrives at a port and has to anchor before discharging its cargo, then someone has to pay demurrage – the Chinese government, no doubt.'

'Demurrage?'

'If a ship is delayed beyond its stipulated time, then the payment for such delay is called demurrage,' I explained. 'It is usually a fixed sum per day or hour agreed to be paid by the charterer of the ship to the shipowner.'

'I'm none the wiser.'

'Look,' I said patiently, 'if you hire a taxi and it has to wait for some reason, then the taxi driver keeps the meter going. The taxi driver will certainly not wait for nothing. It is the same for a ship.'

'So?'

'A shipowner can make a lot of money by sending their ships to congested ports with fictitious cargoes, and then being paid handsomely while the ship is at anchor waiting for a berth,' I explained. 'You do not need to have a fictitious cargo, any low-value cargo in a wreck of a ship will do. A nod and wink between interested parties, then it is almost legitimate. I believe the Nigerians fine-tuned that practice back in the mid-seventies with cargoes of cement to support their building boom.'

'It all sounds too easy,' added Petter thoughtfully, 'How do you know all this, Charles?'

'I was a ship's officer,' I reminded him. 'The first thing we always did when we arrive at a port, berth, or anchorage is issue our Notice of Readiness. That means the ship is ready to work and if we have to wait, then someone must pay.'

'Very interesting,' said Petter. 'At least you have a case study now.'

I always was good at research!

The car took Petter and me to a hotel on the outskirts of town. The hotel manager and Professor Song, who was our host for the banquet, met us at the entrance.

'How do you like our new hotel?' enquired the hotel manager with pride. 'This is a special place, and we normally keep foreigners away from here. You are fortunate Professor Song is an old friend.'

Seeing the bigger picture; pushing the envelope; thinking outside the box; or was it simply perception? Whatever it was, it was obviously not one of my strengths.

What I deemed I witnessed when our car drove up to the hotel was a ruin, an old dilapidated hotel in need of immediate restoration. By the entrance was a fountain in the shape of a fish. It had no water, but only cigarette ends and what looked like the remains of building rubble.

The windows and doors did not quite fit the spaces made for them in the brickwork. They were crudely lacquered, covering bits of cement and other stuff not removed when fitted.

The thick-pile nylon carpets in the foyer were badly marked, particularly with cigarette burns, and whoever laid them did not quite manage to cut them the same shape as the room they shared. The windows were not clean. Nothing was very clean, and not helped by yards of faded, sad-looking, dusty red ribbon hanging everywhere.

'Are you sure this is the right place, Petter?' I whispered.

If you were a worldly academic traveller representing the United Nations and British higher education, work was not all in the classroom.

My colleagues back at the poly did not know about all those banquets and cultural visits that were an important part of my new duties. They did not realise how hard it was having to eat all that food, experiencing new and interesting drinks, and so forth; all in the name of academic collaboration, needless to say.

For example, having to eat a twenty-plus course banquet in a private function room at the top of that new hotel was not necessarily fun. Around the walls were large hand-painted murals of bright coloured blossom and delicate country scenes of ancient China. I admired the scenes. I just wished the real China, the one I saw that day, were, in some small way, remotely similar.

By the side of my bowl were three glasses of varying sizes and a small cup. The small glass was for the Maotai, an infamous Chinese liqueur that tasted like paraffin. The middle-size glass was for the Chinese wine that tasted of nothing. Well, drinking Maotai anaesthetised your taste buds for several minutes, so I might be doing an injustice to the wine. The large glass was for the Tsingtao beer; the beer was good. Lastly, the small cup was for the green tea. I never got round to drinking the green tea. All three glasses were kept full, and you had to be vigilant as to which drink to partake, and when. You did not want to upset your hosts, did you?

I needed not have worried.

All became clearer during the first course because each was no more than a mouthful. Just as well with twenty or so courses. Since it was a formal banquet, rice was not on offer. The translation of the menu by my hosts was not always helpful. For example, 'Sea slugs, delicious,' and, 'Look, black worms,' did not necessarily fill me with confidence. I soon realised it was probably better not to know what you were eating – it all tasted good.

Petter, as guest of honour, sat to the right of Professor Song. Me, I was half way round the table and assumed I was low in the pecking order. There again, I might have got that wrong. I sat next to Professor Sang, the director of contemporary economics division. Professor Sang, a kindly man, explained to me the protocols involved in partaking in a formal Chinese banquet. On my other side was the car driver who also enjoyed the banquet, like the rest of us. Professor Sang explained that was normal because the driver was treated the same as everyone else.

'Some of the students are a little restless,' I commented.

'Not just the students,' Professor Sang replied. 'Intellectuals have been expressing their dissent for some time.'

'Dissent?' I queried.

Surely, people couldn't do such things in China and get away with it?

'We do things...' I could see Professor Sang was looking for the right words, '...more subtly. For example, a leading intellectual or dissident might write an open letter to one of our leaders. Alternatively, they might organise a petition, signed by many, and present it to the National People's Congress. Students may support such actions by placing posters around campus. We can express our dissent in a polite way, but there is a fine line we never cross.'

'And if you do?'

'We must have another discussion,' offered Professor Sang.

'Yes,' I replied, 'I would like that.'

After each of the twenty or so courses, someone had to stand up, carefully choose a drink, and declare a toast, 'Friendship between China and Sweden,' for example. Everyone then downed the drink in one.

By about the eighth course the toasts became less formal, 'Friendship between our wives and anybody else's wife,' and things like that. As a guest at the banquet, along with Petter, I had to make several toasts. You never had any warning because Professor Song, our host, just looked at you. Trying to compose meaningful, worthy, off the cuff toasts, I found, was not my forte. I was pleased with, 'Up with Mao and down with the Maotai.' I wasn't sure if I got the up and down the right way, but I don't think anyone noticed.

To be honest, I don't remember much beyond the thirteenth course. Rest assured, I worked hard for the poly into the small hours of the morning.

Extract from:

THE PRESS
SAT 22 APR 1989
Local correspondent, Peking

ON THE DEATH of Hu Yaobang, the former Communist Party leader, the Chinese government's obituary lauded him as a *staunch communist warrior and statesman* but failed to mention his fall from grace two years earlier. Hu was forced to resign because of his views towards *freedom of speech* and *freedom of press* and his empathy with the student protesters in 1986.

The day after Hu's death on 15 April, a small-scale demonstration in his honour demanded that the government reconsider his public reputation. Public pressure then forced the Chinese government to bestow Hu with a state funeral.

This provided the opportunity for student protesters to show their support for Hu and his views under the guise of mourning, knowing that the authorities cannot be seen publically to assault or harm them in any way. The Chinese authorities hesitated, not knowing what to do, because they could not distinguish between mourning and protests.

The peasants, comprising the majority of the population, angry because many had not been paid for their grain production, also joined the protests along with workers. It is unknown in China for students, peasants, and workers to unify in such a manner. Not only can students get away with far more than that of peasants and workers, their complaints against the government are completely different.

Last week thousands of protesters rushed armed police guarding the Zhongnanhai compound in Peking, where the government leadership lives. Throwing debris, they shouted, 'long live democracy, down with dictatorship,' and arraigned the Chinese leader, the 84-year-old Deng Xiaoping, of outliving his usefulness. Being anxious of casualties, the authorities did nothing, and this resulted in the worse anti-government demonstrations since 1976.

Yesterday, calling for democracy and freedom, 100,000 students marched from their universities to Tiananmen

Square in the centre of Peking, where they flouted police authority and the government's order to disperse. The protesters gathered in front of the Great Hall of the People, China's parliamentary building, where student leaders criticised the communist regime.

Chapter 6

Sunday, April 23, 1989

It was Sunday morning, and Mr Chou kept his word.

We went sunbathing.

'*I* didn't see you at breakfast,' commented Petter, as we got into the car.

English breakfast, in my state...

After about half an hour, the car left the main road, and we passed through a security barrier and checkpoint. The car drove down a narrow road, through secluded woods, for about five minutes. We arrived at what appeared to be a park with attractive trees scattered around. It looked vaguely familiar. I then remembered the murals on the wall where we had the banquet last night. This was a poor representation of old China, a caricature of the real thing. I couldn't quite work out if I felt disappointed or amused.

There was a row of secluded, detached, ranch-style, shabby bungalows with untidy gardens leading onto the beach. We had a bungalow for the day.

Mr Chou had kindly sent Zhuang to accompany us to make sure all the arrangements went as planned. Two stewards provided us with drinks and snacks. Lunch, we were informed, was to be served on the veranda about two o'clock. I was not sure who looked more pleased, Zhuang, who seemed quite overcome by the occasion, or Petter.

'I have never been here before,' Zhuang informed us. 'It is a special place for senior and high-ranking officials and their families in the summer. It is the best beach in this part of China. Mr Chou said you are lucky to come here. He must have pulled a lot of strings.' Zhuang went into the bungalow and watched TV. Obviously, the sun was not his thing.

Petter changed into his swimming trunks and was soon on the beach with a cold drink. He explained that, where he came from, he spent half of the year in darkness. The other half of the year, when it remained light, was infested with insects.

'Let me know when lunch is ready,' requested Petter.

Sunbathing was not my thing either, so I sat in the shade on the veranda facing the sea and, after taking stock of my surroundings, spent the rest of the day preparing my teaching programme for the following week.

Being April, we were the only people around, which was why Mr Chou could arrange for us to visit at such short notice. The place was agreeable, relative to what I had seen so far of Jaliang. I was surprised that the beach was full of stones, rocks, and rubbish; I assumed they would clean it before the summer.

That secluded beach retreat was obviously the better side of communism – if you were a high-ranking official.

Extract from:

THE PRESS
SUN 23 APR 1989
Local correspondent, Peking

YESTERDAY, WHEN CHINESE LEADERS gathered inside the Great Hall of the People in preparation for the state funeral of the former Communist Party leader, Hu Yaobang, whose death sparked off the current spate of protests, over 50,000 students and workers gathered on Tiananmen Square. When the authorities prevented student leaders from gaining access to the funeral service inside the Great Hall, tempers flared and protesters again threw debris and rubbish as rows of police held them back.

Four students were eventually allowed access to the Great Hall but were not allowed to view the body of the former Communist Party leader or speak to prime minister, Li Peng, who is a conservative hardliner at the top of government. Students wanted to hand over a petition, demanding freedom of speech and an end to corruption by Communist Party officials.

Hu's views towards *freedom of speech* and *freedom of press* have greatly influenced students' participation in the current unrest.

Many of the student protesters openly supported Gorbachev, the Soviet president, who is visiting China in four weeks' time to attend the crucial Sino-Soviet summit. They have been enthused by his political reforms, which China has failed to follow.

Chapter 7

Monday, April 24, 1989

'Toast!' I exclaimed. 'You're stretching your luck with that.'

When the little, old, Chinese lady took our orders, Petter handed her a piece of paper. Leaving aside the fact that Petter had been enjoying his pancakes, he considered it was time for a change.

'I asked Professor Song to write this down,' Petter said.

When I glanced at the piece of paper, it seemed to be a very long explanation of toast. It also had some intriguing diagrams thrown in for good luck. Petter and the little, old, Chinese lady eyed each other up, and Petter imagined he had the upper hand on that one. She retired to the kitchen with a wistful look. Petter, I sensed, was looking a bit too smug. We heard a lot of shouting from the kitchen between the little, old, Chinese lady, and the cook, who we had learnt was her husband.

Once the shouting had stopped, the little, old, Chinese lady returned, and she pointed out of the window.

'Toe...' she said, smiling sweetly.

We saw a little, old, Chinese man, the cook, riding away on a large, dilapidated, wobbling bike. He was off to buy bread, I surmised. He looked about eighty, and, until then, I had never seen him. I could not imagine how he had the energy each morning to make all that noise in the kitchen, with the clashing of pans and shouting, and the result only being a pancake and eggs on apple pie.

'Well,' Petter said slowly, 'maybe toast tomorrow.' He looked up at the little, old, Chinese lady, who stood by patiently.

'Omele?'

Petter nodded stoically.

'I don't suppose you're up to speed on the demonstrations,' commented Petter casually.

Since Petter had mentioned it a few days ago, I hadn't taken much notice. I had been too busy preparing for my classes. My first week had been occupied keeping at least one page ahead of the students, which proved to be difficult. They were intelligent, hardworking, and eager.

'Well,' continued Petter, 'the BBC World Service reported that the student protests in Beijing are escalating, and these might spread to other towns and regions. I wouldn't be surprised if you have a few students missing.'

As it happened, my students were all present and correct. Zhuang, the classroom monitor, also sat in the corner. I had noticed before the class started that Hou and his followers were in deep conversation with Zhuang, probably sorting out my photocopying or something.

'It seems you had a good weekend, Professor Charles?' commented Hou. 'Did you enjoy the Chinese seaside?'

'Yes, very agreeable.' I admitted. 'You Chinese seem to know how to have a good time.'

'Some Chinese, not all,' replied Hou.

I then remembered what Zhuang had said about the beach retreat being a place for high-ranking officials and their families. Zhuang must have told Hou about my relaxing day yesterday.

'I am sure you will all become senior officials of the university or industry not before too long.'

Which was probably true? Hou and the others were bright, young students carefully selected to participate on the United Nations programme. They were the high-fliers, the future.

'And be chosen to become a member of the Party first,' added Hou.

'The Party?'

'The Chinese Communist Party,' prompted Hou. 'Only Party members elect our leadership. You cannot join the Communist Party, because they chose you. That is our form of democracy.'

'That sounds similar to how we elect our prime ministers,' I mumbled quietly to myself.

'We have about 47 million members of the Communist Party,' continued Hou. 'Our population is over one billion. Not everyone gets the chance to vote.'

Since I didn't know much about Chinese politics or democracy, I decided it best to get on with my class.

'We are going to explore the complex issues of a Problem Analysis. After I have introduced the conceptual model, you will have the opportunity to review a case study relating to the port of Jaliang. I have recently done some background research relating to the port.'

Okay, not entirely true, I know.

Since Petter had explained to me the difficulties of the port, I decided it would make excellent tutorial material for the students to practise a problem analysis. However, I had to provide some background theory, which was problematic (no pun intended). My notes were back at the poly.

My learning methodology, I decided, would be learning by discovery. Or was it experiential learning?

I recollected attending a tedious workshop delivered by some well-intentioned, middle class, trendy liberal from the school of education. She was wearing a kaftan and bedroom slippers with curly toes. 'It is not what we say that students remember,' she preached, 'it is what they say and do that they remember.'

At the time, I saw flaws in that argument – partly based on the fact I could never remember a thing I said. My own approach to teaching was simply to use a copy of some old, out-of-print academic tome my students could not possibly acquire. They seemed quite happy with me providing notes to copy from the overhead projector. It was, therefore, an excellent opportunity for me to experiment, well away from the poly, with that innovative learning by discovery – or whatever they called it.

Anyway, I didn't have much choice, for I had no notes. I was confident my bright Chinese students would discover something useful.

'In management, and everyday life for that matter, we come across problems of all sorts. Our first indication of the existence of a problem is when we experience or observe the symptoms. That is not to say the symptoms are the actual causes of a problem, they seldom are. Nevertheless, it is apparent that in trying to resolve a problem, most people focus on the symptoms instead of the causes, and in doing so, resolve nothing. We must, therefore, get beyond the symptoms, identify the true causes of the problem, and resolve them.'

Or something like that...

I didn't remember what I actually said, but I remembered seeing some very puzzled faces. I decided to give a very simple analogy to explain my theory.

'A few evenings ago, I was invited to a very nice banquet with Professor Song and other faculty staff. Perhaps I should not say this, but the hospitality of my hosts included the very best of Chinese beverages, for example, Tsingtao beer, Great Wall wine, Maotai, and one or two others. Least to say, next morning I was not at my best!'

Nothing...

I had expected at least a smile from my students.

Nevertheless, I could see the students were listening intently and some were nodding at Hou. I suspected, perhaps, my subtlety was too subtle for the students and I had better elaborate further.

'What I mean is we... eh, I had a little too much to drink, and I experienced a slight headache next morning. Therefore, I took half a dozen aspirins to relieve my headache. The aspirin eventually worked and my headache went away.

'If we analyse this further, the symptom of the problem was having a headache. I took the aspirins to relieve the symptom. We all know the cause of the problem was my having too many drinks. So what is the real solution for my headaches?'

'You take the aspirin before you have the drinks, so you won't get a headache in the first place,' replied Yang.

'That might work, but you are still attacking the symptoms of the problem, be it pre-empting them. No, the cause of the problem is over drinking. If I did not drink too much, then I would not get a headache.'

'Stopping drinking seems to be an excessive solution to the problem when simply taking aspirins beforehand solves the problem quite adequately,' Yang persisted.

I got a little annoyed with Yang because he was missing the point.

'Well... yes, there might well be social and acceptance issues to consider. Nevertheless, problem analysis is all about finding the *causes* and dealing with them and not focusing on the symptoms.'

I was warming up, and my usual safe and comfortable clichés that one normally used back at the poly were in full flow.

'Yang does have a point,' I conceded. 'We also need to consider the wider issues of any proposed solutions. One must take into account both socio-economic and political constraints. Are the solutions feasible? Are they acceptable? Are they achievable?'

'The classroom monitor says you are going to another banquet tonight,' commented Hou, with a grin.

'Yes, that is true. One must do what one must in terms of inter-university relationships. Duty calls—'

'So you will not be drinking much tonight then?' Hou responded.

'Well—'

'Best take the aspirin before you go this time,' added Yang.

'Taking socio-ethnological perceptions into consideration, you might have a point,' I said. 'Now I have a case study for you to consider.'

I had written up some notes about the port of Jaliang based upon what Petter had told me and what I had observed the previous Saturday. I wanted the class to review the information and then identify the problems the port was experiencing. Having done that, they were to identify the symptoms, the causes, and propose solutions. Or should they identify the symptoms before the problem? I was unsure, not having my notes with me. Since it was learning by discovery, it probably didn't matter!

After splitting the class into groups, I gave them the rest of the morning to undertake their problem analysis. They were to make presentations after lunch.

When I returned to the classroom, the students had moved the furniture around, except my desk, which remained at the front.

'The class has agreed to form one group,' Zhuang informed me. 'That's democracy, isn't it?'

'Well—'

'The class has elected an executive committee,' continued Zhuang, 'and the executive committee has elected a general secretary as leader.'

'Fair enough,' I said cautiously, sitting down at my desk.

What I actually wanted was for the individual groups to make presentations and then spend the rest of the afternoon arguing among themselves about the merits of the case and problem analysis.

The class had formed a tight uncomfortable U-shape facing me. Until then, the class had been quite happy sitting in the usual relaxed

33

rows with plenty of space between desks. It was all very well having these liberal democratic U-shape configurations but they were unsuitable for a square-shaped classroom. What did I know? In the middle of the U were Hou, Yang, and Wei, the executive committee. Since Hou was in the middle, I took him to be the general secretary.

Wei stood up. 'On behalf of the students and executive committee, as assistant general secretary, I have the honour of welcoming you to our meeting. It is an honour that you, Professor Charles, an eminent, foreign academic, share with us your knowledge, experience, and research. It is an honour that you allow us to explore our feelings and understanding of western attitudes and beliefs within a Chinese environment. I now ask general secretary Hou to present our findings.'

Following enthusiastic clapping by all, Hou stood up and faced me.

'It is a great honour… (I'll skip that bit). The class considers that the essential and important issues of the case are the economic and political factors that influence our everyday lives. We also took into account the socio-ethnological factors influencing you at the time when you were undertaking your investigations. On this matter, Zhuang was an invaluable source of information.'

I wondered what Zhuang might have said that was of help. He was my classroom monitor, but he seemed to be taking quite an interest in things. He had not been with Petter and me when we visited the port, but he had accompanied us yesterday on the beach.

'The problem,' Hou continued, 'is we do not have the freedom and democracy as enjoyed by those in the West.'

There was now more enthusiastic clapping…

The flaw with that so-called learning by discovery, I remembered, was you could never be sure of the outcome unless you carefully planned the discoveries, which I hadn't done. Fortunately, things seemed to be organised, not what I expected, but well organised. I deemed it sensible to remain quiet and nodded encouragingly to Hou.

'The symptoms to the problem are obvious,' declared Hou. 'Firstly, it is both unfair and undemocratic for senior officials and other cadre to be provided with expensive, imported cars, such as those BMWs you saw in the port on Saturday. In a country where resources are scarce and the yuan is weak against hard currencies, it is economic madness to import expensive cars, never mind the social unjustness of it.'

It was the driver, I realised. He must have talked with Zhuang.

'Secondly, it is also socially unjust for the same senior officials and cadre to have exclusive weekend resorts by the seaside for themselves and their families. This is socially unfair, morally corrupt, and unacceptable.

'Lastly, as an eminent, foreign professor, you are allowed to visit places and see things that are forbidden to ordinary people. You can criticise the People's Republic and our leaders without punishment or retribution. What further symptoms do you need to demonstrate that we in the People's Republic lack freedom and democracy? That is the problem. It is an honour that you are willing to share your criticisms with us and open our eyes. Everything is controlled in China, including the press.'

'Well—'

Unfortunately, a bout of further enthusiastic clapping by the class did not allow me to deny any implied or direct criticism against the People's Republic or its leaders. I would never have dreamt of such a thing. I was not an adventurous person, and back in Pontefract, I normally led a peaceful, if not slightly boring life. In Kuala Lumpur, UNIBO officials warned me never to say anything controversial against the Chinese government. They explained that I was an honoured and invited guest, and I should speak and act accordingly – and enjoy the banquets.

'The solutions to the problem,' concluded Hou, 'are political reforms, end corruption by government officials, and intellectuals should unite with workers and peasants in protesting against the government.'

As Hou sat down, the whole class stood up and applauded, adding a few chants for good measure.

'Down with dictatorship!'

'Long live democracy!'

'Free speech is democracy!'

I made a mental note not to meddle in any further educational nonsense. I would keep to handouts and get students to copy from the overhead projector. Once the clapping and chanting had died down, everyone looked at me with great expectations.

What I wanted to say was the whole case study thing was a big mistake and they had misunderstood everything. I thought frantically to see if I could salvage anything from the fiasco.

'Well,' prompted Wei from the executive committee, after a long pause of silence.

They obviously wanted me to respond.

'Well, eh, what I mean is, your methodology and understanding of problem analysis is – impressive. Your socio-economic and political approach to the problem was – innovative.'

The committee again burst into enthusiastic clapping and seemed pleased with my feedback, which I found perplexing to say the least. By impressive, I meant that they were a little ambitious with their understanding; and by innovative, I meant that with their approach they were living in cloud-cuckoo-land.

'Well, eh, what I mean is,' I repeated, 'you seem to have lost sight of the port itself, which I assumed would be central to your analysis.'

'Oh no,' replied Wei cheerfully, 'we know where the port is. We took your excellent and honoured advice and considered the wider aspects of the case just as you suggested. We are all most grateful for your guidance on this matter.'

This was followed by even more enthusiastic clapping and cheers...

'We all know the road and rail links are inadequate,' added Hou. 'Because of that, cargo cannot move quickly from Jaliang. This is common knowledge. It is typical that the authorities are attempting to resolve the chronic congestion in the port by funding the wrong ministry. We followed your guidance and considered the important social and political issues impinging upon our lives. For this, Professor Charles, we thank you.'

The enthusiastic clapping and cheers were now synchronised, something you often come across while travelling abroad.

Admittedly, I blushed.

The class understood after all. They were only trying to impress me by looking into those wider issues, whatever they were. There might be something in that learning by... (I must look it up sometime).

She in the kaftan and curly toes was forgiven.

That went well, I thought.

'There are no more classes this week, Professor Charles,' mentioned Zhuang, as I was leaving the class.

'Oh?' I queried.

'Everyone is busy,' replied Zhuang. 'This is a pity because we very much enjoy your classes.'

In a way, I was relieved. I had more time to prepare for my classes. I was rapidly running out of material. I had to prepare a teaching plan – now that was innovative teaching.

I went back to my room for some aspirins. I was going to another banquet that evening!

Memorandum

(Telex message)

From   Chou Ke-qiang
         Director of the Office of Foreign Affairs
         Jaliang Number 3 University

To   Deputy Chairman
         Office of Education Foreign Affairs
         Public Security Bureau
         Beijing

Date   24 April 1989

CONFIDENTIAL

DR CHARLES VINCENT

I must report the arrival of a potential undercover provocateur. He is spending several weeks teaching on that meddlesome management project sponsored by the UNIBO office based in Malaysia. Dr Vincent is a replacement for another academic who was withdrawn at the last minute, and this alerted me in the first place.

I always allocate a member of my staff, as a classroom monitor, to the foreign professors. When I mentioned this to Dr Vincent, he appeared unsure, and when I offered him two, he seemed to panic. This made me more suspicious. The classroom monitor reports to me anything untoward.

I checked out Dr Vincent in all our normal traces, but I could find no reference to such a person being an academic of any standing. At best, he is a minor academic from a very minor university.

I could find no record of Pontefract University in any of the normal information channels available to us. To double check, I contacted the British Council in Beijing, but all that the information officer would say was that the place was only good for pontefract cakes, whatever that meant. Vincent also informed the students about the presence of a famous racecourse nearby, which provides some sort of sponsorship, although he did not go into detail. He also referred to teaching in a school of business and that, as you would appreciate, is hardly considered academically credible.

Vincent is supposedly teaching something called cross-management communication. The United Nations has not provided any books for the library to support this subject, and Vincent has the only notes available. When Vincent gave his notes to the classroom monitor for photocopying, we examined them as part of our normal procedure. They appeared to be a random set of articles, with missing pages. The students were given copies of Vincent's classroom transparencies, but these appeared to be bits found in bold from the original notes.

I can only conclude that cross-management communication is both a cover to hide Vincent's lack of academic knowledge and a clever mechanism to allow him to undertake covert operations to destabilise the students.

Until now, the students have not been looking forward to their placements because we have warned them about the inedible food and smells. We also only allow them to travel alone, unaccompanied by any family, which should motivate most to return.

The classroom monitor reported that Vincent has been disseminating subversive information among the students. Vincent was encouraging students to defect to the West during their foreign work placement. He promised them wealth and explained how easy it is to get jobs.

Vincent is encouraging his students to be activists in the protest movement. We are not talking about normal students but highly intelligent, carefully selected graduates who are now leading the protests here in Jaliang.

Vincent allowed his students to leave early on Friday afternoon. I believe that some of them have been contacting other leaders at one or more of the Beijing universities. I suspect that at least two of Vincent's students managed to travel to Beijing over the weekend as delegates, to discuss, with other leaders, a nationwide strike.

Over the weekend, several posters and banners appeared around the university expressing discontent with the government's progress towards democracy. Students gathered in large crowds chanting slogans, such as, 'Down with dictatorship,' and, 'Long live democracy.'

As with other universities, we are expecting demonstrations by students and intellectuals to coincide with the 70th anniversary of the May Fourth Movement. Today, things took a turn for the worse. Students at Number 3 University have joined those in Beijing by boycotting all classes. They have pasted up posters all over the university calling for the boycott to last indefinitely instead of ending on 4 May, as originally planned.

The student movement within Jaliang Number 3 University is now getting out of control as a direct result of the subversive activities of Vincent.

I urgently request your advice.

From: **Deputy Chairman**
Office of Education Foreign Affairs
Public Security Bureau
Beijing
To: **Chou Ke-qiang**
Director of the Office of Foreign Affairs
Jaliang Number 3 University
25 April 1989

Private note (by telex)

DISSIDENT VINCENT

Vincent came to the attention of the authorities when he arrived at Jaliang Airport. He had the audacity to claim diplomatic status on his arrival at the senior officials channel at immigration. He was flaunting his United Nations Certificate.

Other cities are also experiencing similar difficulties as you. For example, on Saturday, in the northern city of Xian, thousands of rioters burned vehicles and houses at the Shaanxi government compound, while at Changsha, in the south, rioters pillaged stores and attacked several hotel employees. The government has officially stressed that students were not involved in the Xian riots but was started by lawbreakers and similarly said that lawless elements in Changsha attacked police and looted shops.

Worse of all, hundreds of professors in Beijing signed a letter requesting that police should not harm the students. In addition, a large group of intellectuals led by Dai Qing, the novelist, signed a petition supporting the students. On Sunday, posters appeared on the Monument to the People's Heroes in Tiananmen Square, and workers signed these. It is unusual for workers to support intellectuals and students; they have their own worries.

At a Politburo meeting on April 20, Li Peng, the prime minister, expressed his view that a small group of people from within has instigated the current student protests.

It is your duty to control all dissidents and rebellious activities at Jaliang Number 3 University.

Chapter 8

'**What** is this?'

Petter was perturbed, if not a little indignant, by what he was being served at breakfast. All he wanted was toast. I know he had a thing about being firm from the beginning, but to practise that on our little, old, Chinese lady who served us our breakfast each morning, was, I considered, being somewhat pedantic.

'It looks like burnt marble cake, Petter. I'll have it if you don't.'

I was having difficulty mopping up my egg yolk with the crust from the apple pie, and the burnt marble cake would just do the trick.

Petter once again closely examined the toast instructions and accompanying diagrams Professor Song had kindly written out for him.

'That diagram there,' I said. 'It looks like marble cake to me.'

'That is toast,' stated Petter, 'with butter.'

'Omele?' said our hostess, before retiring into the kitchen to make an almighty racket with what sounded like a whole army of pan bangers.

I had arranged to see Professor Sang. He had suggested we went for a walk around East Lake, a supposedly noted beauty spot on the outskirts of town, and then refreshments at a popular teahouse.

I learnt to be cautious of beauty spots because the Chinese would visit en masse, particularly at the weekend. These were places where you took family photographs, and where better to pose than at a beauty spot. I had not worked out what constituted one spot to be beautiful, and others not. What I believed to be a pretty and secluded place, the Chinese would shake their heads and say, 'Too quiet.'

Another place afflicted with litter, a pond or fountain long dried up, heaps of stones artistically supporting a dishevelled stuffed panda, hordes of people, and long queues for the ice-cream seller, then they would smile and say, 'Beautiful.'

Luckily, it was not the weekend, and it was a pleasant day for a walk.

I had invited Petter along, but he wanted to go sunbathing again. He had found a particularly peaceful and isolated spot at the back of the university campus with lush green grass, surrounded by almond and cherry trees in full blossom. There was no chance of Petter being disturbed there – too quiet!

East Lake, fed by a small irrigation system from the local canal, had been man-made some indefinite time ago. The irrigation in and out of the lake was only a trickle, and the water appeared stagnant and murky. Water lilies obviously loved the lake. Goldfish, all colours from bright yellow, orange, and brown swam around in large shoals looking through the murk for onlookers to feed them.

'How long have you taught here?' I asked.

'Since the mid-sixties,' he replied.

'You speak very good English,' I commented.

'When I was at university a lot of us learnt English. Many intellectuals my age can speak good English. Since then people never learnt English, but things are changing. The government wants everyone to understand English as part of the Open Door Policy. They have English lessons on the radio and television all the time. English is taught in schools, but perhaps not in the rural areas.'

Puzzled by the expression, intellectual, I asked about that.

'It is just a way of describing someone who is not a peasant or worker. Because they produce the goods and food China needs, peasants and workers are better paid, but that is slowly changing. While intellectuals, including university professors, are lower paid, we have our minds, and can think. This is a freedom difficult to take away, although they tried.'

'You mean the Cultural Revolution?' I enquired.

'I don't want to talk about it.'

I had come across that already. No one wanted to talk about the Cultural Revolution. Until then, Professor Sang was happy, jovial, and proud to be showing me East Lake, the loveliest spot in Jaliang. He suddenly became sullen and glum.

'Chairman Mao, the Red Guards, and the Cultural Revolution are things I know practically nothing about,' I explained. 'People are happy to discuss the Open Door Policy, but what about when the door was closed. It would help my teaching to understand some of these things.'

Professor Sang was quiet for a few minutes.

'It is difficult to defend the Ten Years of Turmoil, as we sometimes call the Cultural Revolution,' explained Professor Sang. 'Because everything happened so recently, I find it uncomfortable to talk about. How can I justify what happened?'

I kept quiet.

'The Cultural Revolution, launched by Mao in 1965 with the help of his third wife, Jiang Qing, attacked all bourgeois tendencies and elements in the Chinese Communist Party, the government, the People's Liberation Army, and all cultural circles.

'That was the first appearance of the Red Guards who were encouraged, by Mao, to criticise and reform from below. They were urged to destroy old customs, old habits, old thinking. They attacked teachers, leaders, and even parents. The Red Guards mostly elected themselves, but they were just students and youngsters from the fields and factories. Chairman Mao told them they were the important ones and not the intellectuals.

'Mao published his thoughts, the 'Little Red Book', as it was called. It was full of slogans and other idealistic opinions used to justify what people did, particularly the Red Guards.

'As university lecturers, we were easy targets for the humiliation and self-criticism campaign of the Red Guard They picked me out because I could speak English, which they considered bourgeois. They cancelled classes and lectures for no reason. During classes, if students did not like you they would make fun or criticise you. You could do nothing about it. I was a young lecturer at the time. I just kept my head down and avoided trouble. If students wanted an easy time, then that was what I gave them.

'It was different for Professor Song, the faculty dean. He was already a professor and much older. They subjected him to severe humiliation and he had to endure struggle sessions. The Red Guards forced him to wear a paper dunce hat and burnt all his books. They made him learn and read aloud the thoughts of Mao. He was resolute, and learning a few slogans was not difficult. The books they burnt belonged to the university. They were for the students. If the Red Guards burnt the books and banned all examinations, then who lost out?

'Professor Song's indifference to the humiliation campaign goaded the Red Guards, and others, to raid his home. They could not cope with his self-reliance. Professor Song's home was vandalised. At first, they locked him up, and then made him clean the toilets. Cleaning toilets is easy work, he said.

'The Red Guards could not break Professor Song's spirit and in the end he was sent away to work on the farms. They sent others with him, but I was lucky. I made a few friends in the Red Guards and had an easy time. Professor Song returned, but others did not.

'Professor Song is still my neighbour. We all know who did what. Professor Song does not hold any grudges, but I know some people who still cannot look him in the eye.'

Professor Sang cheered up. 'We have arrived at the teahouse.'

The teahouse was a dark, highly lacquered, louvre-wooden building by the lakeside.

The staff sat us at a hefty, dark lacquered table, with similarly hefty chairs, next to an intricate fretwork window with views overlooking the lake. The table and chairs were too bulky to be comfortable. We were the only guests, and we were expected. Tea arrived almost immediately.

'This room is for special guests,' explained Professor Sang.

We enjoyed green tea in tall, porcelain teacups, with lids. We sipped the tea carefully so not to swallow the large leaves. They gave us chunks of yellow cake with a similar texture to the breakfast marble cake.

The teahouse looked extremely old and dilapidated, which was attractive so long as you didn't look too closely. Next to the teahouse was an antiquated tall pagoda, painted in bright colours, but the paintwork was faded and peeling. It looked in need of renovation.

'Nice old buildings,' I commented conversationally.

'What buildings?'

'The teahouse and pagoda.'

'They are not old but were built three years ago.'

I must have looked puzzled.

'Teahouses were bourgeois, and pagodas were anti-communist,' explained Professor Sang. 'Being built mainly of wood they were burnt or destroyed by the Red Guards during the Cultural Revolution. The government now wants tourists, and tourists need things to see. Most towns have had to build new pagodas and teahouses.'

I gazed at the pagoda, which, to me, looked dangerous. The Chinese were either extremely skilled at making replica historical monuments or, when left to their own devices, they were just terrible builders. I then remembered the special hotel, the venue of the banquet we had the previous Saturday, where they kept foreigners away.

They were terrible builders...

'Have you any news when students might return to classes?' I asked.

'I don't know,' replied Professor Sang replied. 'Things are unclear. An editorial published in today's *People's Daily* made a provocative denunciation against some of the protesters.'

'What did it say?'

Professor Sang walked over to the man who had served us our tea and cakes. After a brief conversation, he came back with a newspaper and studied it closely.

'You must know about the public mourning of Hu Yaobang's death,' Professor Sang continued, 'when students went to Tiananmen Square and placed wreathes.'

'A little,' I said.

'The *People's Daily* asserts an abnormal phenomenon occurred during the public mourning of Hu Yaobang,' read Professor Sang. 'It points out that an extremely small number of people took advantage of the situation and did not mourn Hu Yaobang's death, but were involved in a well-planned plot to confuse the people and throw the country into chaos. After the mourning, this small group, with ulterior motives, has continued to take advantage of the young people's feeling of grief by spreading all kinds of rumours to poison and confuse people's minds. It also claims that their real aim is to reject the Chinese Communist Party and the socialist system. The editorial goes on to say that this is a planned conspiracy and disturbance.'

'Are they blaming the students or what?'

Professor Sang continued to study the newspaper for a few minutes, and then he placed it on the table, picked up his cup, and sipped his tea.

'In the editorial, the authorities do not point to the students as the culprits but say they are being manipulated by others.'

'What others?' I asked.

'The editorial does not say specifically, but this probably refers to dissident workers, intellectuals, and foreign activists. I am sure some will misconstrue this editorial.'

'Does it say who wrote the editorial?'

'No, but we think it is attributed to Deng Xiaoping, our ruler behind the scenes.'

Chapter 9

Thursday, April 27, 1989

I had considered going into town or perhaps visiting the Friendship Store, but I decided against it. I was supposed to be teaching, so I judged it prudent to hang around looking busy. I therefore strolled around the campus with a pile of documents firmly grasped in my right hand, and I stopped at irregular intervals shuffling my pile around studiously, looking busy.

When Wei invited me for lunch at the student refectory, I agreed. I considered that it would be a good idea to meet students on an informal basis. In any case, I was getting bored with idly ambling around the university campus.

On leaving the guesthouse, I noticed a tree with peculiar large pinkish blossom. I decided to investigate further. When I got to the tree, amusingly I saw the blossom was actually washing hanging up to dry. On closer inspection, I was mortified to see that it was my washing, my white underpants and white shirts draped over the branches, except they were no longer white.

They were pink and my amusing disposition left me.

From the outside, the campus had an appearance much like any other industrial estate – an enclosed compound with guarded gates. Near the main gates were poorly maintained blocks of flats for the staff and a small, commercial area with shops. Inside the compound things looked more like a place of learning with trees, gardens, playing fields, student dormitories, classrooms, and libraries.

On almost every building, tree, and around the playing fields were loudspeakers, which irritatingly droned on for most of the day. How you could ever hope to concentrate in a Chinese university campus was a mystery. The loudspeakers started around daybreak with a wake-up call and then continued until late evening, when it was time to go to sleep. We had a diet of long nagging speeches occasionally broken with catchy Chinese tunes. The only times the loudspeakers stopped were the exact times of classes. Since students had boycotted classes, the loudspeakers never stopped.

I met Wei as arranged. We passed by one of the student dormitories to gather bowls and spoons for lunch. I had assumed all Chinese used chopsticks. That, I found, was not so. At meal times, students and most staff carried enamelled metal bowls and large dessertspoons, taking them to the student refectory or staff dining rooms.

'These belong to Hou,' Wei informed me while handing me a well-used bowl and spoon.

'Busy, is he?'

'Oh yes, very busy,' replied Wei.

I had a sneak look inside a student room. It was tiny and slept eight, four each side on narrow bunks. At the end was a window and beneath it, a single table, and two chairs. What little wall space there was contained the usual posters you would expect to see in a student room. On the table was a large radio-cassette player, blasting out music in competition with the loudspeakers outside. The place was a tip with laundry and clothes hanging on makeshift lines in front of the bunks – providing some privacy, I supposed. On the bunks were books, files, notepads, and things like that.

There was a lingering odour.

I had noticed the smell when I first arrived in China, in the guesthouse, classroom, everywhere. It wasn't an obnoxious smell – but it was there, although it got less each day.

At the back of the dormitory building I saw what looked like a long bicycle shed with a tin roof. The walls were open to the elements top and bottom where I could see wet feet and black bristly heads shuffling and bobbing around. Under the tin roof was a single pipe running the length of the shed with water dribbling over the bobbing heads.

'Male showers,' Wei informed me. 'We only have cold water. It is not a problem in the summer, but the winters…'

The refectory was a large shed-like building, quite narrow but long, with long wooden tables and benches. There was a slight camber on the concrete floor, like on a road. We were among the early diners, and the queue at the serving hatches was not long. There were two large cauldrons. Servers heaped my bowl with rice from the first cauldron and topped up from the second. The ingredients from the second cauldron contained a brownish liquid with irregular lumps of unspecified gristly meat. They also gave me an orange. Not wanting to be too critical, the brown liquid did provide moisture to soften the thick stodgy rice. The students seemed pleased enough, so who was I to complain?

Wei sat on my left and Zhuang, who also accompanied us, sat on my right. Opposite me were other students whose names I had yet to learn. Besides Hou, Yang was also not around.

'I've seen quite a lot of posters around campus,' I remarked, while contemplating the best way to tackle lunch. There was a lot to be said for a traditional knife and fork!

'We are preparing for the anniversary of the May Fourth Movement, which is next week. We are having a big celebration,' replied Wei.

'What is that about?'

'It was a student movement started in 1919, seventy years ago. We also want a memorial to Hu Yaobang who died recently. He was a great advocate for democracy and freedom,' explained Zhuang.

During lunch, we continued to receive lively, Chinese songs through the loudspeakers. I was having difficulty making myself heard and had to raise my voice for the benefit of those around me.

'Are there student associations in British universities?' asked Wei.

'Yes, every university has a student association, but we call them student unions. They mainly have a social role in running the bars, sporting clubs, and things like that. They are also involved in the administration of the university and attend committee meetings. Student unions look after the interests of students.'

I wanted to say they could be a nuisance, but thought better of it.

'Do the authorities control the student unions?'

'No, they are independent and control their own finances. Each year students vote for their representatives. Some of the senior officials, like the president, can take a year out of studies to undertake their duties. It is all very – sort of – democratic.'

Having once been a student, and knowing how students behaved back at the poly, I sometimes found conversations like this difficult to take seriously. Some of the antics students got up to were hardly democratic! Nevertheless, Wei and the others took what I said seriously. They nodded at each other, knowingly.

'Do students in Britain have freedom of speech?'

I was not sure what they meant by having freedom, particularly in speech. Freedom was a difficult concept. If I took into account things like the official secrets act, libel, slander, obscenity laws, heresy, incitement to commit crime, right to privacy, then freedom of speech was limited. We all had freedom, up to a point. It was just a matter of where that point was.

I decided to keep my answer simple.

'Of course,' I replied cautiously. I was the centre of attention, and students were struggling to get in a position to hear what I was saying.

Students appreciated my comments with spontaneous clapping and cheering, with orange peel thrown into the air, cheering enthusiastically.

I was distracted because what I found disconcerting were the eating habits of the students. They casually spat unwanted food, such as pieces of bone or stubborn gristly bits, onto the wooden tables or floor. On leaving the refectory, students emptied the remains of their meal onto the table. Leftover food was everywhere, and the brown liquid stuff slowly dribbled towards my part of the table. Orange peel littered, adding colour to the leftover rice. I tried not to notice. No one else seemed bothered by the mess. Most students had arrived for lunch in their white shirts or blouses, and left the refectory still in a pristine condition – unlike me. The arms and front of my white shirt had brown stains, and my trousers were dappled with odd bits of discarded food.

'Do British students take part in protests?'

'Oh yes, often,' I replied distractedly. 'Well, what I mean is, students in Britain protest quite regularly. We accept that as part their education and growing up, and it can keep them out of mischief.'

I looked around for my laugh, but did not get it. I saw earnest faces, and all were clapping and cheering.

'Do British students participate in democracy?' asked Zhuang. 'Can they elect their government leaders?'

I was uncertain by what Zhuang meant by democracy. Was he referring to the democratic system, social equality, egalitarianism, or what? I took it to be the former, which still caused me problems. There were so many different forms of democracy, and none seemed adequate. In most cases, it was expensive, over-rated, generally corrupt, probably necessary and a comfort for some.

I decided not to share my prejudices with the students.

'Well,' I responded, while trying to avoid a particular bothersome patch of brown liquid, 'anyone over the age of eighteen is entitled to vote to elect our leaders, and that includes students.'

Most didn't bother, I thought while receiving yet another bout of clapping and cheering.

Having finished our lunch, we left the refectory. Wei and Zhuang emptied the remains of their bowls onto the table, and I followed likewise. Some students were casting nervous glances in the direction of the serving hatches. I looked and noticed a couple of the workers, clasping fire hoses, washing down the tables and floor. The water and remains of the meal flowed easily down the cambered refectory floor making cleaning a simple task. I made a mental note to brief the head of estates back at the poly about that innovative cleaning method, as I was sure it would interest her.

We made a hasty retreat from the refectory. The water from the hoses and collective remains of the student meals splashed my shoes and the bottoms of my trousers – impatient lot.

'I hope you enjoyed lunch, Professor?' asked Wei, as we left the refectory. 'We have to go now. Thank you for your support.'

'A meal I won't forget,' I replied truthfully.

I walked slowly back to the guesthouse, still clutching my borrowed, enamelled, metal bowl and large dessertspoon. With the elbows and the front of my shirt covered in brown stains and my shoes and the bottom of my trousers soaking wet with bits of rice sticking to them, I had to admit, I looked a mess. In the distance, I could still hear the students shouting, competing poorly with the loudspeakers.

I passed the tree where my washing was still hanging to dry and accepted with stoicism that the clothes I was currently wearing would soon be experiencing a similar fate.

Memorandum

(Telex message)

From   Chou Ke-qiang
           Director of the Office of Foreign Affairs
           Jaliang Number 3 University

To   Deputy Chairman
           Office of Education Foreign Affairs
           Public Security Bureau
           Beijing

Date   28 April 1989

CONFIDENTIAL

DR CHARLES VINCENT

The activities of Dr Vincent are getting out of hand.

Workers at the university are now collaborating with students in the preparations for the demonstrations of the 70th anniversary of the May Fourth Movement. I suspect that Vincent's classroom monitor is among those workers, and the information he provides me is therefore unreliable.

Yesterday, Vincent was openly giving anti-government speeches in the student dining facility. He was shouting, for all to hear, that it is normal for students to demonstrate for freedom. He said that all students have the right to vote and enjoy democracy. This is both outrageous and an infringement of his status as an honoured guest in this country. I had to put an end to this blatant provocation by using fire hoses to dispel the students. That soon broke up the demonstration.

I highly recommend that the proper authorities either arrest Vincent for deliberate incitement of riots or cancel his visa immediately, and expel him.

From: **Deputy Chairman**
Office of Education Foreign Affairs
Public Security Bureau
Beijing
To: **Chou Ke-qiang**
Director of the Office of Foreign Affairs
Jaliang Number 3 University
29 April 1989

Private note (by telex)

DISSIDENT VINCENT

Party leaders are currently engaged in discussions with students
in an attempt to stop the large demonstrations planned for Beijing
on the 70th anniversary of the May Fourth Movement. What is
problematic is the disparate number of illegal student
organisations now in existence, including an unofficial group
within your own university. The government is talking to selected
student leaders in a conciliatory manner in an attempt to split
the student groups thus making them more cautious of taking to the
streets again.

What is of more concern to the government is the visit of
Gorbachev on 15 May. Student demonstrations in the streets during
this visit would be extremely embarrassing for the government.
Apart from the scale of the demonstrations over the past ten days
or so, what is intolerable to the government is the support the
workers are providing.

The authorities, having threatened a crackdown, allowed a mass
march of students in Beijing to go ahead last Thursday. The march
could have been stopped at the gates of the universities.
Nevertheless, no serious attempt was made to do so, which has
meant a serious loss of face for the authorities. This happened
about the same time as the demonstrations in the student dining
facility at Jaliang Number 3 University instigated by Vincent,
which could not have been a coincidence.

The uncertainty shown by the authorities also indicates
weaknesses within the government and the Party itself. It is your
duty to control all dissident activities within the University.

Chapter 10

'Petter,' I appeased reasonably.

It was a cultural standoff, and I did not want to be involved.

I had not seen Petter for several days. We met up at breakfast and Petter was again being a little bit too pedantic about his breakfast. He was armed with what looked like a loaf of bread.

'I will show you how to make toast,' explained Petter.

'Toe… OK,' protested the little, old, Chinese lady, looking at me.

'Yes,' I agreed, 'toast OK.'

'Look,' Petter replied indignantly, 'I will show you how to make proper toast, and omelettes for that matter.'

'Toe… OK.'

The little, old, Chinese lady, wearing a striking, red blouse, I noticed, stood her ground in the middle of the doorway obstructing entry into the kitchen. Her husband, the cook, hovered menacingly behind armed with a mean-looking egg whisk. Petter wanted to give them cooking lessons, but they were having nothing to do with it. The kitchen was definitely the domain of the little, old, Chinese lady, and her husband, the cook, and no Swedish barbarian was going to alter that.

'You could at least support me, Charles,' complained Petter.

'No chance. I am here every morning, unlike you, and I like my breakfast. Best meal of the day.'

'Mmmm…' mumbled Petter, giving up. His mission for being firm from the beginning was at last faltering, I hoped.

'Omele?' asked our breakfast hostess, with the sweetest smile.

Petter once again nodded stoically.

'That's a flamboyant, pink shirt you're wearing, Charles,' Petter said.

As we finished breakfast, Mr Chou appeared.

'Good morning,' he greeted. 'I am going into town. I can drop you off at the Friendship Store, if you wish.'

Whereas Petter scowled, I thought it was considerate of Mr Chou. I wanted to buy some new shirts. Any colour except pink!

'That is very kind of you, Mr Chou. I would love a lift, and I am sure Mr Lyngstad would welcome a lift as well.'

'I haven't seen you around for a few days, Petter,' I commented, over mid-morning coffee in the Friendship Store.

'No, I suppose not,' answered Petter. 'I've been busy.'

Everyone alleged to be busy, except me; I just pretended to be.

'How are you getting on with the student placements?'

'I have almost finished sorting them out. Would Pontefract Polytechnic consider taking a couple of students on work placement?'

'It sounds like a good idea.'

I might be wrong, but I had the feeling Petter was being a little vague about his activities.

'Things must be difficult for you with the boycott, Charles?'

'A bit,' I admitted. 'I did manage a tutorial on Friday. Mr Chou rounded up some odd students, so I didn't have any continuity.'

That was true. Mr Chou suddenly turned up at the guesthouse, in a bad mood, stating he had gathered up some students and they were eager for my honoured presence in the classroom. I recognised some, but not all faces in the class. They were not my usual students.

'I will have a word with Professor Song. It won't happen again.'

'Have you heard anything on your radio?' I asked.

'I can give you an update, but I don't know much. Apparently, more student demonstrations are expected, so do the best you can. I have heard good things about you from your students, Charles.'

Well, that was as clear as mud.

Mr Chou picked us up at the Friendship Store, as promised, and dropped us off at the guesthouse. Petter disappeared quickly, claiming he had a prior engagement. I was beginning to think he was avoiding me. When I returned to my room, I saw Petter walking away with Professor Song. Hou and Yang, two of my students, accompanied them.

Since I had nothing much else to do, I switched on the television.

After inattentively watching what I initially took to be the Sunday afternoon Beijing opera for a few minutes, I realised that something was not quite right. There was none of the usual wailing-like singing, supported by clicking noises and banging of out-of-tune cymbals. The actors were not in their usual, vivid, traditional outfits, but dressed in what looked like late Victorian clothing.

The acting was dreadful.

After listening and watching a little bit more closely, I realised the actors were not Chinese but western. It took some time for me to identify the language; it was English with strong Welsh accents. I checked this out with the *China Daily*, the newspaper for foreigners, and found the afternoon was dedicated to learning English. The play I was watching was Oscar Wilde's *The Importance of Being Ernest*. The actors were students on some university exchange programme, from Bangor no doubt!

I mused over the words recited by one of the enthusiastic Welsh students; 'Truth is rarely pure and never simple.' Were they telling me something?

Extract from:

THE PRESS
SUN 30 APR 1989
Local correspondent, Peking

STUDENT LEADERS, who have humiliated the Chinese government with mass street protests, had discussions with officials yesterday.

Communist Party officials stated that China would collapse in chaos if the protests continued. However, the government made concessions to the protesters by banning the import of foreign luxury cars and ending the practice of senior officials moving to the summer resort of Beidaihe to escape the heat of Peking.

The student protest movement appears to be deficient in both organisation and focus. For example, a meeting at Peking University broke up in disorder as student leaders squabbled over their demands and who could use the microphone. Students are also demanding, 'Freedom and democracy,' without understanding either.

Despite students claiming success having been able to demonstrate on Tiananmen Square night after night, diplomats consider that the Chinese government handling of the protests has been clever. Superficially, students have been mourning the death of the former Communist Party leader, Hu Yaobang, and the government used this as a pretext to do nothing.

Chapter 11

Monday, May 1, 1989

'Harry!'

I couldn't believe it.

My head of school from the poly had telexed me, via the UNIBO office in Kuala Lumpur, to arrange a time so I could phone him – urgently. Mr Chou kindly allowed me to use the phone in his office. For the past few days, he had been quite helpful. He was always nearby whenever I needed anything.

'Yes,' replied the head. 'I phoned the British Council in London and explained I already had a member of staff in China. I suggested it would be helpful if I could arrange for another to join him. I kind of implied you were negotiating a collaborative agreement between institutions for student and staff exchanges.'

'But—'

'The British Council put me onto the Academic Links with China Scheme, and Harry is flying out on the seventh.'

'Seventh?'

'Stop repeating everything I say. Seventh of May. The academic links scheme does not cover local costs in China, but I am sure you can arrange something at… at, where exactly are you, Charles? I had to be a bit vague with the British Council.'

Harry had been around the poly for some time, but I didn't really know him.

Until recently, he had been a scruffy lecturer with a thick mat of long hair, and known as the bookmaker. He took bets on which members of staff would get the internal upgrades or promotions, and things like that. He was short and tubby, of indeterminable middle age, and originally came from La Réunion, an island somewhere in the Indian Ocean. He turned up for his classes, students never complained about him, and examination papers were marked on time. Harry was a professional career lecturer who seemed satisfied with his lot. He was a mysterious but likable rogue.

For some unknown reason, Harry had recently cut his hair and started to wear smart suits. To the surprise of everyone, he had successfully developed a new undergraduate programme in the financial services sector, which was popular with students. He was the head of school's current favourite, and his reward for his recent endeavours was a week in China.

I was to look after him.

Chapter 12

While sauntering around the campus, I bumped into Professor Sang.

'No classes, Professor Sang?' I asked. It was more a rhetorical question, and I didn't expect an answer. We both knew students were boycotting classes. 'Perhaps you know what's going on?'

'Would you like some tea?' asked Professor Sang, giving a disdainful look in the direction of Mr Chou, who was lurking nearby behind some trees admiring the blossom – not my washing, I might add.

Professor Sang's office was quite large, but almost empty of anything resembling what you would expect to find in the room of a senior academic. He had one shelf containing a small collection of well-thumbed paperback textbooks. At the rear of his office was a large desk. What little there was on the desk was tidy, but not meticulously so.

In front of the desk was a large sofa, facing two winged armchairs. At one end was another larger armchair, signifying seniority. There were off-white towels over the arms and backs of the sofa and chairs to protect the padded, large, floral-print, nylon coverings. The seating looked comfortable. In the middle of the seating was a long coffee table. That arrangement, I had noticed, was common in offices of senior staff and represented more than just a comfortable conversation area. It was an area where guests were formally welcomed and polite conversation took place over a cup of tea.

In the corner of the office was a small table with a shabby, old, plastic thermos flask on top. The thermos flask was part of the furniture in most Chinese public rooms, offices, and hotel rooms. In my room at the guesthouse were two flasks, one containing cold water, for drinking, the other hot water, for making tea. It was someone's job to continually boil water and keep thermos flasks topped up with fresh hot water.

Professor Sang scooped heaped teaspoons of green tea from a caddy into two cups and added hot water from the thermos flask.

Perhaps I should be more precise.

Professor Sang was using a jam jar with a screw lid. That was not odd because most people in China did the same. When you wanted a drink, you unscrewed the lid and sipped your tea so not to swallow the large leaves that unfolded while brewing. You then screwed the lid back on, retaining heat, I assumed – or prevented spillage. As the day progressed, you added more hot water, using the same leaves. The less frugal added more tea to the brew so by the end of the day, the jam jar was crammed with leaves.

My tea was prepared in a tall, decorative, fine porcelain teacup with a snug fitting lid. I was a guest, after all.

Professor Sang sat on the sofa and indicated I should sit on one of the chairs opposite. We both sipped our scorching tea. We exchanged small talk, and I thanked Professor Sang for our recent walk around East Lake.

'I know students are boycotting classes and there are more demonstrations planned,' I remarked, 'but can you explain to me what is going on.'

Professor Sang relaxed back into his sofa. 'I am not sure anyone really understands what the protests are all about. Because the government censors the news, we officially know very little. With the students, things just happen, but mostly unplanned and disorganised. I have a few close colleagues in Beijing and I keep in contact with them, so I know a little of what is happening. I assume you know about the May Fourth Movement?'

'Not much,' I replied. 'It's the seventieth anniversary on Thursday.'

'That is correct. The May Fourth Movement takes its name from the massive, popular protest, by students from Beijing University and other colleges, which took place in May 1919. The Movement instigated the spreading of Marxism in China, and prepared the ideological foundation for the establishment of the Chinese Communist Party.

'The Communist Party is the government here. It is therefore difficult to criticise students for wanting to *celebrate* the May Fourth Movement with a rally. Some students seem to be using that as an excuse to demonstrate and then make demands for other things, even if their demands are unclear.'

61

'You expect that from students,' I added, 'they are never clear with what they want.'

'But they are declaring simultaneously support for the Communist Party and for political reforms.'

'What's wrong with that?'

'The government considers this to be counter-revolutionary and not acceptable. The People's Republic is a one-party state, so how can you have political reform. What is also causing the authorities concern is that students are launching their own organisations. In Beijing, they have established the Beijing Autonomous Student Federation and, as far as I can gather, the students in Jaliang are doing something similar. I don't know where they got such an idea! The government will not tolerate this.'

'Don't Chinese students have their own organisations? As you know, we call them unions.'

'Yes, but they are state controlled. Recently, our leaders clearly asserted that western-style democracy, or even Soviet-style reform, is inappropriate for the People's Republic.'

'Who are your leaders?'

'Interesting question, but difficult to answer. The Politburo and Deng Xiaoping still rule from behind the scenes. Technically, Deng holds no official position and is therefore difficult to oust, but he is still Chairman of the Central Military Commission and therefore controls the military. Zhao Ziyang, who is the Communist Party general secretary, was highly favoured by Deng, but there are doubts about that. Li Peng is the prime minister but is very conservative, a hardliner, and disliked by the students. Yang Shangkun is the President of the People's Republic – we do not hear much from him. We also have Party elders who are retired but influential former officials of the government and Party. Deng is 84 and not in the best of health, and it is considered that his days as all-powerful leader are nearly over.'

'It is all very confusing for an outsider, like me,' I added.

'My friends in Beijing tell me that the leaders are split. Some support the students, except they do not do so openly. Students have had a taste of success and others, intellectuals, are joining in their demands for change. With the leaders weak and split on what to do, the students are able to continue to demonstrate. In spite of that, nothing is coordinated. Some of my friends believe the students are being manipulated for political purposes.'

'So still no classes then…'

Professor Sang smiled at my comment while topping my teacup with more hot water.

'All we can do is provide students with moral guidance and let them know we do not disapprove of their activities. As you say, they are young and impressionable. Being a foreign professor, students look to you for guidance and support. Please remember that.'

Chapter 13

Wednesday, May 3, 1989

Mr Chou had received an urgent message from the British Embassy in Beijing. I was to ring the first secretary (political) immediately. Mr Chou kindly led me to his office where I could use the telephone.

After confirming with each other our identities, the first secretary (political) passed me over to the director of the British Council in Beijing, who did not know how to contact me. The director had asked his colleague, the first secretary (political), to track me down. When my head of school contacted the British Council in London, he was vague about my whereabouts and activities in China.

'What, exactly, are you doing?' asked the director.

I tried to remember what my head of school had said to the British Council, something about collaborations.

'I am in China, or should I say, the People's Republic,' I replied, saying the first thing that came into my head.

'You are as asinine as that head of yours back in Pontypool – or wherever your godforsaken polytechnic might be. I know you are in China. I am in China. We are speaking to each other in China!'

There was no need for the director to raise his voice, although I could see his point about me being in China. I did agree with him about my head of school being asinine, whatever that meant.

'I am at Jaliang Number 3 University,' I replied promptly.

'I know. But what are you doing?' asked the director patiently.

I was in a quandary.

What I was actually doing – nothing much at the moment, but that was not my fault – and what my asinine head told the British Council I was doing are two different things. Mr Chou was present, sitting in his chair, smiling nicely. I had to be careful what I said.

'Collaborating,' I whispered so Mr Chou could not overhear me.

'Speak up, I cannot hear you.'

'Collaborating with associates,' I added in a slightly louder whisper. As chance had it, I remembered Petter's offer about the placements. 'With a bit of luck I should manage to get some students to come back to the UK.'

'If I get this Harry fellow to Jaliang, can you cover his living costs?'

'Not a problem,' I lied.

'What about his itinerary, can you also look after that?'

'I will make sure he meets the right people,' I replied, again in a whisper. 'I have contacts here.'

'I suppose we had better show some support for you polytechnic chaps. Give me your telex number, and I will send you the arrival details. And keep off the rice, it plays havoc with your vocal cords and you obviously already have a problem by the sounds of it.'

Mr Chou was looking at me menacingly as I put down the phone. 'Well?' he demanded. 'Who is Harry?'

'Ah, let me explain…'

After a difficult conversation, we agreed Harry would share my room at the guesthouse as I had two single beds, and I was to cover the cost of Harry's meals from my generous UNIBO living allowance.

Chapter 14

Thursday, May 4, 1989

After breakfast, as I had nothing much else to do, I decided to amble around the campus and possibly walk into town.

When I walked out of the guesthouse compound, it was quiet. The loudspeakers were no longer broadcasting. After a few days, I began not to notice the continuous racket they made, until it stopped.

I then saw what was happening.

Students had lined up, four abreast, preparing for a march with flags and banners held high. At the head of the procession was a large red banner with some sort of slogan in white letters. The procession was dotted with red flags at irregular intervals. A hefty green banner, held high by two heavy bamboo poles, had a prominent position. The students mostly wore white shirts and dark trousers, giving the whole thing a military appearance. University staff, tutors probably, casually leant on their bikes watching the preparations.

I spotted some of my students gathered around the green banner, busy organising this, and arranging that.

'Hello, Hou, I haven't seen you around lately. I assume this is to do with the May Fourth Movement?' I asked.

'Yes, we are celebrating the seventieth anniversary. We would be most honoured if you could accompany us,' invited Hou.

'It would be a privilege if you could be with us this morning, Professor Charles,' added Wei. 'We are going to march into the town.'

Since I planned a walk that morning, I decided I might accept. It was an organised Chinese celebration and not a demonstration, although I had my suspicions about that. I was in China to broaden my experience, and I was still uncertain of the directions to get to the town centre. Anyway, Professor Sang said I should support the students, me being a foreign professor. So why not?

'Yes, I would love to join you,' I replied. 'If we pass near the

Friendship Store I will slip away quietly.'

On the order from Hou, the students marched out of the campus.

There was no random damage to property or heavy drinking. It was a celebration, after all. There was no police presence. The students had their own marshals who made sure everyone behaved and interlopers did not join the procession. There was plenty of shouting. They had speeches with the help of megaphones, followed by synchronised clapping and chanting. I could feel the youthful emotion of the crowd, the energy. They were chanting with passion, sweat on their faces; even I was excited. People on the roadside clapped and cheered as we passed. The whole procession had a festive atmosphere.

A little later, another smaller group, armed with their own banners, joined at the end of the procession. The two groups, while friendly towards each other, didn't mixed.

'Workers,' Wei informed me.

We came to a building where the students used their megaphones to nag at its occupants.

'This is the China News Agency,' explained Hou. 'We are inviting the journalists to join us. We will then march to the municipal buildings to talk with the authorities.'

Because he was also leading the chanting using a megaphone, Hou was having difficulty holding one end of the green banner.

'Allow me to help,' I offered, as I took hold of the heavy bamboo pole. It was the least I could do.

Hou coordinated the chanting of the crowd around him. I also had a go at the melodic chanting, not knowing what I said.

The journalists from the China News Agency joined the procession, and after we exchanged good-natured remarks and posed for photographs, we continued our march towards the municipal buildings. Zhuang took his turn to hold the banner, which was just as well. The banner was heavier than I thought and consequently had been waving around a bit. Fortunately, no one was hurt!

When I recognised the road that led to the Friendship Store, I offered my apologies. I felt the need for a break and looked forward to a Tsingtao beer and a slab of marble cake.

Chapter 15

Friday, May 5, 1989

'**Hello**, Petter. What have you been up to?'

'Oh, you know, busy…' Petter replied in a noncommittal manner.

No, I did not know.

I had not known Petter long, but I liked him, and found him companionable. Having not seen Petter since the weekend, I was surprised to see him at the guesthouse. We had dinner together. I explained about the imminent arrival of Harry. I was worried what Petter might think about Harry arriving, but he seemed not to mind.

'Is Mr Chou being helpful?' asked Petter.

'Yes,' I answered hesitantly. 'He's around most of the time.'

I didn't want to sound too ungrateful because Mr Chou had been helpful – at times. When I asked him if he could cover the living costs of Harry's stay, he seemed a little upset. I suppose it was short notice.

'Do you fancy a walk, Charles?'

'Why not,' I replied.

When I first arrived, I was an excuse for a banquet and a good night out for my Chinese colleagues. Since everyone became preoccupied with the student boycott and protests, I was the least of their concerns. With little to do, I would have welcomed the odd banquet or cultural excursion, especially as Petter was rarely around.

We walked in the general direction of the sea.

Not realising how close some of the docks were, we decided to look at the ships. The whole area looked like a wasteland, except for two unassuming small docks without cranes or sheds. Both docks were empty, except for one ship.

'Not many ships,' Petter remarked.

'These are not commercial docks,' I explained. 'They are used for quarantine, minor repairs, and things like that.'

'Let's go and look.'

As we walked down the side of the dock, despite the darkness, salt, and grime, I could see that the ship had a white hull, with the upper structure illuminated by deck-lights, displaying a white funnel with a broad red band. I saw a yellow hammer and sickle on the red band.

'It's a medium-size, Soviet, general cargo ship,' I said.

'It certainly is,' Petter confirmed. 'We see plenty in the Baltic Sea.'

As we approached, we saw a ship's officer looking down at us from the top of the accommodation ladder.

'Good evening,' shouted Petter to the officer, '*dobri vecher.*'

The officer gesticulated for us to board.

'*Privet,*' shouted the officer in a heavy accent. 'Come aboard and be our guests.'

'Thank you very much,' replied Petter.

'Should we be doing this, Petter?' I whispered.

'Why not?' Petter replied. 'Have you anything better to do?'

I didn't.

I followed Petter up the accommodation ladder. It appeared not to be the safest method to board a ship. I looked down, and all I could see was the dark, oily water of the dock through the ladder steps. All that stopped me from falling into the sea was a rope held up by stanchions slotted into the base of the ladder. The whole thing moved and swayed as we made our way from the dock to the ship's deck.

'Is this thing safe, Charles?'

'Of course it is,' I lied. 'This is a standard ship's accommodation ladder rigged in accordance with international safety conventions, so stop complaining.'

'You should know.'

I did know, and the accommodation ladders I had used on British ships were far sturdier and safer than the one I used that night, but I didn't tell Petter that.

Once aboard, we were welcomed as long-lost friends.

'I am the duty officer and I am pleased to welcome you aboard.'

'The pleasure is ours,' greeted Petter amiably.

His, not mine…

'Follow me,' said the duty officer.

We made our way upward, along alleys, up some stairs, and through doors. On our way through the accommodation, I saw on top of each doorframe, on a poorly polished, brass plate, in Cyrillic lettering, the name of the room or cabin. At the level below the bridge, we arrived at the captain's cabin.

The duty officer introduced us to the ship's captain.

'Welcome, welcome,' greeted the captain, as we entered, 'welcome.'

'A pleasure,' said Petter.

The ship had been laid-up for the past three months because the Soviet authorities had no work for it. The crew had no money and were bored with nothing to do. The ship was at an inconvenient distance from the town centre so walking was not an easy option. Contrary to belief, large ports were not always centres of iniquity, with seedy bars, and the like. Some were, but not Jaliang. The Friendship Store was the only place to go, and that was expensive, they said.

We were the entertainment for the evening.

The captain's cabin was smaller than I expected. It was functional as opposed to being comfortable. With the captain were four other officers, including the duty officer.

We discovered the captain was not Russian like the rest, but North Korean. His only word of English was, 'Welcome.' Fortunately, one of the others, the senior communications officer, spoke reasonable English, and translated things when necessary. It transpired Petter could speak a little Russian, which helped matters.

We sealed our newfound friendship with vodka, neat, and no ice.

That was the general drift of the evening.

Anglo-Swedish-Russian-Korean relations were definitely on the up, not that I remembered much. I was not normally a vodka drinker but we had super-premium Russian vodka from bottles with crudely made labels. I had enjoyed the company of Russians and their infamous vodka before. The trick was, never empty your glass. That way, they could only top you up. Well, that was my plan at the beginning, when I was sober, but who knows what happened after the first few tumblers.

'Cheers,' I said.

'*Skaal*,' said Petter.

'*Budem*,' said the Russians.

'Welcome,' said the captain.

At some stage during the evening, Petter disappeared with the senior communications officer to inspect the bridge. That was a pity, because I wouldn't have minded seeing the bridge myself.

'You must have been on many ships bridges, Charles,' said Petter pleasantly. 'It'll be more hospitable if you stay behind and entertain the captain.'

'Welcome.'

'Cheers.'

'*Budem.*'

There we were in the captain's cabin, one Korean, four Russians, one Brit, and one Swede all happily drinking vodka as if the world was about to end. I suppose the Russians had decided the world had already ended, having been abandoned, from their point-of-view, in that god-forsaken remote part of the world. The room was full of cigarette smoke, stale air, and the smell of burnt scrambled eggs. I did not smoke, but I remembered Petter enjoying his pipe of Swedish shag, or whatever made that ghastly smell.

A true observer of the world would have been able to recall some of the conversations that took place that night, some revealing quote with symbolic meaning, words, or acts that summarised what was wrong or right with the world.

I remembered nothing.

If nothing else, that gathering below the navigation bridge epitomised how a bunch of homesick adults, brought together in some far-flung corner of the world, could drink vodka in excess not understanding a word spoken, but be utterly content in each other's company. That must have some meaning.

I remember waking up next morning thinking I was dead.

How I negotiated that accommodation ladder and returned to my bed is still a mystery.

Extract from:

THE PRESS
FRI 05 MAY 1989
Local correspondent, Peking

IN THEIR FIRST PUBLIC display of hostility towards the government control of the media, journalists yesterday joined students when protesting in several Chinese cities. Student unrest began three weeks ago after the death of the Communist Party leader, Hu Yaobang, who fell from grace a few years earlier.

Protests were held on the seventieth anniversary of the May 4 Movement of 1919, the pro-democratic intellectual insurgency that allowed communism to take hold in China.

Students again converged on Tiananmen Square, Peking's symbolic centre, and heard one of their leaders, Wu Erkaixing, make an unexpected announcement to end the boycott of classes, which has already lasted two weeks. He claimed that they have made their point and they should return to classes. Many protesters argued against this call, thus showing the disunity within the student protest movement.

In Peking, students and journalists claimed they had no further plans for demonstrations. The current Communist Party leader, Zhao Ziyang, when giving a speech in the Great Hall of the People, as students marched towards Tiananmen Square yesterday morning, said that the demonstrations would gradually calm down and students had not incited political instability. He stated that students only wanted to correct errors in the Party and the government, and their demands were reasonable.

Chapter 16

Saturday, May 6, 1989

Petter looked sprightly and cheerful at breakfast, but I was not sure if it was an act. You were never sure with Scandinavians and their reputation with alcohol. He was eating what looked like corn flakes; how did he manage that?

'English breakfast, Charles?' asked Petter congenially.

English breakfast!

In my state...

I made a hasty retreat to the nearest toilet.

Memorandum

(Telex message)

From   Chou Ke-giang
           Director of the Office of Foreign Affairs
           Jaliang Number 3 University

To   Deputy Chairman
           Office of Education Foreign Affairs
           Public Security Bureau
           Beijing

Date   6 May 1989

CONFIDENTIAL

DR CHARLES VINCENT

Dr Vincent blatantly and openly participated in the protests on 4 May by marching with students to the offices of the Chinese News Agency.

Along with student leaders, he demanded that all journalists join the march to the town hall to *criticise* the authorities. Vincent was seen wildly waving the university banner and shouting slogans such as, *tell the truth, and don't tell lies.*

Vincent used one of the student leaders to translate and to speak to the journalists on a megaphone. The student shouted that Vincent was a famous, western professor and was not afraid to be seen supporting them. He said that the journalists were cowards and should be ashamed. The student demanded that the journalists join the protesters immediately. They were to be counted alongside Vincent, the students, and workers. The journalists capitulated and joined the demonstrations and were seen having private discussions with Vincent.

I fear that the British authorities might have arranged for another provocateur to visit the university under the pretence of an educational visit arranged by the British Council. Vincent is in contact with the first secretary (political) in the British Embassy, Beijing, who must be coordinating British subversive activities during the current unrest.

It is obvious that Vincent is getting additional support to provoke further trouble. Vincent was whispering into the phone, but he was unaware that I could hear. I distinctly heard him discussing, with the first secretary (political), about collaborating with students and encouraging them to defect to the West. Vincent also said that he would ensure that the new provocateur would meet the right people.

The name of the second British academic is Harry.

I must also report another and possibly more serious issue. Vincent was witnessed boarding a Soviet ship that has supposedly been laid-up in the local docks for the past few months. Anyone can see that the ship is fitted with an array of communication aerials that can only belong to a spy ship. The local authorities have tolerated the Soviet ship because of the pending visit of Gorbachev in about ten days, assuming it is there to provide support and security for the visit.

Why would Vincent visit a Soviet spy ship under cover of darkness? I will wait for your reply by the telex in my office.

From: **Deputy Chairman**
Office of Education Foreign Affairs
Public Security Bureau
Beijing
To: **Chou Ke-giang**
Director of the Office of Foreign Affairs
Jaliang Number 3 University
7 May 1989

Private note (by telex)

DISSIDENT VINCENT

I received your message late last night but could not reply until this morning.

The landmark visit by Gorbachev is of the utmost importance and cannot be put into jeopardy. During this visit, it is expected that our leaders and Gorbachev will formally end the 30-year-old Sino-Soviet rift and additionally, we expect to gain military concessions from the Soviets.

The visit of Vincent to the Soviet ship must remain a closely guarded secret.

Vincent must not be allowed to meddle with journalists. We do not need journalists demanding press freedom.

I expect that students will be drifting back to classes, so encourage Vincent to get back to his teaching duties. Make sure that the other academic has plenty to do. Arrange special lectures and cultural visits, the usual sort of things. Keep them both occupied at all times.

You must never let the two British academics out of your sight.

Chapter 17

Sunday, May 7, 1989

Harry arrived.

I had requested an official car so I could pick Harry up from the airport, but initially Mr Chou refused. He was adamant Number 3 University was not going to incur additional costs because the university, he reminded me, had not invited Harry. Mr Chou seemed not to understand I hadn't invited Harry either.

He had a sudden change of heart because on the morning of Harry's arrival Mr Chou turned up at the guesthouse with a car. He stated he would accompany me to the airport and unofficially welcome Harry but not on behalf of the university.

'That is very kind of you,' I said. 'I hope I am not spoiling your weekend. I am sure Harry will appreciate your assistance.'

'It is my duty,' retorted Mr Chou sharply.

'We are both grateful for your help.'

He informed me that Harry must give some special lectures because the British Council expected that when they sponsored academics. He would make all the necessary arrangements. That was actually a good idea. What was I supposed to do with him? He also notified me that the boycott of classes was temporary and they would soon return to normal. He emphasised most strongly he would personally keep an eye on us.

I had caught Mr Chou at a bad moment because until then he had been generally polite, but that morning he was grumpy and didn't smile. I assumed he would have preferred being with his family, visiting East Lake, or some other local beauty spot. Perhaps he had other foreigners to look after, but I hadn't seen any.

'Did you have a good night last night?' I asked because he looked the worse for wear.

Mr Chou did not reply but just glared at me. I was only trying to be sociable. I had a lot to learn about my Chinese hosts.

'*H*ello, Charlie, *nee hao, nee hao*!'

Harry had arrived.

'It's Charles, actually,' I replied ignominiously. I never liked the name Charlie, and I was getting used to being addressed as professor. 'This is Mr Chou and he looks after us.'

Mr Chou was obviously still in a foul mood because he just scowled. He went through the motions of welcoming Harry as an honoured, uninvited guest, and stressed he would do his utmost to make Harry's stay the least unpleasant possible. I think that was what he said because he was mumbling his words, but despite that, Harry was not the slightest bit put off.

'*Nee hao, nee hao* – that means hello in Chinese. I bet you didn't know that, Charlie?' Harry remarked.

I didn't.

When I arrived in China, I had decided to play the English foreigner with a modest vocabulary in miming and that seemed to work.

'Call me Harry, Shoe. I can call you Shoe, can't I?' Harry asked.

'Professor Harry—'

'No, no, Shoe, I am not a professor. Just call me Harry. I'm not sure that professors from Pontefract Polytechnic would have much standing in the academic world.'

I quite liked being known as an eminent professor from a very eminent British university, and I would prefer Harry not detract from my recent rise in status. He would be in China a week, but I would remain for another month.

'I am told you are all professors of pontefract cakes, Harry?' commented Mr Chou unkindly.

'That's a good one, Shoe,' Harry replied. 'I can see we're going to get along famously.'

I was a little concerned about Mr Chou's reference to pontefract cakes. I considered his comment rude. Pontefract cakes were a traditional, local confectionery delicacy made from black liquorice, the size of a large coin, but thicker, and much favoured by the older generation and my wife. How did he know about them?

Whereas we met Harry at the airport without mishap, his luggage unfortunately took a different flight path. After completing numerous forms and witnessing a heated discussion between Mr Chou and airport officials, we left the airport with little confidence Harry would ever see his luggage again.

'It's a good job I carry all my money and important documents in my jacket pockets,' Harry informed us.

'Nice jacket,' said Mr Chou, without enthusiasm.

'Made in China,' added Harry, pointing to the label inside.

Chapter 18

Monday, May 8, 1989

The guesthouse had placed a menu on the table, English breakfast, omelette, toast, and Chinese breakfast being the fare on offer.

How was I going to explain the nuances of the menu to Harry? The little, old, Chinese lady wasn't going to tolerate any rebellious notions on her understanding of the menu from Harry. After all, it was successfully tried, and tested on Petter and me over the past two weeks.

Perhaps my description of our breakfast hostess at the guesthouse was a little patronising. I was supposedly a foreign specialist in cross-management communication and should have had some smart socio-ethnically neutral moniker. I didn't.

I didn't know her name, and I had difficulty in getting into a conversation with her. I ate, with gusto, whatever she provided and I smiled a lot. Our hostess seemed pleased with what I did, and she smiled a lot as well. She was small. She was old. She undoubtedly was Chinese and female. My description of the little, old, Chinese lady is, therefore, literal rather than patronising.

Her manner towards Petter was different.

There was no direct conflict or antagonism between Petter and her; she just eyed him up with suspicion, and had the better of him. Petter was never fully happy with his breakfast. When he was around, he got omelette and toast, and he had one of two choices – take it or leave it. Petter chose the former despite finding pancake and burnt marble cake an unappealing culinary combination.

Our hostess was quite relaxed about what time I had breakfast, but not so Petter. His breakfast was on the table at the agreed time. If he was early, he had to wait. If he was late, it just got cold.

Anyway, Harry carefully scrutinised the menu.

'Chinese breakfast please,' requested Harry, pointing to the menu. 'When in China, do as the Chinese do.'

Our hostess went away happily to issue the orders to her husband. I was surprised Harry didn't query the racket coming from the kitchen.

'*Shyay-shyay*,' said Harry, when presented with a large bowl of glutinous mix of rice pudding without the rice. 'That means *thank you* in Chinese. What's that you're eating, Charlie? I can see you've been away from Pontefract for far too long.'

One of Mr Chou's staff took Harry shopping for some basic clothes and toiletries. His luggage had yet to arrive. I lent Harry one of my pink shirts, and I had to admit, he looked somewhat dapper. Harry had flown from London, via Hong Kong, and Mr Chou was adamant the Chinese authorities would deliver his luggage safely.

I was concerned Harry was to travel to town by bus instead of the usual university car. It was Mr Chou's way of reminding me that Harry was, after all, an uninvited guest. The helper Mr Chou had provided spoke little or no English, and I was worried how Harry would manage.

'Have you any contacts in town, Charlie?' asked Harry. 'You can't go anywhere without contacts.'

I was quite helpful there because I had collected a couple a business cards from some of the journalists I met during the celebrations last Thursday. I gave these to him.

'These two chaps speak English,' I said.

Harry was wearing his jacket, which was a little too heavy for the late spring weather we were enjoying in Jaliang

'You might not need the jacket,' I said.

'It's got sixteen pockets and I keep everything I need on me,' Harry informed me. 'Just as well, since I've lost my luggage.'

'What if you lose your jacket?'

'I can't if I keep it on.'

Harry and his helper disappeared towards the back of the university.

I had received a message from Mr Chou informing me classes were to resume that day. All my students had turned up, including Hou and his followers, but I was getting short of ideas for my teaching programme.

Zhuang had already photocopied most of my notes and had handed these out to the students. They, in turn, had read and understood them without my help. They could quote large extracts whenever I asked a question. I just smiled and praised the students on their diligent study.

'Who is Harry?' asked Hou inquisitively.

Everyone wanted to know who Harry was. They were all examining a sheet of paper with bold Chinese symbols.

'Harry!' I exclaimed. 'He is one of my fellow eminent professors. He has come to give some special lectures.'

'Does he specialise in financial matters?' queried Hou.

'Possibly,' I replied cautiously.

To be honest, I was not sure. Back at the poly, our paths rarely crossed. I was vaguely aware he was associated with a group of accountancy lecturers, but we seldom saw them. As you walked down the corridors of the poly, you frequently saw a note pinned to a door apologising for the cancellation of an accountancy class. Most of them had small accountancy businesses and they fitted in their polytechnic duties as best they could.

'He is giving a lecture tomorrow,' Hou said. 'It is called, 'How to make a pot of money through lunatic asylums'. It sounds interesting.'

I was last to know, of course.

'Are you sure you got that right,' I queried.

'The details have been circulated all around the university, and we have a copy here,' replied Hou, indicating the sheet of paper he was holding. 'This sounds interesting and we are all planning to attend.'

'It sounds like an old Confucian proverb to me,' I joked.

Harry had provided Mr Chou with details of his lectures. Obviously, something got lost in translation. I must remember to warn Harry.

'I am unfamiliar with that proverb,' said Wei.

I had to remember to refrain from jokes with the students because, as I had already discovered, it could cause mayhem. I didn't have the patience to explain my reference to Confucian proverbs was just a good example – well, maybe not that good – of English wit and not to be taken literally or seriously. I still have a lot to learn, I surmised.

Since the students were excellent at mathematics, I gave them exercises on quantitative forecasting. I also provided some information on qualitative forecasting. I explained that qualitative forecasting was based upon a high degree of judgement, knowledge of the industry, focus groups, intuition, and things like that – guesswork.

'Central government does that,' Yang informed me.

'That is correct,' added Hou. 'It doesn't involve us.'

'Think of your work placements,' I responded. 'Surely the situation in China is changing with the Open Door Policy? Mark my words, in a few years' time, China will be one of the world's industrial leaders.'

I managed to keep ahead of my students by progressing from linear to multiple-regression, but only just. Multiple-regression requires an understanding of how two or more things might influence another, and that was their difficulty.

The mathematics involved in regression they easily handled, but when it came to judgemental decisions, they were less certain. They wanted an answer with no arguments. I decided to go back to basics and talk about correlation and the relationships between mathematical solutions and judgement.

I gave them one of my standard examples.

I provided a ten-year span of the number of priests who had been ordained in Ireland. For whatever reason, the number of priests being ordained had steadily increased during the time-period in question. In addition, I gave them the number of recorded illegitimate births in Ireland over the same ten-year span, which had also steadily risen.

When the students had quickly done their mathematical calculations, they found the level of correlation between the number of priests being ordained and the number of illegitimate births was extremely high. With regression, they could forecast, to a high degree of accuracy, the future number of illegitimate births by knowing what the planned numbers of ordinations were.

'Is it reasonable to blame illegitimate births on priests?' I asked innocently. 'Or could it just be coincidence?'

'Would priests do such a thing?' asked Wei in astonishment.

I could see the students were a little perturbed by my example, and I had to clarify the position of a priest in Irish society. Most illegitimate births in Ireland probably went unrecorded, but I didn't tell them that.

'Can you vouch for these priests?' asked Hou with scepticism.

I ignored that question for obvious reasons...

'Well, it wouldn't happen in China with our one child per family policy,' said Hou with a grin on his face.

I queried the merit of the example I had chosen, but it was the first that came to mind. Irish priests, well, who can vouch for them?

Hou then provided me with an example of the inappropriate use of statistical data in forecasting.

'I am helping one of my professors in a project he is doing for the port of Jaliang,' he explained. 'We had to do an analysis of the annual imports and exports for the port so the developers could plan what port infrastructure was required for the future.'

That was why Hou knew so much about the port the other day!

'Because of their size, some larger cargo ships are moored to buoys mid-river instead of on berths in the docks. They discharge their cargo into much smaller vessels moored alongside. The smaller vessels then go up-river, or to a berth in a dock, to discharge the cargo. The port authority keeps a record of the tonnage leaving the large cargo ship and again when the smaller vessel discharges the same cargo a second time. The same thing happens, in reverse, when loading. We end up with double counting and official records of cargoes are inflated. That makes it difficult to use those statistics for forecasting and planning purposes.'

'Has your professor resolved the double counting problem?' I asked.

'No,' replied Hou, while giving me an excellent Chinese impression of a Gallic shrug. 'They don't use computers to record statistical data and too many departments are involved. The port officials categorically denied double counting occurs. Nobody would count the same thing twice, they said.'

I made a mental note to ditch the statistics contained in the glossy port brochures they gave me the other day. I hoped to use them in my teaching back at the poly. On second thoughts, I kept them. The story about double counting was a good one.

What followed was a lively discussion between the students, in Chinese. While I felt excluded, they seemed happy enough.

'Harry knows how to make money, right?' queried Yang suddenly.

'Why do you ask?'

I was getting worried about Harry's lecture. He might have been up to his old tricks, taking bets, or something.

'Oh, do not worry, Professor Charles,' replied Wei. 'We were just considering how quantitative methods could help in *financial* forecasting. We do that in business, don't we?'

'Yes,' I replied hesitantly.

When I first arrived, the students would not say anything unless they were certain it was correct. They took no risks. I was the eminent, foreign professor. I would tell them what they needed to know, and that, as far as they were concerned, was that!

The students enjoyed the exercises on quantitative forecasting. All but a few got the same answers, and they enjoyed helping each other out. That, I noted, was quite a change. They were not afraid to take risks, and the class had become more relaxed and definitely more vocal.

I tried to explain the concept of playing devil's advocate as a basis for discussion, but I gave up. I was, after all, a big-nosed barbarian – and that was devil enough for them.

I informed them the next session would be, 'Strategic Management in a Market Economy'. I was on familiar ground with that because I had done it dozens of times. I was not sure what it had to do with cross-management communication, but nobody would be any the wiser.

That went well, I thought.

When I returned to the guesthouse, I found Harry and Petter enjoying a Tsingtao beer in the breakfast room, which served as bar and entertainments room in the evenings. At one end, a table-tennis table and some easy chairs made things more comfortable. If ever there were two rogues up to no good…

'Successful shopping trip, Harry?' I asked.

'Yes, excellent,' replied Harry. 'I have just met Petter, and we introduced ourselves.'

'Beer, Charles?' Petter asked.

'Yes please, it's just what I need,' I replied. 'I've not seen you for a couple of days, Petter.'

'You know me, busy as usual.'

Petter said he had been organising the work placements, but he was up to no good.

We enjoyed our beer and exchanged what knowledge we knew about the current student unrest.

Harry repeated what he had heard before he came to China. The British media had reported the protests in Tiananmen Square. Harry said that the interest in the student demonstrations was because western reporters were in China in large numbers due to Gorbachev's pending visit. Therefore, the coverage of the protests was more extensive than would normally be the case.

Petter occasionally listened to the BBC World Service late at night, the time when reception was at its best. According to the BBC, with live broadcasts from journalists on the spot, demonstrations took place the previous Thursday in several Chinese cities thus embarrassing the Chinese government because of the impending visit of Gorbachev.

'What demonstrations,' I remarked. 'They were just lively celebrations, surely.'

'Students exploited the seventieth anniversary of the May Fourth Movement as a ruse to protest over other matters such as freedom and democracy,' Petter explained patiently.

I had taken part in student celebrations, not demonstrations.

I did think that.

At least, I thought I did...

It was hardly a demonstration. Everything was well organised. I was not into embarrassing anyone, least of all the Chinese government. I decided I had better have another cup of tea with Professor Sang.

'I've got to go now, Charlie' said Harry. 'I am meeting my journalist friends. We'll catch up with things at breakfast.'

'What journalists—'

'Is it that late?' interrupted Petter. 'I also have to leave, Charles. I have a prior engagement.'

I was alone once more, so nothing unusual there.

I saw Mr Chou earlier, lurking around the entrance to the guesthouse, so I thought I might pass some time with him. I knew he considered Harry to be an uninvited guest but that's no cause for being continuously irritable. I reasoned a beer or two might put him in a better mood.

When I looked, he was gone.

I had to make do with my strategic management notes for company; and I had another beer.

Chapter 19

Tuesday, May 9, 1989

I was fast asleep when Harry returned from his meeting with his journalist friends.

'You awake, Charlie?' Harry whispered loudly.

'No.'

'That's okay then.'

After changing into his pyjamas, he spent the next hour shuffling through a pile of paper, preparing for his first lecture. He then went to sleep and snored loudly for the rest of the night, keeping me awake.

Next morning, I was not in the best of moods.

Harry was already up and I found him in the breakfast room. He was sitting with Mr Chou and both were enjoying what I assumed to be an unpleasant wholesome Chinese breakfast.

'I invited Shoe for breakfast, Charlie, I hope you don't mind,' Harry informed me. 'He seems to be a key player here, and you always need contacts. And look, he has brought my luggage.'

Mr Chou explained that Harry's lecture was at eleven o'clock, and he had cancelled my class so students could attend.

'Your lecture is very popular,' remarked Mr Chou. 'Professor Sang will translate for you. If you see him at ten o'clock you can discuss what arrangements you want.'

'I will take Harry to see Professor Sang,' I said.

I helped Harry carry his luggage to our room. While he unpacked, I looked over my strategic management notes, and was grateful for the extra day to prepare for my class.

After a while, Harry started to chuckle.

'What's up?'

'I've been robbed.'

'What do you mean, robbed? It's nothing to laugh about.'

'When I return to Pontefract at the end of the week,' Harry went on to explain, 'I have a short stopover in Hong Kong. My friend, Christopher, lives there, and he is getting married to a local girl, Margaret Chan. While I cannot attend the wedding, I bought them a present. It is an English crystal vase gift-wrapped in a nice presentation box. The tag says, *Congratulations on your Wedding Day*, and I wrote, *Margaret Chan and Christopher*. I also have a card for them.'

Harry was holding the presentation box, with its tag, and the wedding card. And his case was not empty. What was he on about?

'I thought you said you had been robbed.'

'I have,' replied Harry, 'but not everything. On my flight here, the thieves must have stolen my case in transit in Hong Kong. When they opened it and went through my things, they noticed the wedding present and card. The name, Margaret Chan, is obviously a local Hong Kong Chinese name – one of them. They left the present, card, and one set of clothes for me to wear for the wedding. Everything else has gone. The thieves returned my case, and the lost-luggage system found it. I hope the poly travel insurance is good. They certainly have a sense of humour, these Chinese.'

I inspected his case and it was true: one set of clothes, wedding present, and card.

'At least you still have your jacket,' I said.

Harry's jacket had been a topic of continual amusement and frustration. The problem was, much as Harry kept everything in his pockets, he could not remember what was in which pocket. Whenever he wanted anything, he had to search several pockets, at random, to find it. The other problem was Harry could only ever find twelve or so pockets, the rest cleverly hidden, and he kept the important things in those, such as his money and passport.

'Well, it is back to the shops for me,' commented Harry. 'I like to dress well. I have seen some good department stores in town. I bet you know the ropes, Charlie. We'll go shopping tomorrow.'

'I am free in the afternoon. I like little adventures.'

'Excellent. Then it's shopping we will enjoy.'

'I can lend you a shirt to keep you going if you like. It has a brown tie-and-dye effect, you'll like it.'

'What is Petter up to,' Harry enquired. 'He told me about his United Nations project and getting the student placements, but when I pressed him for details, he got evasive. I asked him if he had any useful contacts, but he was vague about that.'

'Petter can be a little reserved at times.'

'Oh, don't get me wrong, Petter was nice enough, and he bought the beers. The interesting thing was, when I was leaving the guesthouse last night, I caught Shoe keeping a close eye on Petter. You read about Chinese officials allocated to keep an eye on foreigners. They all report to the secret services.'

'You've been reading too many novels, Harry.'

'If Petter has been listening to the BBC World Service every evening, he would know a lot more about what is happening around here. He wasn't telling us much, was he?'

'No,' I agreed, 'but as I said, he can be a little reserved.'

'He wouldn't be some Scandinavian agent sent here to stir up trouble, would he?'

Harry could be a teaser at times.

Petter had not managed to get the better of our little, old, Chinese lady who served breakfast. No, I couldn't see him as a spy.

'Whoever heard of a Swedish spy?' I chuckled, 'You'll be telling me they'll be publishing best sellers about Swedish detectives next.'

'It's just a thought.'

'Anyway, Harry, what have you been up to?'

'Those contacts you gave me, they came up trumps. I managed to slip away from Shoe's little helper. He had no idea about shopping. I found a taxi and showed the driver the business cards you gave me, and he took me to the China News Agency building. I soon found the two journalists and invited them to lunch. They asked if they could bring some of their colleagues, and I said, why not, the more the merrier. We had a banquet.'

And to think I was worried about how Harry would manage?

'The restaurant was in a row with others,' continued Harry. 'I told my journalist friends that putting all the restaurants together was not good for business. They disagreed of course. They said if you want to go to a restaurant, then you go to that street because everyone knows all the restaurants are there. Outside were all sorts of animals in cages. I just assumed they were small zoos for the children. 'No,' my journalist friends told me, 'That's the menu.' Snakes are a speciality around here, and puppy dogs, Golden Labradors! I told them I was a vegetarian; well, I certainly was then. Still, we had a good meal.'

'Golden Labrador puppies...' I was obviously sceptical.

'I saw them.'

I wasn't sure about Harry's claim that puppies were on the menu. The thing was, I had noticed, apart from songbirds, the Chinese didn't have pets. Dogs and cats were not in evidence.

'They gave me a list of shops to visit. Number One Department Store, they said, was best for suits.'

'What did you do last night?' I asked.

'I was invited to a meeting with the journalists at the China News Agency building. They picked me up by the main entrance of the university. They were having a discussion about press freedom and wanted me to provide a British perspective.'

What did Harry know about the British press?

'The journalists seem a bit disgruntled about reporting government propaganda,' added Harry. 'They have that naïve notion we have press freedom, and I wanted to explain that there was no such thing.'

'What happened?'

'They were all arguing with each other and I didn't manage to say much. I was going to explain that newspaper proprietors and editors control the press back in Britain and they only employed journalists who represented their views. I would have told them that journalists suck up to the politicians so they can get their stories. I would have explained that journalists go through the rubbish in dustbins to find their stories. If I had half the chance, I would have enlightened them how politicians leak to the press so they can embarrass the opposition or government or other politicians who were becoming a threat. I wanted to tell them in plain words that it's all a bit too cosy for my liking.'

'You didn't say that, did you?'

'I didn't get chance to, unfortunately.'

'It's a good job you didn't,' I said. 'I'm not sure what they would have made of that.'

'I would have told them most people buy a particular newspaper because they know it will report what they feel comfortable reading,' added Harry. 'Take page three of *The Sun*, for example. When you buy that newspaper everyone knows what to expect—'

'It's not the best example to explain to the Chinese, Harry.'

'You're probably right, I suppose But it's the truth.'

While I was a dubious about the authenticity of what Harry had just said, he appeared to know a little about the British press.

'What did you tell them?' I asked.

'I started to say that, in the West, the press has the freedom to report whatever it likes, but I didn't get chance to finish,' explained Harry. 'They started to cheer and didn't hear the rest.'

'What didn't they hear then?'

'I was going to explain that just because the press prints something, it doesn't mean it is true. Our press has the freedom to report whatever misleading information and falsehoods the libel laws will allow. If you are poor, then you are fair game because they know you cannot afford to take them to court. Our affluent leaders of industry and society get a much easier ride because they can afford legal proceedings. Unfortunately, I didn't get chance to explain all that.'

'That was unfortunate,' I reflected absentmindedly. 'Anyway, are you ready for your lecture?'

'Of course,' Harry replied, with unfounded confidence.

'What is the topic of your lecture?' I asked innocently, remembering what the students had said yesterday.

'Making money through institutions. Students back in Pontefract always enjoy this lecture. They like to know how to make lots of money. I told Shoe that when he asked me about my lecture.'

'Institutions?' I queried.

'Financial institutions,' stated Harry patiently.

'Are there any in China?'

'I'm not sure to be honest. I didn't have time to do any research before coming here.'

'Best of luck, I said. 'We should go and see Professor Sang.'

Cowardice made me hesitate asking him about the lunatic asylums. All would become clear, it usually did with Harry; well, maybe not!

'*H*ello, Professor Sang,' I said, 'let me introduce my colleague, Harry.'

'*Nee hao*,' said Harry, shaking hands with Professor Sang.

'Do you speak much Chinese, Harry?'

'Just a few words,' said Harry. 'It's helpful when making contacts.'

'What do you want me to do?' asked Professor Sang.

'Just translate, I suppose…'

'For your translation, please speak in short sentences. Mr Chou informed me you are a specialist in financial matters. Unfortunately this is not my own subject, but I am sure your audience will be very interested in making pots of money, especially using your extraordinary methods in the West.'

'That sounds fine,' Harry replied. 'I'm sure we'll manage.'

'Perhaps you can help me, Professor Sang,' I asked. 'Some of the students were talking about Confucius and his famous quotes.'

'Younger people are not as familiar with Confucian philosophy as my generation,' replied Professor Sang. 'During the Cultural Revolution, Confucius was considered bourgeois and his philosophy was no longer taught in schools.'

'Why was that?'

'What the Cultural Revolution despised most were philosophies on how the authorities should govern,' explained Professor Sang. 'Confucius considered that a ruler who resorts to force has already failed as a ruler. "Your job is to govern, not to kill." Philosophies like that did not go down well.'

'I don't suppose Chairman Mao wanted other thoughts or quotes to compete with his own,' I added.

'Wisdom will grow with our power, and teaches us that the less we use our power the greater it will be,' said Harry.

Professor Sang looked puzzled. Me, I was astonished Harry could quote from Confucius. At least, it sounded Confucian.

'That's a quote by Thomas Jefferson,' added Harry. 'He was an early nineteenth century American president.'

'I know about Jefferson,' commented Professor Sang. 'He wrote the draft Declaration of Independence for the United States, adopted July 4, 1776. Some scholars believe Jefferson modified the original Confucian quote for his own needs.'

'All men are created equal,' added Harry. 'Jefferson drafted that quote while still owning a field full of black slaves.'

'The Declaration also states that when a government becomes destructive then it is the right of the people to alter or abolish it, and to institute new government,' remarked Professor Sang.

I saw flaws in that last statement because you could justify both the Cultural Revolution and the current student unrest by it.

Who was to judge when a government has become destructive?

I supposed that was the role of a democratic process. If not, then any disgruntled group could cause havoc by exercising their *right* in the name of instituting new government.

'Come on, Harry, it is time for you to give your thoughts to our students,' Professor Sang said with a twinkle in his eyes. 'They all want to know how to make pots of money.'

'You Chinese have a good sense of humour,' quipped Harry.

'Any good Confucian quotes I can use to impress my students?' I asked jovially.

'Don't do to others what you would not want yourself.'

That sounded familiar…

'Oh, by the way, some of my journalist friends are coming along,' Harry informed us. 'That shouldn't be a problem, should it?'

'It shouldn't be,' commented Professor Sang.

Harry certainly knew how to promote himself.

I assumed Harry would give his lecture in one of the small classrooms, like mine, and would attract an audience of about thirty. I was wrong. He gave his lecture in one of the university auditoriums with seating for four hundred, and the place was packed. In the corner, I could see Mr Chou; it seemed he also wanted to make pots of money.

I found a seat in the front row.

The auditorium was modern and as good, if not better, than anything we had at the poly. It was an amphitheatre with excellent sight lines, and the acoustics were good. The décor was pleasing with large hand-painted murals framed in wide, dark-lacquered wooden frames hanging on the walls. Behind Harry was a wide, red banner with yellow, Chinese writing. I didn't dare consider what it said. The place had a buzz, and I could see students were excited. The auditorium lights dimmed and several spots picked out Harry and Professor Sang on the raised platform at the front.

Because he had dropped his notes, it was a pity Harry was on his hands and knees picking up sheets of paper. Harry glanced at his audience, squinting at the dazzling lights, one hand raised to protect his eyes from the glare, looking vulnerable.

Harry didn't do looking vulnerable!

Grinning at his audience, he slowly stood up, and received his first round of applause. To my dismay, he was still wearing his jacket. He then demonstrated to his audience, with further applause, its clever layout of pockets. It wasn't a deliberate tactic or anything because Harry was looking for his glasses, and he found them in the seventh pocket.

Once the audience had settled, Professor Sang introduced Harry, in Chinese. Every so often Professor Sang looked at Harry. On several occasions, I clearly heard the words, Harry, Pontefract, racecourse, and cakes. Whatever Professor Sang was saying was popular because the audience showed its appreciation. Professor Sang was a professional.

We were not having the luxury of a simultaneous translation. Harry would speak a sentence or so, pausing when he remembered to, or when Professor Sang coughed. When Professor Sang gave his translation, his length of speech bore no resemblance to the length of time Harry spoke. I found that odd.

Since I could understand Harry, I was chuckling at the humorous bits while he spoke, but doing so alone. When the rest of the audience laughed while Professor Sang translated, I was silent; and they laughed at different places to me.

I was fascinated.

I would like to have recorded Harry's presentation in detail, because it was popular. Nevertheless, I did recall the gist of what Harry said, at least for the first few minutes because after that, things got out of hand.

Harry introduced the concept of western financial institutions but thereafter called them institutions. I never did find out if lunatic asylums featured prominently in what he was saying. Possibly, they referred to lunatic asylums as institutions in China, hence the confusion in the first place. Harry discussed the role of institutions, with particular reference to parliament, the Chancellor of the Exchequer, the Bank of England, and so forth.

Being a good speaker, at regular intervals, Harry asked his audience for questions. He did not want any misunderstandings.

'Are you saying all politicians are lunatics?' asked someone.

Harry took that as gentle banter from the audience.

'You might think that,' Harry responded, 'but I couldn't possibly comment.' He then gave the audience a huge wink. Harry then received his first standing ovation, and there were more to come.

You might argue that the lack of clarity, as practised by most native speakers of English, led to this harmless misunderstanding. To be honest, I was not sure if English was Harry's first language, being originally from La Réunion.

To cut a long misleading story short, while I realised Harry was not really saying that all politicians were lunatics or that government was a lunatic asylum, and, consequently, that was the direct cause of financial chaos in the economy...

...the audience deemed otherwise.

Professor Sang was standing next to Harry with an innocent look on his face – *I only translate – the very model servant!* I knew he had a difficult task on his hands translating for Harry, and he was not a specialist in financial matters, but...

Harry was in his stride. The audience was on his side.

In what I correctly understood to be the context of financial matters, although I could not vouch for the rest of the audience, Harry finished by carefully explaining the importance of freedom of information in the press.

'Journalists, with their noses to the ground and consulting their contacts – you can't overestimate the importance of having contacts – inform their readers about what is happening in the market. They do this freely and without any control from the authorities, otherwise what would be the point?'

I then spotted some of the journalists, who had stood up, and were clapping and shouting words of encouragement to Harry, not that he needed any.

'You,' said Harry, pointing to the audience in a theatrical manner, 'you will then be in a better position to know what to do.'

Harry received another standing ovation, which quickly turned into synchronous clapping, which commonly happened in China.

'Are you saying that press freedom is a representation for democracy?' It was one of Harry's journalist friends.

'Yes of course,' replied Harry, 'financial planning and portfolio analysis by their very nature rely upon up-to-the-minute information, and that is part of what a democratic nation is—'

I heard most of Harry's reply, but because of the applause and stamping of feet, the audience only heard the first three words. The journalist who asked the question then turned to the audience and gave a short passionate speech. I went to see Professor Sang on the raised platform who kindly translated what the journalist said.

'It is time for press freedom,' the journalist said. 'Because of government restrictions, we did not report truthfully on the events since the death of Hu Yaobang last month. This has seriously damaged our reputation. On behalf of all journalists, I apologise to the People.'

'We want to tell the truth and we are forced to tell lies,' shouted another journalist.

'Every aspect of the news is controlled.'

'What has that got to do with financial institutions?' I whispered.

'Oh, lots, according to Harry,' replied Professor Sang, with a mischievous look on his face.

I missed the next bit because Mr Chou stormed over and started protesting with Professor Sang. Professor Sang said nothing but stared at Mr Chou and waited until he had finished. Professor Sang then said something to Mr Chou, nothing much but it was short and obviously to the point. Mr Chou immediately shut up.

Everyone stood and the applause was overwhelming.

'You all heard Harry, so we know what to do,' was the last thing I heard before the journalists trooped out of the auditorium, followed by students, including some of my own – making a quick getaway, no doubt. Within what seemed to be seconds, the auditorium was empty apart from a few bemused looking staff.

That was precisely what happened.

'That went well, Mr Chou, don't you think,' I said.

Extract from:

THE PRESS
WED 10 MAY 1989
Local correspondent, Peking

CHINESE LEADERS had hoped to concentrate their efforts on the impending visit of Gorbachev, the Soviet Union president, when the unexpected happened. Journalists have caused alarm bells to ring with demands for 'press freedom' and calling for talks with government leaders.

On recent demonstrations, students mocked journalists for their coverage of the student protests, who replied they had no choice but had to obey orders and follow the Party line. During the demonstration on 4 May a few days ago, journalists joined students and said they now realised such orders had to end. This was the first time journalists had made a public display of dissent towards the government control of the media and censorship.

Yesterday, the opposite occurred when students, with banners, joined journalists in demonstrations to show their unity. Students went to the offices of the *People's Daily* and accused the paper of reporting rubbish and cheating the people.

From: **Deputy Chairman**
Office of Education Foreign Affairs
Public Security Bureau
Beijing
To: **Chou Ke-giang**
Director of the Office of Foreign Affairs
Jaliang Number 3 University
10 May 1989, 06h00

Private note (by telex)

DISSIDENT VINCENT

Explain immediately what is happening in Jaliang.

I have it on good authority that the journalists at the Chinese News Agency, in Jaliang, are stirring up trouble and that your two British academics are responsible for this. You had specific orders to keep the two provocateurs under close observation.

Behind the walls of Zhongnanhai, the compound for the elite, there is a passionate succession struggle taking place, reformists against hardline conservatives. It is difficult to predict who will win. Some see the current demonstrations as the greatest display of dissent against the Party and a humiliating vote of 'no confidence' against the policies of Deng. This is causing a major distraction and must stop before the visit of the Soviet leader in a few days.

Party leaders are unaware of the activities of the two British provocateurs, but eventually their conduct will be common knowledge, and this will reflect badly on you and your career.

There are forces at work in Jaliang that are prompting the protests.

It must stop.

Memorandum

(Telex message)

From	Chou Ke-giang
	Director of the Office of Foreign Affairs
	Jaliang Number 3 University
To	Deputy Chairman
	Office of Education Foreign Affairs
	Public Security Bureau
	Beijing
Date	10 May 1989 (7:30 a.m.)

CONFIDENTIAL

DR CHARLES VINCENT

On Monday, 8 May, Harry managed to slip away from his escort I had assigned to watch him. I found out later that he had visited journalists at the China News Agency, the same journalists that Vincent met during the demonstrations on 4 May. A group of journalists went, with Harry, to a restaurant, a public place, where the British academic gave a provocative speech about the freedom of press so enjoyed by the West. This was a deliberate and seditious act aimed at spreading discontent among the journalists.

Harry then invited the journalists to a lecture he was presenting at the university. I did not know of that until after the event because if I had, I would have been able to ban all non-university personnel from attending.

On Tuesday, 9 May, Harry presented his lecture. I had arranged for Professor Sang to translate. Initially he was reluctant to do so because he was not a specialist in financial matters. I flattered him by saying that he was the best person to provide an academic translation because of his excellent English.

The lecture itself was a thinly veiled guise to promote subversive western propaganda about democracy and the freedom of the press. Harry invited the journalists to speak and they, in turn, persuaded the students to join them in more demonstrations. That, I consider, was the plan from the outset, but I could not have foreseen this. They cleverly planned the demonstration to coordinate with those in Beijing and other cities.

Once I realised what was happening, I tried to stop Professor Sang translating further, but it was too late. In fact, Professor Sang blamed me because I had made all of the arrangements and insisted that he translated. He also reminded me that most journalists were Party members and I had better be careful.

Chapter 20

Wednesday, May 10, 1989

I was surprised to find all students had turned up for my lecture. They listened, with slight bored indifference, to my well-rehearsed lecture on strategic management. Their reaction surprised me. It was one of my better subjects, and I felt comfortable with the material. Back at the poly, students always took the subject seriously and listened intently. In business terms, strategic management had substance.

'Strategy is always given to us by others. We just do as we are told,' argued Yang. 'We have no choice.'

As I had heard that argument before, I was having none of it.

'Then tell me,' I asked. 'Who gives you no choice?'

'The Party, central government, our leaders,' replied Yang.

'That might be you, one day.'

'Unlikely,' Hou replied. 'We cannot choose where we work.'

'But it might be.'

I could see from one or two faces that some of them were hoping I might be right. I know that to get anywhere in China you had to be chosen to join the Communist Party. I had no doubts some of those in front of me were already members, although nobody talked of it. They were the elite, and if they weren't going somewhere, then nobody was.

'Remember your work placements,' I reminded them. 'You will need to think strategically then.'

I gave them an exercise on a strengths, weaknesses, opportunities, and threats analysis, based on the Chariot Tyre Factory, which was a large local factory I had heard about. The results were not what I expected. Nevertheless, I was encouraged by the possibilities rubber apparently had in China. With the one child per family policy instituted in 1976 and with over one billion population, the opportunities were obvious, they said.

I couldn't argue with that.

'*I*s it possible to have a car this afternoon,' I asked.

'No,' Mr Chou replied emphatically, 'there are none available. You should be preparing for your next classes, not shopping. We don't want another repeat of yesterday's debacle, do we?'

What debacle...

Mr Chou went on to inform us that, after Harry's lecture, students demonstrated in Jaliang with the journalists, calling for freedom of the press. He implied it was Harry's fault. What happened yesterday, even though we saw no evidence of protests ourselves, could hardly be Harry's fault. Mr Chou had cancelled Harry's second lecture, *Snouts in the Rice Bowl*, and stated that he must help me with my classes.

Actually, that was a good idea.

I was losing confidence in my ability to hold the students' attention. They all seemed to have their minds on other things. I was sure, with Harry's help, I could get through the week. I could then spend the weekend preparing for further classes. Despite what Mr Chou said, Harry still wanted to go shopping. He suggested we hang around the guesthouse a bit and then slip away unnoticed.

We spent part of the afternoon conjuring up an adaptation of an old management game that entailed building a tower with *Lego* bricks. These small plastic building bricks click together, the bottom of one onto the top of another. The game goes something like this. The higher the tower, then the higher the revenue, but that involves using more building materials, Lego bricks in this case, thus costs are higher. The aim was to devise a cunning building plan to build the tower as high as possible with the fewest Lego bricks to maximise profit. The tower must be able stand unsupported other than the economical use of building bricks.

'We will call it a pagoda and not a tower,' suggested Harry.

'Good idea.'

'We will have a prize for the winning team. That will encourage competition.'

'Good idea.'

'I will give an introductory lecture on profit and loss, break-even analysis, you know, the basics.'

'Good idea.'

101

'We will call the game – whoever builds the pagoda with most profit will be constant in happiness and wisdom. That sounds Confucian?'

Bad idea I decided, but I didn't want to discourage Harry.

'I'll think about that,' I said. 'But we haven't got any Lego bricks?'

'Not a problem. I have seen them in town or something like them. We can buy some when we go shopping.'

'Good idea.'

Mr Chou spent most of the afternoon lurking outside the guesthouse poking the odd bush. It was difficult to see what he was doing. Surely, he was not watching us to make sure we were working. Late afternoon, we slipped away unseen, through the guesthouse kitchen.

'*Nee hao, zy-jyen,*' Harry said to the surprised little, old, Chinese lady as we passed by, both of us looking guilty I might add.

'**W**hich way, Harry?' I asked.

We were standing by the road where Harry had caught the bus into town the other day. The bus route goes both ways, and I was not sure of my directions.

'I can't remember,' Harry mumbled, looking at his feet.

'We'll try that way,' I said.

We crossed the road and waited by the bus stop along with about twenty or so others loitering nearby. Within a couple of minutes, a bus arrived.

'I noticed that last time,' commented Harry. 'You never wait long for a bus.'

It was the length of two normal buses, concertinaed in the middle, like an accordion, so it could get around corners easily. It was already quite full and I considered it might be a tight squeeze when we boarded.

When the doors opened, there was mayhem.

Those waiting rushed the doors, elbows out, shoulders in, with no respect for those trying to get off who, similarly, were also pushing and shoving. I could see the next bus coming along, and it looked barely half-full. Unfortunately, Harry had already entered the fray, and his elbows were as sharp as the rest.

'Come on,' shouted Harry. 'It's the survival of the fittest here.'

Despite Harry's cry of encouragement, I stepped back until things had calmed down. I didn't fancy my chances against the others, particularly Harry. As it happened, there was plenty room, although some of us had to stand. Harry had managed to get a seat.

Harry pointed to the bus conductor. The conductor sat in a raised seat further down the bus, and I had to go to him. Not many other passengers bought tickets.

I didn't know how much the fare would be or how to ask. I therefore offered the conductor a ten-yuan FEC note, pointed to Harry and myself and said, 'downtown Jaliang,' and smiled hopefully.

The conductor looked at me, then Harry, and at my ten-yuan note in a theatrical manner, not unlike actors in a Beijing opera. He then said something in a voice for all around to hear, not nastily but in a cheery way. I didn't understand, of course. Others around came and looked at the ten-yuan note. One passenger took it to inspect more closely, and passed it around for others to see. When the note had finished doing the rounds, I also examined the note more closely.

The ten-yuan note clearly stated, Foreign Exchange Certificate, and went on to explain, in English, that it could only be used within China at designated places. Buses, obviously, were not one of those places.

One of the other passengers took my FEC note and gave me in return, what looked about one hundred Renminbi in ordinary Chinese currency. I had a good look at the Renminbi notes and saw on one side they all stated, in English, *Zhongguo Renmin Yinhang*. I offered the conductor my Renminbi but he threw his hands into the air in an exaggerated manner. The kindly passenger who had made the exchange removed a note out of my hand and gave it to the conductor. The conductor then gave me two tickets and some change. The tickets were tiny and made from very thin paper.

I made my way back and stood near Harry.

An elderly, well-dressed, elegant-looking woman stood up and offered me her seat with a quick movement of her hand.

'No,' I said, 'I don't mind standing, but thank you.'

I didn't take the seat and the elderly woman remained standing. Everyone on the bus must have been a little puzzled because foreigners normally travelled in taxis, tourist buses, or official cars. Perhaps I was being rude not accepting the seat because it remained empty.

I discreetly studied the woman standing next to me because she looked out of place. She was dressed in beautifully tailored silk clothing reminiscent of pre-revolution, pre-wartime, decadent China, when bankers, businessmen, and western degenerates mingled with the upper-class locals. While her clothing had seen better days, she retained that air of elegance and aloofness about her. Her hair had an intricate hairpin stuck into the tight bun at the back of her head. At the end of the hairpin, three jade birds on fine springs gently quivered with the motion of the bus.

Chinese women, I had noticed, were quite diverse in their choice of clothing. Some wore baggy, faded blue or grey, two-piece suits, buttoned to the neck. These were practical but not very flattering and were a throwback from the days of the Cultural Revolution. Quite popular were trousers and a blouse, especially with the older woman, but not very stylish. By far more fashionable, especially with the younger generation, were western-style clothes. Skirt lengths were just below the knee. With that, they wore short white socks or knee-high pop-socks, which looked odd with skirts.

I put my mind to more mundane matters such as, were we travelling in the right direction? Jaliang Number 3 University was on the outskirts of town, and, although it was getting dark, I could see we were leaving the built-up area. The bus quickly entered the surrounding hills.

'Anything look familiar, Harry?' I asked.

'I don't know,' replied Harry, again looking shiftily down at his feet.

This was becoming the little adventure I had hoped.

Harry, on the other hand, didn't think so...

'This is not right,' he said, looking alarmed. 'There were no hills the last time I went into town.'

'Quite a mystery tour, don't you think?'

'No, I don't think that at all. Where are we?'

'It looks like we are at a tea plantation, but I'm not sure.'

Harry was anxious. We had left the built-up area, and there was no longer any street lighting. Most other passengers had left the bus. It was dark outside and the dim lighting inside the bus cast sinister shadows.

'We're lost!' declared Harry.

At the next stop, Harry suddenly left the bus and it was all I could do to follow. I just made my escape before the doors closed. We were standing in the middle of nowhere in almost complete darkness.

'Harry, what's the matter?' I asked incredulously. 'Why did you jump off the bus?'

'We're lost,' he again complained. 'I don't want to get lost in China. Anything can happen.'

'Like what?' I asked reasonably. 'I was looking forward to finding out where we would end up.'

'We're lost,' he repeated glumly.

Harry then attempted – I could not describe it in any other way – to commit suicide.

The road was narrow, but still with proper tarmac. Coming towards us were headlights from what appeared to be a large, fully laden dilapidated truck. Harry jumped into the middle of the road and started waving his arms around. Fortunately, for Harry, I managed to pull him away before the truck ran him over.

Put it this way…

If you were a Chinese truck driver, minding your own business, tired after a hard day's work, and suddenly, out of the darkness, in the middle of nowhere, in the middle of the road, a plump, little, barbarian foreigner with one of those big noses everyone talked about started jumping up and down, and waving his arms, would you stop?

Exactly.

'Harry, we are not lost. We got off the bus at a bus stop. There is another bus stop on the other side of the road. We will cross the road, and wait for the next bus. This time, we will know it is going in the right direction.' I thought I had better explain slowly.

That seemed to placate Harry and he calmed down. Within a couple of minutes, a bus appeared from the opposite direction to the bus we left. The doors opened, we boarded the empty bus, and Harry sat down.

'I told you it was this way,' Harry remarked.

I let that one go…

As I was becoming a seasoned bus traveller, I confidently walked up to the conductor, requested, 'downtown Jaliang,' smiled, and offered the conductor money. I received two more tickets and some change. The bus meandered into town, picking up more passengers, and we passed the stop where we had joined the previous bus. As we got closer to the town centre, the streets got busier. Occasionally, a shop frontage was completely covered with Christmas tree lights, but all white. The road was full of cyclists and heaving with pedestrians.

'You do know where to get off, don't you Harry?' I asked, half in jest, half seriously.

Harry gave me a look, and smiled.

'We get off when everyone else gets off.'

The bus was full, and passengers were either sitting or standing calmly, chatting to their friends. When the bus came to its final stop, another riot took place. Possibly, there was a forfeit for being last to leave the bus? I put my hand on Harry's shoulder to prevent him joining the scrum. When the last few passengers were about to leave, we nonchalantly stood up and left the bus calmly in our own time.

I felt quite smug and yes, that was a mistake.

As we left the bus, two men in white shirts accosted us. I smiled politely and started to walk away, but they blocked our path. One of the men had a notepad and pen, and the other was talking to us in a very direct manner.

'Any clues what they are on about?' I asked Harry.

'Give them money.'

The man doing the talking was getting twitchy and raised his voice, and everyone within listening distance came to watch. I was witnessing one of the favourite Chinese pastimes – gawping and being nosy about other people's business, particularly foreigners. People were pushing and jostling to get a better view of the action. Quite a crowd was forming. In the middle of that crowd were two barbarian foreigners, and yes, they had those big noses that everyone talked about.

It was inopportune that one of those foreigners in question happened to be me.

The man with the notepad and pen kept pointing to the bus parked by the roadside. Others in the crowd were also pointing at the bus. What had we done wrong? No one had warned us it was illegal for foreigners to ride on a bus.

'You pay off the two in white shirts, and I'll deal with the rest,' offered Harry unhelpfully, while attempting to remove his jacket.

'I'm not sure that will work.'

How, I contemplated, was Harry going to deal with the rest. I then speculated on what Harry would do when he removed his jacket. Since it contained most of his worldly possessions in China, he would never let it go.

The man with the notepad and pen showed me a small slip of paper that I recognised – a bus ticket. They were ticket inspectors.

As Harry was wrestling with his jacket, the man without the notepad and pen, the talkative one, was getting agitated. I racked my brain trying to recall what I had done with the bus tickets.

I remembered.

I raised both my hands, chest height, palms facing outwards in a non-threatening manner, smiled nicely, and hoped body language was universal. I then put my hand on Harry's shoulder to try to calm him down before he hurt himself.

'Don't panic and all will be revealed,' I explained to the two agitated men in white shirts, knowing they couldn't understand a word I was saying. I just hoped my voice sounded reassuring.

I put my hands into my pockets and rummaged around for a bit until I found what I wanted. I extracted a tiny ball of paper no bigger than the head of a knitting needle and, slowly and meticulously, unravelled it until two bus tickets appeared. I was, after all, English, and I would never dream of dropping litter in a public place. Everyone in the crowd watched in anticipation. I then gave the man, the one without the notepad and pen, the two bus tickets to inspect. He duly inspected the two tickets, conferred with his partner who entered something into his notebook, and returned the tickets to me.

Both men gave us big smiles. The talkative one said something in a quite pleasant manner; what exactly, I didn't know. I assumed he said something along the line of, 'That wasn't too hard, was it. We only wanted to see the bus tickets, all this excitement over nothing!'

Everyone in the crowd laughed, and someone provided a commentary to the others who could not quite see what was happening. Again, I didn't know what was actually said, possibly, 'The foreigners had tickets, fancy that, how did they get them?' or words to that effect.

Within seconds, the two men in white shirts walked away. Everyone had had their fun and got on with whatever they were doing before.

'I told you paying them off would work,' Harry remarked. He had missed what had happened, and I hadn't the patience to explain.

'Where is this Number One Department Store you were telling me about?' I asked.

Harry, I could tell, was in his element. He had a smile from ear to hideous, barbarian ear.

'Follow me,' he said.

Intuition told me that was not the best thing to do...

'Harry, why are we walking in the middle of the road?'

'It's the safest place. Look, there are no footpaths.'

That was true, but still...

The road was crammed with cyclists going in both directions but on the correct side of the road. In the middle of the road was a no-man's land where cyclists didn't bump into each other. It was there that Harry insisted we walk, but I was not convinced.

When I attempted to get to the side of the road facing the cyclists, as proper, I realised it was a bad move. One cyclist, in an attempt to miss me, ran into another, and there was an almighty pile-up. Cyclists were having an intense argument, with several pointing at me. A crowd quickly gathered to watch the fun, but we didn't hang around.

We beat a hasty retreat – in the middle of the road, of course.

*R*egardless of me telling Harry about the Friendship Store, it had to be Number One Department Store or nothing.

'They only take Renminbi at Number One, and the coffee is good at the Friendship Store,' I reasoned.

'I keep telling you, Charlie, you need contacts,' replied Harry, while taking out of his jacket pocket a huge wad of Renminbi. For the record, it took him quite some time to locate his Renminbi – pocket six for those who are interested.

Harry knew his way around Number One Department Store. He explained he had visited there with his journalist friends, having neglected to inform me of that before.

There was nothing to set aside that department store from any other, except it was the largest in Jaliang. It was crowded and shoppers were buying. Shelves were piled high with everything made in China. Washing machines, a new product line crudely made from plastic and poorly designed, were selling fast. Colour television sets, electric sewing machines, cassette tape recorders, radios, and ghetto blasters were all popular items. The demonstration on the karaoke machine had attracted quite an audience; not us, I might add. Unlike the Friendship Store, shop assistants were attentive.

The open-plan third floor had nothing but men's suits, all colours, shapes, and sizes. While some were crammed on long, horizontal rails, others were on wide, circular hanging rails, all mounted on castors. They needed to be, because the place was so full you had to move the hanging rails around to pass through. By each rail was a female shop assistant, so the place looked busy before customers arrived.

'The good thing here is Chinese men are not very tall and the more elderly tend to be a bit fat, a bit like me,' Harry explained. 'The buttons are poor quality, but I can change those when I get back home.'

He was right.

What I meant was – Harry was a bit fat and not very tall. I couldn't comment on the buttons, obviously.

'Back in Pontefract, I pay a fortune to gets suits tailored to fit me,' continued Harry. 'Here, the place is full of them.'

Harry spent the next hour rummaging through the rails checking all the materials, colours, and styles. I stood back in amazement and watched Harry at work. Three shop assistants followed him, which was handy, because he handed over any suit that caught his eye.

'The problem is, there are no changing rooms,' said Harry, 'and I am not buying any suit without trying it on.'

That wasn't a problem for Harry, much to my dismay.

Harry eyed up one of the wide circular rails.

'That'll do,' declared Harry.

He then squeezed through the suits and entered the space in the middle. His head and shoulders appeared just above the height of the suits, which were hanging in a neat circle around him. Harry had aroused the attention of some of the shop assistants.

'Surely, you aren't going to try your suits on there?' I said.

He wasn't and he climbed back through the circular hanging rail. 'Not enough room in there, unfortunately.'

Thankfully...

He wasn't beaten.

Harry re-arranged the whole floor space. He wanted four straight rails of suits positioned to make a fort, with him in the middle. Surprisingly, the shop assistants seemed to understand what he was up to and helped him.

'That's better.'

Harry had attracted quite an audience. Almost all of the shop assistants were strategically positioned with good views of him, not forgetting the other shoppers who couldn't resist an entertaining gawp at a foreigner.

Me, I was trying to be as inconspicuous as possible.

'Don't look,' declared Harry to his audience. 'Cover your eyes.'

Harry gave a demonstration of covering his eyes with his hands and then made all the shop assistants do likewise. If any shop assistant did not comply, Harry pointed at her, wagging his finger, and demanded in a stern voice, 'Don't look!'

There was Harry, in the middle of his makeshift changing room, with a large audience, all with their hands covering their eyes, absolutely captivated with what was going on. Harry happily undressed in the middle of his fortress and tried on his selection, one by one. I saw more than one pair of eyes mischievously peeking through their fingers.

'Too big!'

'Wrong colour!'

'Poor material!'

'Don't look!'

To my utter horror, there was more to come.

Harry's head disappeared below the level of suits and, after a delay of a few seconds, a confident, out-of-tune, baritone voice from the direction of the makeshift changing room was heard to be singing the 'Stripper' – assuming *da da-ing* could be classified as singing.

I could not believe it.

Suddenly, through one of the rails appeared a stocky, brown, hairy leg, foot covered in a black sock, waving to the tune of the 'Stripper'.

The fingers of the hands, covering the eyes of the shop assistants, slowly opened. With hands still covering their faces, twenty or so fascinated Chinese females were peeking through their fingers, thoroughly mesmerised by Harry's performance.

So was I.

With perfect timing, the little black-socked, brown, hairy leg disappeared and Harry's head popped up.

'Don't look!' whooped Harry, 'I can see you're all looking.'

Harry bought three suits, six shirts, four silk ties, ten pairs of underpants and matching vests, and countless socks. He also bought a leather briefcase for work, five sets of Chinese look-alike Lego bricks, and a new suitcase for carrying all his new belongings in. He managed to find his money in pocket nine and insisted his jacket had seventeen pockets, and not sixteen.

Me, I had a thoroughly enjoyable and entertaining evening.

Chapter 21

Thursday, May 11, 1989

I didn't have a class, so Mr Chou informed me at breakfast.

I was relieved because I did not feel quite ready for the management game I had hatched up with Harry. Contrary to Harry, who wanted to launch the build the pagoda management game without further ado, I considered it prudent to spend more time preparing the detail.

'Look, Harry, these are not Pontefract students,' I tried to explain. 'They're intelligent and will be quick to notice anything not quite right.'

Harry was to prepare his cameo pieces on profit and loss, break-even analysis, and other accountancy tricks. He was also to prepare some exercises on basic accounting skills that were not generic to the West. A key area for the game was the decision criteria to assess the height of the pagoda – revenue, against the number of bricks used to build the pagoda – costs. Harry volunteered to do that.

I know cynics back at the poly, not familiar with modern management techniques, considered building towers with children's building bricks was a waste of time. Much as I might have had some sympathy with that view, building the tower had provided the backbone of management training for as long as I could remember. Those who participated took it very seriously. Believe me, many a promising career had abruptly ended on the collapse of a pile of Lego bricks. There were so many intricacies, boardroom plots, backstabbing, and other nuances in the game, that from experience, I had learnt to curb my scepticism.

I was to prepare an introductory session on a market-led economy, which I did not mind. I did something similar in one of my regular sessions back at the poly. I just needed a Chinese flavour to it. Harry and I went our separate ways, and we agreed to meet in the evening for our final preparation.

I decided to undertake some serious research.

It was time for another visit to see Professor Sang.

When I arrived at Professor Sang's office, he was having a meeting with Professor Song, the faculty dean.

'I am sorry to disturb you,' I said. 'I will come back later?'

'We are having a cup of tea,' replied Professor Sang. 'Please join us.'

Professor Sang prepared my tea in the porcelain teacup. He and Professor Song were both using jam jars.

'I apologise for your classes being disrupted,' said Professor Song.

'Things are certainly lively,' I admitted.

'Professor Sang is keeping you informed, I believe.'

'Yes he is and I am grateful for his assistance,' I replied. 'Gorbachev is to visit Beijing, I hear.'

'Negotiations for his visit started a long time ago,' said Professor Song, 'but the Soviets have had to make many concessions. The visit is supposed to be a tribute to Deng Xiaoping. He is 84, and this would be one of his final legacies to the People's Republic. It must be a bitter blow for Deng because he is confronted by unprecedented student demonstrations and disaffected intelligentsia. The demonstrations on Tiananmen Square must be difficult for him to accept. Gorbachev, when he arrives, will find he is the students' hero. His portrait has been posted on a wall near the main entrance to the university.'

'Your English is excellent, Professor Song,' I said.

'I studied at Cambridge,' replied Professor Song. 'Can we help you?'

'I am planning a management game, with the help of my colleague, Harry. I'm gathering some background information on the Open Door Policy and the developments of the market economy in China.'

I certainly did not want to inform Professor Song we were going to do the building the pagoda with Lego bricks routine. What would he think, being a Cambridge man?

'Your colleague Harry is very nearly as popular with our students as Gorbachev,' joked Professor Song. 'As he is leaving soon, I have organised a small banquet on Saturday evening as a token of the faculty's thanks. I must go now, but Professor Sang will be able to help you with our Open Door Policy.'

After Professor Song left, taking his jam jar with him, Professor Sang topped up my teacup with more hot water from the thermos and then settled down in the sofa opposite me.

'What do you want to know?' asked Professor Sang.

'Just some basic information, nothing too complicated,' I answered.

Professor Sang went to his desk and after shuffling through one of his drawers, returned with an old copy of the *China Daily*, the newspaper for foreigners.

'This provides a few basic facts,' offered Professor Sang.

> The Open Door Policy of China was announced by Deng in 1978. It included earmarking four southern cities as Special Economic Zones, which were Shenzhen, Zhuhai, Shantou, and Xiamen, to take advantage of their geographic proximity to overseas Chinese communities such as Hong Kong, Taiwan and Macau and for their vast overseas connections.
>
> Foreign investment is being encouraged and new factories are being established in the Special Economic Zones. Central Government is offering tax privileges, reduced imports tariffs on raw materials and tax exemptions for the importation of certain capital goods. There are plans of other areas also being designated special economic zones.

Excellent research on my part, and I even had it in writing!

'Thank you,' I said gratefully.

'Maoist policy created large communes providing equal work and equal pay,' Professor Sang went on to explain, 'but these became extremely inefficient. Deng is reforming China's huge agriculture system by breaking the large communes into smaller organisations, with quotas to fulfil. Farmers also have more freedom to choose what crops to grow and what animals to rear. In the new free markets, farmers can sell their excess crops.

'If you get up early in the morning, there is a street near the main entrance of the university where you will see a free market. People are allowed to sell their wares freely, not only farmers either. You will see furniture makers selling their wares and all sorts of other goods available. The market usually ends before breakfast.'

That explained why I had never seen it.

I made a mental note to tell Harry about the free market.

'Joint ventures with foreign investors are also being encouraged,' continued Professor Sang, 'and that is increasing productivity.'

For the first time since arriving in China, I appreciated the relevance of Petter's project. Our talented students, who were studying western business practices, would eventually influence the curricula taught in universities and business practices in China thus contributing to the Open Door Policy. I felt a heavy weight on my shoulders, a responsibility. Until then, my main concern had been day-to-day survival, keeping ahead of the students. I now saw myself as a tiny splinter in the huge wooden wheel of Chinese progress; I was part of it.

'I still don't understand why the students are so restless,' I remarked. 'Surely they should be supporting all these reforms.'

'Unfortunately, political freedom does not come with market reforms,' observed Professor Sang. 'That is one of the main reasons why the students are protesting. The students know Gorbachev has introduced political reforms, in the name of Glasnost, in the Soviet Union, but Deng has not done so in China.'

Chapter 22

Harry wanted to go to the free market, but I had no intention of going.

Unfortunately, Harry didn't do getting up early quietly. He was excited and singing, and since we were sharing the same room, I was wide-awake.

'Come on, Charlie,' Harry cajoled, 'you are awake now, so you might as well join me.'

I did, and that was Harry's plan all along.

It was still dark when we found the free market. There were stalls on both sides of the road, packed with all sorts of goods. It was hard to believe that all that activity took place every morning while I was still asleep in bed. Whenever I had previously passed that street, it was clean and had very few people around.

The place was not buzzing, but it had an honest purpose. People were going about their early morning tasks before breakfast. They were carrying their woven baskets and inspecting the goods before sealing the deal. Customers didn't hang around. They had to get their shopping done, have breakfast, get their children to school, and then go to work.

Bananas were obviously in season and displayed on wide, shallow, wicker baskets balanced on top of wooden benches. Stallholders piled onions on sacks on the road. Large cockerels strutted around in metal pens, unaware of their eventual fate of tasting delicious. There was plenty of everything. One metal barrow had long, slimy fish. Stallholders weighed their goods on wooden hand scales, balanced in the middle with their fingers. It looked inaccurate and both parties poked the scales, but nobody argued.

What caught Harry's eye were the stalls selling clothes. He bought two pairs of padded trousers, which according to Harry, were necessary for the harsh winters back in Pontefract.

It started to get light.

I spotted an elderly man, between two stalls, sitting on the ground with his legs crossed, selling something on a small table. I looked and saw his wares were just odd pieces of loofahs.

'How much?' I asked, but he didn't understand.

I held out a handful of Renminbi and pointed to two short lengths. The man took a few coins but it wasn't much. I offered him more, but he was having none of that. He had his price, and that was that.

Harry then walked in a particular direction, so I just followed him.

'Breakfast!' announced Harry, as we came upon a row of stalls, with plastic tables and chairs placed in front.

On the stalls were a variety of cooking pots, fires, stoves, and food on display for inspection, and the smells were delicious. The place already had quite a few customers, and most were slurping the usual glutinous mix of rice pudding without the rice. The stallholders looked at us in surprise. We paused, not knowing what to do. Harry did the honours by miming chopstick movements and rubbed his ample stomach with a big grin on his face. That did the trick. A stallholder quickly cleaned the table nearest to us, knocked off the debris from two chairs, and invited us to sit.

'I'll choose breakfast,' I offered.

'I am in your capable hands.'

'Is there anything you don't want?' Harry could be a bit fussy.

'No sticky rice water, snakes, or puppy dogs.'

I considered it prudent to patronise the stallholder who had wiped our table. I chose tea and savoury rice wrapped in vine-leaves.

I went to the next stall and saw a pile of round woven palm-leaf containers about two or three inches deep. These were stacked one on top of the other, with the bottom container placed neatly over a pan of boiling water, where the steam passed through the weave of the containers. The stallholder obliged by showing me the contents, which were dumplings and looked tasty. I ordered and pointed to our table.

The next stallholder had an open fire with burning charcoals, but no food. The stallholder pointed towards the meat and fish stalls further up the market. I had to buy from there, and he would then oblige by grilling it over his charcoals. That was a good arrangement and together we walked over to the other stalls. I chose two plump carp and two lean cuts of meat of, well, difficult to say really, but the meat was dark.

The final stall had black noodles that smelt irresistible, and I promptly ordered two bowls.

I finally sat down to a glass of hot, sweet, black tea and, with Harry for company, enjoyed the best breakfast yet.

When we finished eating, we ambled back to the university, content with life and the world in general. We were ready to educate our students with the build the pagoda management game.

As we passed the guesthouse breakfast room, I felt a small pang of guilt until I saw the little, old, Chinese lady smile, and wave at us. I could see we were not expected. Word we were feasting in the free market must have got around. We saw Petter scrutinising his plate; what was he trying to order now?

'See you tonight, at six,' shouted Petter, as Harry and I attempted a quick getaway.

'*C*an I observe your class?' asked Mr Chou. 'I am particularly interested in your modern teaching methods.'

'No, Shoe, you cannot observe,' replied Harry. 'However you are most welcome to participate and join one of the teams.'

'You are lucky,' I added mischievously, 'because we are going to demonstrate the very latest western management training techniques. It's best to experience this first-hand, not watch.'

I could see Mr Chou was looking at us suspiciously, but at least he stopped scowling.

Harry gave his introductory lecture on profit and loss, break-even analysis, and provided some basic accounting skills. I provided my standard lecture on a market-led business environment where goods and services had to be orientated towards customer needs.

Leaving aside the fact that Chinese industry operates within a centrally controlled, command economy, the shops were full. They could buy whatever was on offer with what little surplus cash they had. Harry was proof of that. Within a small business environment, my students, and most Chinese generally, were very much at ease. It was at the central government level where the students became more cautious.

I read out my little cameo piece about the Open Door Policy from the *China Daily*, and dropped vague innuendoes about Deng's reforms. I insinuated I knew about Deng's reforms, that I knew they knew, and therefore I wouldn't bother anybody about such things since we all knew anyway. I think I got away with it.

'We are very familiar with your Open Door Policy,' I bluffed, 'and we enjoyed the benefits of your free market only this morning.'

Nobody laughed, but I saw a few smiling faces.

'We know,' shouted Zhuang, from the back.

There were few secrets around here, I reflected.

'Was the meat tasty?' asked Hou.

'It is a local speciality,' Wei informed us.

'Delicious,' I replied.

'What was it?' Harry whispered. I could see he was now worried.

'Mutton,' I whispered back.

I lied, of course. Knowing Harry's obsession about the locals eating puppies, I didn't want to tell him that I didn't know what the meat was.

I outlined the essential elements of the build the pagoda management game. I could see bewildered faces, until Hou spoke up.

'The building bricks are emblematic symbolisms of western-profit-motivated culture and the competitive nature of the business environment,' he remarked. 'That's right, isn't it?'

'Yes,' I replied guardedly, because I didn't understand a word of what he said.

'And as Harry explained,' continued Hou, 'western organisations are profit-motivated, keeping down costs at all times, no matter what?'

'Yes,' I again replied guardedly.

'And from what Harry said the other day,' added Yang, 'business organisations can only truly operate when you have freedom of speech and freedom of information.'

'I don't recall Harry saying that,' I said, 'not exactly—'

'Didn't Harry say that the British press publishes financial information about companies, banks, interest rates, market trends, and other things? Is it not true that anyone, with funds, can invest freely in the market?' persisted Yang. 'Isn't that the same thing?'

'Yes,' replied Harry. 'Information has value and power in business.'

'In our case, our leaders keep all important information to

themselves,' pronounced Hou. 'That is how they keep power and why corruption is rife. The press can only print what it is told to print.'

'Well, you know what Confucius said,' Harry offered brightly. 'The only good politician is a dead politician.'

I was little dubious about that one but, nevertheless, he got a round of applause from the students.

Harry handed out the decision criteria sheets.

The first sheet had a graph showing the relationship between the height of the pagoda and revenue. The higher you built the pagoda – then the higher the revenue.

The second sheet had a graph showing the relationship between the number of bricks used to build the pagoda and costs. The fewer bricks used – then the lower the costs.

The key to the game was in the method of construction. The highest pagoda did not necessarily mean the highest profit; it depended on the building technique. If you used too many bricks, no matter how high you build the pagoda, you could easily make a loss.

Apart from the tangible objective of attempting to maximise profits, the game also involved vague intangible benefits such as participation in teamwork, planning, negotiation, listening skills, and the like. We are told these are skills needed by modern companies.

We divided the class into five teams, and they had an hour to prepare. When the teams returned to the plenary session, each had ten minutes to present their business plan, objectives, and building technique. The team then had ten minutes to build their pagoda, where no part could be prefabricated.

As a game facilitator, or referee, there was little to do, as the game took on its own momentum. At the end, we did a simple numeric calculation. Firstly, we measured the height of the pagoda and consulted the revenue chart. Secondly, we counted the number of bricks used and consulted the cost chart. Finally, we deducted the costs from revenue and the difference between the two figures was profit – or loss. The team with the greatest profit won.

We then send the teams away for a post-rationalisation session. They then considered their performance with the benefit of hindsight and learnt from their experience. From that, individuals would be better able to function as a team having learnt the importance of group-work and other such unworthy nonsense.

Life was never like that!

The losing teams invariably accused the others, especially the winning team, of cheating. Once that was out of the way, retribution between individual team members took place. For example, one team member would accuse another of using too many bricks thus increasing costs, and hence they lost.

I found it interesting to record the results because they were not typical of what happened back in Pontefract.

For the sake of brevity, when you clicked one brick into another, one on top of the other, management specialists referred to that as the standard construction.

Team one opted for a non-standard construction where they could gain greater height with fewer bricks. That, they argued, was a more aesthetically pleasing design to the eye. Their pagoda was symbolic of modern China in as much as it was cheap to build. Regrettably, by using a non-standard construction, the brick-clicking mechanism was vertical instead of being horizontal and they could not devise a method for fixing the base of the pagoda to the ground. The pagoda never did stand up, but we did admit it looked pretty when laid along the ground.

Team two argued there was already an abundance of pagodas in China, particularly around Jaliang. It made no economic sense to build another, as no one would visit it. What Jaliang wanted was a new and unique tourist attraction, which competed with the Great Wall, the Forbidden City, and the Terracotta Army. They constructed a Disneyland China, which contained miniatures of the above three attractions. Unfortunately, they ran out of bricks and went bankrupt. They admitted that running out of building materials and going bankrupt might have been all right before, but they might not be able to get away with it in the future. Nevertheless, we all admired the half-completed Disneyland China, particularly the caricature of Minnie Terra.

Team three, they admitted, argued too much and could not agree what to do. They did manage to sell their surplus resources – in their case, all their building bricks – to team two and four and therefore made a hefty profit. That, they concluded, was the way for the future.

Team four used the standard construction following the advice of Mr Chou, who proclaimed that in modern China, big-is-beautiful, and Jaliang must have the highest pagoda. Consequently, they bought all surplus bricks from teams one and three and cleverly built the highest pile of building bricks I had ever seen. Sadly, the pagoda fell down in the last few seconds, contrary to the belief I had accidentally nudged it. Even if the pagoda had remained standing, team four was bankrupt, having used too many building bricks. In conclusion, one student quickly stood up and explained that their presentation was a parody of the old ways that were no longer applicable to the modern People's Republic. She added that the act of the pagoda falling down was a symbolic gesture not missed by those present.

Team five approached the problem from a mathematical perspective and spent most of their time working out equations for Harry's revenue and cost graphs – not easy with Harry using non-linear equations. In their presentation, team five attested they knew the precise number of bricks to use and the exact height that the pagoda should be to maximise profit. The problem was, however, they did not know how to assemble the bricks to construct the pagoda, try as they did. In their defence, they argued, given more time, they could devise another mathematical model to formulate an optimal construction plan for their pagoda. When asked how much more time, they considered six months sufficient, and the use of a mainframe computer.

We declared team three the winner, and I had no doubt they would soon become the largest asset strippers in the Far East. They looked bemused when Harry presented them with their prize, a miniature glass pagoda in garish colours.

'That went well, Mr Chou, don't you think,' I said.

'*I*'ll get the beers,' I volunteered.

'Your management game was a success, I hear,' Petter remarked. 'The students are still arguing among themselves. Professor Song is very pleased with what you are doing.'

'We had some fun, I can tell you,' Harry said. 'Charlie, being a professional, knows all the tricks. I have never seen the one where you accidentally knock over the pagoda. I don't think anyone noticed.'

'Very clever...'

I was going to argue that I never did such a thing, but since both Harry and Petter believed I was being professional and clever, I let it go at that. We talked about nothing in particular, enjoyed the cold beer, and our conversation eventually came around to the student unrest and political situation in China.

'Everyone is talking about the coming visit of Gorbachev,' mentioned Harry. 'He's quite a hero with the students.'

'Yes,' I added, 'it appears that Deng is not a happy man. Things are not going according to plan.'

'That's correct,' agreed Petter, in a contemplative tone. 'Gorbachev chose to visit Beijing on Deng's terms, like when foreign visitors had to kowtow to emperors in the past. The summit is supposed to be Deng's swan song, so he can finally retire with a success. With the student protests, it looks like Deng is a lame duck leader now. Apparently, more student demonstrations are planned when Gorbachev arrives, or so it is rumoured.'

Petter knew what was going on, but why was Harry smirking?

'Harry, what are your impressions of China?' asked Petter.

'I have been to Bombay and other towns in India,' replied Harry meditatively. 'What I remember are the extremes – slums and palaces. I have seen neither here.'

'India had never been my favourite place, I have to admit.'

'This sounds like an excellent project that you and Charlie are involved with,' commented Harry. 'Whose idea was it?'

'The Swedish government had allocated funding to UNIBO, but it could not come up with a suitable project that was acceptable, until I came along,' Petter replied. 'I proposed the project to UNIBO in Kuala Lumpur, and they liked it. They discussed it with the Swedish government, which happily accepted it. UNIBO employs me as the project manager, and everyone is happy.'

'How did you get Jaliang No 3 University to participate,' I asked.

'Professor Song is an old colleague. We wanted a reliable Chinese university and he agreed to host the project in his faculty. It took a long time to get permission from Beijing, but Professor Song bent a few arms. The problem with most UN projects is that they are failures and a waste of money. They often don't take into account cultural differences. We didn't want that to happen with this project.'

'I know about a project that didn't take into account cultural differences.' I said.

'Wait, I'll get more beers before you tell us,' Harry offered.

'I knew someone who worked for an aid agency in Rome,' I continued, once Harry had returned. 'He was involved in a project developing fisheries in Somalia a few years ago. The Somalis were suffering from droughts, traditional crops were failing, cattle were dying, and famine was rampant. Apparently, there are abundant fish stocks off the Somali shores. Someone deemed it would be a good idea to develop the fishery industry in Somalia, using all that abundant protein that was swimming around just off the coast. That would solve the famine. They employed consultants, bought fishing boats, made specialist nets, developed harbours, everything.

'What the consultants didn't appreciate was why hungry Somalis didn't eat all that abundant fish in the first place. The Somali tribes are traditionally herders, keeping sheep, goats, and a few camels. The more camels a man has, the greater his prestige. The Somali diet consists of milk, camel, goat meat, and rice. To serve a Somali herder or rural worker with fish is an insult, like serving pork to Muslims.

'In the end, the army was used to force Somalians to live in newly constructed fishing villages. They had a choice, catch fish, sell it, eat it and live, or starve.'

'That sounds a little far-fetched, Charlie.'

'It's true.'

'So you know a little about Somalia,' Petter commented amiably, 'interesting.'

Harry had discovered that some Chinese coins could float on beer. I know because I lost a bet and had to get the next round of drinks.

'I often wonder who benefits from aid,' reflected Petter, sipping his beer. 'Paradoxically, most aid is in the form of a loan, be it on generous terms, and has to be paid back to the original donor. For example, if the British government gave aid to, say, Kenya, it would insist that it could only be spent on British equipment and consultants. Everyone gets a cut, but it's called commission! Once the money has gone, it then has to be paid back. Since it was British equipment bought, who provides the spares and maintenance in the following years?'

'The British, of course,' answered Harry.

'So who actually benefits?'

'It's an indirect subsidy to British industry paid for by Kenya,' added Harry. 'It makes good business sense.'

'That's a bit cynical,' I said.

After swapping a few more yarns, we compared the relative merits of Tsingtao beer against a popular Shanghai brand. Tsingtao, we found, was far superior, and we each had two bottles of the Shanghai brand to verify that.

Rest assured, we put the world to rights that night, but not China. The People's Republic, we agreed, was far too big a place to put right that evening. That would be another night with a few more beers.

Petter, unavoidably, according to him, was to be away the coming weekend, but said he would be back soon.

Drowsy after good company, and possibly a Tsingtao beer too many, the last I remembered when falling asleep, was Harry whispering, 'I told you he was a spy.'

Chapter 23

It was Harry's last day.

Mr Chou offered to take us sightseeing in one of the university cars, which was a sudden change of heart. Until now, Mr Chou had been uncompromisingly sullen towards Harry. Possibly the success of our management game had tempered Mr Chou, and he, at last, accepted that I did not intentionally knock down his pagoda.

'Well,' I said, in a high-minded and supercilious voice, 'that might not be convenient, Mr Chou. You could have given us some advanced warning because we have made other arrangements.'

Harry looked puzzled, as we had not made any specific arrangements, apart from one last look around the shops. In any case, Harry's enthusiasm for shopping was on the wane. His new suitcase was already full.

'But all of the arrangements have—' responded a flustered Mr Chou.

'That may well be, Mr Chou,' I replied, cutting him off mid-sentence, 'but it would help if you could arrange for a car to take Harry to the airport tomorrow morning. That would allow us to change our arrangements.'

I was learning how to negotiate with Mr Chou. Until then, he was adamant that the university could not provide a car for Harry. There were protocols to follow, and Harry was an uninvited guest, after all.

'I was just going to inform you that I did manage to pull a few strings and arrange a car for Harry,' answered Mr Chou carefully. 'It will be available after breakfast.'

Mr Chou recognised a quid-pro-quo when he saw one.

'That is very considerate of you.'

'Let's get going,' affirmed Harry, 'I haven't done much sightseeing.'

I might have underestimated Mr Chou's sense of humour. We visited four pagodas, and he insisted we climbed to the top of every one.

Professor Sang accompanied us to a restaurant that specialised in the local cuisine. Two students, Hou and Yang, also accompanied us, which was a nice touch. We travelled into town by bus where I impressed the others with my grasp of the ticket procedure.

Harry was worried about what he was going to eat. The meal he had enjoyed with the journalists was still at the back of his mind, let alone what he imagined he might have ate when we had breakfast in the free market the other morning.

'As honoured guests, we must eat everything placed in front of us,' I whispered. 'Our host would have carefully chosen the menu on our behalf, and we are expected to eat it on his behalf. That's the deal.'

'What exactly is the local cuisine?' Harry asked.

'Oh, delicious things,' responded Professor Sang a little vaguely.

'Just eat it, Harry,' I whispered menacingly.

'But—'

'Just eat it.'

'You don't get foreigners here,' Professor Sang informed us.

We arrived at a restaurant in a part of town I had never visited. Professor Song, our host for the evening, decided against having a formal banquet because we were all good friends. He chose an informal setting where we could enjoy ourselves. He waited at the entrance, welcomed us, and took us to a reserved table at the far end.

I had only ever seen Professor Song wearing the dark-blue trousers and tunic I associated with Chairman Mao. There were still plenty about, but mostly worn by senior officials. That evening, Professor Song was wearing grey slacks and a white shirt. I was wearing one of my pinkish white shirts with one of Harry's new ties he had loaned me. It matched quite well, he believed. Harry insisted on wearing one of his new suits.

I had to smile.

Harry had copied the Chinese habit of not removing the suit-maker's label stitched to the outside of the sleeve, just a few inches above the cuff. That habit appeared to be quite fashionable in China, particularly among younger men.

The restaurant was long with a single row of tables on each side of the room. Through the middle was a wide aisle where the waiters rushed up and down, which was unusual. In most restaurants in China, nobody appeared to hurry at all, and service was casual. Our table was round with one of those smaller, slightly raised, round platforms that revolve in the middle. There was a similar table to ours across the aisle, where another group were enjoying a good night out without the ladies. At the other end of the restaurant were swing doors leading into the kitchen.

We had Tsingtao beer preferably to the normal assortment of wines and spirits I had come to expect at banquets. It was a much more informal affair, an evening with friends. Conversation was light-hearted, nothing serious. Harry delighted our hosts with some of his shaggy-accountant tales.

We had small porcelain bowls and chopsticks – no enamelled tin bowls and spoons here. The swing doors from the kitchen burst open and a waiter brought a large bowl of boiled rice and placed it in front of Professor Song. Being host, he served Harry and me with rice, gave a serving to himself, before swinging the revolving central platform so that the others could serve themselves. Hou and Yang tucked in with appetites that would make any mother proud.

The swing doors opened again, and another waiter placed two further dishes in front of Professor Song.

'This is a local delicacy,' Professor Song informed us.

Harry looked uneasy.

'Normally, they would show us the snake before slitting its throat so honoured guests can drink the blood, but I do not go in for that sort of thing. I hope you don't mind.'

'Not at all, not at all,' replied Harry, 'it's not the sort of thing I go for either.'

'In this dish the snake has been delicately steamed to retain taste and flavour,' explained Professor Song. 'The other has been caramelised.'

Professor Song served us from both dishes. I tried a piece of the caramelised snake and it was delicious, being crisp on the outside with a firm texture on the inside. I didn't like the steamed snake as much; it reminded me of jellied-eels I had once tried in my youth.

'The caramelised one,' I declared, 'is delicious.'

'Another piece for you then,' offered Professor Song, carefully giving me another generous portion.

Harry was having a hard time. He started with the caramelised snake, but I could see he was having difficulty. He passed the offending morsel from one side of his mouth to the other. Not knowing what to do, he eventually swallowed it.

I must give credit to Harry for his ingenuity. It was obvious he did not intend to eat the steamed snake – no matter how delicately it was cooked. Under cover of one of his humorous stories, he carefully buried his portion beneath the rice.

'I see you have finished, Harry,' commented Professor Song, who then served Harry with another piece of the delicately steamed snake.

Harry's face was a picture. His worst nightmares had come true.

Harry carefully examined the situation and realised there was no more room beneath the rice. He looked at me for assistance, but received none. There was no way out. Harry carefully picked up his delicately steamed morsel with his chopsticks, stared at it for a couple of seconds, popped it into his mouth, and swallowed it. I doubted if it ever touched the sides.

'Well done, Harry,' said Professor Song, congratulating him by filling his glass with more beer.

I might have been mistaken, but I was sure I detected the faintest of smiles on Professor Song's face. Was he having a little fun with some Chinese humour?

Using the same porcelain bowl, we had several other courses, including hot greens, button mushrooms, peanut paste, baked carp, and juicy dumplings. The kitchen doors once more flew open, and our waiter trotted down the aisle with a platter held shoulder height and again placed it in front of Professor Song.

Harry looked even more uneasy.

I looked at sparrow-size birds, plucked, and crisply deep-fried in a light batter. They still had their head and legs intact, hence my recognition of the birds potentially as being sparrows. Seven birds littered the platter in a haphazard way, just as they had come out of the deep-frying pan.

Everyone looked pleased with what they saw; everyone except Harry. He now realised he had nightmares he did not know existed.

Professor Song kindly gave Harry and me a quick demonstration on how to eat our next course. 'Pick it up like this,' he said.

Like this involved holding the head with one hand and both legs with the other, and eating everything in between, bones, the lot. The sparrows were tender, and cooked in a light batter to a crispy perfection.

'Delicious.'

Harry, looking glum, picked up his sparrow in the manner shown, and slowly chewed without delight.

There were six on our table and seven birds on the platter.

It could be Professor Song had discovered we had done the build the pagoda management game, and blamed Harry. It could be Professor Song had a wicked sense of humour. It could be the seventh bird was for Harry, being the guest of honour.

Harry got the seventh sparrow, and he ate it.

Why would Harry bravely eat something he obviously did not like?

Apart from me reading him the riot act about eating whatever was placed in front of him, we were in China, unfamiliar territory, and uncertain how to behave. They called us eminent professors when we knew we were no such thing. Everything was a ceremony, with protocols, and no one had told us the rules. We did not want to offend, and everyone was being kind.

'The last course will arrive soon,' we were informed.

Harry looked uneasy. Hidden at the back of my mind were Harry's objections when he ate with his journalist friends a few days ago.

Puppy dogs – Golden Labradors – that was it!

According to Harry, they were a local delicacy – a real party treat!

I also became uneasy.

Suddenly, the restaurant lights went out.

The doors to the kitchen swung open and a waiter appeared with a large platter raised above his head. I swear that what I saw was a roast puppy, four paws, and tail dangling over the edge of the platter. At the four corners of the puppy were sparklers, lit and throwing their playful twinkle all around.

Everyone in the restaurant started synchronised clapping, including the staff, everyone, that was, except Harry and me.

Harry had my sympathy because I then knew how he had felt throughout that informal and cosy banquet. How were we going to get out of that situation because I wasn't going to eat any puppy dogs? I decided I would get Harry to do the fainting trick and then I could help him and both of us escape.

'Faint, Harry,' I whispered.

'What?'

The waiter, with the platter held high above his head, ceremoniously marched down the aisle, everyone applauding. He stopped by our table.

'Harry, faint now, please.'

'What?'

As it happened, Harry didn't faint.

The waiter promptly turned to the table next to us and served the celebration meal with gusto and style. Admittedly, the restaurant lights were out and the four sparklers were distracting, but it was a roast puppy on that platter suffering the fate of tasting delicious.

A waiter served us another large bowl of boiled rice.

'This is a traditional dessert,' declared Professor Song.

'A marvellous meal,' Harry had the audacity to say.

Everyone had a generous portion of rice and scoffed it down with their chopsticks, with porcelain bowl held close to their lips so no rice escaped. Harry, of course, could not quite manage to finish his dessert!

After the last course, Professor Song gave a short speech about how Harry had enriched student life over the past week, and things like that. He gave Harry a gift, a nice bronze medallion, on behalf of the faculty. As senior guest present, I gave a short speech and said some nondescript platitudes about the United Nations, friendship between friends, and Number 3 University; nothing memorable...

Harry, I could see, was deeply moved by the occasion.

'Professor Song,' Harry said quietly, 'thank you. Thank you for having me. I have learnt a lot from the students and your staff. This has been one of the most memorable weeks of my life.'

The banquet over, Professor Song stood up, shook our hands, and promptly left the restaurant. While Professor Sang visited the washroom, Harry and I chatted amiably with our two students.

I saw one or two faces pressed against the restaurant window, looking in. It was a better class of restaurant where prices were far too high for your average worker. Nothing stopping them having a good gawp, especially if foreigners were involved.

We left the restaurant with Professor Sang with Hou and Yang still eating at the table. There was food remaining and they were determined to finish it off.

You would think they didn't know when their next meal was going to be.

Memorandum

(Telex message)

From   Chou Ke-giang
            Director of the Office of Foreign Affairs
            Jaliang Number 3 University

To   Deputy Chairman
            Office of Education Foreign Affairs
            Public Security Bureau (PSB)
            Beijing

Date   14 May 1989 (8:00 a.m.)

CONFIDENTIAL

DR CHARLES VINCENT

On Wednesday, 10 May, Vincent and Harry managed to give me the slip. I had been keeping them both under close observation all day until I had to attend to some urgent matter. It was during this brief interlude that Vincent and Harry covertly left the university by the back entrance. I observed them catching a bus travelling in the opposite direction to the town centre. I was unable to pursue the provocateurs but noted the number of the bus. Later, I was able to interview the ticket official who clearly remembered the two foreigners because they had been involved in illegal money changing. When I asked where they disembarked, he stated they left the bus unexpectedly, without warning, in the middle of nowhere.

It is obvious that the two British academics were using transport exit techniques to ensure that no one followed them. I can only deduce that they were covertly meeting other unknown persons at a predetermined destination. Because of more recent developments, I think I can deduce who the academics met and for what purpose. I will come to this later.

While I have been keeping Vincent and Harry away from students, I had to allow at least one class. Teaching, as you are aware, is the official purpose of both their visits. Most students have returned to classes, and it would appear strange if Vincent and Harry were no longer teaching.

On Friday, 12 May, I requested if I could observe the two academics, feigning interest in western teaching techniques. Harry insisted that I could not observe their class, but must participate as a student. This was a means to humiliate me, but I had no alternative but to accept.

Harry commenced the class by, allegedly, quoting from Confucius – *kill all politicians!* We all know that Confucius had some strange notions on how the authorities should govern, but that, I know, was not one of them.

Vincent cleverly split the class into small groups and separated them into isolated locations where I could not observe what was happening. The two academics are well trained.

The class was to participate in some form of modern western management training involving the use of children's building bricks. I believed that I could beat the two academics at their own game because the session involved building a pagoda as high as possible. I have a child with similar building bricks, and I am familiar with their use. I was able to build a pagoda higher than the rest. I could see that Vincent was astonished with my pagoda. Instead of allowing me to win, he deliberately knocked it down and insinuated that this was symbolic of communist ideals. I was, again, humiliated in front of students.

On Saturday, 13 May, I managed to stay with the two provocateurs most of the day by using the guise of taking them on a sightseeing trip. Foreigners fall for this every time.

In the evening, I left both academics in the guesthouse, thinking Harry would be packing his luggage in preparation for his departure the next day. I quickly visited my office to check for messages. When I returned, I discovered that they had again slipped out of the university by the back entrance. I undertook a frantic search of Jaliang and eventually found them in a restaurant with two of their students. The academics were obviously providing the students with a *last supper* because early this morning, with others, both students began a *hunger strike*, vowing to starve unless senior officials meet their demands.

It is obvious that Harry's intent is to stir up discontent with the journalists. Vincent is now free to coordinate the hunger strike. That must have been the purpose of the covert meeting last Wednesday evening.

Chapter 24

Sunday, May 14, 1989

I was already missing Harry.

After breakfast, Mr Chou arrived with a car, as promised. I said he didn't need to accompany us to the airport because he looked terrible. I began to speculate on what Mr Chou got up to in the evenings.

'It is my duty,' he informed us.

When Harry checked in for his flight, he found his tickets in pocket four, which was quite good. When asked for his passport, I let him get to pocket eleven before producing it. I considered it prudent to keep it myself but omitted to inform Harry. I was worried in case his jacket really did have seventeen pockets because upon close inspection, I could only find fifteen.

Mr Chou must have pulled a few strings because he carried Harry's hand luggage and escorted him onto the aircraft.

I began to think the student unrest was dwindling, but things changed. A small group of Jaliang students decided to support their Beijing colleagues and start a hunger strike. I did not even know there was a hunger strike in Beijing but, apparently, it started the day before to coincide with the arrival of Gorbachev.

Heading the hunger strike were Hou and Yang. No wonder they were eating everything left on the table!

With having too much time on my hands, I contemplated the series of events that had happened over the past few weeks. I began to notice that demonstrations and protests occurred when Petter was not around. Where did Petter go? I had also noticed that the university was always in the forefront of the current unrest in Jaliang. The students, my students, were always in the thick of things, particularly Hou, and his colleagues Yang and Wei.

I had seen Hou and Yang with Petter, and they were leading the hunger strike.

Harry couldn't be right, could he?

Could Petter really be a Swedish agent sent to stir up trouble?

I remembered Petter's knowledge of Gorbachev's visit and Deng's swan song becoming a dead duck, or something like that, but he could have got that from the BBC.

Which students accompanied us at Harry's farewell banquet? Hou and Yang.

What about Professor Song having had a rough time during the ten-year Cultural Revolution, and how he was a stalwart, or words to that effect, and survived, yet had never told the tale.

What about the editorial Professor Sang read to me a couple of weeks ago, when it stated that intellectuals and foreign activists were manipulating students?

What were Petter and Professor Song up to?

What about the Soviet ship?

It was Petter's idea to visit the ship, and go aboard, and he disappeared with the senior communications officer for some time, if I remembered correctly. Petter could also speak a little Russian.

Was Petter involved in some conspiracy to help the Soviets save face with the Chinese? I remembered Petter's words during our last conversation. The Soviets, in diplomatic terms, had had to kowtow to the Chinese, but now Deng was publically humiliated.

It then dawned on me.

Petter was not a Swedish spy; that was absurd.

Petter was working for the Soviets.

Extract from:

THE PRESS
SUN 14 MAY 1989
Local correspondent, Peking

STUDENTS BEGAN a hunger strike yesterday to coincide with the arrival in China of Mikhail Gorbachev, the Soviet president. The night before, intellectuals indulged students with an extravagant 'last supper' in preparation for the hunger strike.

Thousands of students marched into Peking's Tiananmen Square, and hundreds pledged to starve until the government meets their demands for genuine talks and political reforms. Students declared they were willing to die for democracy and the glory of China.

Chapter 25

Monday, May 15, 1989

'**There** are no classes today,' Mr Chou informed me at breakfast.

Mr Chou's sullen mood hadn't altered.

I appreciated he was never happy about Harry arriving, but he had left. Anyway, everyone liked Harry, except Mr Chou of course. Harry's contribution to the academic debate was both positive and provocative. What more could a university want?

'What do you plan to do?' Mr Chou continued sourly.

'I don't know.'

'I advise you to prepare for your classes.'

'And when might classes be?'

Mr Chou did not answer but left me to finish my breakfast undisturbed.

After breakfast, I decided to walk around the campus and see what was happening.

It was eerily quiet.

I walked towards the university main entrance because there was a crowd of students staring at the wall to the left.

Students were looking at a selection of posters.

Most were handmade in large Chinese lettering but some were professionally printed. By far the most popular were cartoons of some kind, and students were pointing and laughing at these. I decided to take a closer look. There were six or so cartoons with caricatures of what looked like a selection of Chinese leaders. I recognised Deng, the Party elder, who ruled from behind the scenes. The cartoons with their writings and slogans were clearly symbolic of popular feelings towards the leaders in question. They were similar to the political cartoons in the British press.

I saw Mr Chou lurking near the main entrance talking to some of the security guards, but I decided against asking him to explain the cartoons. I gave him a smile and a wave, and since it was such a nice day, I continued my walk.

As luck had it, Professor Sang was sitting on a bench in the shade of a cherry blossom tree. The blossom was almost over and the fallen petals lay around him. As he was reading a book, I hesitated; I didn't want to disturb him. He happened to look up, and he gave a wave. I waved back, walked over, and sat on the bench beside him.

'This is a beautiful spot you have chosen,' I said. 'Are you reading anything interesting?'

'You spoke of Confucius a few days ago,' replied Professor Sang. 'I thought I might remind myself of his teachings.'

'The students are still active,' I observed, 'but the hunger strike is more serious, isn't it?'

'Throughout the protests the students have often outsmarted the government, and they have done it again. Food, you might have noticed, is something we Chinese take very seriously. The fact that our brightest students are starving themselves will be hard for families and the Chinese people to deal with, especially with our one child per family policy. That will bring greater attention to the student movement. The hunger strike is also well timed. Gorbachev has brought the international media to Beijing, and, no doubt, the hunger strikers will steal the limelight.'

'What do the students hope to achieve?'

'I believe they want the government to retract the 26 April editorial. I read it to you at the teahouse by East Lake. They also want a televised discussion with government leaders. The students consider they have the upper hand. The government had planned a formal welcoming ceremony for Gorbachev on Tiananmen Square today, but it had to be cancelled because it is currently full of hunger striking students.'

'Beijing I can understand, but why go on hunger strike here, in Jaliang?' I said. 'There is no international media here to report it.'

'They want to show solidarity with their Beijing colleagues. The students and journalists from the China News Agency are supporting each other. Other government agencies are also supporting the students. That is extraordinary.'

'There is obviously a lot going on.'

'You might not be aware,' continued Professor Sang, 'but yesterday afternoon, Professor Song made an announcement demanding that the government give students fair treatment. Other famous scholars and writers made similar announcements, but mainly in Beijing.'

Professor Song, Petter's close accomplice! What were they up to?

'Will Professor Song get into trouble?' I asked.

I was hoping Petter was not a bad influence on Professor Song. If things went wrong, Petter could no doubt claim diplomatic immunity and start flashing his blue United Nations Certificate about, but poor Professor Song would remain in China.

'No, his words were very considered,' he replied. 'What can be fairer than asking the government to be fair? This is a coded message letting everyone know the students have support, without excessive risk to themselves.'

'Do you know when classes might start?' I asked.

'Not until Gorbachev leaves on Thursday, at the earliest. There will not be any classes while the hunger strike is on.'

I was at a loose end. I wanted to make the most of my time in China, but I had seen all the sights around Jaliang, including the pagodas. I asked Professor Sang for his advice.

'You should visit one of China's most beautiful cities, Suzhou. You can get there by train and if you leave very early in the morning, you can do the trip in one day.'

'That's a good idea,' I replied. Admittedly, I hesitated when I heard the word *beautiful*, but only briefly.

'I can arrange for one of your students to accompany you.'

We plotted my escape for the next day.

Chapter 26

Tuesday, May 16, 1989

I woke up excited.

I was excited because I liked adventures. I also felt uneasy because I was leaving my hunger-striking students to their fate. What could I do?

Wei, who surprisingly was not on hunger strike, was my accomplice and appeared as excited as I was. She was dressed in an amber coloured skirt with a bib and shoulder straps over an attractive white blouse. She wore short, white, ankle socks with frills, and silver, low-heeled shoes. She was slim, as were most Chinese females, and had delicate facial features without blemish or wrinkle. She had her hair cut in a fashionable, but practical, short bob. Without sounding patronising, in Chinese terms, Wei was dressed to kill.

We left the university, via the back entrance, and caught the bus into town. The buses were quite busy, even at that time in the morning. Our plan was to go straight to the railway station, buy tickets for Suzhou, and have breakfast before joining the train.

I found buying train tickets was not as easy as it sounded, even with Wei to help me. First, it was always advisable to book train tickets in advance, as they were in huge demand. There were two classes of seats, soft and hard. Soft seats were primarily for foreigners and senior officials, and hard seats were for the rest of the population. Fortunately, they allocated you a seat number when booking.

Wei showed me the small queue for the soft seats and advised me that I had better make the booking and not her, because she could not buy soft seat tickets.

The soft seat official could speak broken English, and informed me there were no soft seats available for the train I wanted. It was already fully booked.

When I asked if there were hard seats available, the official looked surprised. He said there were hard seats available, but was I sure I wanted one? When I stressed that hard seats were fine, he then pointed to the numerous other queues to my right. That, he informed me, was where you bought tickets for hard seats.

When I joined the queue for soft seats, there were only two or three people waiting, which wasn't too bad. The queues for hard seats were some twenty or so yards long. We would never catch the train we wanted. The soft seat ticket official carefully explained that most people booked their tickets in advance, as the other people were doing. Since I was a foreigner, and obviously not to know, he would pull strings and get me hard seat tickets without having to join another queue.

When asked if I could also buy a soft seat return ticket, that is, a ticket from Suzhou back to Jaliang, he looked at me in exasperation. In the People's Republic, he explained, return tickets were not possible. How would he know what tickets had been sold in Suzhou? What I had to do, on arrival in Suzhou, was to go immediately to the ticket office and see what was available. When I enquired whether I would be able to return to Jaliang that evening, he replied that he wouldn't know, would he, and the only way to find out was to go to Suzhou.

'*I* managed to get two tickets, but only hard seats. All the soft seats were booked,' I explained.

'Never mind,' replied Wei.

If Wei was disappointed, she didn't show it. We were both excited about the trip and a hard seat was not going to spoil that.

'What about breakfast?' I asked.

'The train leaves in about twenty minutes,' Wei informed me. 'It is best we buy something and eat it on the train.'

We went to the railway buffet, and I let Wei buy what looked like a feast for the whole train, rather than a snack for two. I gave Wei our train tickets and followed her to the platform, where, at regular intervals, there were queues of other passengers behind wooden signs. Wei explained that on our tickets was the train carriage number, and we must wait in the correct queue. Our train was on the platform, but passengers did not board.

On the platform was a fierce looking woman who blew her whistle and furiously waved a red flag at anyone queuing in a careless manner.

She was wearing a faded, baggy, blue uniform and an official hat.

'That's the platform official,' said Wei. 'So don't make her cross.'

Looking at the fierce looking platform official, I didn't intend to make her cross. Wei found the queue for our carriage and, until I stopped her, was about to join. When made to queue, the Chinese did so in an economical and harsh manner. Queuing is regimented, no personal space at all, with a hand on the shoulder of the person in front to keep balance and maintain a minimum degree of modesty.

'Are we guaranteed our seats?' I asked.

'Yes, of course.'

'Then why are we queuing?'

'Because if you don't, you make the platform official cross,' answered Wei.

I had in the back of my mind the queuing etiquette used for buses, and being crushed in the stampede for the train doors was not what I wanted. We had tickets, and our seats were booked. What was the rush? I decided we would loiter at the back of the platform until it was time to join the train.

That made the platform official cross. She blew her whistle, waved her flag, and shouted at us. I didn't understand what she said, so I gave her a nice big smile.

'She said that the soft seats are at the other end of the train,' Wei informed me. 'I told her that we could not get soft seats. She said we should get in the queue. I told her we were going to the toilets, and she agreed that was wise. The toilets are this way.'

I judged it best not to argue and went to the toilet. Upon our return, the queue for our carriage was longer. I again refused to join and feigned interest in one of the posters on the wall at the back of the platform. The platform official came across and said a few brusque words to Wei, but left us alone.

'What did she say?' I whispered.

'She said you were a stubborn foreigner,' replied Wei, quite proudly.

I agreed with Wei that if she were going to translate for me, then she would tell me what other people said, without any form of sanitised translation. This, I said, would make it interesting for me. That, Wei remarked, would also make it interesting for her.

A klaxon blew.

I knew that was the signal to join the train because there was a stampede for the doors. The stampede was not a riot, more a habit than a necessity. Because I sensed she also wanted to make a dash for the door, I lightly placed my hand on Wei's shoulder. After all, we all had guaranteed seats. Once the other passengers had boarded the train, we casually embarked at leisure. As we approached the door, the platform official blew her whistle to get us to move more quickly, but I noticed a smile on her face.

The first thing I saw on boarding the train was the toilet door open. The toilet was a hole in the floor about four inches in diameter. The smell wasn't too bad, and, in spite of some attempt to clean the toilet before our boarding, I saw that years of poor aiming by users had taken its toll. I was thankful for Wei's earlier suggestion.

Although passengers had pre-booked seats, that, I found, had little meaning. Passengers wanted to be with their friends and family for the journey who, despite pre-booking, were unable to get seats together. The reason why there was a minor stampede for the doors was for passengers to stake their claim, irrespective of what their tickets said.

What followed was a lot of haggling and shouting, but Wei could stand her ground in any argument. We ended up with two seats together and, happily, I had a window seat.

Made from slatted wood, the seats were hard. We were six seats around a table, with three seats facing each other, much as any other train, but more cramped. There was a similar table for six on the other side of the carriage, across the aisle.

I could see that I was attracting some attention from the other passengers, and Wei was exchanging some light-hearted banter.

'What is the foreigner doing in hard seats?'

'They had sold out of soft seats,' replied Wei.

'So it is true about their noses, huge isn't it?'

'Who is he?'

'Oh, just an eminent professor from England,' replied Wei.

'Does he smell? I can't smell him from here.'

'They say they all smell in the West. It's the diet, you know.'

Etcetera...

As soon as things settled, everyone started to unpack their parcels and bags on the tables in front of them, and Wei was doing likewise. It was time for breakfast. After a minute or so, the train pulled away from the platform.

Sharing our table was a family of three and an elderly man with a briefcase. The parents of the family had a small daughter aged about four. The daughter was everywhere, as you would expect. She was wearing pink tights, a white vest with pink trimming, and white ballet slippers. Although her hair was cut short like a boy, she was unmistakably a little girl. After considering me very funny, she quickly lost interest and watched Wei carefully laying out our breakfast on the table. We had oblong chunks of marble cake, crispy savoury rolls of several flavours, what looked like pancakes stuffed with rice, and a few other things. Along with our large bag of fruit and cartons of orange juice, we could have fed half the carriage.

What followed was a session of swapping and bartering. We managed to get rid of the marble cake and in exchange, had jam jars of hot tea, with lids of course. I was not hungry, but managed a crispy savoury roll and half of a stuffed pancake. Wei ate about four times as much as me, but we still had to give most of our breakfast away.

'You are their favourite, big-nosed, smelly foreigner,' Wei said.

The carriage was in a state of complete devastation – mess would have been too polite a word – with the remains of fruit and food scattered all over the floor and tables. With packages and paper bags abandoned, drink cartons left half drunk, and the tables awash with leftovers, I was reminded of lunch a few weeks ago in the student refectory. The other passengers seemed not to be bothered. Most of the male passengers were wearing white shirts but these remained clean. The females were dressed in their best and again were spotless.

The young daughter of the family sharing our table was sitting on my lap, half asleep, having demolished two chunks of marble cake. I couldn't smell that badly.

'Where are you working?' asked the elderly man with the briefcase.

'I am teaching at Jaliang Number 3 University.' I responded.

'Number 3!' he exclaimed. 'A hunger strike, that is dreadful. It is the government's fault for not listening to reason.'

There was general agreement among the other passengers, and they continued their discussion as I dozed off with the small girl still on my lap. My last recollections were seeing workers bending over in paddy fields through the carriage window.

'*P*rofessor Charles, we have arrived.'

I woke up suddenly. Having left my lap at some stage, the daughter was with her parents, who were gathering their luggage, parcels, and other oddments together.

'We now know why you foreigners snore so loud,' teased a passenger tapping her nose.

That received quite a few laughs.

'Suzhou has twenty-three famous gardens. You must see some,' one of my fellow passengers advised.

'No, it is twenty-five gardens,' responded another, 'and a pagoda.'

'The layout of the gardens in Suzhou is symbolic, and each is different,' added the third.

'They are beautiful.'

My heart sank...

We all shook hands and said our farewells.

We left the train, went straight to the soft seat ticket office, and got two tickets for our return journey later that evening. It was still early morning, I had eaten, was refreshed, and my clothes had not suffered too much damage. It was a warm sunny day and the sky was blue. We had the whole day ahead to enjoy.

Wei removed a map of Suzhou from her bag, and while sitting on a bench under the shade of a sycamore tree we planned our day.

'Suzhou is the prettiest town in the whole of the People's Republic,' Wei enlightened me, reading bits from the information on the map, 'although some argue that Hangzhou is prettier. Suzhou is the Venice of the East, with more canals and rivers than any other town. It is famous for its gardens and has a fine pagoda.'

'We'll skip the pagoda.'

'Suzhou is also famous for its stuffed dumplings.'

'Excellent, that's lunch sorted.'

Nearby was a taxi rank with a miscellaneous collection of cars that looked both hot and uncomfortable. Opposite was a gathering of bicycle rickshaws with padded passenger seats. I saw one old man with a colourful painted rickshaw, which was by no means of the latest design, but it looked well cared. I decided to hire the rickshaw for the day and see Suzhou in style.

When we approached the aged rickshaw driver, our negotiations were quick and amiable. I asked how much for the whole day, which surprised him. Nobody hired a rickshaw for the whole day, but he gave his price.

'Ridiculous,' I responded.

'That's fair,' he replied.

I offered him double his price with lunch thrown in. That, I could see, puzzled our aged rickshaw driver because that was not how you haggled for a price.

'Agreed,' he said, 'You are in good hands because no one knows Suzhou better than me.'

'I never doubted it.'

'Did you know,' he continued, 'that there are twenty-one famous gardens in Suzhou?'

'No,' I answered truthfully, 'I didn't know there were twenty-one!'

We agreed a plan for the day, which included enjoying the best dumplings in town.

Suzhou was shabby but attractive. The outskirts of the town consisted of low-lying buildings, with lots of trees. Wei said there was quite a bit of industrialisation around Suzhou. The roads and pavements into town were wide and clean. We passed some street cleaners with their twig brooms. They had a large wooden, open-boxed, barrow on what looked like bicycle wheels pulled by two long handles from the front.

'What did you think of Harry's attempts at speaking Chinese?' I asked, while enjoying our leisurely tour of the town.

'Interesting,' replied Wei. 'But there are many Chinese dialects.'

'How many?'

'I am not sure, exactly,' Wei said, 'but they are roughly classified into seven linguistic groups, where each group contains several dialects. There are, of course, languages of the minorities, such as Tibetan,

Mongolian, and Miao. The dialects of the seven groups are quite different, as different as Spanish and French. For example, a Mandarin speaker in Northern China cannot understand Cantonese.'

'What was Harry speaking then?'

'Mandarin,' said Wei, 'but it was difficult to tell sometimes. Speaking Chinese is a bit like singing where each syllable has a tone or movement of pitch, which is important to the meaning of the word. An incorrect intonation can completely change the meaning.'

'With so many dialects, how do you understand each other?'

'Mandarin has been the official national language since 1913,' Wei explained. 'Fortunately, there is one thing in common for most Chinese dialects; they share the same writing system. People can communicate quite effectively in this way. Many non-Mandarin speakers can speak a little Mandarin, but with a strong accent.'

Wei made me practise some basic words in Mandarin while we were sitting on our bicycle rickshaw, meandering around Suzhou.

The town centre consisted mostly of two-storey buildings, partly made from wood, and the rest stone or brick, painted white but with a distressed look about them. The roads were in need of minor repair, but nothing life threatening.

We stopped at a small street stall, frequented by bicycle rickshaw drivers, for some tea. The tea was waiting in glasses with a round piece of card placed on top to keep out the flies and, presumably, for keeping it warm. They made the tea in a hefty enamel kettle, topped up from a large, red, plastic thermos kept under the table. That was definitely a Chinese fast-drink establishment! We sat on wooden benches under a plane tree while our rickshaw driver told the others tales about his barbarian client who couldn't barter to save his life.

After the third famous garden, The Master-of-Nets Garden, I had to say, enough, no more.

I found Chinese gardens followed a common pattern. Popular were small pavilions, piles of finely shaped stones placed artistically next to a lily-pond, ornate arched bridges, waterfalls, and narrow pathways creating, according to Wei, an illusion of vastness within a small area. The planting was harsh, symbolic, and lacking in colour.

They were not your quintessential English gardens.

Lunch was at a small restaurant.

It was popular with locals and not the place that would attract foreigners or tourists. It was hardly a restaurant, but no more than a collection of wooden tables and benches spilling out of a small room onto the wide pavement and street. The street was unsuitable for cars, with leafy sycamore trees providing much welcome shade from the midday sun.

'Come on, make room for the foreigner, show your famous Chinese hospitality,' nagged the rickshaw driver, 'and no comments about his nose, because it has been following me around all morning.'

The other lunchtime diners shuffled around to make room in a shady position on the pavement.

Inside the restaurant, I could see a table where three dumpling makers practised their art before passing on the finished products to the cooks. I had seen the steaming method before when I had breakfast with Harry at the free market, but here they sprinkled spices and finely chopped herbs on the dumplings. They also quickly boiled dumplings in what looked like a mixture of well-seasoned vegetable oil and water, and others they baked.

'What do you fancy?' asked our rickshaw driver, who was also a splendid host. 'I tell you what, I will order a selection and tell the cook to keep them coming until we have had enough.'

'Why is he eating here?' asked one of the other diners in an inquisitive manner.

'Because I promised I would give him the best dumplings in town – none of that rubbish they serve in foreigner restaurants and hotels,' replied the rickshaw driver. 'And no smelly jokes either.'

'Well, you have come to the right place,' commented another, who was sharing our table. 'Can he use chopsticks?'

'Yes, he can,' Wei replied.

'I better wash some,' offered one of the cooks jovially. He picked up a pair of chopsticks from a discarded plate on another table, swirled them around the sink in murky water, shook off the excess, and placed them on the table in front of me.

'Voilà!' he said, but obviously some Chinese version.

Wei and the rickshaw driver hunted around for their own

chopsticks, which seemed to be the normal practice. Diners were using chopsticks to manoeuvre whole dumplings from plate to mouth; others just used their fingers. I would have preferred to use my fingers; it would have been much easier. I felt it would be unkind not to use chopsticks since the cook had gone out of his way to provide them.

To describe what we ate as dumplings was probably misleading because each stuffed morsel was different and a few were hand-wrapped in a kind of pastry. They made some from gelatinous rice and others had names like, dumplings with cowpeas, stuffed with three shredded delicacies, and white turnip. My particular favourites were the sweet dumplings, soaked in honey. The cook kept them coming, as promised.

'Delicious.'

I surprised our rickshaw driver with my appetite. I managed to out-eat him but not Wei. Where she managed to put all those dumplings was a mystery. I could hear our rickshaw driver, along with Wei, exchanging light banter with the others nearby. I washed lunch down with tea served in a tiny, but chipped, porcelain cup without a handle.

After lunch, Wei wanted to visit some of the other gardens because Suzhou was famous for them. That suited me. I preferred to walk around alone, just poking around and generally being curious.

'Where shall we meet?' I asked.

'Don't worry,' answered the rickshaw driver. 'I'll find you.'

Wei happily went away with the rickshaw driver.

Suzhou had a labyrinth of canals, which connected with the Grand Canal. Most canals had grey-tiled terraced houses built alongside, with faded whitewashed walls streaked with green mould. You could cross the canals using picturesque arched bridges.

The wider canals had steps built into the wall, leading from a veranda in front of the houses, down to a landing space, for junks, presumably. Some verandas had chickens pecking around, pots with plants, and long bamboo poles used for hanging washing to dry over the canal. There was the occasional bamboo birdcage with a canary adding song on the veranda. Earlier, I had noticed shops selling birdcages and all kinds of songbirds.

The narrower canals, with residential buildings either side, had stepping-stones jutting out of the canal wall. The top stepping-stone was level with the door that opened into the house. The bottom stone stopped short of the canal so that a small junk could fit below, allowing you to step on and off easily. There, houses had no verandas, but windows and small balconies facing the canal, pale blue being a popular colour. The windows were mostly open to catch what little breeze there was, with washing hanging to dry. The canals were empty apart from rubbish floating around, but that looked in keeping. The water in the canals looked greenish-brown with the reflection of the houses on the still water.

The narrow canals now had no commercial purpose, and there were no junks. By chance, I came upon a small archway opening to a tiny courtyard, with steps leading to a canal where women were washing their laundry.

Outside of the residential area, wider canals were still in commercial use. I saw wooden junks side-by-side, their bows tied to the canal bank and sterns jutting out into the waterway. The covered sterns looked add-ons to the original structure. Some of the junks were empty. Others were full, but I couldn't see what they were carrying because they covered their cargo with canvas tarpaulins. A single sculling oar at the stern powered the smaller junks, although the larger ones had engines.

While walking along a narrow alley, I saw a small girl sitting on the kerb concentrating hard on her hands. She was smartly dressed, for a special occasion perhaps, and sitting on a plastic bag to keep her clothes clean. When I looked closer, I could see she had a small jar of nail varnish by her side, and was painting each nail with care. I thought of my own daughters, who would borrow their mother's nail varnish and similarly hide away, undetected. The little girl never even noticed me. The smell of the canals must be stronger than the smell of a foreigner!

I came across a dilapidated, wooden building with huge red doors. It had one of those intricate, two-tier roofs with upward-curving pointed eaves on what was, basically, a simple building. There was a gathering of elderly men, having a good gossip, sitting on the steps leading to the building. One man had a wooden crutch and from the way he was sitting, a deformed leg. Two others had black, plastic sunglasses and, presumably, were blind. As I stared at the building, one of the elderly men told me it was a Confucian Temple, but I might have misunderstood.

I found a street stall and treated myself to a glass of tea. The elderly couple that served me nodded and smiled, and the old man offered me his stool, which I accepted.

'*I* visited nine gardens,' Wei informed me, looking pleased.

'I walked around the canals and looked at the old houses,' I said, also looking pleased, but Wei looked unconvinced.

Our rickshaw driver took us on a leisurely scenic route back to the railway station, travelling alongside one of the larger canals for part of the journey. At the station, I paid the rickshaw driver our agreed fee. I tried to give him extra, but he wouldn't accept it.

Our aged rickshaw driver had a strong pair of legs, and an old trusty bike. He hadn't let us down.

'*S*oft seats!' declared Wei, as we walked towards the platform.

The queuing regime at Suzhou station was not as regimented as Jaliang. In any case, we were travelling soft seats. The platform official was not about to tell the elite cadre to join the queue and to be quick about it. Our train arrived on time, and we boarded without any stampede for the doors. At the end of the carriage, there was a small pantry with an antiquated water boiler, which looked dangerous.

The soft seats were just that...

We had large armchair seats with padded armrests and despite showing their age, were comfortable. In front of us was a small table with a dainty white tablecloth that had seen better days. I had a window seat facing forward and Wei sat opposite. The seat next to Wei was unoccupied. Next to me was a smartly dressed man in a well-cut, grey Mao-style suit. He also wore a white shirt where the white collar was showing just a fraction above the high collar of the Mao jacket. His black shoes were immaculate, which was rare to see in China.

'*Nee hao*,' I said to our travel companion, and he nodded and smiled back in a friendly sort of way.

Soon after we had made ourselves comfortable, the carriage steward placed tall porcelain cups on the table in front of us, the type with lids.

Our cups already had tea leaves inside. The steward then came along and filled our cups with boiling water, and he topped us up at regular intervals for the duration of our journey.

As soon as the train started, Wei fell asleep. I considered waking her because she had looked forward to travelling soft seat.

'Can you speak Chinese?' asked the man next to me in good English.

'No,' I replied. 'I have been practising saying hello, goodbye, and thank you. That's all I know.'

'You must have seen some of the famous gardens in Suzhou. There are over one hundred gardens, but most are in need of renovation.'

'I saw three gardens, but I'm not an admirer.'

'You need to visit the Yellow Mountains to appreciate a traditional Chinese garden. These mountains are peculiar shaped, weatherworn, craggy, granite peaks. When they rise above the clouds, the light effects make striking views, with peaks covered with plants and vegetation. There you will see the Welcome Pine, which is famous. Such scenes of nature have influenced Chinese art for centuries, particularly traditional landscapes, and this has inspired garden design. In a Suzhou garden, every view is a work of art.'

'I found Suzhou attractive, particularly the canals,' I said.

'Suzhou was a centre for the silk industry, and still is to a certain extent. A lot of the houses alongside the canals were used for weaving.'

'If you don't mind me asking, what do you do?' I was inquisitive.

'I am a senior official from the Ministry of Agriculture, the vice-chairman of the regional council, which coordinates the export of grain. I live in Jaliang, but I am away a lot,' he answered. 'Are you a tourist?'

'No, I am a visiting professor at Jaliang Number 3 University. One of my professor friends suggested I visit Suzhou and kindly arranged for one of my students to accompany me.'

'My son is studying at Number 3 University.'

'What a coincidence.'

'It must be awkward for you with all the student unrest.'

'Yes it is, and it is sometimes difficult to know what is going on. Things are not always clear, but I pick up information when I can. I have a colleague who occasionally listens to the BBC World Service, and he keeps me informed.'

153

'I also listen to the BBC, although the authorities do not like us doing so. It offers a different perspective of Chinese news, more factual but not necessarily understanding what is happening behind the scenes.'

'Do you understand what is happening?'

'Not behind the scenes. I am a Party member and loyal to the government, but I have sympathy with some of the students' complaints. We expect our journalists to tell us the truth, not everything, I know, but they should report everyday matters accurately. Zhao Ziyang, the Communist Party leader, suggested at a Politburo meeting a few days ago to agree to the students' demands against corruption and for more freedom of the press. Who can disagree with that? Who wants corruption? Others, it seems, think differently.'

'Others?'

'Hardliners who want to crush the protests. The student demonstrations have humiliated Deng Xiaoping, and he will be after revenge. With the international media in Beijing covering the Gorbachev visit, he cannot do anything.'

'What are your son's views about the protests?' I asked.

'My son has joined the hunger strike, and I am worried about him. That is why I am travelling back to Jaliang. Being a foreign professor, you might have some influence. You must talk to the student leaders and persuade them to end the hunger strike.'

'I know some of the students on hunger strike,' I replied cautiously. 'I promise to speak to them.'

I had a worried father sitting next to me, a Party member, a senior official, and he turns to me for help. We sipped our tea and contemplated nothing important, and while doing so, I looked out of the train window. I saw a series of what looked like rectangular, man-make lakes.

'What are those?' I asked.

'They are fish ponds. Because of our overfished seas, stocks are getting low. Over half the fish we eat comes from freshwater ponds.'

'What types of fish do they grow?'

'Silver carp, grass carp, bigheads, and black carp are popular species grown in the ponds. We are famous for our integrated fish farming techniques. Wuxi, which is not far from here, is a town that specialises in fish farming with colleges and a university that teaches our techniques to both Chinese and foreign students.'

'I can see lots of animals and ducks.

'They are part of the integrated fish farm production. In fact, the manure from pigs, cows, and poultry is good organic fertilizer for fish farming. It is quite normal to construct pigsties, poultry coops, and pens for geese and ducks on the embankments or on platforms above the ponds. This way, fresh manure can enter the pond easily thus avoiding having to transport or carry it. About 45 kilos of manure can be converted into one kilo of fish.'

'That doesn't sound very appetising.'

'Geese and ducks can be reared on the ponds,' continued the worried father. 'Pond embankments can be used for fruit trees, soft fruit and vegetable cultivation, or for raising pigs. The slopes of the embankments are useful areas for growing fodder crops. In winter, they drain the ponds and scrape out the sludge to fertilise the grass and crops. They cut the grass to feed the fish.'

'Are the fountains just to look nice?' I asked.

'No, they are necessary to aerate the water and provide oxygen. When ducks swim, play, and chase each other that also aerates by disturbing the smooth surface of the pond.'

At banquets, the beautifully cooked carp had invariably been the highlight of the meal. I then found out my fondness of carp had contributed in the disposal of farm manure. I made a mental note to avoid the carp at future banquets and meals.

'Wei, your snoring was louder than the sound of the train,' I chided.

'I don't snore, do I?'

As we walked from the railway station, things were not the same as they were that morning. It was dark and the noise was disquieting.

'There's a lot of shouting,' I commented. 'What's going on?'

'Demonstrations,' replied Wei brightly. 'I should have been here. When I explained about Suzhou, my friends said I should go. I must go and find them now. They said they were going to protest outside the municipal buildings and make things very uncomfortable for those inside. We are hoping to get a lot of support from the workers.'

'I am sorry you had to miss the protests.'

'That's okay,' said Wei. 'I had a nice day. It is not often I get the opportunity to visit Suzhou. You must see what we are doing.'

It was evening and I had nothing else planned, so I agreed to accompany Wei. I remembered my promise to speak to the students about ending the hunger strike, and I hoped I might get the opportunity to do that.

We found Wei's friends, including Zhuang, the classroom monitor, sitting outside the municipal buildings.

'*Nee hao,*' I said, sitting on the ground next to Zhuang.

'We appreciate you joining us, Professor Charles. We are getting support from workers, journalists, intellectuals, and many others.'

'They are from the Ministry of Education,' someone said, pointing to a small group of people not far away.

'Including the big one,' added Zhuang, indicating the large woman with the group.

Large women in China were uncommon, which was probably why Zhuang pointed her out. I did notice one or two of the others in the group were quite attractive.

'Having you with us will boost our morale,' added Wei.

I wasn't there to support the protests or boost morale. Foreigners in China should keep their noses clean, no matter how big they were.

Most of the protesters were sitting on the ground in an orderly way, a bit like a school assembly. A student with a megaphone led the chanting. The dim lighting picked out the white shirts and blouses of the protesters. Flags were fluttering in the slight evening breeze. A few students held lanterns on poles, casting red shadows over the heads of those nearby.

Although it was dark, I could see other protesters gathered around flags chanting protests with their leaders. While the body of protesters was one, there were different sections. Students in another section wore red bands tied around their heads with a slogan of some sort in bold white lettering on the front.

'Why are they wearing red bands on their heads?' I asked.

'They are from another faculty and the headbands help others to recognise them. The flag represents their faculty,' explained Zhuang.

'This is our flag,' Wei informed me, pointing to a red flag above.

That explained how Wei found her friends so easily; she had just to look for the flag.

'What about the green banner?' I asked, pointing to it just a few yards away. I remembered helping carry it a couple of weeks ago.

'That's the flag of the Jaliang Autonomous Student Federation.'

'Why do you keep within faculty groups?'

'To make sure there are no infiltrations from outsiders. We can recognise most people from our own faculty. That way the authorities and troublemakers cannot mix among us. We know what we say and do and the authorities cannot accuse us of doing anything wrong. We have a right to protest.'

I saw a table with a crowd of students around it.

'What are they doing?'

'We are signing a petition requesting the government in Beijing to start discussions with student leaders,' replied Wei. 'Some university professors have also signed, including Professor Song. It would be an honour if an eminent, foreign professor like you were to sign.'

When put like that, how could I refuse? After I signed the petition, the students cheered and clapped.

I blushed.

'Some students only print their names because they are afraid of repercussions,' Wei explained. 'They can later claim they didn't sign the petition and someone else must have added their names.'

Now she tells me.

The students sat in front of several, drab, grey, multi-storey, concrete buildings enclosed within a high wall with wrought-iron gates. Despite the noisy protest, the gates were wide open, but no one attempted to enter. A single security guard stood casually by the gate protecting the municipal buildings.

Two student leaders entered the municipal compound, and with a megaphone, standing next to three, gleaming, black, foreign cars, they nagged those inside. I couldn't work out if they had any effect because people were coming and going from the buildings, not at all impeded by the protesters outside.

'I was hoping to meet some of the hunger strike leaders,' I said.

'Hou and Yang – they are back at the university,' Zhuang answered. 'Some of the other hunger strikers have been taken to hospital, but they are okay.'

'I can arrange for you to see Hou and Yang,' offered Wei.

It was noisy, and I was starting to feel a little queasy. Since the Friendship Store was not far away, I decided to go and have a cup of coffee. I had been drinking tea all day and as nice as it was, I needed something a little stronger.

Chapter 27

Wednesday, May 17, 1989

I woke up after a restless night having visited the toilet on several occasions. Was it the chopsticks, dumplings, a surfeit of green tea, or some dodgy milk I had with the coffee at the Friendship Store? As I passed the breakfast room, I saw Mr Chou sitting at a corner table, sipping tea.

'I am not eating,' I informed my breakfast hostess, who looked at me expectantly. Since she did not understand, I did not bother to go into the details of my queasy tummy.

Mr Chou, who must have heard me, choked on his tea. I was touched that he was concerned about my state of health.

I met Wei by the university main entrance, as arranged. I was going to see Hou, Yang, and some of the others, and attempt to convince them to end their hunger strike.

'What do the posters say?' I asked Wei, pointing to the wall to the left of the main entrance.

'Oh, they are mostly condemning Deng,' Wei answered vaguely.

'What does that one say?' I again asked, pointing to a large banner.

'Deng Xiaoping disappear, you are too old.'

'And that one?'

'Clean up the political rubbish!'

'Why is there a pile of broken glass over there?' I asked.

'Deng Xiaoping's name in Chinese sounds like, little bottle,' Wei explained. 'The smashed glass represents the broken power of Deng.'

We walked across the campus to a block of student dormitories. The ground floor was for the hunger strikers because it was close to the university clinic. If needed, medical help was at hand, and I felt happier knowing that. Some students wore white headbands, like a kamikaze pilot, with a slogan written in red, looking like blood. One slogan was in

English, 'Die for Democracy,' it said.

Hou and Yang were both sitting at a table, near the window, in a cramped dormitory sharing with two others. They were part of the production of posters and banners. I noticed that they had an ample supply of water.

'Are you sure this is the best thing to do?' I asked. 'I came across a very worried parent yesterday and he asked me to speak to you. I don't pretend to have any influence, but I must discourage you from continuing the hunger strike.'

'We are together, twenty of us, all volunteers,' replied Hou. 'We represent all faculties and must continue. It is our duty.'

'We, the children, are ready to die,' quoted Yang. 'That was the call from our colleagues in Beijing.'

'Wu'er Kaixi and other Beijing student leaders have already had discussions with senior government officials,' explained Hou. 'Yan Mingfu, who is a senior official close to Zhao Ziyang, and another, I forget his name, met student leaders last Saturday, and urged them to be more moderate and to give up the hunger strike. It was supposed to be televised but the students were tricked.'

'We think Zhao and Yan were anxious that, with the visit of Gorbachev taking place, the hardliners might move to crush the protest movement,' said Wei.

'It is difficult to know what is going on in other parts of China,' Yang commented. 'There are many student groups saying different things. We are not organised.'

'Yesterday, for example, while we were demonstrating in Jaliang last night, Wang Dan and Wu'er Kaixi, who are student leaders in Beijing, were urging everyone to end the hunger strike,' exclaimed Wei indignantly. 'Fortunately, other leaders outnumbered them. Yan Mingfu, accompanied by Wang Dan, went to the Square yesterday to make further appeals.'

'Wang Dan has been a popular leader,' explained Yang. 'He published an article in a student magazine last month criticising the government and supporting the recent developments of eastern European countries. He's not so popular now.'

'We need representatives in Beijing,' stated Hou.

'We are not looking to overthrow the government,' added Wei, 'but we want to see changes. We started our protests by supporting the Party and socialism. Deng turned that against us by his public condemnation in the *People's Daily*, saying we were against the socialist system. That is not true.'

'We heard that a group of Beijing university presidents signed an open letter advising that discussion between the government and students would be a good thing. We have popular support,' stated Hou.

'We are writing slogans for our posters,' said Yang. 'Do you have any ideas, Professor Charles?'

'None come to mind,' I replied guardedly.

'This one is inspired by you,' Hou informed me. 'The only good Deng is a dead Deng.'

I never said that, although I couldn't vouch for Harry.

'We don't literally mean dead but politically dead, and that slogan is linked to Confucius,' Yang said proudly. 'We like symbolic slogans.'

I walked away from the dormitory block and did not know what to think. What I had seen so far had been well-ordered demonstrations, with a bit of light banter, but then students went on hunger strike. Last night I had witnessed the residents of Jaliang supporting the students, their apparent martyrdom bringing people to the streets; or was it just inquisitiveness?

With my tummy being unsettled, I decided to return to my room and take things easy.

Extract from:

THE PRESS
WED 17 MAY 1989
Local correspondent, Peking

IN THE LONG AWAITED Sino-Soviet summit meeting
yesterday, Gorbachev and China's aging leader, Deng
Xiaoping, ended their 30-year discord.

For the second day of demonstrations, students and
workers marched into Tiananmen Square with their flags.
They chanted anti-government slogans demanding 'freedom'
and 'democracy' causing embarrassment to the Chinese
government. In an extraordinary turn of events, workers also
left their jobs in nearby offices and factories to join the
students on Tiananmen Square.

In a move to alleviate its embarrassment, the government
sent a senior official, Mr Yang Min Fu, to plead with students
to leave the Square.

Large demonstrations also took place in Shanghai,
Nanking, and other major cities.

Memorandum

(Telex message)

From   Chou Ke-giang
           Director of the Office of Foreign Affairs
           Jaliang Number 3 University

To   Deputy Chairman
           Office of Education Foreign Affairs
           Public Security Bureau
           Beijing

Date   17 May 1989

CONFIDENTIAL

DR CHARLES VINCENT

I now have evidence that Dr Vincent is largely responsible for the student unrest in Jaliang.

Yesterday, Vincent gave me the slip in the early hours of the morning and disappeared for the whole day. When I finally traced his whereabouts, he turned up among the leaders of yesterday's demonstrations taking place outside municipal buildings. While outside the municipal buildings, he publicly signed a student petition as a symbolic gesture against the authorities.

In a clever move, Vincent has joined the student hunger strike thereby ensuring that he has the full confidence of the protesters. In addition to this, I saw him conspiring with other hunger strikers, helping them with slogans for the posters that students are displaying by the main gate. One of the posters referred to the death of Deng, our leader.

I urge you to ensure that my report is made available to those responsible within the *Public Security Bureau* so that punitive measures can be taken to remove this provocateur from the People's Republic.

From: **Deputy Chairman**
Office of Education Foreign Affairs
Public Security Bureau
Beijing
To: **Chou Ke-giang**
Director of the Office of Foreign Affairs
Jaliang Number 3 University
18 May 1989

Private note (by telex)

DISSIDENT VINCENT

You obviously do not appreciate the situation in Beijing. The world media is here to cover the Sino-Soviet summit, which makes the government and our leaders vulnerable to the following:

1.　humiliation by the protesters actions, and
2.　criticism if the authorities make any move against the protesters.

Whatever is happening in Jaliang is of no consequence because it is not being reported or covered by the press. You must ensure that all subversive activities against the government in Jaliang are contained and not allowed to escalate any further.

The resources of the Public Security Bureau are fully stretched with the troublesome Beijing universities. I must emphasise that our priority is containing the subversive activities of the protesters in and around the capital Beijing.

Please continue to provide regular updates on the current situation in Jaliang.

Chapter 28

There was a continuous knocking on my door and when I answered, there was Petter. I had slept fitfully throughout the night and when dawn came, I slept heavily, until he woke me.

'Come on, Charles, it is lunchtime.'

I invited Petter into my room, excusing myself for only wearing my pyjama top and underpants. I had given up on my pyjama bottoms due to my frequent visits to the toilet. I gave Petter a quick update on what I had been doing since last seeing him and a brief account of my current state of health.

'So, Petter,' I asked, 'any news?'

I tried to sound casual, but I had not had much experience in getting information out of Soviet agents. I still could not take in that Petter might be a spy. Petter was sitting cosily in the armchair and was calmly filling his pipe with his ghastly shag. He looked the most unlikely spy.

They said that about Philby, Burgess, and MacLean, hadn't they.

'You don't mind if I smoke?' asked Petter, while lighting his pipe.

'No, not really,' I replied with a heavy sigh of resignation, while opening the window.

'Things are just about wrapped up here, and I am leaving on Saturday,' Petter informed me. 'I have a few things to do in Beijing before returning to Sweden.'

'Wrapped up what things exactly?' I asked as innocently as I could, without sounding too hostile.

'The arrangements for the student work placements, of course. Go and have a shower, Charles. It will do you the world of good.'

While having a shower, I started to worry. Was I in danger if Petter suspected that I suspected that he was a Soviet agent? The hot shower cleared my head. I realised that the only thing I was in danger from were the ghastly fumes from Petter's pipe.

Despite feeling fragile, I joined Petter and Professor Song for lunch.

'What you need is a bowl of rice, garnished with finely chopped fresh herbs,' Petter advised, as we walked towards the university main entrance. He put his arm around my shoulders in a friendly way while he offered me his advice, but, in doing so, he made me stumble.

'I could manage a bowl of rice, I think.'

Nearby, Mr Chou was taking a particular interest in one of the flowerbeds. Professor Song also noticed and paused to give Mr Chou a cold and hard stare.

'I didn't know Mr Chou had an interest in gardens,' I commented.

'He doesn't,' Professor Song replied casually. 'He always did take too much interest in other people's business. He can be a bit zealous.'

'Do I remember you once saying he was a Red Guard activist during the Cultural Revolution,' commented Petter.

'Yes, he took it all too seriously, but that was a long time ago,' replied Professor Song.

Students were still reading the posters stuck on the wall to the left of the main entrance. Professor Song must have seen me looking because he was smiling.

'There appears to be more posters,' I remarked.

Professor Song took me to the wall and after examining a few posters, read out some of the latest editions.

'Deng Xiaoping, you are terribly old. You may be healthy but you are senile.

'Missing person! Has anyone seen Li Peng?

'We have lost Zhao Ziyang.

'The only good Deng is a dead Deng.'

'Please can you explain them to me?' I asked.

'The first slogan is merely rude towards our leader, a sentiment held by many. The next two draw attention to the refusal of the prime minister and Party general secretary to speak directly to the protesters,' explained Professor Song. 'That last slogan is strange. It has a comment stating it is a parody of an old Confusion quote.'

'I think it means politically dead. It is symbolic,' I offered quickly, and on reflection, a little too quickly.

'You understand Chinese symbolisms, not many foreigners do.'

I tried not to look guilty, but I couldn't stop blushing.

'You've got some colour in your cheeks at last, Charles,' Petter noticed. 'You must be feeling better.'

'What do you think of our student protests?' asked Professor Song.

'Chinese students are better at organising protests than their British counterparts,' I replied, after giving this some consideration.

We walked for about ten minutes, past the street where the early morning free market took place, to a small restaurant not far away.

'This is one of my favourite restaurants,' Professor Song said. 'It is close to the university and convenient for lunchtimes. It is really a private house but the owner does good meals for a few select people.'

It was to be Petter's farewell banquet, but he had requested a simple and quiet meal with friends. I was touched to be included.

Petter explained that I was feeling a little fragile. Professor Song suggested I had a herbal drink instead of beer. Because I wasn't ready for beer yet, I agreed. I didn't think I was ready for the herbal concoction either but, much as it tasted horrid, it had no ill effects.

'Professor Sang has been keeping you informed about things, I hear,' commented Professor Song.

'Yes, he has been extremely helpful and kind. I'm afraid I haven't been doing much teaching lately,' I said apologetically.

'You have been helpful in more ways than you think,' he added.

'What will happen next?' asked Petter.

Professor Song paused before answering. 'The students have already achieved much. They have the support of the workers, journalists, and many intellectuals. Just two days ago, our leaders had to change their plans for the arrival of Gorbachev. Instead of an official welcome on Tiananmen Square, Gorbachev had to enter the Great Hall of the People by the back entrance. That was humiliating for Deng.'

I was watching Petter closely. He was smiling; I was sure of it!

'The students are having a certain measure of success with their calls for press freedom,' continued Professor Song. 'On television last night, the news gave a lengthy and objective report on the demonstrations and this took priority over Gorbachev and his ill-fated visit.'

'What will be the outcome?'

'That is difficult to judge, but Chinese history shows that

suppressors of student movements come to no good end. Prominent intellectuals have urged the government to recognise the legitimacy of the new student federations, promote political reform, and eliminate corruption. They want the government to respect freedom of the press, thought, and assembly. That is a lot for the government to legitimise.'

'Which prominent intellectuals are these?' I asked.

I still had a problem with references to intellectuals, never mind prominent intellectuals. What did it mean? I was also mindful that they referred to me as an honoured guest or eminent, foreign professor and the like. The truth was I knew I was merely seminar fodder at a northern polytechnic.

'People like Yan Jiaqi and Bao Zunxin,' answered Professor Song.

'And yourself, of course,' I added, with a twinkle in my eye.

Professor Song smiled nicely, and I took that to mean that while I might think that, he most definitely was not going to comment.

'Is the carp to your liking, Petter?' Professor Song asked.

It was.

It wouldn't have been to my liking, knowing what carp are fed in the fish ponds. I was pleased with my bowl of rice, garnished with fresh – I was not sure what, to be honest, but it was green, definitely.

I started to feel better.

*P*etter had enjoyed a siesta to sleep off his lunch, and it was the evening. We were in the guesthouse breakfast room, playing table tennis.

Buses to downtown Jaliang were no longer reliable because of the protests, so a visit to the Friendship Store was out. When I broached with Petter about asking Mr Chou for the use of an official car, he was against it. That was a pity because I had spotted Mr Chou with a torch, inspecting some nearby trees.

We considered what to do.

We contemplated having another game of table tennis, but neither of us was very enthusiastic.

'I'm bored,' declared Petter.

'Give me a five-point lead and we'll have another game.'

We had already played a couple of games and established Petter was far superior at ping-pong than me. In Petter's home village in the Arctic

Circle, for entertainment during the dark, winter evenings, most villagers assembled in the village hall, and table tennis was a popular activity.

'Can you hear music?' Petter's head shot up, vigilant, looking for the source of the music.

'Yes.'

'Strauss, a Viennese waltz,' Petter remarked knowledgably.

The music was not coming from the campus loudspeakers. Of late, the loudspeakers had been erratic and mostly used for chants and speeches by students.

'Follow me,' said Petter.

My heart sank. Look what happened when I followed Harry.

Petter entered the kitchen, but I was reticent to follow because his recent history of entering had not been successful. Our hostess, the little, old, Chinese lady, was around. On the plus side, I had not seen her husband, the whisk wielding pan-banging cook.

'Omele?' queried the little, old, Chinese lady, who was evidently surprised to see us in the kitchen.

Petter cupped his ear and swayed in tempo with the music. He then raised both his hands and hunched his shoulders in a semi-Gallic shrug. Petter's skill in miming had obviously improved, because the little, old, Chinese lady pointed to a door at the other end of the kitchen. I had been in the kitchen before, with Harry, but we took another door, which led outside.

'Ah,' Petter beamed, 'in the old building.'

I looked puzzled.

He explained that the old building attached to the foreign-visitor guesthouse was for Chinese visitors. It used to be for foreigners before they built the new guesthouse, and on previous visits, Petter had stayed there. The kitchen served both wings, which explained the amount of unaccountable noise emanating from it each morning.

I followed Petter down a short corridor before turning right through swing doors into what appeared to be a large dining hall. The tables had been pushed to the far end of the hall, which was in darkness. At the end of the hall nearest the entrance, where there was plenty of lighting, the chairs were set around the perimeter. In the corner was a bar. To the side of the bar was a table with an ancient record player on top. If modern Chinese washing machines were anything to go by, the record player was probably the very latest in modern Chinese electronics.

The record player was the source of the Viennese waltz.

I was fascinated.

There was a group of mostly middle-aged Chinese, doing some form of conga dance, Chinese style, a human chain moving around, inside the circle of chairs. The men wore white shirts without a tie, and dark trousers, and the women were dressed in frocks of one kind or another. The peculiar thing was they still looked Chinese. The group appeared to be swaying to the music but the synchronisation was terrible.

The group noticed us entering. Some waved, others grinned, but the winding line of the Chinese conga dance continued undisturbed. At the front was a large woman who waved us in. We were welcome.

'Beer?' Petter asked, walking towards the bar.

I went and sat at a table, not at the back, but in that gloomy area between the light and dark ends of the hall. I was trying to work out what was going on. Was it some form of Chinese dragon festival, or what? There was no one dressed as a dragon and the music was wrong; Strauss, Petter had said.

Petter arrived with two bottles of Tsingtao beer and quickly filled his own glass. I paused to consider if I should drink beer. I felt almost back to normal, but I didn't want to stretch my luck.

'What's going on, Petter?'

'See the well-built woman in the front,' Petter pointed out, 'she is giving dancing lessons. She is directing from the front and the rest are following, trying to copy her movements.'

The well-built woman in the front had her arms in the air, as if holding an invisible partner. Her left hand was in front of her ample bosom, and her right hand held high, as if reaching for an object on a shelf. I deemed she was pretending to be the dragon because she certainly looked like one. The person behind had their left hand on top of the well-built woman's left shoulder and right hand similarly help high. That posture continued down the line, some having confused their left and right hands. I had seen nothing like it before.

'This is interesting,' I said. 'I have never seen traditional Chinese dancing before.'

'That,' remarked Petter, with a big beam on his face, 'if I am not mistaken, is supposed to be a waltz.'

I had not taken Petter to be the dancing kind.

He informed me that during the dark winter months, in that godforsaken village in northern Sweden, not only did they play ping-pong in the village hall, but also ballroom dancing was a feature of their entertainment. I had images of village halls all over the Arctic Circle, with locals ping-ponging and stomping away to Strauss and the like. My parochial life-style back in Pontefract, I had to admit, had not really prepared me for the sophisticated wider world.

Petter could hardly contain himself. He quickly drained his glass of Tsingtao, walked boldly to the dancing area where no Swede had gone before, grabbed a strikingly attractive, tall woman, and led her skilfully into a waltz. She looked familiar although I could not place her. Petter's partner struggled for all of ten seconds before picking up the movement and rhythm. They glided around the room with grace and style.

The others stopped to watch Petter and his partner, and some even applauded. Members of the dancing class quickly positioned themselves behind either Petter or his partner, mimicking them. The troupe followed them around the hall attempting to copy every step.

Imagine it.

Petter would execute a quick turn and, a yard or so behind, the troupe would attempt to follow, but would take the long route, most not quite making it. Some abandoned following and went into corners to run through the movements individually before having a go on the dance floor.

I could not believe it.

There, the dancing guru from the Arctic Circle was happily giving a demonstration of Swedish ballroom virtuosity to a group of total strangers staying at the Chinese-visitor guesthouse.

Everyone was happy.

Wrong.

Not quite everyone.

Because, until our arrival, she was the centre of attention, the well-built woman who originally led the dancing had a face like thunder

I must justify what I mean by being well-built, as no belittlement was intended. I had observed that most Chinese females were invariably slender, even in old age. When you witnessed a fine example to the contrary, it was noticeable. The woman in question was by no means fat – more like an ex-shot putter whose previous muscle was turning to fat.

Petter decided to change partners and grabbed another strikingly attractive woman, but not so tall. As before, Petter's new partner quickly picked up the steps and they glided around the room. Petter's original partner became popular as she passed her newfound skills to the others. All were having a good time.

I realised where I had seen some of the dancers before. It was the evening of the protests when I returned from Suzhou. Zhuang and others had pointed out a group of officials from the Ministry of Education.

In a way, I felt a little foolish. All those evenings I had been alone in the guesthouse, the only foreigner staying, feeling a little homesick and sorry for myself. All I had to do was walk through the kitchen where there was a bar, lively entertainment, and company.

I decided to have some beer. As I filled my glass, I did so clumsily and when the bottle hit the side of the glass, a clear chink echoed across the hall...

...and that was to be my undoing.

Not many in the hall would have heard the chink, as most were too busy having a thoroughly good time. One person did hear the chink and I could see she then remembered that two foreigners had entered the room. Her eyes followed the direction of the chink, and in the gloom, she could make out the other foreigner who was not dancing.

Me.

I knew how Paul felt on the road to Damascus, or wherever, when the bright light shone on him. It happened to me. I had deliberately chosen to stay in the gloom, well away from the dancing. I did not dance and until that moment, I never intended ever to do so.

If destiny were on my side, then the strikingly attractive, tall woman would have been the one who glanced in my direction. No such luck.

The ex-shot putter whose previous muscle was turning to fat, the dragon look-alike, stood up with an irresistible smile and boldly walked where, I had always hoped, no woman would ever go. There was no escape. She grabbed me and I was frog-marched towards the dancing area right into the centre of things.

Where her left hand was previously, she firmly fixed me between such hand and ample bosom. She firmly grasped my left hand in her right hand, some place above head height in the general direction she intended I should travel.

And off we went.

The dancing skills of my partner were only marginally better than my own, and it took me most of my time to stop from tripping.

The other dancers who had given up following Petter saw their chance and got behind me. I looked over my shoulder and saw about five would-be ballroom champions, hands held high with an invisible partner, but eyes firmly fixed on my feet. While dragged round the floor by my new bosom partner, my dancing pupils dogmatically attempted to follow me, copying my every step.

Beer flowed freely. The cost of a bottle of Tsingtao was a fraction of what we foreigners normally paid. As drinking beer had no ill effect on my fragile constitution, I joined in the fun.

The dancing group were indeed officials from the Ministry of Education. They were there to collate the government annual educational statistics. Since internal communications in China were unreliable, representatives from all the provinces got together once a year to aggregate their figures. That year, it was the turn of Jaliang to be host. Sadly, they had not reckoned on there being student protests. It had restricted their recreational activities, especially in the evenings. Hence, that night they decided to give themselves dancing lessons.

Quite a few of the Ministry of Education officials could speak English and were eager to practise with me. Admittedly, Petter's grasp of English was superior to mine; he was Scandinavian, after all. I had noticed that with many Europeans and Asians. They spoke English so correctly it gave them away. That was in stark contrast to native speakers, like me, who had never received formal English lessons but just picked it up along the way.

I was a native speaker and therefore in demand. In any case, Petter was too busy providing dancing lessons to anyone willing. The image of a tall, distinguished looking Swede dancing around the hall with a little, rotund, middle-aged, Chinese man, was one I would never forget. How he managed to smoke his pipe at the same time was still a mystery!

The ex-shot putter was proficient in English. Her name was Miss Ma Qian, but for fun, she wanted me to suggest an English name because that was popular in China. I initially suggested, Tamara, but she looked at me suspiciously. She asked if it was an English name, and how did I spell it. I quickly said that I meant to say, Tammy – and that sounded very English. Tammy, Miss Ma informed me, sounded nice.

The shorter of the two strikingly attractive women, who had been one of Petter's initial dancing partners, was a friend of Tammy. Both worked in Beijing, in offices quite close to Tiananmen Square. Her name was Miss Li Pei-Zhen. When she wanted an English name, I said it was not necessary, as Leigh sounded English anyway.

I could not say my dancing technique improved that night, but it did not matter. I made a mental note to watch out for future Chinese *Come Dancing* teams touring England. If they had leading hands held bizarrely high, and they had peculiar feet movements, then who knows…

Extract from:

THE PRESS
THU 18 MAY 1989
Local correspondent, Peking

WITH THE CHINESE Government's inability to resolve the dispute with the student protesters, it will be interesting to see who comes out on top in the current leadership struggle. So far, there has been neither a crackdown nor conciliation with the protesters thus adding fuel to the suggestions that there is a power struggle within the ruling elite.

Deng, despite his popular Open Poor Policy reforms, is disliked by the people. Zhao Ziyang, having publically stated that the demonstrations would gradually calm down, has suffered loss of face, and Li Peng has reinforced people's belief that he is both inept and lacks initiative.

It is believed that depending upon how the government finally handles the demonstrations will indicate who has gained power and who will fall from grace.

Chapter 29

Friday, May 19, 1989

I woke up early and decided to have breakfast in the free market. As it was dawn, I thought I would have a walk to gain an appetite.

I came upon a small park close to a residential area and noticed a group of elderly people wearing their baggy, faded suits, apparently doing nothing, just standing there. I was wrong of course, because when I got closer, they were moving, but very slowly. There was a person in front who was leading the others. I realised it was an early morning gathering of *t'ai-chi*. I sat down under a tree nearby, and watched the slow graceful movements of the early morning exercise session. I could hear the soft tones of traditional Chinese music in the distance, but I might have imagined it. There was a faint layer of early morning mist, so the park had a calming, spiritual feel about it. I watched the sun slowly rise and cause picturesque reflections in the mist.

I felt good.

Afterwards, I enjoyed a leisurely breakfast in the free market.

When I visited the hunger-strike students, both Hou and Yang were missing, and I began to worry. The other students around the dormitory did not speak English so could not help me. I noticed the odd carton of orange juice and empty yoghurt pots lying about. At least they were not being too pedantic about things. I immediately made my way to the university clinic where I found Yang receiving medical attention.

'Are you all right?' I asked Yang. 'What about Hou?'

'I was feeling faint and they brought me here,' replied Yang, smiling weakly. 'Hou and Wei have gone to Beijing. We needed representatives there. We are never sure what is happening or if the Beijing student leaders are hearing our views. We also wanted to deliver our petition to the authorities in Beijing.'

'Was Hou well enough to travel?' I asked.

'It was agreed Hou can go on semi-hunger strike while travelling, but he will return to full hunger strike when he arrives in Beijing,' replied Yang. 'We want to show that students from Jaliang are true supporters of the protests. Students in Beijing think that the protests only involve them and provincial students do not matter.'

On leaving the clinic, I decided I would talk to Mr Chou and find out what was happening about my teaching programme – or lack of it. I would also request if I could use his telephone to confirm my return flights, scheduled to return to London, via Beijing. If there was nothing much happening in Jaliang, I decided I might as well leave a few days early and do some sightseeing around Beijing, and visit the Great Wall, Ming tombs, and the Forbidden City.

I did not need to look very far because Mr Chou appeared to be doing some weeding in the flowerbeds close to the clinic. I was impressed with senior staff multi-tasking and willing to lend a hand at the more menial tasks. I couldn't see that catching on back at the poly.

'Good morning, Mr Chou,' I said. 'You're looking a little off-colour. Why don't we go to your office and have a nice cup of tea.'

'What!'

In Mr Chou's office, there was the usual plastic thermos flask full of boiling water. He spooned a measure of green tea into our porcelain cups and added hot water. I settled myself, uninvited, into the large armchair at the end, the place of honour, which unsettled Mr Chou.

'What about my teaching programme, Mr Chou?'

'What!'

'Will there be any classes next week?'

'What!'

'It will be my last teaching week, according to my schedule. And some of my students have already gone to Beijing,' I explained.

'What!'

'I think it best if I prepare an examination paper for the students,' I proposed. 'I will ask Professor Sang to invigilate when things have settled down a bit. The students have copies of all my notes.'

'What!'

'Good, that's settled then. Can I use your phone, Mr Chou?'

That went well, I thought.

On leaving Mr Chou's office, I saw Tammy and Leigh strolling around the campus, and I gave them a wave. They waved back and walked over to meet me.

'Good morning,' I said. 'What a beautiful day.'

It was.

I had an enjoyable early morning walk, ate a hearty breakfast at the free market, ascertained my students had not starved to death, and judged I might have got the better of Mr Chou. Yes, it was a beautiful day.

The weather was also good.

'Hello, Professor Charles.'

'Shouldn't you both be adding up your numbers and things like that?' I asked light-heartedly.

I had tried to get my friends from the Ministry of Education to call me Charles, but they wouldn't. I was a professor and that, according to them, was that. I did not want them to know I was merely a northern polytechnic lecturer. In truth, I quite liked them calling me professor. All the same, I had no illusions, once back in Pontefract, it would be back to, 'oi, you...'

'We finished our work yesterday,' Tammy informed me. 'We are deciding where we should meet next year. After that, we will be saying our farewell speeches. We fly back to Beijing tomorrow.'

'I have a lot of preparation to do,' added Leigh. 'I am getting married in two weeks.'

We sat on the bench, in the shade of the cherry blossom tree, where I had met Professor Sang the other day. The blossom had faded and where it had lain on the ground, it had mostly blown away. Nonetheless, it was still a nice spot.

'What are your plans, Professor Charles?' asked Tammy.

'My teaching programme has finished,' I replied. 'I think I saw you in town the other night during the demonstrations, near the municipal buildings. I was told you and some of your colleagues were supporting the students.'

'That was not strictly true,' Leigh responded. 'We had visited the local education offices as part of our official programme and were caught up in the demonstrations. We were waiting for our bus to find us. The students seemed pleased to see us, so we stood around and watched. Do not get us wrong, we support the students, but we are not sure what they want.'

'Have you any news about the protests?' I asked.

'A little,' said Tammy. 'We have been in touch with our colleagues back in Beijing. Our offices are very near Tiananmen Square and they can see what is going on. Since the visit of Gorbachev, students have taken to the streets in Beijing on most days. The hunger strike has encouraged a lot of support from the Beijing residents, but it is difficult to gauge what level of support that is.'

'Our colleagues said that, yesterday and the day before, huge crowds, including workers, government officials, journalists, and hospital staff, marched in the streets and on Tiananmen Square in support of the students,' added Leigh. 'Early yesterday morning, Zhao Ziyang, Li Peng, and others visited students in hospital suffering from the effects of being on hunger strike.'

'But don't the students disliked Li Peng,' I asked.

'That is true,' said Leigh, 'but our leaders want to be seen doing the right thing. There is also a leadership struggle going on, so who knows what is really happening?'

'About midday yesterday, Li Peng held talks with student leaders at the Great Hall of the People,' Tammy went on to inform me. 'There were about eleven students, including Wu'er Kaixi and Wang Dan. Wu'er was amusing because he is a little fat, which is unusual for someone so young, and was wearing hospital pyjamas. He was not intimidated by premier Li.'

'Was anything agreed?' I asked.

'No, nothing was accomplished as far as we can make out. At least, not on television,' replied Leigh.

'Everyone just seemed to quibble,' added Tammy.

For a country that claimed poor communications, everyone seemed to be quite well informed. That was probably an unfair observation because the people I met were the elite, government officials who were well-connected, or Party members. If things did not work or went wrong, they blamed poor communications. Meanwhile, the people that mattered communicated with each other without much difficulty.

I explained that, next week, I planned to visit Beijing for a few days. Both Tammy and Leigh considered that was an excellent idea and offered to show me around some of the sights. They gave me their office telephone numbers because neither had phones at home. When I arrived in Beijing, I was to phone Tammy.

Tammy and Leigh had to go to complete their farewell ceremonies. They both hoped next year's venue for the annual collation of Ministry of Education national statistics would be a more pleasant location. Jaliang, they both agreed, had been disappointing – apart from the dancing lessons, of course.

After lunch, I visited Professor Sang to beg his assistance with the examination arrangements for my students. He gladly agreed to help. He offered to take me for a walk the next afternoon.

I also wanted to see Professor Song, the faculty dean, to inform him of my decision to end my teaching programme. Unfortunately he was busy with Petter and two others, one being Mr Cheng, the assistant deputy port director, and the other a representative from the Chinese National Shipping Line.

I then remembered the conversation I had with Petter in the Friendship Store after we visited the port three weeks ago. He seemed very interested in that Nigerian scam, where ships with fictitious cargoes were paid handsomely to wait at anchor – no, surely not.

What was Petter up to?

Memorandum

(Telex message)

From Chou Ke-giang
Director of the Office of Foreign Affairs
Jaliang Number 3 University

To Deputy Chairman
Office of Education Foreign Affairs
Public Security Bureau
Beijing

Date 19 May 1989

CONFIDENTIAL

DR CHARLES VINCENT

Last night, I witnessed Dr Vincent spreading propaganda and bourgeois liberalism among officials from the Ministry of Education. This clandestine meeting was no accident, as we saw the very same officials with Vincent during the demonstrations outside the municipal buildings a few days ago.

The conniving academic then had the nerve to inform me that he had sent some of his hunger-striking students to Beijing, obviously to stir up further trouble with the protesters. These students are planning to deliver a petition, the very one that Vincent has signed, to the authorities in Beijing.

Further to this, I overheard Vincent arranging to travel to Beijing because he had interesting things to do. We all know what he will do. He will make contact with his fellow conspirers and continue causing trouble.

Vincent will arrive in Beijing on Tuesday. He will then become your responsibility.

Chapter 30

Saturday, May 20, 1989

I accompanied Petter to the airport.

Mr Chou insisted on coming and provided an official university car. Professor Song, who also came, said, with controlled patience, that he could have arranged that. Mr Chou responded by saying he was the director of the Office of Foreign Affairs and it was his duty to see that all arrangements for foreign guests went smoothly.

After checking in, Petter had about an hour before his flight was due. He said he would wait in the first class lounge. Professor Song and Mr Chou took their cue and said their thanks and official farewells. Mr Chou presented Petter with an official gift from Number 3 University, and Petter provided the usual polite platitudes. The gift was noticeably large and well wrapped. I suspected that Petter and Professor Song had already said their farewells.

'Join me in the lounge for a few minutes, Charles,' said Petter.

'I will wait for you outside,' stated Mr Chou in an authoritarian tone.

Professor Song and Mr Chou nodded their heads to Petter, promptly turned round, and left the departure terminal without further ceremony. In China, a farewell was a farewell with none of the lingering around. On the way to the lounge, Petter took a small detour to a large rubbish bin and, without breaking his stride, dumped his official gift from the university.

'This way,' said Petter.

When we arrived at the lounge, I decided I would have words about his insensitive action. 'You can't do that,' I said indignantly.

'Do what?' replied Petter, looking puzzled.

'Dump the gift.'

'Oh that,' replied Petter, in what I considered was a patronising manner. 'Look, these people show no consideration. At the last minute, they unload on you some cumbersome, unwanted gift. I have already checked in, and my arms are full with hand luggage. What am I supposed to do?'

He had a point, but only just…

'Besides,' continued Petter, 'I have been to Jaliang several times, and I am sure I already have what Mr Chou gave me. At home, rooms are full of gifts presented to me over the years. I now make a habit of never looking at them. Inspecting gifts is a mistake. If you open one before dumping it, you might think it's not that bad or your mother might like it. Better to dump it at the first convenient opportunity.'

I looked around the lounge and tried to work out what was first class about it. I then remembered, although it had international flights, Jaliang was a provincial airport, and Petter was on an internal flight to Beijing. It was just a place for senior officials to escape the queues and hordes elsewhere in the airport.

'Professor Song is pleased with what you have achieved, Charles,' complimented Petter.

'Oh,' I responded bashfully, 'thank you.'

I intended to inform Petter that I had no alternative but to curtail my teaching programme and planned to spend time sightseeing around Beijing, but I never got round to it because I was uncertain of my contractual obligations. I explained that Professor Sang would invigilate my examination when things have settled down.

'You're well organised, Charles. I like that,' complimented Petter.

'Some of the students have gone to Beijing,' I said. 'They want to make sure their views are represented.'

'Yes, I know,' replied Petter nonchalantly.

A Soviet agent provocateur would know, wouldn't he? He was using my innocent students as his accomplices. At times, Petter appeared to be indifferent to what was happening, then at other times he seemed to know too much. It was possible that someone had told him about Hou and Wei, but he could have shown a little more concern. I didn't know what to think.

'Are you all right, Charles?' Petter asked. 'You look as if you have seen a ghost.'

'A surfeit of English breakfast,' I responded.

The truth was I hadn't seen a ghost, I had seen a spy, a Soviet agent.

He was sitting calmly in front of me filling his pipe with that ghastly stuff of his. I was sure there was a *No Smoking* sign just behind Petter, but noticed no one else was following that rule.

'So what are your plans, Charles?'

'On my way home, I plan to spend a few days in Beijing and have a look around.'

'Splendid, Charles,' said Petter. 'Who knows? We might bump into each other.'

I was about to suggest we exchanged hotel details, but then he stood up, shook hands, and strode off in the direction of the toilets. How were we going to meet? He obviously wasn't going to give me the details of where he was staying. There again, a Soviet agent wouldn't, would he?

When leaving the terminal, I found Mr Chou waiting with the car. He informed me that I was lucky because he had arranged a special sightseeing trip for me to visit the countryside, taking in the delights of rural achievements and—

'Not today, My Chou,' I replied. 'I am far too busy.'

As Professor Sang and I walked out of the main gate, there was a lot more student activity.

'Things have escalated and there are more marches planned today,' explained Professor Sang. 'Because of their inability to contain the students, our leaders were humiliated. By the time Gorbachev left for Moscow last Thursday, the students had disrupted his programme many times. The hunger strikers on Tiananmen Square totally upstaged the summit. Our leaders are very status-conscious and that caused an immense loss of face, particularly for Deng.'

'What about the other leaders?' I asked. 'Isn't there a political struggle going on?'

'Zhao Ziyang and Li Peng, both visited students on Tiananmen Square yesterday afternoon. Zhao told the students he had come too late, was sorry, and deserved their criticism.'

'So what happens now?' I was going to Beijing, so wanted to know.

'It doesn't look good. Yesterday evening it was heavily rumoured that the government will declare martial law in Beijing, and that prompted large numbers of Beijing residents to take to the streets. It is also rumoured that Zhao Ziyang has resigned as Party leader in protest against martial law. Last night, Li Peng gave a broadcast on television blaming conspirators behind the students for instigating the turmoil. He also called for serious measures to end the riots.'

When Professor Sang mentioned conspirators behind the students, I immediately thought of Petter, and he had just flown to Beijing to stir up further trouble.

'Have you any idea who these conspirators might be?' I asked. Professor Sang seemed to be knowledgeable on these matters, so no harm in asking.

'I don't suppose there are any specific conspirators,' he replied. 'Since last month, one thing has just led to another. When government leaders hesitated to take robust action, this encouraged other student groups and intellectuals to join in, and the whole protest movement has taken on its own momentum. The arrival of Gorbachev provided a good opportunity for the protesters to embarrass the government. The government could not risk taking firm action against the protestors with all the attention of the world press nearby. We have an impasse and it is difficult to know what will happen next.'

After considering that, it was possible for agitators, such as Petter and Chinese intellectuals, to stir up trouble. Chinese students were impressionable and easily influenced and often did things they otherwise would not do.

'You will be pleased to know that yesterday evening the students ended their hunger strike,' added Professor Sang.

That was good news.

We were wandering around a part of Jaliang I had never seen. It reminded me a little of Suzhou but without the canals. The houses had a more traditional feel about them.

'We call this area, China Town,' Professor Sang informed me.

That was it...

It looked how you imagined China to be.

We looked in some shops, and one sold those tall porcelain teacups with lids. I bought two, one for my wife, and the other for Professor Sang. I planned to give him it as a gift when I left, but I didn't tell him.

The narrow streets were quiet and shaded by sycamore and plane trees. The locals were sitting on chairs outside their houses or shops, gossiping about this and that. Some of the elderly men were playing a board game, possibly draughts. Being a foreigner, I drew a few glances and no doubt became a minor topic of conversation for a moment or so. 'Does he smell?' and, 'So it is true about their noses then,' and other such things.

Professor Sang was walking with a purpose, not fast, but we were going somewhere specific. The first place he took me to was a bookshop. There were rows and rows of paperback books. Although sold as new, they already looked worn. Professor Sang was looking for something. The shopkeeper went into the back and returned with three pristine hardback volumes, which he wrapped up in old newspaper and tied with string.

I bought two books of old Chinese paintings of traditional mountain scenes and buildings.

Professor Sang explained that Chinese painting had a long history and was one of the oldest artistic traditions in the world. Originally, paintings were ornamental, with patterns or designs, rather than depicting physical recognisable forms of people or scenes. Traditional painting techniques used a brush dipped in black or coloured ink, similar to calligraphy. They introduced oil painting to China about the same time as the start of the May Fourth Movement, in 1919, when students and intellectuals protested against the old warlord government.

'Wasn't the appreciation of art considered a bourgeois tendency?' I bantered jovially.

Professor Sang smiled. 'During the Cultural Revolution, art schools were closed, and the publication of art journals and art exhibitions were banned. A lot of art was destroyed during that time, but fortunately, much survived.'

'These look like scenes of the Yellow Mountains,' I commented casually while browsing one of my new purchases. 'The Welcome Pines are particularly attractive.'

I was looking at a series of landscapes, and recognised where I had seen them before. They were in miniature in the gardens of Suzhou, particularly one garden whose name I had forgotten.

Professor Sang just smiled.

We carried on a bit further and came to a walled pond, teeming with goldfish. In the middle of the pond, on stilts, was a wooden two-storey teahouse, with lacquered windows; it might have been old, but I wasn't sure. It had an intricate roof with those traditional upward-curving pointed eaves. On the curvy bits at the end of the eaves were a row of little ornamental pottery animals that looked like lions and dragons. Normally, a building like that would look quite plain without the roof, but not this. The wooden walls were painted dark red and turquoise. The dark red picked out the detail of the fretwork that lined the turquoise-coloured boarded walls. The windows were dark red, with turquoise curtains fluttering in the wind.

To get to the teahouse, we had to cross a narrow bridge, again made from detailed lacquered wood.

'It is time for afternoon tea,' said Professor Sang.

Inside the teahouse, we found a table, though I suspect some of the other guests had vacated it to make room for me.

'Foreigners and tourists never visit this place because buses and cars cannot get here,' explained Professor Sang.

The tea came in a small, reddish purple, clay teapot and was poured into small, clay teacups.

'The teapot is very old,' explained Professor Sang. 'It is made from a particular type of clay only found in the Yixing part of China.'

'It certainly looks well used.'

'They are never glazed. The pot absorbs the oils from the tea leaves and, over time, develops a glaze appearance, especially the inside.'

'The tea tastes good.'

'Yes, the tea here is special. The clay absorbs the flavour, smell, and colour of the tea. The flavour of the tea improves with the age of the teapot. A good teahouse, like this one, will only ever use a single flavour of tea to a specific teapot, so that the flavour of the tea is not spoilt. There are not many traditional places like this remaining.'

It was a splendid place.

Later that afternoon, the campus took on a festive atmosphere. Students were preparing for their demonstrations in an orderly and organised manner, which appeared out of place with their resentment towards the government, government leaders, and grievances in general.

I sat on the bench near the main entrance and watched the preparations. I did not want to be alone in the guesthouse, as I was the only guest remaining. All my companions had left and I felt quite abandoned, and I did not want to keep bothering Professor Sang. Mr Chou was about, but he was not what I considered fun!

'Hello, Yang,' I said, as he came across. 'You seem to have made a remarkable recovery. Surely you're not going on the protest march?'

'Oh, I will be all right,' replied Yang. 'My friends are with me.'

I then noticed Zhuang, the classroom monitor, who was arranging the green student banner between two bamboo poles. Zhuang waved and I waved back. I saw quite a few of my other students getting ready for the march, and we all waved. The students started chanting. What they were shouting, I didn't know, but I pretended to be the conductor.

All harmless fun...

'Perhaps you would like to join us, Professor Charles?' asked Yang.

Since I had nothing better to do, I agreed to accompany them for part of the journey into town. Professor Sang did say we needed to show our support, or words to that effect. I had in mind a quick visit to the Friendship Store.

'We will be honoured by your company,' remarked Zhuang.

'The honour is mine.'

When the march set forth, I joined Yang and Zhuang by the green banner. When passing Mr Chou, I informed him I had some business in town. Being polite, I asked if he would like to join me. He looked like he was going to have an apoplectic fit, and I took that to mean, no. I just wanted to buy him a beer.

The march into town was orderly, with a lot of chanting synchronised by cheerleaders using megaphones. As we went along, Jaliang residents joined in support, but only at the rear. Marshals kept the students together and maintained discipline. People were cheering from the sides of the road. Traffic was at a standstill, and someone said that taxi drivers were on strike. They used buses for ferrying demonstrators around. Some buses were flying banners and adorned with slogans on the sides. People greeted each other cheerfully and gave each other victory signs. It had the feeling of a public holiday and not a demonstration against the government.

The route of the protesters went past the China News Agency building, and I thought that would be a good place to leave the procession. I would find Harry's journalist friends. Harry had kept the business cards I lent him, all in the name of keeping good contacts, no doubt. I remembered their names were Luo and Xia.

I did not need to look far as most journalists were outside waiting for the protesters to arrive. Some joined the procession and others cheered. My two journalist friends gave a friendly wave and I went across to see them. I promised Yang and Zhuang I would catch up with them later.

'Professor Charles, what a surprise,' exclaimed Luo. 'We did not expect to see you again. What are you doing?'

'I am a little weary and in need of a drink,' I explained.

'Please come inside,' offered Xia. 'We are on duty and have to write the editorials. We are not sure what to do, follow the official party line, or report freely.'

The office had several desks and the biggest clutter I had ever seen. To one side were the usual armchairs for entertaining guests and official visitors, but again, these were haphazard and piled with old newspapers and magazines. In the corner were several plastic thermos flasks topped with boiling water. Luo cleared a chair for me and went to make some tea. They called Xia away and I was alone. Most of the newspapers and magazines scattered around were foreign, mostly in English.

Luo returned with our tea in jam jars and I felt accepted, a friend, and not just another foreign visitor.

'We get some of our world news from the foreign newspapers, but we are careful what we report,' commented Luo. 'I am pleased to see you are still supporting the protesters. You are the only foreigner in Jaliang doing so.'

'I just want to provide some moral support,' I said vaguely. I was certainly no hero. I did not really understand what the student grievances were, apart from the generalisations of wanting more freedom, and things like that.

'I am writing a general, background piece on the current unrest, and

Xia is covering today's protests. That's why he has been called away,' Luo informed me.

'The protests seem to have taken the government by surprise,' I observed.

'My informants tell me our leaders were warned months ago by the Public Security Bureau to expect trouble in May. Unfortunately, our leaders were in a heated power struggle. Because of that, they have been too divided and hesitant when making decisions. Deng is old and his power seems to be in decline. Zhao Ziyang, the Party leader, has been plotting against the conservative hardliners led by the premier, Li Peng.'

'So what happens now?'

'Who knows? The students believed the government would make concessions before the arrival of Gorbachev. The government speculated that the protests would dwindle, but they were wrong. With the hunger strike and the visit of Gorbachev, the protest movement has gained momentum and has put the government in a difficult position. Without help from the Beijing residents and workers, the students couldn't have persisted for so long.'

'What about the power struggle?'

'Zhao appears to have lost his struggle against the hardliner premier, Li Peng, who has mobilised the army and declared martial law in Beijing. Li said he was speaking for the government and the Party, indicating that he was now in command, but that is highly unlikely. Deng Xiaoping is behind the crackdown. Authority in the People's Republic resides in individuals, not in positions.'

'There's a lot happening in Beijing!' said Xia, who had just returned. 'Leaders have ordered troops to move into Beijing, but they are being stopped on the outskirts by sympathisers. The commander-in-chief of the crack thirty-eighth army refused orders to enter Beijing. Troops of the twenty-seventh army, north of the city, declined to enter the suburbs and promised not to return. It is incredible.'

'The leaders chose the wrong time to attempt to enforce martial law in Beijing,' observed Luo incredulously. 'It is the weekend. No one is working today, so people can quickly take to the streets. The army is unlikely to turn against the people.'

Someone shouted and called Luo away. I could see they were both busy and decided to leave them to it.

'Look, I am writing tomorrow's feature and it would be good if I could include you,' shouted Xia as I was leaving. '*Eminent foreign professor leads demonstrations* – that would make a good headline.'

I turned round to say that I did not think that would be a good idea, but he was gone.

I smiled.

I was getting the hang of the Chinese dry sense of humour.

After leaving the China News Agency, I made my way towards the Friendship Store. Sadly, because of the demonstrations, it was closed.

I ambled around the back streets, well away from the bustle and noise where the demonstrations were taking place. I found an empty bench shaded from the late afternoon sun by the broad leaves of a plane tree and sat down for a rest. After a few minutes, an elderly man came from a door behind me. He placed a small bamboo cage, containing a canary, on the step and after nodding politely, he sat on the bench next to me. We both enjoyed the late afternoon, changing into evening, listening to the occasional burst of song from the canary.

I watched some of the local children playing. Three small boys sat on the kerb opposite and, under cover of talking to each other, gave me the once over. They could have been three small boys from Pontefract, or anywhere. Two were wearing jeans and the third, in the middle, wore shorts. With their elbows on knees and trying to look casual, I could see quick glances in my direction. After a few minutes, they left, so I couldn't have been that interesting.

Some of the other residents brought out stools and chairs and sat outside to enjoy the cool evening, catch up with the gossip. I heard a radio playing Chinese pop-songs, but the music was not loud. It got dark quickly and the street took on an entirely different look, all shadows, and dim lights. There was faded red bunting hanging between some of the trees and over the odd doorway, lit by the lighting from the houses. I heard the chanting and clapping of the demonstrators in the distance, their noise travelling in the calmness of the early evening.

'*Shyay-shyay*,' I said to the elderly man when leaving. He looked at me in surprise, nodding as I left.

I slowly made my way back to the university. I could hear the noise of the protesters who, I assumed, were also making their way back, but I managed to keep ahead of their progress. On the side of the road were a few small traders selling dumplings, noodles, and other things. I managed a small feast for my supper from those traders who saw me as an easy target because I didn't haggle much over the price. When I arrived back at the university, it was dark. I returned to my bench, near the entrance, to wait for the return of the protesters. I had said I would see them later, and I didn't want to break my promise.

The noise of the protesters, as they approached the campus, seemed much louder than before. If I didn't know what it was, the noise would have been intimidating. When the students trooped through the main gate, some looked tired, but most retained the festive air of a holiday, a good day out. I walked towards the area where I saw the green banner and waved at Yang and Zhuang. They insisted I shook their hands and those of their friends nearby. They were jubilant. I declined Yang's offer to join his group for drinks in the dormitory. Drinking warm Chinese Fanta, in a cramped dorm with over-excited students, was not my idea of a Saturday night out.

Extract from:

THE PRESS
SAT 20 MAY 1989
Local correspondent, Peking

EARLIER TODAY, the Chinese government declared martial law in Peking after the start of a military crackdown in an effort to stop the continuous anti-government student protests. This partly confirms rumours that China's hardliners have gained the upper hand in its internal power struggled, further verified by the belief that Zhao Ziyang, the Communist Party leader, has offered his resignation.

Troops, when marching towards Tiananmen Square, were stopped in their tracks by the residents of Peking on the outskirts of the city. On Tiananmen Square, student leaders declared there would be no backing down from the demonstrations and they would fight on for victory. However, this signalled the end of the hunger strike over the last week, which had disrupted and humiliated the government during the visit of Gorbachev.

Chapter 31

After a late breakfast, I again sat on the bench near the main entrance. I had decided it was an excellent, strategic, nosey position. I saw all that was happening but at the same time kept a certain amount of privacy. That, I concluded, was why Professor Sang often chose that spot.

I was surprised to see students about. Quite a few waved at me, some came across to shake my hand, and others wanted photographs with me.

I decided to walk to the teahouse in China Town where Professor Sang had taken me the other day and quietly read a book. I managed to secure a small table in the corner with a window overlooking the pond. They provided me with a continual flow of tea and nice snacks.

The other guests saw I was busy reading, and apart from the odd stare, they left me alone.

Actually, I received quite a few stares!

Memorandum

(Telex message)

From   Chou Ke-giang
              Director of the Office of Foreign Affairs
              Jaliang Number 3 University

To   Deputy Chairman
              Office of Education Foreign Affairs
              Public Security Bureau
              Beijing

Date   21 May 1989

CONFIDENTIAL

DR CHARLES VINCENT

It has been a disastrous weekend.

On Saturday, Dr Vincent led the student activists on a successful protest into town. Once the march was under way and gaining support with the local residents, Vincent slipped away into the China News Agency to conduct a press conference with local journalists known to be sympathetic towards the protest movement. At the end of the demonstration, Vincent congratulated the protest leaders on their achievement.

Today, Vincent had another success. He has taken on a cult-status with students. The *Jaliang Daily*, which is the local newspaper, published a feature article headlined, '*Eminent foreign professor leads demonstrations*'. It shows a photograph of Vincent waving the unofficial student banner to the cheers of students and journalists around him.

I must warn you that special agent Vincent will soon arrive in Beijing and if he is half as successful there as he has been here, then you are in for some trouble.

From: **Deputy Chairman**
Office of Education Foreign Affairs
Public Security Bureau
Beijing
To: *Chou Ke-giang*
Director of the Office of Foreign Affairs
Jaliang Number 3 University
21 May 1989

Private note (by telex)

DISSIDENT VINCENT

The Public Security Bureau has noted your last two messages.

Since Jaliang is a long way from Beijing, none of Dr Vincent's activities is being reported by the press in Beijing or by the world media.

Unfortunately, the world media remains in Beijing, ignoring the fact that the Soviet leader has already returned to Moscow. The Public Security Bureau cannot be seen to be hostile towards an eminent academic, employed on a United Nations project, without positive and irrefutable proof of his clandestine activities against the government.

Once Vincent arrives in Beijing, his activities will be closely monitored. Knowing what he is really up to will help the Public Security Bureau identify some of the protest movement ringleaders.

Chapter 32

Monday, May 22, 1989

Mr Chou was waiting for me at breakfast but declined my offer for him to join me. Since it was my last day in Jaliang, he had made several appointments on my behalf as part of my leaving formalities.

'What appointments?' I asked.

'Do not worry, I will accompany you.'

'I already have appointments, and I am having lunch with friends.'

'I have made arrangements for you to visit a special pagoda,' Mr Chou pleaded. 'You like pagodas.'

Mr Chou was obviously not himself. His shirt was not its usual spotless white and needed a good iron. Possibly, he had had a falling out with his wife. I had noticed in the mornings, recently, especially at the weekends, he had been looking the worse for wear, probably because of late nights out with friends. No wonder his wife wasn't happy.

'I have seen enough pagodas,' I said. 'What appointments have you arranged this morning?'

I was to have a photograph with the university president, tea with the staff from the Office of Foreign Affairs, and then the senior librarian was going to give me a personal tour of the library facilities.

'I can manage that, Mr Chou.'

*T*he president of No 3 Jaliang University wore a formal blue Mao suit with his jacket unbuttoned, showing an open-neck white shirt. He sat with his legs crossed and one arm over the back of the chair, and since he was quite tall, he did so easily. You knew who was in charge. Others in the room were fussing around with tea, biscuits, and other things. A photographer was one of those being fussy as he kept taking pictures from all angles with his large camera. The president formally introduced himself through an interpreter. I took it to mean that he could not speak English, but I was wrong.

'*Nee hao*,' I said, 'my name is—'

'Oh, we all know who you are, Professor Vincent. Apparently you are quite a celebrity here,' interrupted the president in perfectly good English. He glanced at the coffee table where my tea was cooling, near the newspapers.

Why the interpreter?

Why all the flattery?

I took the hint and sipped my tea. Everyone had fine porcelain teacups. This wasn't the occasion for using jam jars.

'The students were marvellous,' I said. 'They did all I asked.'

'Evidently so,' replied the president casually.

Mr Chou, who was sitting politely at the other end of the coffee table, almost choked while drinking his tea.

The president must spend half his day exchanging small talk with visitors, and I felt sorry they had encumbered him with me for fifteen minutes. He did not touch his tea.

Through his interpreter, the president gave a short speech about the importance of academic exchanges and respecting other cultures. The interpreter was not as proficient in English as the president was, so I did not really follow what he said. After his speech, the president handed me a tourist guide of Jaliang and a copy of a Number 3 University's prospectus – both in Chinese.

I responded in my usual haphazard, mumbling fashion. In my speech, I emphasised the importance of cultural mobility, how honoured I was to have had the opportunity to influence Chinese students in what little way I could, and how I hoped to do great things in Beijing. I said I would be grateful for any useful contacts they had.

I got some peculiar looks and again poor Mr Chou almost choked while drinking his tea.

Forewarned by Mr Chou that an exchange of gifts was expected, I presented the president with a copy of the Pontefract Polytechnic's student prospectus and hoped that he did not look inside. He did.

The first few pages of the prospectus were aimed at gaining the attention of prospective British students escaping from home for the first time. The emphasis was, therefore, on students having a good time in the Pontefract clubs and pointing out the fact, in the most unsubtle way, that the beer in the students' union bar was exceedingly cheap.

Everyone gathered around the president, pointing at pictures, laughing, and generally having fun. I just sat po-faced with a weak smile, nodding my head at anyone who happened to glance in my direction.

One picture was getting particular attention, the one in the union bar showing the annual pontefract cake eating competition. They gave students a bag of pontefract cakes to eat followed by a free pint of beer. The more pontefract cakes you ate, then the more free beer you got. The one who ate and drank the most was the winner. A confectionary manufacturer, with a factory nearby, sponsored the competition.

'So it is true then,' stated the president with a mischievous look on his face. 'You are a professor of pontefract cakes.'

'Ha, ha…ha,' I responded, still attempting a weak smile.

I could do without that Chinese wit.

*T*ea at Mr Chou's was a desperate affair, but I got through it.

*I*nitially, I was not at all interested in the tour of the library. As it happened, I found it fascinating.

While there was a central library, each faculty had a mini-library, which specialised in books generic to its academic area of interest. The faculties funded their mini-libraries and administered them in their own way. All libraries kept the same opening hours, nine to twelve, and one-thirty to five, the same times as all classes and lectures.

One faculty decided not to use a conventional book index or catalogue but had its own peculiar method. The exterior of the mini-library was like a shop-display window where all the book spines, showing title and author, were visible from outside the library. Students browse all titles from outside and if any caught their eye, they would write down the details, enter the library, and make their request. The beauty of that, a proud librarian informed me, was the student knew immediately their requested book was available, as they had just seen it. More importantly, it ensured students were not cluttering up the inside of the library.

I made a mental note to inform the head librarian back at the poly of that ingenious system. I was sure she would see its potential.

Lunch was informal and held in one of the staff dining rooms. Professor Sang acted as host on behalf of Professor Song, who unfortunately had another lunchtime engagement, but I was to see him later that afternoon. When Professor Sang informed Mr Chou he was not invited, I felt sorry for him. He looked as if he were going to cry.

Yang and Zhuang, who were representing the students, shook my hand and asked if they could have a photograph with me. Several of the photographic poses involved Yang and Zhuang holding up a newspaper. They said it had an article written by one of Harry's journalist friends, but it was all in Chinese. Some of the staff also wanted photographs taken with me. I had noticed the Chinese interest in photography before, especially in the parks and other beauty spots, so I was not surprised. Professor Sang watched with mild amusement.

Lunch was wholesome and plentiful.

Similar to the practice in the student refectory, anything uneaten they carefully spat onto the plastic tablecloth in a neat pile next to the bowl. The students did something similar, but not so carefully. I realised why they did that. For lunch, we had several courses but used the same bowl. If the bones, gristly bits, fish heads, and what-have-you were left in the bowl, then there would be no room for the next course. In any case, who would want fish heads mixed up with the shredded beef?

We decided to skip the speeches as we were among friends and just enjoyed the beer.

I left lunch shouting, 'Beijing here I come,' with my right fist held high. Although I did not deserve the cheers and clapping that followed, nonetheless, I blushed.

When I arrived at Professor Song's office, he politely dismissed Mr Chou stating we had some academic matters to discuss, which were not of his concern. Mr Chou just stood looking astonished as the office door closed, with him on the other side.

I looked around to see if I could get any clues as to what he and Petter might have been up to – none.

'I appreciate your positive contribution to the activities and well-being of the students,' remarked Professor Song.

He must have been referring to my state-of-the-art teaching

techniques and management games, which seemed very popular.

'Thank you.'

'You teach in the school of business at Pontefract, I believe,' said Professor Song.

'Yes.'

'That is an inopportune title as it does not translate very well into Chinese. *School* has connotations with schoolchildren, not with a university. The term *business* represents very small businesses such as shops, restaurants, and artisans. If asked, I would suggest you say you teach in a faculty of management, as that is far more impressive. People will understand what you do.'

'Thank you.' At least that clarified why I got odd looks when I gave details of what I did back in Pontefract.

'I like my academic visitors to reflect on their experiences,' said Professor Song. 'You must have some interesting views to share.'

What I had in mind to say, with the exception of Professor Sang, was most conversations I had in China were essentially one-way. I was the one being questioned, interrogated, and queried for any information, be it academic, political, social, or whatever. They sifted that information, any useful bits noted, and the rest discarded. At least, that was my impression.

On the one hand, I realised I was the so-called eminent professor from the West cordially invited to provide them with what few titbits of useful information I had. On the other hand, I normally found an exchange of ideas more fulfilling, where both parties bartered information and experiences, putting things into context. They might gain and so might I; that was my wish.

It appeared my Chinese hosts already had a context, and they were checking if they could add anything useful. My students were an exception because they had been, at times, quite candid. Perhaps I lacked the intellectual capacity to recognise or absorb anything useful that came my way.

While that might have been an interesting conversation, I kept quiet.

'I had a very interesting tour of the library facilities this morning,' I said in what I hoped was a reflective manner. 'Your students use library facilities far less than students back in Britain.'

What I wanted to say was in Jaliang students could never use the library facilities, because they were only open when classes were taking place. Nevertheless, I didn't want to appear rude.

'That is an interesting observation,' replied Professor Song. 'I have noticed that myself and consequently instigated an audit of the student usage of library facilities.'

I was pleased with myself, having found a common topic to reflect upon with Professor Song. Perhaps I might have some influence on the future teaching techniques in China.

'I have decided to take remedial action to resolve this problem,' he continued. 'I shall reduce my faculty library expenditure. Why waste money on facilities that are never used?'

I was stunned.

'In any case,' concluded Professor Song, 'we are all professors and we know what our students need to know, so we tell them in classes. So what do they need books for?'

I mulled over that proposition but couldn't find fault with it!

When I left, Mr Chou was still standing where he was before, he hadn't moved. I showed him the bronze medallion Professor Song had given me, which was similar to the one Harry received. It was well made and fitted snugly in a silk presentation box. Unfortunately, all I could give in return was another copy of the poly student prospectus.

'Haven't you got a home to go to?' I said to Mr Chou.

He looked hurt, and I regretted my insensitive comment because of my suspicion he might be having problems with his marriage.

As it was late afternoon, I decided it was time to go and pack.

*L*ater that evening, I met Professor Sang by the bench, near the main entrance, to thank him for all his help and to say farewell. I suggested we met at the bench, as I had grown attached to that vantage position. We both sat and enjoyed the cool evening and admired the stars in the cloudless sky. It had been a humid and stuffy sort of day.

'It's been much quieter today,' I commented casually.

Students were still bustling about, but with none of the chanting or waving of banners as we had witnessed over the past few days.

'It must be difficult for students to keep up their momentum,' he commented. 'They need encouragement and inspiration. They have had that obviously but all the attention is focused on Beijing.'

'Are there any further developments in Beijing?' I asked.

'There are rumours circulating about everything, so it is difficult to know what is really going on. On television yesterday evening, the martial law enforcement authorities, and other leaders, spoke in conciliatory terms, but they also stressed the importance of maintaining law and order. From what I can gather, the army has not entered Beijing. I believe there are still lots of protesters about, particularly around Tiananmen Square, but I am not sure they can keep it up for much longer.'

That sounded like good news. Without sounding too cynical, I wanted to see as many of the sights in and around Beijing as I could without too much disruption.

I presented Professor Sang with his gift of a porcelain cup to replace the jam jar he normally used in his office. I had not wrapped his gift. It appeared to be the Chinese habit of not opening gifts in front of guests but they took them away and opened them in private. I had considered why they did that. I concluded that the reason was not to cause embarrassment if the gift was of poor quality or the recipient did not like what they just received. I wanted to see Professor Sang smile at my choice of gift for him. In any case, we were friends and it was an informal occasion, after all.

'It is for you to use and not for guests,' I explained.

'It is normal for guests to be offered the best cup,' he replied, 'but I will try and break with tradition and use it myself.'

The cup I had chosen, while a nice example of porcelain, was not extravagant, and would not cause Professor Sang too much embarrassment to use.

Professor Sang then presented me with a large parcel wrapped in an old newspaper, tied with string.

'Please open it,' he said.

I realised I had seen the parcel before; it was in the bookshop in China Town. I untied the string and saw the three volumes Professor Sang had bought the other day. They were hard-back with crisp clean covers, printed in English, and called, *A Dream of Red Mansions*.

'This is a classical Chinese novel written in the mid-eighteenth century during the Ching dynasty. The novel is the product of class contradictions and struggle in that period of Chinese feudalism. It is about political struggle – a political-historical novel. If I promise to use my porcelain cup, then you must promise to read all three volumes.'

We made our pact.

We shook hands and Professor Sang strode off into the darkness without looking back. I felt sad and, for the first time, thought about why the Chinese always say farewell so abruptly. I always believed the Chinese showed no emotion; but perhaps they did, not wanting others to see it. At least, I hoped so.

Chapter 33

Tuesday, May 23, 1989

Mr Chou insisted he accompanied me to the airport for my early morning flight. After checking in, I followed Petter's example and said I was going to the first class lounge.

'Good idea.' Mr Chou replied. 'I will accompany you.'

That didn't work then!

We exchanged small talk. I had a coffee in a cardboard cup. Mr Chou had a cup of tea and some famous Great Wall marble cake.

'What hotel are you staying at in Beijing?' enquired Mr Chou.

'I'm not sure to be honest,' I replied.

It was written on a scrap of paper in one of my pockets, but I didn't want to search for it then. I had decided that once on the flight, I would get myself organised.

I had left the university in a rush. A large group of students came to the guesthouse and gave me a send-off. I recognised some as my students and others from the student protests, the rest I did not know. That touched me. I insisted Mr Chou joined me for a photograph with the students. Initially, he was a little shy about it, but I would not take, 'No,' for an answer.

When they called my flight, Mr Chou presented me with an unwieldy, official Number 3 University gift, similar to what Petter received when he left.

From its shape, I recognised what it was.

When I had tea in Mr Chou's office the day before, I noticed, in the corner, a row of identical large ornaments. They were in some kind of glass display case about two feet in diameter and three inches thick. With glass front and back, held in place by a highly lacquered black surround, they looked very fragile. Inside the glass case was an extremely fine embroidered picture, very delicately done and stretched to fit the casing. I had seen some fine examples of Chinese embroidery in the Friendship Store, when shopping with Petter. These had traditional Chinese themes, exquisite landscapes, scenes of lakes, and so forth. Those in Mr Chou's office were all identical pictures of a fluffy kitten amusing itself with a ball of wool, all in garish colours.

I presented Mr Chou with my last copy of the poly student prospectus. I said to look at the photographs because everyone else seemed to find them amusing.

Mr Chou accompanied me onto the aircraft thus robbing me of any opportunity of following Petter's example of finding the nearest rubbish bin to dispose of my unwanted gift.

What I found confusing where I sat in the front of the aircraft, in first class, was it looked identical to that in the rear, economy class. I saw one or two other passengers missing seat belts but the cabin crew took no notice. At least the air-conditioning was working. As I was feeling a bit chilly, I put my pullover on.

And another thing, it was definitely a smoking only flight.

Once airborne they served us a drink, a little carton of orange juice. In first class, we had a plastic cup to drink our orange, but those in the rear, in economy, had a straw. I would have preferred a straw, because when squirting the orange juice into the plastic cup through the little hole meant for a straw, it made an awful mess.

About halfway through the flight they gave us all a cardboard box, which contained lunch.

Lunch was a cheese roll, a large slab of pink and green cake, a packet of crackers, an apple, a chocolate bar, a toothpick, a novelty toy, and another carton of orange juice. I could see I was getting the hang of China because I had automatically kept my plastic cup, which was just as well because I never received another one. My fellow passengers were pleased with their lunch boxes. Instead of eating them straight away, most kept them to take away, probably as souvenirs for their families.

The children, as you would expect, wanted to eat straight away and not wait, and that was causing quite a disturbance. Since I had recently enjoyed what I hoped to be my last English breakfast, I offered my lunch box to a woman with a troublesome child. At first, she declined my offer, more out of politeness because I was a foreigner, but she did not need much persuasion. To my surprise, she did not give it to her child, but added it to her souvenir collection. At least the child became less troublesome – probably the fright of a big-nosed foreigner speaking to its mother did the trick!

My act of kindness, if you could call it that, sparked off conversations around me, similar to when I had travelled hard seat to Suzhou. Two rows behind me was a fellow foreigner, who I had noticed when boarding because he wore a pale pink shirt like me.

With the light banter going on, the other foreigner looked to see what all the fuss was about and on seeing me, nodded in recognition. Since I wanted to stretch my legs a little, I went to exchange gossip with him. Apparently, he was on his way home and had a connecting flight in Beijing. He was a little annoyed with the student protests because he had not been able to buy all his presents for his family, particularly his grandmother, who always had expectations when he returned from his trips abroad. He was hoping to find something in the duty free shops at Beijing airport, but he reliably informed me that things there were hideously expensive compared to what you pay in the streets.

I told him I had the answer, my official Number 3 University gift, for which he was grateful.

When the fasten seat belts sign came on for landing, the most extraordinary thing happened. The flight was almost full, but there were a few seats not in use. Passengers began hopping between seats to be near the exit doors. As a seat became vacant, then another passenger would take possession. The cabin crew made a token effort to stop it but appeared to be merely going through the motions. We landed with a few well-rehearsed bumps and rapturous applause from all passengers, including myself. I had to admit, I was pleased to be on *terra firma* once more. As the aircraft slowed down and began to leave the runway, passengers queued, with their hand luggage, by the exit doors, accompanied by half-hearted shouting from the cabin crew.

'Welcome to Beijing,' the announcement said.

When the doors opened, there was a free for all, a mad rush to escape. I sat and waited until the aircraft was nearly empty before moving, unlike my fellow foreigner who joined in the rush from the outset, clutching his cumbersome official Number 3 University gift. I just hoped it didn't break because I forgot to mention it was fragile.

On leaving the aircraft, things were not very organised at the domestic terminal. There was no conveyor belt for the luggage, which they just dumped at the end of the hall. Since several internal flights had just landed, the luggage hall, security, and customs were in disarray.

Upon retrieving my luggage, I followed a rowdy group of men, who seemed to know the ropes. I ended up in the queue for Chinese nationals. The woman who inspected my passport realised my mistake, but she saw I had a valid visa and reluctantly let me through. She must have supposed I was with the rowdies because they gave her a hard time when she was inspecting my passport. They seemed pleased I was able to buck the system.

One of the rowdies spoke English and asked me where I was going. I gave the name of my hotel but no one recognised it. They assumed it must be somewhere near the centre because most foreigners seem to stay around there. They were being picked up by a bus and kindly offered me a lift, which was as well, because the queue for taxis, I could see, looked chaotic. Mr Chou had informed me that the best thing to do, upon arrival at the domestic terminal, was to walk to the international terminal where foreigners could get taxis more easily – and cost more, no doubt. The bus ride was fine.

They dropped me outside a large hotel for foreigners, which was not where I was staying. I went inside and ordered a taxi to take me to my own hotel, which wasn't far away. I sat down in a comfortable easy chair in the spacious foyer, drank chilled bottled water from a crystal glass, and gazed around me. It then struck me what was puzzling; I was no longer in China. It could have been a hotel anywhere, modern, plush, and impersonal. Apart from the staff, I saw only foreigners.

Ignoring the excessive amount of cigarette burns, my hotel had a comfortable, dated feel about it. The foyer still had the clean lines of art deco architecture despite the poor attempts at modernisation. The arches and high ceilings in the foyer lacked the elegant chandeliers of bygone years, and the black-and-white tiled floor had seen better days. Surprisingly, the mahogany staircase leading from the foyer had remained intact. There were large, battered, brass ashtrays on wooden pedestals, and spittoons in the corners, all well used by the look of them. The other hotel guests were Asian executives in dark suits and black shoes.

I tried, without success, to get some tourist information at reception. They gave me directions to the hotel shop. The shop didn't have much tourist information but they managed to find me a Beijing bus map, in Chinese. The kindly assistant annotated the map, in English, with the main landmarks and the numbers of the main bus routes. Apparently, my hotel was neither in the town centre nor on the outskirts. It was somewhere in between, near the main road going towards the airport. The town centre was a short bus ride away. He also gave me a tourist leaflet, in English, about Tiananmen Square, which included some of the basic dimensions, names of buildings and surrounding roads.

I phoned Tammy. She still wanted to show me around Beijing and would be free at the weekend. Leigh, despite being busy with her wedding preparations, would also accompany us.

I said I had about ten days before my return flight home.

Tammy had an excellent idea. A friend of her cousin, whose name was Sam, worked in the China Travel Service and was responsible for Japanese tourists participating in side trips from Beijing. It took me a few minutes to work out that side trips were a local name for tours or excursions. Would I be interested? I was indeed.

Sam was responsible for the booking arrangements to attractions nearby, mainly by train or bus. I quickly learnt that *nearby* was a relative term because, since China was a large country, travelling nearby could be a long journey. Interestingly, Sam offered me a three-day side trip to Qufu, the hometown of Confucius, leaving by train in the morning. How could I resist.

I was to pay the going local rate, give Sam an under the counter commission, and we had a deal. Because of the recent protests and unrest, quite a large number of the Japanese had cancelled their once-in-a-lifetime trip to China, so there was plenty of availability. I was to be an honorary Japanese citizen for a few days. All I had to do was keep quiet about our little arrangement.

Harry was right.

You did need contacts.

*D*espite Tammy wanting to show me around, I could not resist a short bus ride into the town centre, which happened to be Tiananmen Square.

The bus map, with its annotations, was excellent. I pointed to my destination on the map to anyone about, allowed time for him or her to scrutinise the map, and then he or she pointed me in the right direction. With a similar approach on the bus and a few Renminbi in my pocket, I was fully mobile.

I left the bus just before it arrived at Tiananmen Square and walked the remaining hundred yards or so. I walked past a bicycle park with hundreds of bikes in disorderly rows. Nevertheless, an attendant issued tickets and each ticket carefully examined before retrieving your bike.

I stopped at a corner of Tiananmen Square and studied my leaflet.

From where I stood, the Square was across the road, Chang'an Avenue. The avenue was empty of traffic and was at least eight lanes wide. I walked a little further and saw an underpass, which rose on the Square itself. To my right was Tiananmen Gate, the entrance to the Forbidden City. I recognised that because hanging above the Gate was the large portrait of Mao. I walked a few yards more and turned facing the Square. I faced south and saw the Square across the wide avenue, with Mao's portrait immediately behind me.

The Square was China's symbolic centre of power and had played a lively role in Chinese communist history.

On the Square, I saw a tall flagpole flying the national flag of the People's Republic, red with a large yellow five-pointed star and four smaller stars arranged in a vertical arc towards the middle of the flag. The flag was unveiled for the very first time on October 1, 1949, where, from the platform above the Gate, Mao had formally announced the founding of the People's Republic of China. From there, he had addressed the crowd on important occasions.

Even after death, Mao was larger than life, gazing over the Square.

Ignoring the happenings on Tiananmen Square, it looked vast and bland, with wide avenues on all sides. My tourist leaflet explained that the Square was over one hundred acres in size and could easily hold a million, although I could not visualise so many people together.

On further study of my leaflet, I ascertained to the west of the Square from where I looked was the Great Hall of the People with all its huge columns where all the upheaval had taken place during the recent visit of Gorbachev. To the east of the Square was the Museum of Chinese People's Revolution. At the far end of the Square, despite being a long way from where I stood, Mao's Mausoleum dominated the skyline again with great columns holding up its flat roof. In the middle of the Square, I saw the Monument of the People's Heroes where there was quite a lot of activity.

The flagpole, Monument, and Mausoleum were more or less in line down the middle of the Square. About fifty yards on each side of that line, I saw a row of impressive lamp posts, holding up clusters of round white shades; some held large loudspeakers, for crowd control and special announcements. In the distance was a line of small flagpoles across the Square in front of the Monument, but it was too far to make out the detail.

The Square had the appearance of a shantytown common on the outskirts of many cities around the world. There were temporary shelters between the tall flagpole and the Monument, with flags and banners of all colours and shapes draped everywhere. The Square wasn't busy. People were sitting on the steps of the Great Hall of the People under the watchful eyes of police officers.

There were many buses parked haphazardly around the Square, but these weren't for tourists.

I studied those on the Square but I couldn't make out who were students, peasants, workers, intellectuals, journalists, or tourists. Surprisingly, white and light-coloured shirts were prominent, which was hardly sensible for a protest. The whole place had a festive atmosphere, but not quite. While I did not sense antagonism, I knew things could change quite quickly in China.

I heard loudspeakers blaring around the Square. There appeared to be two separate systems competing with each other. At irregular intervals, there was shouting and chanting from those on the Square, but the volume was lost because of the vast space.

I turned, facing north, to view the portrait of Mao, which I considered a bit garish. If Mao were alive, standing on his rostrum surveying the Square, what would he have thought? Would he have recognised all the elements of a struggle with which he was so familiar?

Below the portrait of Mao, around Tiananmen Gate, there was quite a bustle of people. Many were tourists, but not foreigners. People were trying to get photographs so they could include the gate, Mao's portrait, and their friends in the same frame. Having your photograph taken there, I surmised, must be as good as it gets for the wistful communist. Some of the crowd were wearing badges of Mao, miniatures of the portrait above. Was that nostalgia for the days of Mao? Others were walking past with a purpose, with plastic briefcases, officials between buildings, perhaps.

I was about to cross the avenue onto the Square to investigate further, but disturbances near the gate with lots of pushing and shouting distracted me. At first, I couldn't see what the commotion was about, but then I saw that the portrait of Mao had been defaced with paint or something. I saw three dribbling marks disfiguring the face of Mao, one on the left eyebrow, another high on the right forehead just below the hairline, and the last on the left side of his neck. As things began to look ugly, I decided to leave. Clouds were building up overhead and the sky was turning a dark and ominous yellow. It looked like bad weather.

That evening, as I walked around the streets near the hotel, I couldn't get a feel of the place. The main roads were wide and apart from my hotel, buildings were low. Beijing being the capital, I had expected to see many shops, but I couldn't see any. I saw blocks of residential flats, concrete and surrounded with green grass, functional, rudimentary, but not too unpleasant.

I went back to the hotel bar and enjoyed a couple of beers with a Chinese Singaporean businessman and two Dutch postgraduate students on their way home from Shanghai.

The Singaporean informed me he was there to negotiate a joint-venture agreement with the Chinese. Joint-ventures agreements had built all the decent, new hotels, he informed me. His negotiations with the Chinese were going very slowly. They wanted hard currency and technical expertise, but were reticent to talk about marketing, exports, and profit.

The two Dutch postgraduate students said they had just completed an Erasmus funded six-month study trip in Shanghai to investigate

Chinese transport systems. They had chosen the proposed Shanghai underground system as their topic.

Apparently, the transport system in Shanghai was congested, and that was before taking all the new development and planned growth into account. The solution, as proposed by the Shanghai authorities, was the new underground network.

The two Dutch postgraduates had undertaken a demographic survey of where the local population lived and the position of the existing and proposed new industrial zones where people would work, taking into account shopping areas etcetera. They could find no clear correlation between the findings of the demographic survey and the proposed routes for the underground network. They were baffled. It took them some time to work out that at the extremities of the proposed underground routes were where the cadre and elite had their compounds, particularly middle-ranking and senior officials. The proposed underground system, if completed under the present plans, though useful, would not resolve the congestion. They admitted that the cadre and elite would enjoy a quick and comfortable journey without the crowds.

'That's China,' they said.

From: **Deputy Chairman**
Office of Education Foreign Affairs
Public Security Bureau
Beijing
To: **Assistant to Chairman**
Public Security Bureau (*PSB* Beijing)
23 May 1989

Internal memorandum

Subject: DISSIDENT VINCENT

I must inform you of the presence of a British provocateur in Beijing.

Until now, the provocateur has been undercover, supposedly teaching at a provincial university in Jaliang. He is in possession of a blue United Nations Certificate that extends to him certain privileges and immunities, so I have had to act with caution. Since Jaliang is well away from Beijing and the interest of the media, I kept myself updated on the situation but took no further action. Several incidences have now prompted me to review my initial assessment of the activities of the British academic.

Firstly, a feature article in the Jaliang Daily published by the China News Agency openly described the activities of the British academic but without naming him. Luckily, they printed a photograph of the academic in the Jaliang Daily, so we were able to identify him. The Jaliang Daily insinuated that the academic has been involved in clandestine activities for several weeks, and he is now a local cult figure.

Secondly, the academic is now in Beijing. My initial plan was to closely monitor his activities and observe whom he meets. I had received specific details of the academic boarding an internal flight from Jaliang to Beijing. I had instructed the security officials at the airport in Beijing not to apprehend the academic but to closely monitor and follow him.

The security officials at the airport mistook another foreigner to be the academic. They claimed that the unsuspecting foreigner was wearing a pink shirt, as briefed, and carrying a large gift given to the academic minutes before boarding. What gave credence to the foreigner being the British academic was

214

that, immediately upon disembarking, he dumped the gift into the nearest rubbish bin. They clearly heard broken glass. As you appreciate, this practice is common among ungrateful foreign guests.

Clearly, the academic is not what he claims to be. He is a well-trained provocateur who managed to give the PSB the slip, and he has now gone undercover. I am now frantically searching all hotels in Beijing frequented by foreigners to find the so-called academic.

Lastly, on another issue, my informants in Jaliang tell me that the director of the Office of Foreign Affairs at the provincial university in Jaliang may well be an accomplice of the British academic. They were photographed together, arm-in-arm with student ringleaders only yesterday. In addition, they had cosy drinks, in private, on several occasions. <u>I will deal with that matter later</u>.

I will keep you fully informed on any further developments.

Chapter 34

Wednesday, May 24, 1989

Sam neglected to mention that the train journey to Qufu was over eight hours. Luckily, we travelled in soft seats. An officious woman who insisted we called her by her English name, Ann Kong, escorted us. She was pleasant enough, so long as we did things her way. That was fine for my fellow Japanese travellers because they liked things organised and orderly. I was nothing but a continual irritation for Ann. For a start, I couldn't speak Japanese, and her English was rudimentary. For no reason other than to be obstinate, I refused to call her Ann and addressed her as, Miss Kong.

Because of our very early start, we had breakfast in the restaurant car after about an hour travelling. Ann took us to our reserved tables, and preferably to sitting with a group of elderly Japanese, I shared a table with a man wearing a smart tailored, navy, Mao suit, a senior official of some sort. I could see that Ann was going to give me a hard time for sitting at the wrong table, but when she saw my breakfast companion, she thought otherwise. One of the stewards immediately served me with breakfast from one of the other tables laid out for us before we arrived. I assumed it was a Chinese version of a Japanese breakfast, and, whatever it was, it was cold. The tea was also cold.

'*Nee how*,' I said politely to my breakfast companion.

'Would you prefer fried eggs on toast?' asked my breakfast companion, in faultless English, who must have recognised the resigned look on my face.

'Is that possible?' I replied dubiously.

If you were a senior Chinese official, a member of the elite, then anything was possible. He called over one of the stewards and gave a few brief instructions and within minutes, I had a plate of hot fried eggs on buttered, hot toast, and hot coffee. Contacts!

'Where are you going?' I asked.

'Tianjin. It is an interesting place with a colourful history.'

'Why is that?'

'Mainly because foreign invaders had occupied Tianjin for the past hundred years or so, until the communists took over in 1949.'

'Who were the foreign invaders?'

My companion thought about that before giving me his considered reply. 'It is a long list and includes the British, French, Russians, Germans, Belgians, Austro-Hungarians, Italians, Americans, and the Japanese. The area also suffered during the Second Opium War, the Boxer Rebellion, and the Second Sino-Japanese War.'

'Oh, those foreign invaders...'

'The *Tianjin Church Incident* was a curious event,' he continued. 'In 1870, a church, built by the French, was implicated in the kidnapping, neglect, death, and improper burial of Chinese children. The local population also accused the nuns of bottling children's eyes. Furious protesters burnt down the church and the nearby French consulate.'

'The French do eat strange things,' I added.

'There was a misunderstanding over some jars of pickled onions.'

I laughed...

'After the Japanese occupation ended in 1945, Tianjin became a base for the American forces. There was a spate of rapes by American soldiers, and that triggered demonstrations by thousands of students in early 1947. The American troops pulled out of Tianjin later that year.'

'Did the foreigners leave anything positive?' I asked.

'Architecturally there is an influence. There are thousands of buildings and villas built by the foreigners, which provide an exotic beauty to Tianjin.'

'Is that a positive influence?'

'I live in one of those villas,' my breakfast companion replied, with a twinkle in his eyes. 'Where are you travelling to?'

'Qufu,' I replied.

'Kong Fu Zi, of course,' he said.

I was going to ask what he meant by that strange remark, but we arrived at Tianjin where he left the train. I liked his stories.

Chapter 35

Friday, May 26, 1989

The past two days had been a pleasant and peaceful break from Mr Chou and the misfortune of having to live up to the reputation of, supposedly, being an eminent, foreign professor.

I soon learnt that Confucius was the Latin rendering of his Chinese name, Kong Fu Zi, by the Jesuits in the sixteenth century. Kong Fu Zi literally means Master Kong.

Qufu was a small rural town dominated by the history of the Kong family. One fifth of the Qufu residents had the surname Kong and all were, allegedly, descendants of the sage himself, including, I assumed, our tour guide, Miss Kong. After our initial familiarisation tour of Qufu, I made a pact with Miss Kong. If she left me alone, I would leave her alone to look after the others, the elderly Japanese.

Qufu had three official attractions, although I disagreed; it also had another. The first attraction was the Confucian Temple, the largest in the world. It actually took up about twenty per cent of the town itself and was one of the largest architectural complexes in China, comparable with the Forbidden City, in Beijing. The next attraction was the Kong Family Mansion. It was another huge complex where the descendants of Confucius lived in noble splendour. I felt a little sorry for Confucius himself, who was an orphan and grew up in poverty.

The Confucian Forest, or Kong Family cemetery, the last official attraction, I found, was wild, wooded, and atmospheric. To enter, we had to go through several gates and the place was immense, nearly five hundred acres in size. In the middle was the tomb of Confucius, surrounded by his descendants buried under domes of earth and thousands of upright engraved stone slabs. There were statues of goats, tigers, and horses among the unkempt grounds.

While the official attractions were nice, what I found most pleasing was that there were no high buildings. I discovered that the local authorities did not permit buildings to exceed the height of the main building of the Confucian Temple. It made Qufu a pleasing place to stroll around, particularly as parts of the Confucian Temple or Mansion were never far away.

I managed to hire a bicycle and toured Qufu at leisure.

In conversation with one old man who wanted to practise his English, I learnt that Qufu didn't suffer too badly during the Cultural Revolution. Realising the importance of Confucius, the residents of Qufu took to the streets and built barricades to prevent advancing zealous Red Guards destroying the city's heritage.

If I were a Kong, I would have taken to the streets and helped build the barricades.

Extract from:

THE PRESS
FRI 26 MAY 1989
Local correspondent, Peking

STUDENT LEADERS on Tiananmen Square are running out of ideas to motivate other students, their main demand being to remove the prime minister, Li Peng, from power. But to leave the Square would be to admit defeat. Earlier skilful organisation by the students is turning into chaos, where the unofficial union has virtually disappeared. Disheartened students are returning to campus, criticising their leaders for their continuous absence from the Square. They believe that the political situation is changing and that some of their leaders have gone into hiding.

Determined students are remaining on Tiananmen Square, having established their Command Headquarters in improvised tents around the Monument to the People's Heroes, with accounting, propaganda, and communication departments.

Chapter 36

Saturday, May 27, 1989

After a very early start, I arrived back at my hotel in Beijing around lunchtime. After unpacking, I had a quick snack before meeting Tammy that afternoon, under the portrait of Mao.

By chance, in the hotel foyer, I saw my Singaporean drinking acquaintance I had met a few days earlier.

'Were your negotiations successful?' I asked.

'Eventually,' he replied. 'They wanted to know what's in it for them. I tried to explain about the new employment opportunities, technology transfer, the impact of earning hard currency, the multiplier effect on the local economy, the usual, but they looked at me as if I were mad. No, they said, what's in it for *them*? I should have realised earlier, it would have saved a lot of time and frustration.'

I arrived early at Tiananmen Gate and saw that Mao's portrait was no longer defaced. There had been a good clean-up job, or they had changed the portrait.

I looked around and little had changed since Tuesday, except most of the buses had gone. There were fewer people around and things were quieter. The wide avenue that separated Tiananmen Gate from the Square was slightly busier, mainly with bicycles. People were still posing for their photographs under the portrait of Mao, much as before.

I decided to use the underpass and crossed over onto Tiananmen Square. On the stairs leading from the underpass to the Square, I saw posters and slogans pasted to the walls, eagerly read by those passing. It was Saturday, the weekend, and a good day for seeing the sights.

Others, like me, just ambled around the Square, taking photographs, and generally seeing what was going on, which wasn't much. Some were pushing their bicycles, having a good look around.

Students were just getting on with their tasks and chores, whatever they were. Some, when they saw me, grinned and gave me the victory sign with two fingers.

I gazed at some of the temporary shelters, made from bamboo poles and plastic sheeting, at the end of the Square nearest Tiananmen Gate. Other makeshift tents made from a dark brown material looked more robust than the plastic. Waving in the slight breeze were flags and banners, mostly tattered, some red, others white, printed with yellow or black slogans, all leaning at lopsided angles above the shelters. I also saw large multi-coloured beach umbrellas made into temporary homes, which looked out of place among the makeshift tents. There was a pile of folded blankets placed on plastic sheeting so not to get dirty. They probably handed these out in the evening for those sleeping on the Square, but I was guessing. There were many large, grubby looking, plastic water-containers.

The Square was a mess with rubbish strewn everywhere. I could see portable toilets, not particularly well hidden. I didn't need to see them because the smell gave them away.

As I got nearer to the Monument, I saw a large makeshift shelter among the others, with a table outside, where students handed out leaflets to those passing.

'Professor Charles?' said a familiar voice.

It was Wei, who looked remarkably well, considering.

'Hello, Wei,' I replied. 'I was hoping to find you and Hou. I was worried about what had happened to you both.'

'Oh, we are both all right,' commented Wei. 'Hou has gone to a meeting.'

'What are you doing?' I asked.

'I am helping in the propaganda tent,' replied Wei. 'That way we can find out what is going on.'

'Surely your parents are worried,' I added. 'Shouldn't you go home?'

'It was a good thing we came,' said Wei, avoiding my query. 'These Beijing students believe they know better than us from the provinces, just because they get the attention of the foreign press. They are disorganised and always arguing among themselves. What are you doing here, Professor Charles?'

'I wanted do some sightseeing before returning home,' I explained.

'I am meeting a friend in a few minutes. Why don't you come with me and then you can tell me what's been going on.'

At first, Wei was not sure. She did not want to leave the Square as until then, either she or Hou had taken it in turns to maintain a presence. Remembering Wei's excellent appetite, I promised her tea and cakes in a nearby hotel, and that did the trick. Wei grabbed a pile of leaflets from the table and told her colleagues that she and her foreign professor friend were going to distribute them around the Square. She stuffed a pile of leaflets in my hands to confirm her story, and I obliged by handing them out to anybody nearby. I found I had a remarkable success rate in handing out the leaflets, but I put that down to my being a foreigner of the big-nose variety and catching the recipients of such leaflets off their guard. Wei was less successful and eventually gave me hers to hand out.

'Last week,' explained Wei, 'helicopters flew over the Square and dropped leaflets on us.'

'What did they say?'

'It was just a list of communist slogans selected by Li Peng. Some of the students shouted, "Down with Li Peng," but intellectuals who were around at that time put them up to it. When they declared martial law, the authorities told us to leave the Square or face attack. We ignored the warning, of course.'

'So what have you been doing?'

'A student from Tianjin arrived at the Square about the same time as we did. He assessed the situation and called a meeting for all the universities from the provinces. We elected him leader of the Autonomous Federation of Universities from Outside Beijing. We tried to join forces with the Beijing Autonomous Student Federation, but the Hunger Strike Committee, led by Chai Ling, didn't approve. Some of us wanted to hold elections for our leaders, one student, one vote, like in British universities, but we were told that elections were not practical under the circumstances.'

'I know about Tianjin,' I informed Wei, 'it has had a history of student unrest.'

As we approached Tiananmen Gate, Tammy was gave me a wave.

'This is your friend!' exclaimed Wei incredulously.

I did the introductions. I felt quite pleased with myself, enjoying the company, walking between my two Chinese friends. Recently, I had been feeling lonely, despite the polite nods from the elderly Japanese on the side trip to Qufu.

'I will show you around the Forbidden City,' said Tammy.

I was surprised it was business as usual in the Forbidden City. Just yards across the avenue, on Tiananmen Square, protesters were attempting to change Chinese history, and here, crowds were jostling to get the best position for their photographs.

I looked up at Mao, above the gate.

'I see they have replaced the portrait of Mao,' I said. 'I was around when someone threw paint over it a few days ago.'

Wei looked a little crestfallen and upset. I felt guilty for not visiting the Square earlier.

'I would have visited you then, but there was a disturbance and I wasn't sure what was happening—'

'It isn't that, Professor Charles. They were three activists from Hunan province,' explained Wei. 'They threw ink. One was a teacher, one a newspaper editor, and the last one a factory worker. Students grabbed them and took them for interrogation before handing them over to the police. They came to support the protest movement and look what we did in return.'

'If charged as counter-revolutionaries, they will spend the next twenty years in prison,' added Tammy, which I didn't consider was a helpful comment, under the circumstances.

'The name of the person who handed the three activists to the police is commander Huang,' continued Wei. 'She is the leader of the Dare-to-Die Squad, which protects our leaders on the Square. Someone said she is a public relations student from the China Social University. Hou wanted to challenge commander Huang about what she did, but he couldn't find her. Hou never gives up easily, so he decided to go to the China Social University to see if she was there. Most of the Beijing students had never heard of the place, but apparently, it is a small privately run college in the east part of Beijing. Hou found it down an alleyway and sneaked in. He asked around but no one had heard of her. He also found out that the place didn't even teach public relations. We believe she was a government agent who had infiltrated the students on the Square.'

'Perhaps she gave a false identity to protect herself,' offered Tammy, who was obviously trying to be helpful because we could both see that Wei was upset.

'What do they say?' I asked, pointing at two huge hoardings, one each side of Mao's portrait.

'Long live the unity of the peoples of the world,' replied Tammy.

'Long live China,' added Wei, while pointing to the other side.

'When was it built?' I asked, nodding at Tiananmen Gate.

'It was first built about 1417 during the Ming dynasty when the Forbidden City was rebuilt. Mao reinforced the building above Tiananmen Gate so he could watch parades and other events on Tiananmen Square. It is also called the Gate of Heavenly Peace.'

'What about Tiananmen Square, when was that built?'

'The government built it in the late fifties for official parades and public meetings,' Tammy explained.

'The Monument of the People's Heroes is the central feature of the Square and built at the same time. It commemorates all those who died during all of the revolutions since 1840,' added Wei.

Tiananmen Gate was open and we marched through. There was someone at the gate, who might have been a ticket collector, but he appeared not to do much and most people, like us, ignored him.

'Is this the Forbidden City?' I asked.

'No, we need to walk a little further,' Tammy replied. 'This is the entrance to the Imperial City where privileged courtiers used to live. The area where Tiananmen Square is now was the outer city for rich commoners, contained within a walled enclosure.'

We passed a temple, a couple of palaces, the Working People's Theatre, and then stood before another huge gate with high walls.

'This is the Meridian Gate, the main entrance to the Forbidden City,' declared Tammy. 'This was the imperial palace for the emperor and his close family and attendants. At one time, Mao wanted to level the Forbidden City and build offices for himself.'

Upon entering, I was undecided whether I was impressed or disappointed. It was like visiting a pagoda, a popular tourist spot. You were supposed to be impressed. The paintwork was slightly tawdry and peeling. The city was immense and went back about a thousand yards. There was a series of large buildings, each shaped like a squat pagoda, but much wider. Between buildings were vast courtyards.

'The first imperial residence on this site was built in 1274 by Kublai Khan,' Tammy informed me, 'but it was levelled to the ground by the conquering Ming. Less than a century later, in the early fifteenth century, Emperor Yung Lo rebuilt it. It was not until 1911 that the once-forbidden palace was open to every Chinese citizen.'

'How many emperors lived here?' I asked.

'Over the five-hundred-year period there were twenty-four.'

'It looks big and full of draughts,' I commented.

'It officially has 9,999 rooms, but I think it is less.'

'That seems a lot.'

'These are not conventional rooms. Here, a room is a space between four pillars.'

I was none the wiser, as usual.

From the Meridian Gate, we came to the Supreme Imperial Gate and then the Gate of Heavenly Purity. I could not take in all the historical aspects of the Forbidden City with all of its palaces, halls, gates, and courtyards. I found myself gazing with ignorant curiosity.

'They must have been nice,' I said, looking at some private, enclosed, unkempt gardens.

'Concubines would have lived there, in boring luxury, purely for the pleasure of the emperor,' Tammy informed me. 'There were lots of concubines, so if they didn't catch the eye of the emperor, they would die a virgin.'

As we left the Forbidden City, walking through Tiananmen Gate, we could see the high flagpole on the Square itself.

'Every morning, at daybreak, the flag is hoisted by a ceremonial guard. This is popular with out-of-town visitors,' said Tammy.

I looked and could just make out the five yellow stars on the red flag as it gently flapped in the breeze. I wondered if the daybreak ceremony, with the soldiers, still took place during the demonstrations.

We turned right and walked down Chang'an Avenue.

'Those tents belong to the Gongzilian, the Beijing Workers'

Autonomous Federation,' Wei informed me, pointing across the avenue to the corner of Tiananmen Square. 'Some students think they are just ordinary workers, crude, and stupid. I read some of their leaflets and they are very practical. They want things like wage rises, equal rights for women workers, better housing, and cheaper food.'

Flying above their tents was a crude, red-and-black banner. I could also see what looked like a public-address system.

'The Gongzilian is a small workers' organisation that started a few weeks ago,' added Tammy. 'It raises issues such as the right of workers to establish their own labour organisations, and the right for workers to represent themselves. And they are dangerous issues to consider.'

After a few minutes, we passed the north end of the Great Hall of the People, which was across the avenue.

'The Great Hall was built to commemorate the tenth anniversary of the People's Republic. Inside are numerous meeting halls, designed to represent every province. It is very symbolic, but some say the workmanship is poor. It is where all meetings, congresses, and official gatherings of the Party and government are held.'

We crossed Nanchang Avenue, and after a few more minutes stopped outside a gated compound.

'This is the Xinhuamen Gate,' explained Tammy, 'the main entrance to the Zhongnanhai compound where our leaders live. Inside is the nerve centre for the Chinese Communist Party, the State Council, and government of the People's Republic. The compound is nearly as big as the Forbidden City, and it has several lakes.'

Protesters had gathered outside, a few sitting next to the guards. One protester was leading the chanting with a hand-held megaphone, but they appeared to be merely going through the motions. The guards didn't look particularly perturbed. They were just standing there looking resigned to the noise they had to endure. Onlookers stared, no doubt amused that the protesters could get away with making such a din outside the leaders' main entrance.

'The Chinese White House,' I said, hoping to sound humorous.

'More like the Chinese Kremlin, the new Forbidden City,' added Wei with feeling. 'Ordinary people are barred.'

The Xinhuamen Gate was another one of those squat pagoda

buildings. It had a large flagpole immediately in front proudly flying the Chinese flag. The gate was set back from the road, with eight columns in the front holding up the structure above. There were two entrances barely a car's width; they must use another entrance. On each side of the compound entrance were eight-foot high lions and one had a poster hanging from its mouth.

'What does that say?' I asked, pointing at the poster.

'Li Peng, resign,' Wei answered.

I had to smile. Would they tolerate a poster on the gates outside 10, Downing Street saying, Margaret Thatcher, resign?

I got closer so I could peer through the entrance, but a wall, with a large slogan, shielded my view. I assumed I might be too close to the entrance for the comfort of the guards, but they merely watched me with bored indifference.

'And what does that say?' I again asked, pointing at the slogan.

'Serve the People,' replied Tammy. 'It was written by Mao himself.'

Wei looked but did not say much. That had been the site of some of the recent demonstrations. Guards with belts and clubs had attacked protesters there in April. Some of the recent hunger strikers had also camped outside, but they had been ignored.

It was normal for leaders and elder statesmen to live in nice surroundings. China was no different.

Wei would not go to a hotel for lunch, especially one for foreigners. We had to find a place frequented by workers. Tammy worked close to there, so took us to a pleasant little place about ten minutes' walk away. It was an up-market coffee shop frequented by intellectuals and middle-ranking officials.

'I have nothing against foreigners or hotels,' explained Wei. 'The people in Beijing donated money to support us. There are rumours that some of the Beijing student leaders have been spending money on meals in expensive restaurants.'

The coffee shop had a display cabinet full of sickly, sweet looking cakes, and an apple pie. I ordered coffee, Tammy tea, and Wei a coke. I also ordered a selection of cakes, but not the apple pie.

'When are you returning to Jaliang?' Tammy asked Wei. 'I am sure your parents will be worried.'

'Some of us are not leaving,' stated Wei pointedly, 'unlike others.'

'What do you mean?' I enquired.

Wei was busy destroying a pink sponge cake with layers of mock cream, jam, and a thick covering of icing sugar, sprinkled with hundreds-and-thousands. Tammy was not far behind. Having a sweet tooth myself, I entered the fray, but I was a poor third in that contest.

'The leaders from the Beijing universities have been arguing among themselves,' Wei said between bites. 'Last night, the Beijing Autonomous Student Federation had agreed to leave the Square, tomorrow, and return to classes. Hou has gone to another meeting to argue against that.'

'Leaving sounds like a good idea,' I said.

'And the Beijing student leaders keep changing,' Wei said, ignoring my comment. 'Last Wednesday, Wu'er Kaixi was voted out as president of the student protesters. He wanted all students to leave the Square, but that wasn't acceptable. There were rumours about him. They said he had connections with Deng Xiaoping's son, who is very corrupt. They said that Deng was using his son to communicate requests for us to leave the Square. Wu'er Kaixi was one of the ones urging the students to end the hunger strike. We have a new leader, Chai Ling, who was head of the Hunger Strike Committee. Other leaders are Feng Congde, who is Chai Ling's husband, and Li Lu.

'The main problem is that our leaders are disorganised, and they almost rival the authorities in officiousness and bureaucracy. They cordoned off the area around the Monument and called it the Tiananmen Square Command Headquarters. They give each other names like commander-in-chief and talk like army generals.

'The leaders elect student guards, pickets, to provide security around the Headquarters and broadcasting station. Other leaders, with their own guards then try to take over the Headquarters and broadcasting station. Whoever controls the broadcasting station is in charge.'

Orwell's 'Animal Farm' came to mind.

'How do you know all this,' I asked.

'I help in the propaganda department, so at least we can find out what is being said. They formed the Joint Liaison Group to coordinate the pro-democracy movement and it includes representatives who are intellectuals, workers, and residents of Beijing. Do you remember Hou telling you about Wang Dan? Although he resigned as leader some time ago, he is a member of the Joint Liaison Group. We do not agree with what the group wants to achieve, which is getting the government to act in accordance with the Constitution. The government should do that anyway. We want to reform the Communist Party system. It should be more accountable.'

There was no stopping Wei. All her pent-up emotion and frustration was coming to the surface. Until now, she probably had no one to tell, no one to listen.

'We received enormous sums of money in donations from workers and from supporters overseas, but our finances are in a mess. People are just taking money from the box without keeping records, which isn't right. In the evenings, you can hear loud music, people shouting, and dancing. The Gongzilian must think we are corrupt capitalists.

'Because we are from the provinces, the Beijing students think their demands are better than ours. They come to Tiananmen Square and strut around as if they own the place and then go home or back to their dorms or visit their favourite restaurants or clubs.

'Many of the students from outside Beijing are disillusioned. Today, the numbers are the lowest since I arrived.

'I have to go now. I don't like to ask, but can you buy as many of those cakes as possible so I can give them to my friends.'

After Wei had left, Tammy and I had another drink.

'The problem with the protest movement,' Tammy told me, 'is that it contains people with varying agendas. There are intellectuals hanging around the student leaders feeding them with confusing ideas.'

Petter?

'I just want to get on with my life and be as comfortable as possible,' continued Tammy. 'But what I hate is corruption. For example, when you hear about the teenagers of party officials spending fortunes in a Beijing club that just shows the loss of the moral authority of the Party.'

'Do you know anything new about the leadership struggle?' I asked.

'On Thursday evening Li Peng appeared on television. It was a symbolic appearance because we then knew the hardliners, like Li Peng, had gained the upper hand over the moderates, such as Zhao Ziyang. I suspect Zhao has lost his post. Deng Xiaoping is still in charge. That is not the outcome most people wanted, especially the protesters.'

'What will happen now?' I asked.

'I am a Party member and a middle-ranking official from the Ministry of Education. Some of my colleagues, and other senior officials, have sons and daughters who are students on the Square. This is the same in most ministries. Our leaders are not about to cause harm to their children or those of their colleagues, are they? At first, because Deng's Open Door Policy now exposes students to the outside world, my colleagues dismissed the protests as adolescent high spirits. These students are the elite, particularly those from Beijing. Most are already marked for higher things, and they know it.

'The situation is changing because the ordinary people, the workers, have seen the students getting away with things. They are now supporting and joining the protest movement, particularly the residents of Beijing. For a few days, the state-controlled press reported the news accurately, before the authorities clamped down once more. It gave ordinary people a brief glimpse into press freedom, and they liked it. When they declared martial law, the Beijing residents erected makeshift barricades to prevent the army from reaching the Square. I never saw this myself, but some of my colleagues did. By mid-week, they removed the barricades, and things returned as before.

'Although Deng's Open Door Policy has stimulated economic growth in China, it has increased social inequality. Only a few enjoy the new wealth, while the ordinary worker experiences frozen wages, rising prices, and falling living standards. The support from the workers has more to do with a protest against inequality and wanting more socialism, and this has threatened is the authority of our leaders.

'The students are not a significant threat. Government has always been tolerant towards them. All the authorities want is for the students to leave Tiananmen Square and return to their studies. No doubt, some students will receive bad work allocations and the ringleaders, if they atone in the correct manner, will only receive short jail sentences.'

'And if they don't atone or leave Tiananmen Square?' I asked.

'Please, when you see your students again, warn them to be careful. I heard some student leaders are already contacting western embassies about asylum.

'The residents of Beijing have sensed greater freedom and hope. It can be dangerous for the workers and peasants, particularly the Gongzilian, to have too much hope. What our leaders fear the most is the working class organising unrest and dissent similar to Poland's Solidarity, the Polish disease. The Communist Party will stop at nothing to maintain its monopoly of power.'

From: **Deputy Chairman**
Office of Education Foreign Affairs
Public Security Bureau
Beijing
To: **Assistant to Chairman**
Public Security Bureau (*PSB* Beijing)
27 May 1989

Internal memorandum

Subject: DISSIDENT VINCENT

After frantically searching for the British academic, we have had
two sightings of him.

On Tuesday 23rd, minutes before criminals defaced the portrait
of Mao Tse-tung, they saw Vincent in that vicinity. That could not
have been a coincidence. He quickly disappeared with all the
commotion going on and they were unable to follow.

Early today he was on Tiananmen Square at the protesters'
propaganda tent, and then walking away with a student leader.
Unfortunately, we do not have her name. Vincent had the impudence
to hand out propaganda leaflets in and around Tiananmen Square and
more audaciously within the Forbidden City itself.

When approaching the Forbidden City, Vincent met another
provocateur, a tough looking woman, probably an underground
intellectual from Hong Kong, whose identity we failed to discover.

After distributing leaflets around the Forbidden City, they
took particular interest in the Zhongnanhai compound where our
elite leaders live. Vincent continued to hand out leaflets outside
of the compound which, on later inspection, contained seditious
information against the premier, Li Peng. We think Vincent took
notes of the security arrangements at the compound entrance and
consequently we increased security with immediate effect.

We managed to follow Vincent and his co-conspirators to a
coffee shop popular with intellectuals. Vincent and his
accomplices then left separately and went in different directions
and the PSB officer did not know who to follow. He stayed and
questioned the staff in the coffee shop but obtained no further
clues on what Vincent was planning.

Chapter 37

Sunday, May 28, 1989

Tammy and Leigh met me in the hotel foyer shortly after breakfast.

Sam from the China Travel Service had arranged a minibus trip to the Great Wall and the Ming Tombs, stopping at some nice place for lunch between visits. Again, I got the trip at local rates, and I gladly paid the commission.

The gossip at breakfast was that movements in and out of Beijing were difficult under martial law. When I broached that with Tammy and Leigh, they just shrugged their shoulders and said the driver knew the best routes. Their excitement was infectious, and I was looking forward to seeing the Great Wall.

Our journey out of Beijing was uneventful, the suburbs having no great architectural merit to warrant note. I looked out of the window and saw the locals going about their daily lives. Children were playing as any other children might. Parents were gossiping with their neighbours, possibly about the students who did not know what was good for them. Grandparents were sitting in the shade, just watching the world go by, as was I, but from the other direction.

Once we were clear of Beijing, I could see the hills in the distance, shrouded in mist and pollution.

'That is where we are going,' Leigh informed me.

'How are your wedding plans?' I asked.

Leigh was getting married in seven days' time. Back in England, a bride-to-be and her mother would be making frantic last-minute arrangements. A bride's father would be trying to keep as low a profile as possible, usually with little success. Leigh appeared to have not a care in the world.

'My fiancé and our parents are doing all the arrangements, so there is nothing to worry about,' she replied.

'What are you wearing for the wedding?' I asked.

I was curious. I had noticed, at weekends in Jaliang, that brides wore traditional western wedding dresses, with frills and veils. That seemed to be the fashion.

'A white wedding dress, of course,' Leigh replied, as if I were some idiot. 'We are having the reception in a popular restaurant not far from the Forbidden City. We had to book weeks ago. I live with my parents in a residential area to the west of Beijing, and the wedding procession will pass the Gate of Divine Military Genius, at the northern end of the Forbidden City. It will be romantic.'

'And the honeymoon?' I asked.

'My fiancé has made those arrangements and has kept them a secret. We only have a few days from work so the arrangements better be good, or there will be trouble from day one,' replied Leigh.

I visualised Leigh, startlingly beautiful in her wedding gown, and almost envied her fiancé, pleased for his good fortune.

'Where did you go for your honeymoon?' Leigh asked Tammy.

I didn't know Tammy was married.

'My husband couldn't get the time off work,' answered Tammy. 'We did manage a nice weekend away after the wedding.'

'Have you any children?' I asked.

'I have a little girl,' replied Tammy.

'Why didn't you bring your family?' I asked. 'There's plenty of room in the minibus.' I felt selfish for taking up so much of Tammy's time away from her family over the weekend.

'I was going to bring my family and surprise you,' Tammy replied. 'To be honest, I was not sure about the martial law restrictions. My daughter was looking forward to meeting you, she has never met a—'

'...smelly, big-nosed, barbarian before,' I finished.

'I don't think you smell, but your nose—'

'Look!' exclaimed Leigh, pointing to the hills.

It was a remarkable sight. Clearly visible was a distinct line rising up and down the hills in a capricious manner.

We arrived and the minibus driver dropped us off. I walked up to the wall and read the plaque by the steps, *Great Wall of China, renovated in 1975*, it said, or words to that effect. I was slightly disappointed because there was nothing ancient about what I was looking at.

'The real wall is too dangerous to walk on, so this section has been restored for the tourists,' Tammy explained.

'So how do we get to the real wall?' I asked.

'We walk.'

We climbed the steps to the top of the wall where there was a wide path and areas for taking photographs. The height of the original wall was about twenty feet, and the pathway on top was wide enough, Tammy informed me, for five horsemen riding abreast. There were plenty of others enjoying the renovated wall and its views, but not foreigners. I was the only foreigner around. These were your normal Sunday morning sightseers enjoying a famous beauty spot and taking photographs as evidence.

The views were spectacular, but I wanted to walk on the real, ancient Great Wall of China.

'Follow me,' said Tammy.

I did hesitate...

After walking for a bit, we were alone. Then we came upon some sort of official who was blocking our way.

'We cannot go any further,' said Leigh. 'We are not allowed.'

There was a sharp exchange of words between him and Tammy, and I could see that the official was not going to argue. Without being too unkind, I wouldn't want to argue with Tammy either.

The renovations came to an abrupt end. Before me was a pile of rubble snaking up and down the hills in a haphazard fashion. With intrepidness on my part, but foolishness in the eyes of Tammy and Leigh, I managed to scramble over the stones and rubble for a few yards. I could genuinely claim to have walked along the ancient Great Wall – without twisting my ankle, I might add.

'This was built by China's first emperor, Shih Huang Ti, in the third century B.C.,' explained Tammy. 'The Great Wall stretches from the sea to the deserts of Sinkiang. Parts were actually built before by various feudal lords to guard mountain passes, but the emperor ordered all the previous constructions to be joined to make one wall.'

'That explains its erratic route,' I said.

'Most of what remains of the wall is the result of a rebuilding programme undertaken during the Ming dynasty, apart from the recent renovations for tourists.'

'Why did they want to make one continuous wall in the first place?'

'It was to protect the fertile plains to the south from the marauding nomads of the northern steppes. The wall did provide some protection against foraging gangs of warriors, but had little effect once the nomads united under a strong leader.'

I could see it would not be easy to get horses of foraging gangs over a twenty-foot wall and even harder to make your escape with flocks or herds of captured animals, but building such a wall seemed to be a lot of effort to achieve that. Did Hadrian know about the Great Wall? I was sure there must have been lessons to learn from the emperor's mistakes.

In the end, the Great Wall was just another botch policy by government.

For a leisurely lunch, Tammy took us to a rural farming commune where she had distant relations. We ate under the shade of a sycamore tree much to the amusement of the local children fascinated by my chopstick skills. Noodles were not easy.

Lunch was noodle based and flavoured with garlic and ginger. We had diced duck, black bean sauce, stewed pork, white cabbage, spring onions, bread, and dumplings.

'This is typical northern Chinese cooking,' explained Tammy.

The Ming tombs were a disappointment.

Since the tombs were much nearer Beijing and it was the afternoon, there were a lot more sightseers around. We had to queue with the rest. The location of the tombs was pleasant enough, being in a valley sheltered on three sides by hills in the distance. We approached from the south, along the Sacred Way, a route lined with large statues of animals, mythical beasts, and human figures. Tammy didn't know if the statues had any meaning, but given time, I was sure the local archaeologists would come up with something.

The Sacred Way led to the tomb of Yung Lo, the builder of the Forbidden City. His tomb had the appearance of the Forbidden City in miniature, and therefore offered no surprises. Yung's tomb was the first to be constructed followed by twelve others built nearby. Since most of the tombs remained sealed, we could only visit the underground tomb of the Emperor Zhu Yijun, which was a much more modest affair. We queued to enter from one side and went down some steps into the tomb. There was nothing much to see inside, apart from a shoddy replica coffin and some empty chambers. There were families posing for photographs by the coffin arguing with the official trying to stop them. We then went up some more steps, out the other side, and that was it.

What was nice about the tombs was the area had not been commercialised for tourists, not yet anyway. The gardens and courtyards were generally in neglect, and the Sacred Way was more like an untidy country lane.

I had a nice day, with pleasant company. I arranged to see Tammy and Leigh later in the week before I flew home. I made a mental note to buy Leigh a wedding present, something nice but not extravagant, as that would embarrass her.

Chapter 38

Monday, May.29, 1989

I decided to visit Tiananmen Square and try to persuade Wei and Hou to return to Jaliang. I was uneasy because of what Tammy had said.

'Tell them to be careful.'

Before leaving the hotel, I bought a bag of food and drinks for the hungry protesters. Wei was always hungry.

The first thing I noticed when I arrived was there were fewer people on the Square.

Since someone had organised a reasonable clean-up job, the place looked tidier. The rubbish bins were still overflowing. I saw discarded polystyrene burger containers. I looked to see if the polystyrene containers had the McDonald's emblem, but they didn't.

I had a walk around the Square.

Near Mao's Mausoleum, I saw an encampment of new bivouac tents, mostly red but some were blue, and a sign that said, *Donated by Hong Kong Polytechnic*. The tents were sturdy tubular affairs arranged in neat rows and looked out of place among the other makeshift tents.

I found Hou near the propaganda tent and saw Wei handing out leaflets. Both looked tired.

'What's the matter, Hou,' I asked. 'What has happened to your face?'

'Hello, Professor Charles,' Hou said, ignoring my query about his face. 'Thank you for coming. We appreciate your support.'

'Lunch,' I said, handing over my bag.

Hou looked inside and smiled gratefully. Wei and the others came across and propaganda was temporary postponed for lunch.

'You're all still here then,' I said, stating the obvious.

'We have been busy,' Wei informed me.

'What have you been doing?'

'On Saturday morning there was a meeting of the Joint Liaison Group,' said Hou. 'I am not a member, but I wanted to listen to what was being said. It was agreed we would all leave the Square yesterday, but then amended that to Tuesday, which is tomorrow. That would be a moral triumph, they argued, and after a victory march, we would return to classes. The Joint Liaison Group drafted a ten-point statement for the press. Chai Ling and other leaders were present, and the decision was unanimous.'

'Some of us were not happy with that,' added Wei.

'It seems like a good idea to me,' I said.

'When we returned to the Tiananmen Square Command Headquarters,' continued Hou, 'Chai Ling informed everyone it had been agreed we were leaving on Tuesday and a statement would be issued to the press. Then an argument broke out. Li Lu, Chai's second-in-command, was surprised, because, just two days ago, we had agreed at a meeting with over three hundred colleges to maintain our presence on the Square.'

I had to admit I was confused about who said what about when they were leaving. The leadership on Tiananmen Square was obviously weak and disjointed.

'Li Lu argued it would be too dangerous to leave. We would have achieved nothing, and there would be repercussions,' Wei added.

'Someone then make changes to the ten-point statement. It just became a mess,' said Hou. 'Wang Dan read the statement to the press. He got to the eighth point, paused, and quietly read that the Joint Liaison Group has proposed suspending our peaceful demonstrations on Tuesday, 30 May.'

'Everyone was furious,' said Wei. 'Li Lu objected and then Chai Ling changed her mind about ending the protests. There was another meeting, and the statement again modified. Someone read the statement to the press saying that unless the authorities convene the next meeting of the National People's Congress immediately, then we would remain on the Square until June 20, when the next meeting is due. It is difficult to know what is happening because there are too many committees making decisions.'

'Wang Dan resigned from the Joint Liaison Group and left the Square,' said Hou. 'Well, leaving the Square might be all right for the Beijing students, but we're not leaving. Leaving the Square without any concessions from the government means surrender.'

'Chai Ling threatened to resign as commander-in-chief. She said she was tired and felt guilty about agreeing with the Joint Liaison Group,' said Wei.

'She left the Square and went to a hotel, with a supporter from Hong Kong, for a shower and a change of clothes,' added Hou disapprovingly. 'We think she also had a secret meeting with an American journalist.'

'Despite that, Chai Ling agreed to continue as commander-in-chief.'

'We marched yesterday and another is planned tomorrow,' said Hou.

'Was there a march yesterday?' I asked surprised. 'I was around Beijing but saw no evidence of anything. Things looked normal to me.'

Hou frowned.

'It was not as successful as we hoped. Not many joined us, but they did cheer from the roadside. We heard that the authorities are warning workers, with threats of reprisals and punishment, not to support us.'

'Some of us distributed leaflets around university campuses,' added Wei. 'We want students to start another hunger strike in front of the Great Hall of the People, here on the Square, and near the gates of Zhongnanhai. We also demanded changes to our constitution.'

Lunch was finished and the others from the propaganda tent returned to their duties, but Wei and Hou remained with me.

'Look, are you sure you are doing the right thing?' I asked. 'You could look at the situation differently. You have made your protests, disrupted the Sino-Soviet summit, embarrassed the government, and got support from the people. Importantly, you have stayed on Tiananmen Square disregarding martial law. If you leave the Square now, at your choosing, surely, you will have won a significant freedom – your right to protest without government interference. Once you have made this precedent, what is to stop you doing it again, but a little more organised?'

I had a plausible argument. I considered it a better approach to saying, 'Shouldn't you go home now? You've had your fun.' I was uncertain what they hoped to achieve. They were making demands for all sorts, but I could see no logic in what they wanted.

'We will consider what you said and discuss it with some of the others,' Wei replied.

'There are not as many students on the Square,' I added gently.

'There are rumours that the authorities are taking names, and if we continue our struggle, this will jeopardise our future careers,' said Wei.

'So students are leaving.'

'A few,' admitted Wei weakly. 'It is the Beijing students who are the ones who want to end the protests. Hou had a fight with some of them, as you can see.'

'What if, through fear or lack of interest, the whole protest movement just fizzles out?'

'We recognise your style of questioning from your classes, Professor Charles. You are playing devil's advocate,' said Wei.

'I heard that student leaders are trying to claim political asylum at some of the foreign embassies.'

'We didn't know that,' responded Wei.

'We still have some friends in Beijing, from the Art Institution,' said Hou suddenly. 'Come and see us tomorrow and we will show you we are not beaten.'

'And don't forget to bring lunch.'

After leaving Tiananmen Square, I decided to tour Beijing using my trusty bus map.

Some routes and buses were busy, but I used my well-tested technique of waiting to board until last. If a bus were full, I would wait a few minutes for the next one, which was invariably empty. I moved around in a random fashion, just seeing what I could discover.

Beijing, I found, was flat with predominantly low-rise buildings. The streets appeared unusually wide, and apart from Tiananmen Square and its surroundings, I could detect no centre or shopping areas. Beijing did not feel like a town in the western sense, but a sprawling suburb lacking character. There were no slums or upmarket areas. Everywhere was more or less clean, but never sparklingly so. I could feel no attachment to Beijing like the one I had for Jaliang, Suzhou, and Qufu.

From: **Deputy Chairman**

Office of Education Foreign Affairs

Public Security Bureau

Beijing

To: **Assistant to Chairman**

Public Security Bureau (*PSB* Beijing)

29 May 1989

Internal memorandum

Subject: **DISSIDENT VINCENT**

Vincent has again broken cover.

We observed him conspiring with others on Tiananmen Square.

He went straight to the propaganda headquarters of the protesters, called all students together, and gave an impromptu speech. I had instructed 24 hours surveillance of the area around the propaganda tent with English speaking undercover police, and this diligence paid off.

Vincent told students to control the situation with cunning.

He made clear they must not allow their protests to collapse through lack of interest because their protests will be seen as a failure. The alternative, he explained, is that they all leave the Square together, immediately, in an orderly fashion.

After doing so, they could declare publically that they have made a significant success towards freedom by choosing when to enter Tiananmen Square, demonstrate they can embarrass the government, as they did over the Sino-Soviet summit, then leave at a time of their choosing without any intervention by the authorities. In doing that, Vincent said the protesters would have set a precedent, and later, they could coordinate further demonstrations, but better organised, with apparent impunity from the government.

This would be a dangerous precedent, particularly when the residents of Beijing were quick to support the protesters before the authorities started to exert pressure on them.

Vincent then left the Square, but our undercover police were unable to follow him.

243

Chapter 39

I bought food and drink for a late lunch, then caught a bus to Tiananmen Square.

It was my practice to stand in front of the portrait of Mao and Tiananmen Gate, looking over the Square.

I then saw it.

It was a miniature Statue of Liberty, rebelliously standing between the Monument and the end of the Square from where I gazed. Flags and banners, different sizes and colours fluttering in the early afternoon breeze, crowded around the statue. It had provoked a lot of interest because the Square looked busier than the day before, mostly people just staring at the statue. I looked around at Mao's portrait, and wondered what he would have made of it all; not much, I bet.

I crossed the avenue instead of using the underpass. It was quicker.

As I approached the statue, which looked to be about thirty feet high, I recognised a face staring up at it, in a haze of smoke, head-and-shoulders above the rest.

It was Petter smoking his pipe.

All my fears of him being a Soviet agent immediately returned. There he was, right in the middle of things, stirring up trouble.

'Petter,' I said incredulously, 'what are you doing here?'

'Hello, Charles,' said Petter. 'I might ask you the same thing.'

I recognised the technique from some of the spy novels I sometimes read; you answer a question, with a question!

Actually, he had caught me off-guard.

I was supposed to be teaching in Jaliang. Instead, I had cut short my programme to go sightseeing around Beijing. Petter had employed me to teach, and there I was, by his side, admiring the Chinese replica of the Statue of Liberty. I decided not to pursue what our activities had been. Petter was certainly not going to tell me what he had been up to, and I was a little coy about what I had been doing.

'What do you make of that?' I asked, looking at the statue. 'It's well bolted to the ground and will be difficult to remove.'

'I can see that the representation is based upon the Statue of Liberty. There is a resemblance,' Petter answered casually, 'but as a work of art, I might query its merits.'

…as a work of art, he might query its merits. What was he on about?

What I saw was a poke in the eye for the Chinese government and its leaders. There it was, standing proud, right under the nose of Mao, outside the Chinese Houses of Parliament. What had Petter's involvement been in this? I hoped he had not been using my students, as tools, in his subversive underhand activities for the Soviets.

'It is very provocative,' I said.

'And, as we speak, will be headline news around the world.'

I didn't know if Petter looked gleeful, or thoughtful. It was difficult to tell with that pipe sticking out of his mouth.

'But still provocative,' I persisted.

'But clever.' There is no way the government can come out of this looking good. Can you imagine the TV pictures and newspaper photographs showing the Chinese army pulling down the offending statue and all the symbolism that would entail? Leaving it is a reminder of the protesters' audaciousness. Or so I was informed.'

'By who?' I demanded.

'Exactly,' replied Petter, 'and he is standing over there.'

Hou – I should have known.

Hou stood among a group of other students. He looked pleased with himself, tired, dishevelled, and had smears of white plaster on his arms and clothing. I walked over to him, and he shook my hand enthusiastically, as did his student friends around him.

'So this is what you wanted me to see?'

'It is a memorial to democracy,' Hou announced, 'and we named it the Goddess of Democracy.'

'Here's lunch,' I said.

Hou then disappeared with the others.

'Did you know Hou and Wei are both here, Petter?' I was not going to let Petter off the hook that easy.

'I knew they had come to Beijing, but I did not know they were still here,' replied Petter indignantly. 'Because I have been busy, this is my first visit to Tiananmen Square. I am returning home on Thursday evening, so I considered a little sightseeing wouldn't go amiss.'

Should I have reported Petter to the British Embassy? What would I have said? Well, he was an expert dancer, smoked a pipe, drank lots of vodka, spoke Russian, and visited Soviet ships. Oh, and he was a little evasive about what he got up to. Yes, he was definitely a Soviet agent – even Harry said so.

'You seem very friendly with everyone, Charles,' added Petter, with a glint in his eye. 'This is not your first visit to Tiananmen Square, is it?'

What did he mean?

'We should see if Wei is all right,' I said hastily, ignoring Petter's question. 'Follow me.'

Surprisingly, Petter did.

'You seem to know your way around, Charles.'

What was he implying?

Wei was by the propaganda tent, also looking tired but not as dishevelled as Hou. She appeared to be arguing about the wording on one of the leaflets, but it could have been a normal conversation between friends. It was sometimes difficult to tell in China.

'Hello, Professor Charles,' said Wei, when she saw us coming. 'You have brought Mr Petter. It is nice to have new people coming to show their support.'

'How many times have you been here, Charles?'

'I have given lunch to Hou,' I said apologetically to Wei, while ignoring Petter once more.

'Don't worry, he will save some for me,' Wei replied cheerfully. 'Did you see our surprise? Hou helped the art students to erect it, and the authorities made no attempt to stop them.'

'You look tired, Wei,' I said.

'It has been another long night and everyone is tired,' replied Wei. 'Things are now different. The Goddess of Democracy has raised our spirits, and people are coming to see what is happening. Nobody is leaving the Square today.'

'What are the loudspeakers ranting on about?' asked Petter. 'How can you think with all that noise going on?'

'The loud ones belong to the authorities. They are telling us that the erection of the statue is contravening city building regulations, and even in America, students would not be allowed to build statues outside Congress. The authorities have been urging us to leave the Square. The other loudspeakers belong to Command Headquarters and the Gongzilian, and we broadcast our own messages.'

'What are all the flags for?'

Everywhere there were flags and banners of all shapes and sizes, particularly large red flags with yellow Chinese lettering. I was used to seeing them, but it was obviously Petter's first visit to the Square.

'They represent the universities and faculties of the protestors on the Square. It lets people know who is here. It also makes it easy to find each other, especially visitors to the Square. We just look for the flag. That one near the Goddess belongs to Beijing University, Faculty of Chemistry. That one is Beijing Teachers University and next to it is Beijing Normal College, Department of History. Over there is Qinghua and Mid-South Industrial. And this one is Jaliang Number 3 University.'

'The flags are very nice, Wei, but there have been arrests,' Petter commented casually.

'There are rumours, but it could be propaganda from the government to frighten us.'

'They are not rumours, Wei,' Petter said gently. 'They have arrested motorcyclists, couriers for the protest leaders, relaying information about the movements of the army and police.'

Petter seemed to know a lot. What was the cunning Soviet agent up to? Admittedly, Hou and Wei had not seen Petter on the Square until now. What did that prove?

'We have read about arrests in the Beijing Daily,' conceded Wei. 'Last night the police arrested Shen Yinhan, a Gongzilian leader, outside the Beijing Hotel. They also arrested two other Gongzilian leaders, so we started a protest outside Police Headquarters not far from here. There have been no arrests on the Square. I'd better go and speak to Hou about this – and have lunch.'

'Be careful,' I said, as she disappeared in the direction of the Goddess of Democracy.

'This is a smart hotel, Petter,' I commented while sipping an excellent gin and tonic.

After Wei had left us, we had a brief walk around Tiananmen Square, but I could see Petter was not comfortable. He was convinced people were watching us. I pointed out that this was quite normal because people in China, I explained, had this thing about our noses. Petter said he did not mean them, but others. It then dawned on me. Perhaps the police were onto Petter. Perhaps being suspicious was part of his Soviet training. In any case, Petter found a taxi, which was not easy, and suggested we had a drink. The hotel he chose was very plush and definitely out-of-bounds for most Chinese.

'This was built as a joint-venture project with a consortium from Hong Kong,' said Petter between mouthfuls of apple pie à la mode.

Apple pie – I let that one go.

We were in the lobby, as Petter insisted on calling the hotel foyer, facing the main entrance where he kept glancing. I realised that if the police were following Petter, then what better way was there to spot your adversaries.

'What do you make of the protests?' I asked. If a Soviet agent didn't know, then who would?

'It is difficult to say,' answered Petter reflectively. 'There are regular briefings by students to journalists in some of the hotels around the Square. The western media readily go to print with what the students are saying without checking their stories or obtaining further corroboration. I suspect that the journalists' enthusiasm for a good headline has given some students an inflated sense of their self-importance. Some of the media-savvy student leaders can play to their audience like professionals, particularly on television. You must admit, what you see on Tiananmen Square and around Beijing has an immediate visual impact. Who needs proper analysis?'

'How do you know all this, Petter?'

'I am staying in one of those hotels.'

'What do the students want? Wei and the others keep saying they want democracy. They also say they still support the Communist Party but want to modify it. It doesn't make sense.'

'I doubt if they have any particular ideological or political goals, apart from those promoted by the dissidents and intellectuals who hang around the student leaders.'

'Aren't you being a little cynical?'

'Look,' said Petter, 'the students call themselves a pro-democracy movement. That is a phrase used by the western media, but nobody has tried to find out what sort of democracy the students have in mind. That would be a good story.'

I had lost touch with what the western press and BBC had been saying, and I could make neither head nor tail of the demands made by Wei, Hou, and the others on the Square.

Anyway, I had a much more urgent problem.

'I am looking for a wedding present, nothing extravagant. Have you got any ideas?' I asked. I explained it was for Leigh, one of his dancing partners back at the guesthouse, in Jaliang.

'There is a shopping mall with a few gift shops at the back of the hotel,' Petter informed me. 'Just give them half what they ask, in US dollars, and be tactful.'

Petter winked and I nodded!

'We must do something about Hou and Wei,' I said. 'They are our responsibility, and we need to get them back to Jaliang.'

'I know,' replied Petter, 'leave it with me.'

Petter left to finalise some details he was dealing with, and I went to the mall at the back of the hotel. Things were hideously expensive. I took the young shop assistant to a quiet corner and asked her, 'How much?' in a hoarse whisper, with a wink, showing her a discreet handful of dollars. For some reason she took offence and I had to leave quickly. It certainly didn't deserve all the fuss they made.

Wait until I next see Petter.

From: <u>Deputy Chairman</u>
Office of Education Foreign Affairs
Public Security Bureau
Beijing
To: <u>Assistant to Chairman</u>
Public Security Bureau (*PSB* Beijing)
30 May 1989

Internal memorandum

Subject: <u>DISSIDENT VINCENT</u>

We are almost certain that Vincent was behind the scheming charade of the erection of that annoying statue on Tiananmen Square today. On several occasions, we observed him talking to some of the students responsible for the erection of the statue.

Despite the fact that things were confusing on the Square at the time, with crowds watching, we heard Vincent declare that there was no way that the government could come out of this looking good. Vincent examined the statue's fixtures to the paving and was overheard stating that it would be difficult to remove.

It has not been possible to get the names of Vincent's student co-conspirers. Students are suspicious of any strangers hanging around, and we have instructions to keep a low profile on the Square and not to further provoke the protesters.

We were unable to follow Vincent as he once again implemented anti-surveillance techniques. On entering a shopping mall, he managed to cause a minor disturbance and then escaped in the resulting chaos.

Extract from:

THE PRESS
WED 31 MAY 1989
Local correspondent, Peking

STUDENT LEADERS have managed to revitalise and motivate other protesters yesterday by erecting a 30-foot high replica of the State of Liberty, nicknamed the Goddess of Democracy, in the middle of Tiananmen Square.

This coincided with the first reports of arrests in Peking since martial law was declared 10 days ago.

What appears to be of concern to the government is the participation of workers and ordinary Peking residents in the protests. While an assurance of no reprisals was given to students if they stopped their protests, this was never extended to the rest of the population. There are already reports of reprisals where workers are being fined or threatened with loss of job if they participate in the demonstrations.

Chapter 40

Wednesday, May 31, 1989

I woke up worried...

To begin with, I was worried about Wei and Hou. I somehow felt responsible. Aside from my grave suspicions of Petter working for the Soviets, he said he would deal with Wei and Hou, and I trusted him. If an undercover Soviet agent couldn't sort it, then who could.

What was a more pressing worry was my wish to buy Leigh a wedding present. I decided to visit the assistant in the hotel shop who had annotated my Beijing bus map to see if he had any ideas. He said he knew of a shop that sold fine porcelain, but not for tourists, more for your senior official with a dollar or two to spend.

The shop assistant told me that most shops were on the ground floor below residential blocks and not necessarily signed. They didn't need signs because everyone knew where they were, which explained why I had not seen many, apart from the odd grocery store. He carefully annotated my map showing me a round trip that took in the shopping area in question, a bit of the suburbs, and ended at Tiananmen Square.

I boarded the correct bus, at the right stop, but somehow got off at the wrong place. I knew the shopping area in question was a low-level building, on the same road as the bus route, and at a crossroad. All I had to was investigate low-level buildings at crossroads.

My getting lost was fortuitous because Beijing revealed some of its secrets. I discovered all sorts of shops, but I never did find the porcelain one frequented by dollar-flushed senior officials.

I bought Leigh a silk tablecloth with delicate hand embroidery of bamboo and plum blossom — none of your fluffy kittens there, as favoured by Mr Chou! The woman in the shop wrapped the tablecloth in silk and tied it with a silk ribbon. I was pleased with my purchase.

There was evidence of the army around Beijing, but not in great numbers. I passed some parked cattle trucks, with soldiers lounging around, smoking, and larking about just as you might expect. The local residents took no notice of the trucks or soldiers. When I walked past, the soldiers took no notice of me until I said, '*nee hao*,' and they looked at me in surprise.

I found a place for a late lunch where others were still eating. By the entrance was a glass covered counter displaying several types of noodles. A casually dressed man loitered near the entrance, and I took him to be a waiter. He looked a bit puzzled at my entering because it was not a restaurant for foreigners. Nevertheless, he just ignored me, which I felt was impolite.

Sometimes in China, service could be a little lacking. I smiled, pointed to my mouth, rubbed my stomach, and sat down at a clean looking, empty table. The waiter continued to stare at me.

'*Nee hao*,' I said, hoping to break the ice but, funnily enough, that didn't work.

Maybe he wanted my order.

Easy…

I stood up, took the waiter firmly by the elbow, and marched him around the restaurant. When I saw a tasty dish on a table, I pointed to it, making sure the waiter confirmed my request, although he seemed reluctant to do so. Still, I was persistent. After half a dozen or so points, I judged that might be enough. Finally, I ordered a beer; I could do that.

'Tsingtao,' I said.

After a heated discussion with another waiter, the truculent one who took my order left the restaurant. Looking more professional, with a tea towel over his left shoulder and wearing an apron, the new waiter went about his tasks diligently.

They promptly served me hot green tea, and within a couple of minutes, I got a bowl of flat noodles, hot and steaming. Most tables had noodles. Possibly, they were what the cook staked his reputation on, his signature dish. What followed was a selection of dishes that bore no resemblance to those I had pointed at, but it didn't matter. The food was hot and delicious and served in small tasty portions. Although I never got my beer, I had no cause for complaint.

After lunch, I ambled around aimlessly, and then I paused to get my bearings. According to my map, I was on the outskirts of Beijing. I needed to walk a bit further to find another bus route in the direction of Tiananmen Square. The area was not heavily built up but was dusty and without much vegetation or trees.

I crossed the road where there was a row of cattle trucks similar to those I had seen earlier. In some of the trucks were ordinary people, just sitting there in boredom, some asleep. Others were walking to and from an area behind a residential block near a large building where people were milling around and shouting. Whatever they were doing, they were doing it without enthusiasm or passion. Perhaps they had missed lunch.

I saw three men in white shirts, dark trousers, and black shoes, which normally signified your Chinese office-worker or intellectual. They looked too old and smart to be students going for a peaceful afternoon demo. They were obviously being nosy, like me. I suspected they were not standing there by accident.

'*Nee hao*,' I said. 'What's going on over there?'

The three men looked at me suspiciously, exchanged words among themselves, before the little one at the end spoke.

'What are you doing here?' he asked, in broken English.

'I'm lost,' I replied, showing him my bus map.

The three men had a good look at my map, and I pointed to the route I was trying to find. It so happened I wasn't lost at all.

'What's going on over there?' I again asked.

'There has been a pro-government rally,' explained the little one, 'but we think this has been organised by the authorities so they can show it on television.'

The little one conferred with his two colleagues, before continuing.

'We talked to some of the demonstrators and a few said they were brought here in army trucks. Others said they were sick and tired with the students complaining because everyone knows they are privileged. We heard the demonstrators shouting slogans supporting the prime minister, Li Peng.'

The other two were looking around anxiously and obviously had had enough. They tugged on the sleeve of little one who, in turn, shrugged his shoulders before walking off with the others.

The buses were not as regular as they had been and I had to wait a bit. It was dark when the bus dropped me two streets away from

Tiananmen Square, and, as I approached, I sensed things were different.

I had only been in the area during daytime, when the roads around Tiananmen Square were almost empty. I stood on the side of the road, near the Museum, and looked across to Tiananmen Square. I could not see the Square, just the tall Monument in the middle, odd flags waving in the evening wind, and the head of the Goddess of Democracy in the dim light. The whole area had a peculiar atmosphere, as if expecting something to happen but not knowing what.

The road was crammed with cyclists, thousands of them, just cycling around Tiananmen Square. Were they supporting the protesters on the Square, or were they inquisitive, just having a good look after work?

I decided it would be impossible to cross the road to get to the Square and when I checked the underpass, it was crowded with people reading the posters on the wall. I assumed if Wei and Hou were on the Square then they would be safe enough.

As I walked away from Tiananmen Square, I noted the contrast; a street or so away, things appeared normal.

I strolled around the area to the east of Tiananmen Gate where there were a few hotels. I decided I might go into one or two, and find a vantage point overlooking Tiananmen Square, but I failed to do so. Other buildings blocked views of the Square.

From the top-floor balcony of the Beijing Hotel, I could make out the northern end of Tiananmen Square but the distance was too great to make out any detail. The upper part of the Monument, rising above the roofs of government buildings, was just visible in the gloomy light. I couldn't see its base, where the students were. Looking at my map, the Monument must be nearly three-quarters of a mile away.

On leaving the hotel, I got lost in the lifts, which were confusing. I eventually caught a bus back to my hotel, enjoyed a beer at the bar, and went to bed.

From: **Deputy Chairman**
Office of Education Foreign Affairs
Public Security Bureau
Beijing
To: **Assistant to Chairman**
Public Security Bureau (*PSB* Beijing)
31 May 1989

Internal memorandum

Subject: DISSIDENT VINCENT

Vincent appears to be able to move around Beijing and its suburbs without fear of apprehension by the authorities.

We observed him talking to journalists who we suspect are sympathetic to the protest movement in the area of today's pro-government rally. Later, we saw him near Tiananmen Square monitoring the events taking place at that time. He entered several hotels, where foreign journalists are known to be staying, and was seen seeking out vantage points over the Square. I can only conclude that Vincent is now coordinating a propaganda campaign, against our leaders and government, through the world media.

It is my view that it is highly likely that Vincent is one of the masterminds behind the protest movement from the very beginning and will stop at nothing until he has fulfilled his objectives.

It is imperative that the authorities take the initiative and clear Tiananmen Square of all protesters before they leave of their own accord.

Once again, the provocateur implemented anti-surveillance techniques and we were unable to follow him.

Chapter 41

Thursday, June 1, 1989

When I arrived at Tiananmen Square, everything had changed.

The roads around the Square were once again empty. I scrutinised the Square from my normal vantage point, near the portrait of Mao, and suspected there were even fewer protesters than before. People were still posing for photographs by the gate, manoeuvring to get the portrait of Mao in the picture. The Goddess of Democracy was not attracting the crowds as before. Only a few people stood and stared.

I crossed the avenue, and found Wei at her post by the propaganda tent. She appeared to be all right, and I mulled over how she always managed to look clean and fresh. Other protesters on the Square, mainly the male students, seemed to favour the bohemian look, with shirt open at the front, tails flapping behind, looking grimy.

'Good morning,' I said brightly. 'Where is Hou?'

'He is sleeping,' replied Wei. 'We had another busy night, especially Hou. There have been more arrests, so Hou and some others marched to the Public Security Bureau Headquarters to demand their release. We wanted to know who had been arrested, and why.'

'There are fewer people today.'

Wei shrugged.

'Early this morning there was an attempted kidnapping of Chai Ling and her husband Feng Congde,' Wei said quietly. 'They were asleep in their tent at the time, but they yelled and others came to their rescue.'

'Who did that?'

'We think it was students from outside Beijing. There were complaints about their leadership style and messy finances, so some took radical action. There are rumours this has happened before.'

'Why did they do it?'

'To change the leadership, but it is difficult to know for certain.'

I shook my head in disbelief.

'We heard the authorities have been bribing students, so it might have been some of them that did it,' added Wei. 'There are government agents on the Square, taking notes and names. We have to be careful.'

'I'm going to look around, then buy some lunch,' I said.

'Cream cakes, please.'

I walked around Tiananmen Square and found it much as it was before. There were quite a few men in clean shirts, others pushing bicycles, women wearing nice summer frocks, and smartly dressed couples walking together. Hardly students, but these were the minority.

I noticed a man, with a short-sleeved white shirt neatly tucked in his grey trousers and holding a rolled newspaper close to his face, staring at me. I walked over to ask him what was going on, but he moved away.

I walked towards the Monument of the People's Heroes.

I remembered Wei telling me it was the base for the leadership of the protesters, and I decided to investigate further. As I attempted to step over the makeshift barrier enclosing the Monument, someone quickly came across and told me that the area was out-of-bounds. He was confident but a bit too officious for my liking. I quickly showed him my blue United Nations Certificate. I didn't know if he recognised it as such, but he scowled and marched away as if saying, 'I don't have time for this and have much more important things to do.' I knew my certificate would come in useful – eventually.

I crossed the barrier and looked around.

I paused at the base of the Monument to take in my surroundings. To the north was the Goddess of Democracy and further, the portrait of Mao above Tiananmen Gate, looking on. The steps up to the Monument were in two sections, one podium placed upon a larger one, with a paved platform between. To the left of the Monument, in the middle paved area, were makeshift tents.

At the top of the first flight of steps were some officious-looking protesters, equally spaced in a line. They were trendily dressed, some with arms folded, and all looking onto the Square. They were pickets protecting the Command Headquarters. They did not bother me.

At the base of the Monument, and slightly to the left, was an imposing square poster, predominantly blue, with a strip of pale green on top, with writing in black Chinese symbols. In front of the poster was an orange tent, one of those from Hong Kong. Above the poster were two huge red banners with yellow lettering, one above the other, taking up the width of the Monument. Below the banners, above stone friezes of scenes of some sort, was a grey metal loudspeaker. I could see more loudspeakers on the sides of the Monument.

Some of those around were smartly dressed. One was carrying a bulging briefcase under his armpit. They were doing nothing in particular, just looking. Were they journalists or intellectuals? Others were obviously students from their dress – veterans from the hunger strike, maybe.

I went up to a student.

'What does that say?' I asked, pointing to the gold calligraphic inscription on the northern face of the Monument.

He looked puzzled at my question, but looked at the inscription, nonetheless. To my surprise, he replied in English.

'The people's heroes live on forever,' he said.

'And those?' I again asked, pointing to the two red banners with yellow lettering.

'The top one is demanding a meeting with the government and the resignation of Li Peng. The lower banner is demanding an end to martial law. They are difficult to translate exactly.'

'What are these?' I persisted, pointing to the carved stone friezes at the base of the Monument.

'Scenes from Chinese history,' he replied, scrutinising the base more closely, 'The Boxer Uprising; the Opium War; the Anti-Japanese Invasion; and the Civil War.'

The carved friezes represented highlights of revolutions since 1840. I remembered Tammy telling me that. There was an element of irony because all around us was another revolution, of sorts, taking place, and I wondered how history would record that.

'How long do you intend to stay?' I asked.

'Some of us want to leave at the weekend,' he replied.

'Who is that?' I asked, pointing to the officious student who attempted to prevent me crossing the barrier. He was with a group of others, discussing important student matters.

'Feng Congde,' he replied. He did not elaborate further and edged away. I did not want to press him.

I talked to one of the intellectual-looking types, a self-assured, smartly dressed man. He seemed to be gazing at the horizon, or maybe looking at the Goddess of Democracy and speculating, as I had, what Mao would have made of it all if he were still alive.

'Can you help me,' I asked. 'Over there near the new tents, the pink flag by the rubbish bin, which university is it?'

He scrutinised the flag for a few seconds before replying.

'That is interesting. It belongs to Yanbian University in eastern Jilin Province, near the North Korean border. It is a provincial university at Yanji, in the Yanbian Korean Autonomous Prefecture. It takes students from the Korean minority in Northeast China.'

'What's going to happen now?' I asked.

'I don't know,' he answered, 'but in the end, this whole incident will be nothing but a spit in the ocean in China's long history.'

What a strange reply.

At the top of the steps, on the right hand side of the Monument, was a man with a large television camera on its tripod, facing the Goddess and the portrait of Mao. He was tall, with long, fair hair, and had a beard. He was unwilling to talk at first.

'Where do you come from?'

'Sweden.'

Alarm bells rang in my head, because Petter was also from Sweden – coincidence maybe.

'What are you doing here?'

There was a long pause before he replied.

'If anything happens, then I won't miss it.'

After that, the man refused to talk and ignored all further queries, but just stared ahead.

It then occurred to me what everyone was doing. They were all waiting for something to happen, but they did not know what.

I had heard foreign journalists were still around, despite Gorbachev having left China some time ago. I found it odd that there were not many other foreigners, besides myself, on Tiananmen Square. I recognised none as being western journalists. They must be in nearby hotels interviewing contacts and doing whatever else they do.

I hung around the Monument, with the rest, waiting for something to happen; but nothing did. From where I was standing, Mao appeared to be hiding in the distance, behind the Goddess, with the tall flagpole between, the red flag of China proudly on display, high above. I left the student Command Headquarters and walked towards Mao's Mausoleum, which was closed and remained untouched by the protesters. It was much quieter there.

I left the Square by crossing the road on the west side. I walked down a street just south of the Great Hall of the People. I wanted to find the coffee shop Tammy had taken me to the other day. I had to buy lunch.

Within a minute of leaving Tiananmen Square, life was normal in central Beijing – just another day. Apart from the usual cyclists, by the roadside were tables where people were just passing the time of day playing cards and having a gossip. Some of the men had their trouser legs rolled up to their knees to keep cool; it was a warm day. Turning round, I could still see the end of Tiananmen Square, which was a different world to this.

As I entered the coffee shop, I could smell the sickly, sweet looking cakes, and they still had apple pie. At first, they did not understand what I wanted. I wanted everything, the whole lot, including all the cold drinks. I had Harry to thank because I still had the remains of his Renminbi in my pocket. The coffee shop wouldn't part with everything because it didn't want to disappoint its regular customers, but I didn't do too badly. I carried one box of food and drinks, and the coffee shop arranged for someone else to carry the other. It was a bit of a struggle. My helper was reluctant to cross the road to get to Tiananmen Square, but he did.

I had arranged to meet Tammy and Leigh near the propaganda tent but that was before they erected the Goddess of Democracy, and I was not sure if they would come. Knowing my arrangement with Tammy and Leigh, I had arranged for Petter to meet me at the same place and time. I chose a spot among the makeshift tents at an intersection, with the Goddess to the north, the Monument to the south, the Museum to the east, and the Great Hall to the west. When I found Wei, I sent her to find Hou and to borrow a couple of those blankets I had seen a few days ago. I then saw Petter approaching. Apart from being tall, his pipe gave him away. I waved, and he came across.

'What are you doing, Charles?' asked Petter.

'We're having a picnic,' I declared.

Petter raised his eyebrows ever so slightly. I knew he would prefer a comfortable hotel to have his lunch, but he did not say anything.

'Petter,' I said, 'I want a straight answer from you. You haven't been entirely straight with me, have you?'

'I admit I have been a little elusive,' he said.

'Elusive?'

'There are so many opportunities these days, and China has more than most,' he continued. 'Do you remember Mr Cheng from the port of Jaliang? He was very helpful in making introductions.'

I then remembered telling Petter about the demurrage swindle fine-tuned by the Nigerians in the mid-seventies, where they paid shipowners handsomely while waiting for a berth with a fictitious or low-value cargo. He wasn't considering doing such a thing, was he? I again remembered he took a lot of interest in that Soviet ship, the one with lots of vodka. If that was the case, then he had been more than a little elusive – that was fraud.

Maybe Petter wasn't a Soviet agent after all, just a Swedish crook.

'Petter, you're not thinking of involving Mr Cheng with illegal activities, are you?'

'Certainly not,' Petter replied indignantly. 'The Chinese government is encouraging joint ventures and Mr Cheng has been very helpful.'

'Joint ventures...' I repeated slowly.

'You know the project involves student placements in western companies and I am responsible for arranging them. Well, I had done most of that before arriving here, but I considered I might be able to develop the idea further.'

'Go on.'

'In China, there are industries with well-trained personnel who would be very employable at a fraction of western salaries. I wanted to tap into this market. For example, shipping companies in Scandinavia have to pay crippling high crew salaries, so why not employ well-trained

Chinese. Other industries include the offshore oil and gas industry, possibly the port industry itself. I was offered twenty mathematicians, all speaking English, by one Chinese university.'

'So you're not working for the Soviets?' I blurted.

'Certainly not... not yet,' he replied carefully. 'You could be onto something. The situation in the Soviet block is very unstable, so who knows what might happen in the next year or so. I am sure they would welcome joint ventures. You have given me something to think about.'

Who could have thought Petter was a spy?

'Were your discussions successful?' I asked.

I was beginning to recover my composure, and I knew a little bit about joint ventures from my Singaporean drinking partner at the hotel.

'Not exactly,' he replied cautiously, 'it is early days yet.'

'Did you explain about the multiplier effect in the local economy, hard currency earnings, and so on?' I asked. I did not want to go into too much detail, as I couldn't remember everything my Singaporean friend had said. I could tell my line of questioning surprised Petter.

'I did try and explain the benefits.' I could see Petter was faltering.

He was not successful.

'I suppose you had the usual problem of trying to explain what was in it for them. That can cause confusion, I believe.' I added, whimsically.

Wei and Hou arrived with the blankets and interrupted our conversation. I asked them to spread the blankets on the ground and place the contents of the two boxes in the middle.

Petter took me aside.

'What about you?' he said. 'Haven't you been a little mischievous?'

'What do you mean?'

'From what I heard, you have been promoting riots and subversive activities at Number 3 University from the day you arrived.'

'What do you mean?'

I know I was sounding repetitive, but I did not know what Petter was on about, hence the question.

'Who was it spreading subversive information in the classroom and encouraging students to defect to the West during their work placements?' I could see Petter was having some fun at my expense!

'What do y— '

'Who was it preaching about western democracy in the student refectory and caused a riot?'

'That's not how I remember it!'

I decided I had better vary my answers a bit.

'Who was it carrying the student flag during the demonstrations in Jaliang, providing support and encouraging the students?'

'There might have been a misunderstanding, I admit.'

'Who was it who introduced the journalists from the China News Agency to the student leaders? The list is endless, Charles. I even heard you have become a cult figure in Jaliang.'

Petter was enjoying himself and I didn't understand what he was saying. Admittedly, when I arrived in China I was a little naïve, but what Petter was saying was absurd. How could I be a cult figure?

'That's all a little bit over the top,' I protested.

'You are right,' Petter admitted, 'but Professor Song and the students thought otherwise.'

'Professor Song, the faculty dean!'

'Professor Song is a bit of an old rascal with one or two old scores to settle. He understands that the students are very impressionable and take things too literally. He asked Professor Sang to keep an eye on you and to keep you briefed as to what was happening. With your British sense of academic liberalism, events took their own course, so to speak.'

I was mortified.

Things were never what they seemed. Who told me that?

'You mean I was unwittingly used to stir up trouble. Was that why you had all those meetings with Professor Song?'

'We did talk about you, but not much. Professor Song was helping me with my joint venture schemes. He introduced me to other universities and some local industries. One or two of the students were helping me with background research.'

Things began to fit into place...

'If it is any consolation, Charles, we think you have done an excellent job,' added Petter. 'Your management game was a masterpiece, especially when you manoeuvred things to humiliate Mr Chou. Professor Song was laughing for days when he heard about that.'

'Professor Charles, your friends are looking for you,' said Wei.

It was Tammy and Leigh over by the propaganda tent, but they had already spotted Petter and were coming over.

Lunch was set, and there was food to feed half the students on the Square. Wei and Hou gathered some of their friends.

'I wasn't sure you would be able to make it,' I said to Tammy. 'You remember Petter, don't you?'

'Of course.'

Tammy explained that the authorities were making it difficult for people to support the pro-democracy movement, especially those who had left their jobs to attend protest rallies. It was lunchtime, and she explained that, being from the Ministry of Education, she and Leigh had promised their colleagues they would do the patriotic thing. They would encourage students to leave the Square and return to classes.

'You must leave the Square and return to classes,' Tammy informed students nearby, 'but not until after lunch.'

We all sat in the midst of the makeshift tents, with flags of all shapes and sizes, predominantly red, flapping around us. It was warm, and I could see most of Beijing's tourist attractions nearby, including the Goddess of Democracy. I had most of my friends in China around me. Only Harry and Professor Sang were missing. In the distance, I could see Mao looking down from Tiananmen Gate. He was not quite a friend, but had been company, nonetheless.

I served Petter apple-pie.

The coffee shop had done us proud. Apart from the cakes, we had a selection of savoury dishes prepared ready for the lunchtime rush.

Conversation was jovial and light-hearted and, for a short time, we forgot about the recent turbulence so evident around us. For no apparent reason, the loudspeakers on the Monument began to play Beethoven's 'Ode to Joy'. I had heard it before, the day when they erected the Goddess of Democracy. Petter then stood up and walked over towards Tammy.

'Madame,' said Petter, taking Tammy by the hand, 'would you care to dance? I don't think I have had the pleasure.'

Tammy bounced up and grabbed Petter much as she did me some weeks ago, but there the similarity ended. They moved around delicately to the music and with much applause from onlookers.

My dancing lessons with Tammy must have worked!

'Please, everybody,' I shouted, 'if I can have your attention for just one minute. Leigh is getting married on Sunday, and I would like us to wish her and her fiancé all the very best for the future.'

I handed Leigh her wedding present and she looked slightly embarrassed, but radiant. Everyone clapped, and I got a hug from Leigh, Tammy, and Wei. It was like that on Tiananmen Square that day.

The food was soon gone, and Tammy and Leigh had to return to work. I explained I was flying home that evening and needed to pack and get to the airport. Petter had a later flight. We said our farewells. Students started to drift away, but Petter asked Hou and Wei to remain.

'What I am about to say is not negotiable,' Petter said, 'because you are returning to Jaliang. What you have done is commendable and we are proud of you both. You still have examinations to do, and you have to prepare for your work placements. You are both young and will be able to make an impact on the social order in China, when you are older and in senior positions.'

Petter produced airline tickets for flights back to Jaliang for Hou and Wei and sent them to collect their few belongings. He was not leaving the Square without them.

We all left via the underpass. Petter didn't want to be knocked down by a cyclist on his last day. He was personally taking Hou and Wei to the airport in case they had second thoughts, particularly Hou because we could see he was upset.

'I might have another project for you, Charles,' shouted Petter, as his taxi drove away, 'Somalia.'

Chapter 42

Sunday, June 4, 1989

I walked into the lounge and saw my family staring at the television watching the evening news.

I was horrified!

I saw armed troops, tanks crushing barricades, and buses and trucks on fire. In the background, I heard gunfire. The commentary talked about a brutal attack on Tiananmen Square, massacres, and the unofficial death toll being over 1000, with many more injured. There was a blurred picture of an armoured vehicle knocking down the Goddess of Democracy, a replica of the Statute of Liberty built by students on Tiananmen Square only last week.

The commentary said tanks and armoured personnel carriers had driven onto the Square indiscriminately crushing temporary shelters with many students still asleep inside. Another account said that as students left the Square, troops had fired on them, felling the first row of 100, and then the second.

I switched between channels and one commentator from the BBC reported that while watching from the Beijing Hotel, he saw troops shooting at students at the Monument in the centre of the Square.

Nothing made sense.

I was there just a couple of days ago.

Extracts from:

THE PRESS
SUN 04 JUNE 1989
Local correspondent, Peking

THE CHINESE GOVERNMENT ended several weeks of pro-democracy protests in a massacre today when elite troops made an attack on Tiananmen Square, with countless killed and wounding thousands while randomly firing at protesters.

Atrocities occurred in other parts of Peking as troops in armoured vehicles and tanks smashed into barricades set up by the residents. About one million people had taken to the streets but troops, who had orders to end the demonstrations at all costs, open fired at anyone in their way.

TELEVISION BROADCAST
SUN 04 JUNE 1989
World editor, Peking

'TROOPS AND TANKS moved towards the Monument, shooting first in the air and then, directly at the students themselves, so that the steps of the Monument and the heroic reliefs which decorate it were smashed by bullets.'

THE PRESS
SUN 11 JUNE 1989
Local correspondent, Peking

AS THE TROOPS entered Tiananmen Square that fateful morning on 4 June, people with their hands held in V-for-victory signs were singing in groups. Within minutes, almost all of them were dead. Students, huddled around the Monument, linked hands, and sang the Internationale. Troops cut them down with machine-gun fire, line after line after line.

Chapter 43

Friday, June 23, 1989

I received a letter from Leigh. Her wedding went well, which was nice. For some people, it appeared life in Beijing carried on as normal.

Ministry of Education
Statistics Department
Beijing

16 June 1989

Dear Professor Charles,

With my husband, we would like to thank you for our wedding present. We were delighted to receive such a fine tablecloth made by traditional methods, because these can be difficult to get (and expensive).

We had a lovely wedding (4 June) and everything went well. After the marriage formalities, we all had to travel across Beijing for the reception in a famous restaurant. We managed to do this despite the army crackdown in Beijing. We travelled in a procession of cars and passed quite close to the Forbidden City, and it was romantic. We could hear gunfire all around us as if in honour of our wedding. We were all excited.

Our honeymoon arrangements were memorable, so my husband had a good start after all!

Tammy sends her best regards.

Yours sincerely

Leigh

Chapter 45

Wednesday, July 5, 1989

I received another letter from China, this time from Wei. Both she and Hou were well, it seemed. I was worried about them.

Number 3 University
Dormitory 7A
Yoga's Road
Jaliang

26 June 1989

Dear Professor Charles,

   Best wishes from all of your students at Number 3
University.
   Professor Sang arranged for our examination on
cross-management communication last Friday. We found it
very interesting. We are now preparing for our foreign
work placements, and I hope to go to New York. I could
have gone to Pontefract, but I chose New York because I
wanted to have a placement in industry and not a
university. I looked at an atlas and found Pontefract.
It is quite close to the old York, you never told us
that.
   After Hou and I left you in Beijing, Mr Petter took
us to the airport. Despite Mr Petter's best endeavours,
once he made sure that we had checked in for our
flights, Hou still managed to slip away unseen and he
returned to Tiananmen Square. He just couldn't leave.
   As for myself, I was tired and didn't think we could
achieve much more, so returning to Jaliang was a
relief. I arrived back at Jaliang and told all my
colleagues about our experiences. I am sure you have
seen the news and know what happened shortly after we
left Beijing.
   We were all relieved when Hou managed to return
unharmed to Jaliang a few days after the troops cleared
Tiananmen Square. He told us what happened, but we have
to be careful because the authorities want to arrest
all student leaders involved in the protests.
   Hou was on Tiananmen Square right to the end.
Although things were very confused, I will tell you
what he said.

   On <u>Friday, June 2</u>, the day after you left, four
intellectuals started another hunger strike, in a tent
near the Monument of the People's Heroes, to show that

272

they could face the same kind of dangers as the students. They were not to eat for two or three days, and then others were to replace them. They were; Liu Xiaobo, a writer and professor; Zhou Duo, an official from a computer company; Zhao Xing, a sociologist; and Dejian, a rock-singer from Taiwan. Other intellectuals also gathered around the Monument in support.

There were rumours of People's Liberation Army (PLA) troop movements around Beijing, some close to the Square. The troops seem to be inexperienced, poorly dressed, unarmed, and young. Hou did not see them because he remained on the Square. Someone said there was a traffic accident where a military jeep ran into pedestrians and cyclists, killing one or two and seriously injuring others. That seemed to rally the residents of Beijing.

Residents of Beijing made it difficult for troop movements and criticised them for attacking the people. Students gathered outside the Police Headquarters and the Zhongnanhai, the residence of the elite. There were rumours of arrests all over Beijing.

Saturday, June 3, was confusing. There were clashes between troops and protesters as the army converged on Tiananmen Square. At first, the army was not very organised. The residents of Beijing gathered in large crowds and built barricades. Troop movements ended in uncertainty. There were rumours that soldiers had shot people in the streets; Hou could hear gunshots. Despite not knowing what was happening, Hou remained on Tiananmen Square.

The government broadcasted warnings on television. 'Stay at home. Keep off the streets. Keep away from Tiananmen Square.'

Everyone was aware that something was going to happen that night.

The residents of Beijing were determined and they made things difficult for the troops. Most believed that the PLA was *their* army, and it would not do anything to harm them, but they were wrong. Later, things changed as armoured troop carriers moved towards the city centre, pushing aside the makeshift barricades. Large crowds tried to block the path of PLA troops in the western suburbs such as Muxidi, Gongzhufen, Fuxingmen, and Liubukou, but then things got ugly. The PLA killed many Beijing residents for their resistance.

By late evening troops had reached Chang'an Avenue. These were well dressed and heavily armed, unlike those the day before. Hou and his friends realised that the bullets were real; they were expecting rubber bullets.

Some student leaders, like Wu'er Kaixi, left the Square and never returned. Most of the students who were still on Tiananmen Square, like Hou, were from the provinces. The majority of the Beijing students had already left and had returned to campus or home. Parents had been arriving all day to take them home, sometimes forcibly.

Hou could hear gunfire from the direction of the southwest corner of the Square, where there was a confrontation between troops and Beijing residents, but he couldn't see what was happening. It was night, and with the vastness of the Square, it was impossible to see everything. There must have been casualties.

At about 1.00 a.m. on Sunday, June 4, troops had blocked off the northern end of Tiananmen Square. Most students on the Square congregated on the steps of the Monument. They were calm, frightened, and waited for the inevitable to happen. The government loudspeakers accused them of being counter-revolutionaries and demanded they leave the Square immediately.

Hou was not frightened but he couldn't remain with the others at the Monument, just waiting. He drifted around and found comfort in being near foreigners who were cautiously keeping an eye on things. At times, he considered making a desperate dash to safety, but fear of what might happen prevented him doing so. He realised he should have done that hours earlier.

Hou saw the Gongzilian tents in flames at the northwest corner and was worried about what had happened there. There was gunfire, flames, and smoke from the direction of the Forbidden City and Chang'an Avenue, and there must have been casualties. Most troops arrived from the west along Chang'an Avenue.

At first, there were a few foreign journalists and

camera crews around, but Hou saw most of them leaving quickly as the PLA arrived, including the BBC.

Around 2.15, there was a long burst of gunfire from the direction of the Forbidden City; it seemed to last a long time. People dropped to the ground for safety. Hou couldn't work out what the troops were firing at, because he saw no one injured. He thought the troops were trying to intimidate those on the Square, and it worked.

By about 2.30, it was eerily silent although those on the Square could still hear distant gunfire. The medical tent of the United Medical College, staffed by volunteer doctors and medical students, which stood in isolation between the Goddess and Museum on the east side of the Square, was still functioning and treating the wounded. There were student pickets sitting around the tent, providing protection.

By 3.00 troops had cleared the northern end of the Square. Other troops gathered in front of the Museum to the east and the Great Hall to the west.

Hou saw foreign journalists, or they might have been a film crew, inspecting the tents around the Goddess; someone said they were Spanish. There couldn't have been many remaining in the tents, not asleep anyway. Over by the Great Hall, there were Beijing residents milling around, but Hou couldn't see if they were merely watching or haranguing the troops.

Chai Ling was heard over the student loudspeakers saying, 'Those who want to leave, should leave, and those who want to stay, should stay.' There were many people gathered around the Monument, including angry workers who told the students about some of the killings in the streets.

After some discussion with the students, two intellectuals, Dejian, the rock-singer, and Zhou Duo, went to negotiate with army officers. That was about 3.30 or so. They took off their vests using them as white flags. It was agreed that the army would give the students time to vacate the Square peacefully, but they must do so by daybreak. Dejian might have spoken to the officers more than once.

Around 4.00, the authorities switched off the lights on the Square. It was dark and everything was quiet.

Among the students, who remained seated on the Monument steps, there was divided opinion on what to do.

In the darkness, flames from burning vehicles from the north and south ends of the Square looked menacing and the smoke was causing sinister shadows. Through the smoke and the dark-orange light from the flames, the flags and banners were like waving silhouettes in slow motion. In front of the Forbidden City, army vehicles, tanks, and troops were just visible, moving like ghosts through the eerie light and smoke.

Suddenly two busloads of students arrived from the southeast corner of the Square. Hou believed they were mad, but he was pleased they did. If they could get onto the Square, then it should be possible to get off.

The student loudspeakers came to life. Feng Congde and some others had been busy reconstructing the student broadcasting station on the southeast corner of the second level. The students sang songs, like the Internationale and the Chinese national anthem, to raise their spirits.

Someone set fire to tents and rubbish between the Monument and Great Hall causing more smoke. One of the leaders shouted over the loudspeakers. 'Keep order and stay calm. We must create no pretext for them whatsoever.'

After about fifteen minutes, lights in front of the Great Hall and Forbidden City came on, throwing a gloomy light over parts of the Square. Troops rushed out of the Great Hall, crossed the road, and took a position in front of Mao's Mausoleum, behind the Monument. The only exit from the Square was by the southeast corner, behind the Mausoleum. Troops near the Museum fired warning shots.

Several people gave impromptu speeches on the student loudspeakers. A leader from the Beijing Autonomous Student Federation said that they must on no account leave and they would now pay the highest price for democracy, their blood. A leader from the Gongzilian, in a rough voice, pleaded that they should all leave immediately, otherwise there would be a bloodbath. Chai Ling told an old Chinese story about a colony of ants and a fire, but Hou didn't listen.

'We have won a great victory, but it is time to

leave,' said Dejian over the loudspeakers. He also said
that they had already shed too much blood and they
could not afford to lose any more. He promised that he
and the other intellectuals would remain at the
Monument until all students had left.

Most students were sitting on the Monument steps,
some writing their last wills and letters to their
families.

Minutes passed, and all the students could feel the
tension. Tanks started their engines on the northern
end of the Square.

Incredibly, two foreigners slowly climbed the
Monument steps, avoiding students seated closely
together. They got to the top level, had a look around,
and slowly descended on the side nearest the Museum.
One must have been a journalist because he was taking
notes.

Around 4.30, a voice vote was quickly organised by
Feng Congde. It was dark and frightening and people
were scared, uncertain about what might happen.
Students had to shout, 'go', or, 'stay', at the same
time. Those wanting to leave were ashamed and did not
shout very loud, but the two sides sounded about the
same; some claimed that the 'stays' were louder.

Fortunately, reason prevailed, and Feng Congde
announced they would leave.

As the vote ended, troops, but not many, were moving
around on the top level of the Monument and they shot
out the loudspeakers on the north side. They must have
approached from the northwest. Some of the students on
the north side may have missed the final decision
because they couldn't hear it. The loudspeakers on the
south side of the Monument were still working.

A tank or heavy army vehicle toppled and smashed to
pieces the Goddess. Hou wasn't sure when that happened
but someone said it was still dark.

At 4.40, the authorities switched on the lights on
Tiananmen Square, possibly so that the students could
see to leave because they had to do so before daybreak.

At dawn, shortly after 5.00, led by their leaders,
students stood up, reluctantly left their position on
the Monument steps, and then, slowly, walked off
Tiananmen Square by the southeast corner. Students were

crying as they left, some were obviously in shock, and others shouted slogans, a last show of defiance. Those in the front walked in rows, arms locked. They left with mixed feelings, uncertain if they had won a victory, or were beaten.

As students started to leave, a small unit of camouflage troops rushed up to the highest level of the Monument and shot out the remaining loudspeakers. Some were firing warning shots into the air and they roughly pushed students down the Monument steps. Despite that, some foreigners and intellectuals stayed behind.

The strangest thing then happened. A small group of foreigners – journalists, a few diplomats, and Hong Kong Chinese – who were a few yards away from the Monument started applauding as the students left. Two of those applauding were the foreigners who had climbed up the Monument steps not so long ago.

Some of the students were carrying banners from the universities in Beijing, which was odd, because most of the students were from the provinces. As they left, marching past Mao's Mausoleum, soldiers kept their distance. Hou was near the end of the line.

Someone said that tanks ran over tents crushing those still asleep inside, but Hou didn't see that. How could students be asleep in tents with all the fear, excitement, and noise? There were some reluctant stragglers, but troops helped them on their way.

By 5.30, most students had left the Square.

That was how the students vacated Tiananmen Square, no bloodshed, and no massacre.

A few of the foreigners remained on the Square, along with the rock-singer Dejian and other intellectuals. They witnessed the students leaving. The medical tent was still there, manned, and attending to the wounded.

Once Hou left the Square, he went to the left and ran. He made his escape though the back streets in the direction where the hotels were. Most of the others turned right, heading west along Qianmen Avenue, past Kentucky Fried Chicken, before heading north.

Many people, workers, students, and bystanders died that night. They did not die on Tiananmen Square, but in different places and under different circumstances.

Hou hung around the back of the Beijing Hotel because, although it was close to Tiananmen Square, people could still move around. When it was fully daylight, he saw that the PLA had sealed off Tiananmen Square.

Shortly after 9.00, a crowd started to gather on Chang'an Avenue, in front of the Beijing Hotel. Some of them were parents looking for their children who were involved in the protests on Tiananmen Square. Some were holding hands and walked towards Tiananmen Square, facing the tanks and the guns of the soldiers. There was some shouting, then suddenly, around 10.00, soldiers started to shoot at the crowd while they fled east, along Chang'an Avenue. It was as if the crowd had crossed an invisible line unacceptable to the officers in charge. It was clear that some soldiers were firing above or to the side of those fleeing, but not all. Hou saw fatalities and many wounded.

Hou had nowhere to go and he refused to take refuge in any of the Beijing colleges. Luckily, some of the kitchen staff from the Beijing Hotel fed him and provided protection.

On Monday, June 5, Hou did a brave and stupid thing.

Having slept and had breakfast, Hou decided to look around and see what was happening. Since leaving Tiananmen Square, there had been sporadic gunfire, some close, some further away. People were still walking around, some carrying on as normal, and others in defiance despite the clampdown by the PLA.

Around midday, Hou saw a column of at least fourteen tanks leave the northern end of Tiananmen Square and rumble east along Chang'an Avenue. He was standing on the north side of Chang'an Avenue, not far from the Beijing Hotel. He was watching the tanks, trying to work out what they were doing. Suddenly, out of the corner of his eye, he saw a man in the middle of the wide avenue directly in front of the path of the tanks. Hou didn't see where he came from but he seemed to walk casually from the other side of Chang'an Avenue. The man didn't look like a student because he was smartly dressed in a white shirt and dark trousers. He was carrying what looked like two flimsy, white plastic bags in his right hand and a darker bag in his left hand, which could have been a coat.

The man just stood in front of the leading tank. The tanks stopped in a neat line, their turrets at the same angle, as if on parade.

The man waved his right arm, his two bags sailing through the air, as if saying, 'I've had enough,' although Hou didn't actually hear what he said. All Hou could think was, they'll kill him, without a doubt.

The leading tank didn't try to run him over, it turned to the right to go round, but the man just jumped in front of the tank. The tank turned the other way but again the man stepped in front of its path. They did this a couple of times and then the tank stopped and turned off its engine.

The man put all his bags into his left hand, climbed on to the leading tank, and banged on its hatch, shouting at those inside. After a while, the man jumped down from the tank. The tank engine started and it moved a few yards forward but the man just ran in front of the tank, which again stopped.

There was an impasse.

Another man rode on his bicycle to the one in front of the tanks to try to persuade him to leave, before it was too late. When two others went to assist the cyclist, Hou couldn't hold back and ran to help with the others. They all hustled the tank man away to the south side of Chang'an Avenue and quickly disappeared. Hou just ran but nobody followed.

Hou decided it was time to leave Beijing.

On that same day, we in Jaliang marched in protest at what was happening in Beijing. The army did not intervene at all.

There were bad skirmishes between the people and the army for several days. There have been many deaths, particularly among the ordinary workers and residents of Beijing. Troops also received casualties in some of the skirmishes.

Arrests started immediately, including students and particularly those with links with the Gongzilian. The government has compiled a Wanted List of leading participants in the protest movement - no, our names

are not on the list. Pictures of the most-wanted
protesters were shown on television – no, we haven't
seen Hou's picture. Many student leaders have managed
to leave China and others are in hiding.

I only wonder what would have been the outcome if
the students had left Tiananmen Square earlier, as you
suggested.

Regards

Wei

Remember Mr Chou; for some reason they dismissed him
from his position, but nobody knows why. Zhuang is now
temporary director of the Office of Foreign Affairs.

Chapter 47

Friday, July 7, 1989

'**Charlie**,' greeted Harry warmly, '*nee hao, nee hao.*'

I had arranged to meet Harry in the student union bar. With one thing and another, I hadn't had chance to speak to him properly since returning from Beijing. He was wearing one of the new suits he had bought at No 1 Department Store back in Jaliang, suitably accompanied with matching shirt and tie.

'I thought you were going to change the buttons.'

'I was,' replied Harry, 'but I got attached to the original ones.'

'Beer?'

'Of course'

As usual, the bar was quite full. The music was loud, and 'Sealed with a Kiss', sung by Jason Donovan, was obviously popular.

'How did your teaching go after I left Jaliang?' Harry asked.

'Well, both Petter and Professor Song said I had done an excellent job,' I replied. Petter did say that to me on Tiananmen Square, and with any luck he might have meant it.

'That's marvellous, Charlie.'

'What have you been doing?' I asked, 'Anything interesting.'

'I have a plan that could be beneficial to both of us.'

'Go on,' I replied cautiously. One should always be cautious of any plan of Harry's.

'Remember the build the pagoda management game we did?'

'Yes, I remember it well.'

'I'm sure our innovative Chinese management games, like build the pagoda, will be highly sought after by local industry. We are leading international management specialists now.'

'Go on.' I had a premonition that my life was about to change.

'Well,' continued Harry, 'I talked to the head of school about us offering short courses for local industry based on our Chinese know-how. Doing business in China is becoming the smart thing to do and managers want to prepare for this. They'll pay good money. He was most impressed with *our* proposal. What do you think, Charlie?'

Our proposal…

'Are you sure Pontefract is ready for building pagodas?'

'I've seen some of my contacts at the Chamber of Commerce and at the Pontefract Council offices,' retorted Harry with a wink, gently nudging me in the ribs with his elbow.

'I know, you can't do without contacts,' I added.

'My contacts at the Chamber are supportive about promoting Sino-British business interests,' continued Harry with enthusiasm. 'Specialist short courses on China are what the Chamber needs, I told them; and they agreed. The first course is booked for early September; you are available then, aren't you, Charlie? Pontefract Council is even considering sending a delegation of local councillors to China on a fact-finding mission. They want us to organise that. China's the future now. The head of school has agreed a 50:50 split on all consultancy fees with PRIME. That's fifty per cent for us, Charlie, and we keep our full university salary as well. Think about it.'

'PRIME?'

'Pontefract Regional International Management Enterprise – that'll be the name of our management consultancy company.'

I thought about it over the next couple of beers, and the more I drank, the more receptive I became to Harry's plans, particularly the fifty per cent bit. Perhaps I had become academically stale and was always looking for an easy life. I should make use of my knowledge of China. I managed to survive six weeks in Jaliang with bright Chinese graduates and that must count for something. Surely, I could manage a motley collection of local Pontefract businessmen.

'Fifty per cent, you said?' I wanted to make sure I heard correctly.

'Yes,' confirmed Harry.

'Harry,' I said slowly, 'that idea of *ours* about offering short courses to local industry…'

'Yes,' said Harry innocuously while sipping his beer.

'I think it might be a good idea.'

I probably had had a drink too many, but I meant what I said. It was time for new challenges, and who better to do that with than Harry?

'Excellent,' replied Harry with a glint in his eye. 'This will be a little adventure, and I know you like little adventures.'

'Let's go for it, and September is fine.'

'We have lots to prepare,' Harry informed me.

'I like the name PRIME but I think, Pacific Rim International Management Education, would be a better title.'

'Good thinking, Charlie.'

We shook hands on the deal.

The bar was packed. Students had finished their examinations and were celebrating the end of academic year before returning home for the summer. I could hear a small group of students planning a camping trip to the Lake District, but two others, who were planning to travel around Yugoslavia, bettered that.

'You must tell me about the Tiananmen Square massacre, Charlie. Rumour has it you were there.'

'I actually left a couple of days before the Chinese army moved in to clear the Square,' I corrected. 'I should tell you there was no massacre on Tiananmen Square.'

'I can't hear you, Charlie...'

It was noisy. The loudspeakers were blasting out, 'Hand on your Heart', by Kylie Minogue, and the student end-of-term festivities, British style, were in full swing.

'There was no massacre on Tiananmen Square,' I shouted.

It so happened at that precise moment Kylie had stopped singing, and I needn't have shouted; but I wasn't to know that, was I?

Quite a few of the students in the bar looked at me in surprise. Some were listening to what I was saying.

'But I read it in the papers,' responded Harry with theatrical exaggeration, beaming at the students around.

'Harry,' I said patiently, 'with your views about the freedom of the press, you should know better.'

'What do you mean?'

'I had a letter from Wei, one of my Chinese students, who told me what happened. There were skirmishes around the Square and no doubt, there were a few fatalities, but there was no massacre of students on Tiananmen Square. The students were escorted off the Square by the army, under extreme duress, obviously, but mostly unharmed.'

'Oi, you, that's not true,' yelled a student nearby. 'I saw it on TV. That reporter with grey hair said he saw soldiers shooting at students. Hundreds were killed on Tiananmen Square.'

'Thousands,' added another.

'You're in denial,' accused the previous student.

'Sometimes the press can be a little lackadaisical and doesn't always allow the truth to get in the way of a good story,' I shouted back.

'Don't you believe in freedom of the press?' someone else yelled.

'My colleague will explain to everyone all about the freedom of the press,' I responded, pointing to Harry.

'Don't bring me into your argument,' Harry informed me light-heartedly, looking down at his shoes with his hands in his pockets.

Traitor...

'Lecturer denies freedom of the press,' shouted the student, and others joined in.

'Look,' I said as best as I could above the noise of the music, which happened to be Jason Donovan again, 'I am not denying there was a massacre, I'm just saying it didn't happen to students on Tiananmen Square. There was a massacre of ordinary workers and residents, and some students no doubt, all around Beijing under different circumstances. That's the real story.'

'Freedom of the press,' continued the boozy banter from students, but not very coordinated, I must add.

'Where's Beijing?' somebody commented absently, looking puzzled.

Although students couldn't hear me clearly, I decided to persevere.

'Listen,' I bellowed. 'The Chinese army killed many innocent people that night and the following days. Ordinary workers and Beijing residents were the majority who lost their lives. People in China saw that the students were getting away with things and that gave them hope. They started supporting and joining the protest movement. They were out protesting against hardships, rising prices, government corruption, years of repression, and this threatened the authority of the Chinese leaders and government. They were probably the target intended by the government, not the students. The Chinese government doesn't want to encourage freedom or democracy for the ordinary people, the workers, who make up most of the population. Who do you think the government needs to control?'

'Lecturer denies democracy,' roared yet another student.

'I didn't say that,' I said quietly to myself, because no one could hear me clearly. I wasn't going to give up easily. I stood on a chair so those in the bar could hear me better.

'Before the army moved into Beijing that fateful weekend,' I continued, 'some of the protesters had already decided they were going to leave Tiananmen Square. They were already drifting back to their homes and campuses. The reality is this. The Chinese government would never tolerate students occupying Tiananmen Square, allow them to make their protests, humiliate its leaders, undermine its authority, and then watch placidly while they leave at their own choosing. To maintain its authority the government had to remove the students from the Square. The residents of Beijing tried to prevent that but the army butchered them in the streets. That's the tragedy that hasn't been told.'

I looked around and realised not many were listening. Some students were pointing at me and giggling. They must have considered me slightly drunk.

'Students just returned to their classes and studies,' I persisted. 'They are the elite and the future leaders of business and government. They made their protest and most will now quietly get on with their lives and careers. What have they achieved, if anything? Unfortunately, the student leaders are in trouble. Arrests started immediately.'

And many people were dead...

I couldn't continue, not that many were listening, or taking much notice. I was weary. Everything just caught up with me, my time in China, my teaching, the protests, the massacre. I tried to visualise the residents of Beijing taking to the streets to disrupt the progress of the army and butchered for doing so. Evidently, Leigh and her wedding entourage had snaked its way through the chaos without a care in the world. I remembered the students I had seen around the Monument to the People's Heroes in Tiananmen Square and wondered what had happened to them. Had they escaped, were they in jail, were they...?

That was it, my last stand.

I realised, concerning the ostensible Tiananmen Square massacre, I had experienced and seen more than most. Beijing was, after all, a long way away. The world according to Pontefract was not ready for the realities according to me, Charles Vincent, one time visiting professor to Jaliang No 3 University.

The music stopped and it was quiet at last. I smiled wryly and stepped down from the chair.

'That's better,' said Harry, with a mischievous grin. 'You were trying to tell me something, Charlie.'

I found I quite liked the name, Charlie; it was growing on me.

'Harry,' I said, after a wistful pause, 'what do you know about Somalia?'

About the author

For many years, TG Snowball was a travel-hardened minor academic managing British higher education with collaborative partners worldwide. He has also been involved in various projects as a consultant for the United Nations.

Being a professor, he has about fifty or so academic publications (journals, readers, conference papers, and so on), which includes short spells as a technical editor for a shipping journal.

Travel has been the nature of his career and he has visited over eighty countries, including spending about eight months in China, and working in Oman and Israel among other places. He currently spends the summer months in the south of France, swimming, drinking the local wine, and writing.

www.TGSnowball.co.uk

Pirates *of* Provence

TG Snowball

Young adult fiction

SUMMER IN THE SOUTH OF FRANCE

Charlie arrived at the airport in Provence to collect his four grandchildren. They thought they would be staying in his villa for the summer, as usual, but little did they know.

And that's where their adventures began!

'Beignets, beignets – les meilleurs de toute la Côte d'Azur…'

'A compelling and humorous insight into family relationships'

'A must read for adults'

The Cheats

TG Snowball

Adult fiction

SPRING 1999, ISRAEL

The diaries of two minor academics from a very minor university.

They are sent to Israel with the instruction to sort out a large financial debt discovered by the external auditor. As you might expect, things are never simple in Israel. They stumble upon unimaginable academic mayhem and things only get worse.

They follow a serendipitous role of haphazardly discovering problems and concocting cunning plans to resolve them.

'How can this be?'

One often wonders...

'Black humour at its best'